# JACK STEEL

THRILLER

# STEEL FORCE

BOOK ONE

**GEOFFREY SAIGN**

## Books by Geoffrey Saign

### Jack Steel Thrillers

*Steel Trust*
*(free on website)*

*Steel Force*

*Steel Assassin*

### Alex Sight Thrillers

*Kill Sight*

Interior design by Lazar Kackarovski

Printed in the United States of America
ISBN: 978-1-070553-89-4

At the end of this book you will find a special gift for my readers: the FREE BOOK: STEEL TRUST—how it all began for Jack Steel. Thank you!
Geoff

*For Mom and Dad...*

*"If you have men who will exclude any of God's creatures from the shelter of compassion and pity, you will have men who deal likewise with their fellow men."*

~ St. Francis of Assisi ~
(1182-1226)

# PART 1

## OP: KOMODO

# CHAPTER 1

**Komodo: 2200 hours**

MAJOR JACK STEEL CLENCHED his jaw as the plane splashed down on the quiet waters of the lake. He pulled the black Lycra hood at the back of his neck over his head so only his eyes and mouth were visible. Even though his black fatigues were vented, he still sweated profusely.

Stepping out from behind the massive kapok tree, he waited. He would finally get answers. Everyone at the site was to be terminated, but he hadn't signed on to murder unarmed civilians.

The twin-engine DeHavilland Twin Otter float plane was almost impossible to see except as a dark shape moving against the far tree line. Painted all black and gutted for weight so it could carry extra fuel, it also had no registration numbers on it.

The aircraft angled over to the shore, the engine noise overwhelming the rainforest sounds until it was cut. A side cargo door slid open with a rasp and a rope was tossed out.

Steel caught it and pulled the aircraft into the shore, securing the line around a tree. Picking up his silenced SIG Sauer MCX Rattler, he gripped it with both hands. The folding stock made the rifle-caliber machine gun easy to conceal and it had little recoil.

A large hooded figure jumped out of the plane into a few inches of water, also holding a Rattler. Steel recognized the height of the man. Colonel Danker.

Danker nodded, using Steel's call sign for this mission; "PR," which stood for *point & recon*. The call sign wasn't very inventive, but Danker had assigned it.

Heavily muscled with a gravelly voice, at six-five Danker had three inches on Steel.

"Good to see you, BB." Steel heaved a silent breath, finally relaxing. Danker was U.S. Army and always did things *by the book*, thus his call sign of BB. Steel trusted him.

Everyone else on the Op worked for Blackhood, the private security contractor that signed their checks. But Danker would know all their profiles and made sure they had excellent skill sets for the Op.

Over a year and a half ago Steel had been asked to resign from the Army to join the secret Blackhood Ops program to target terrorists. The missions had been named Blackhood Ops to further distance the U.S. military and put the private military contractor on the hook for responsibility. Except for Danker, the U.S. government wanted no ties to these missions.

Four more hooded men exited the plane, one of them its pilot. Steel didn't know their identities, and they didn't know his—another precaution to maintain Blackhood mission secrecy.

He led them a dozen yards from the shoreline vegetation into the trees, where they squatted in a tight circle.

Each man was equipped with a Rattler, Glock 19, fixed blade knife, and a belt pouch that contained a night monocular scope, first aid, and a GPS tracking unit should things go bad. They also all had small wireless radios, earpieces, and throat microphones. The guns all had their identification numbers erased.

In addition, Steel had a Benchmade 3300BK Infidel auto OTF blade in a small, horizontal belt-sheath built into the inside back of his belt. For his fixed blade he carried a seven-inch Ka-Bar— he liked the leather handle. A small sling bag on his back held rations, a soft-sided canteen, and some first aid supplies.

He looked at Danker. "There are unarmed civilians at the building."

Danker nodded. "Brief us."

From his pouch Steel brought out a piece of white folded plastic and an iridescent red marker. He marked off the position of the site and guard positions.

Glancing around the circle, he said, "Two guards on the roof, two at each of the building's two entrances, four more in the jungle. We'll be coming in due east of the objective. The building has two main wings. Our target will be in the south wing."

He showed them the position he would lead them to, then made quick suggestions on how to take out the guards and secure the area and building. Finding optimal strategies was one of his specialties and he didn't expect any objections.

"All civilians should be inside at this time of night." He looked up at Danker.

The colonel said softly, "No warm bodies. No one leaves the site. I'll take care of the primary target. Radio silent unless you're in trouble."

Steel's neck stiffened. He stared at Danker, but the colonel was already upright, waiting. Standing, he whispered, "There are at least four noncombatants at the site, including a Franciscan friar."

Danker spoke matter-of-factly: "Orders stand."

Glancing at the other four sets of eyes, Steel saw only acceptance. "Our drones will record it."

Danker shook his head. "No drones tonight. Take point, PR."

Fifteen years of following orders compelled Steel to nod and move past the others as he returned the plastic and marker to his pouch.

Leading them at a brisk pace through the rainforest, he walked up the gently sloped mountain. The heat produced rivulets of sweat over his torso. He clenched his jaw. Civilian casualties were unavoidable in any conflict, but his job was to protect them, not actively target them. That view had inspired his entire military career. It was the cornerstone of his life.

Current U.S. military command accepted more civilian casualties in certain scenarios, but this wasn't a bombing run. Here they could control the outcome.

He had no problem killing armed guards to get to a terrorist, but he trained to avoid civilian casualties. Danker hadn't even asked how many nonmilitary personnel were on the premises. The colonel didn't care.

Danker had more intel than he did about the Op and the terrorist. Still, Steel had enough missions under his belt to recognize the difference between uninvolved civilians and those supporting terrorists. The female cook and maid were pushing fifty and were never armed. Like the driver and friar, they didn't act, talk, or move like terrorists in hiding worried about an attack.

His trust in the mission evaporated. Danker was following orders, but Steel questioned the motive of whoever gave them.

He gripped his gun. *No warm bodies.* This wasn't a planned assassination of a known terrorist. It was going to be a massacre.

# CHAPTER 2

## Komodo: 2230 hours

THE FLUORESCENT NEEDLEPOINT OF Steel's wrist compass guided him, but he didn't need it. He had traversed this same trail for two nights in a row to make sure he could do it with speed when the time came. Blackhood intel indicated the terrorist would be here for five days.

A laughing falcon gave its intense *ha-ha-ha-guaco* call in the distance. From much closer came the low-pitched guttural rumbling of a gray-bellied night monkey. Insects buzzed and hummed everywhere.

Normally Steel would drink in the teeming life that enveloped his senses. He had a deep abiding love of nature, however now it just reminded him of home and brought a lump to his throat. Light rain pattered his shoulders and head, mixing with the sweat running down his face.

He wondered where they were. To protect Op secrecy, Blackhood operatives were never given mission locations or terrorist names. Even the GPS unit was rigged so it didn't show numerical coordinates, but they could track him. Real-time tracking via satellites wasn't used on Blackhood Ops to avoid any record and to minimize the number of personnel aware of the Ops.

Over the last three days he heard the guards speak Spanish but couldn't place the dialect. Thus, except for seeing a photograph of the primary target, he knew next to nothing about Komodo

Op. And the high canopy and the overcast sky prevented any fix on location using star sites.

When he considered the current conflicts and problems, and everyone in power in Central and South America, he concluded they might be in Venezuela. Nicolas Maduro and his predecessor, Hugo Chávez, had supported Hezbollah and Al Qaeda. Their embassy had even sold passports to operatives of ISIS. Chávez had openly sided with North Korea, Iran, and Syria, and had accelerated his efforts to create a coalition against the U.S. Maduro had continued his legacy. The current mess in Venezuela and U.S. interference might favor terrorist support.

Maybe Blackhood Ops had decided to take out someone in Venezuela's armed forces that interfaced with terrorists.

That might explain Danker's orders of *no warm bodies*. Even though ISIS had been routed from Iraq, they still had a web presence and there were splinter groups. This might be a preemptive strike to give anyone in the Venezuelan government with terrorist connections a warning: *We can hit you anywhere we want, even in your own country.*

Maybe one of the civilians was related to someone in the Venezuelan government—Komodo Op might be a personal message to that person. If so, Steel still didn't like being used for an agenda he hadn't signed up for.

Holding up a hand, he stopped behind a tree, listening for anything beyond the pattering of rain and sounds of insects. None of the other men spoke. In moments he continued on.

During reconnaissance he had assumed they had decided not to use a missile drone to avoid civilian casualties. Now he knew they just didn't want this Op traced back to the U.S.

It was the presence of the Franciscan friar that had first triggered his concerns. The diminutive man wore short hair and a brown ankle-length habit with a hood. An image out of the Middle Ages. The friar's simple robe had a waist rope with three knots in the hanging end, signifying vows of poverty, chastity, and obedience, and that he was a Franciscan friar.

Every evening the friar took a walk in the forest, often stopping to pray. Once during the day, the friar had taken a stroll with the target, who dressed in civilian clothing. Neither were armed. The guards had remained in their positions, seemingly unconcerned about the target's increased vulnerability. That also didn't fit a terrorist camp under heightened security.

In some countries, like Iran, religious leaders sponsored terrorism. Steel wouldn't hesitate to treat them as criminals. But why would a Franciscan friar associate with terrorists? And this friar seemed to have an affinity for the rainforest and wildlife. Birds flocked into trees near the friar. Steel had even witnessed a songbird landing on the man's shoulder. Amazing.

His own affinity for nature probably created a bias on his part, making him feel protective toward the friar. Maybe that was misguided. Yet there was also something familiar about the man that Steel couldn't quite grasp.

When he considered his choices, he had to work to remain relaxed. If he showed resistance, he would be prosecuted. Black-hood operatives were under military jurisdiction and could face court-martial. Or maybe Danker would shoot him. He wouldn't put it past the colonel.

Even though he trained obsessively with his virtual reality program back home, the other four men accompanying him were elite soldiers. He couldn't manipulate them, and he couldn't stop this mission. That made his hands sweat.

His feet made no sound on the forest floor as he tried to think of some way to avoid what was coming. His improvisational skills, usually something he could rely on, didn't produce a solution that seemed satisfactory.

He started to withdraw. Just like at home when he faced Carol's anger and depression. He swallowed. He didn't want to lose her. And he didn't feel loved by her. An unequal balance of power that he felt helpless to change. He exhaled and let it go.

As he walked down an incline he leaned back, looking for anything out of place amid the trees—many of which were supported by three-to-five-foot-high buttress roots that kept the trunks vertical in shallow soil.

A lone howler monkey gave an eerie bellow from the valley below. Most likely to protect its territory or mating rights.

Stopping, he braced his palms and torso against a hollow strangler fig tree, scanning the terrain ahead. Intuition, something he relied on in everything he did, tightened his gut. Nothing felt right.

Still he didn't believe in the Kobayashi Maru principle. He trained in his virtual reality simulations under the belief that there was always a way out of even seemingly impossible situations. He focused on his own motto for when a plan blew up: *Stay calm, assess options, look for a solution.*

The others watched and waited.

He signaled left and right. The men spread out, Danker to his right. Taking the middle left, Steel crouched and stepped carefully over the soil. The others would circle around to the back and sides of the building.

In a few minutes Steel stopped behind a large tree. Using the carry strap, he positioned the Rattler against his back and lowered himself to his knees, and then his belly. Motionless, he looked ahead for any signs of movement. Crawling around the buttresses, snakelike, he pressed his hands and arms into the thick detritus. A rich brew of earth filled his nostrils.

He had practiced this part of his plan each day he was here, visualizing the enemy in a position similar to what the guard held now. This was also a maneuver he had repeated a hundred times in his VR sims. Using one foot and arm at a time, he quietly pushed and pulled himself forward. In minutes he spotted the faint outline of the guard sitting on one of the waist-high tree buttresses of a hundred-foot fig tree.

Moving at an angle, he kept crawling until the tree hid him from view.

All the guards wore nondescript tan uniforms and they never changed their nightly positions. Their lack of caution felt amateurish, supporting his doubts about the mission.

He paused at the back of the gnarled tree. No sounds. Methodically he drew himself to his knees, then his feet. Moisture and sweat beaded his face and hands, and the light rainfall patter disguised the quiet whispers of his movements.

Drawing his fixed blade knife, he gripped the handle and slipped over each buttress in turn until only one separated him from the guard. He checked his watch: twenty-three-hundred.

Taking a deep, silent breath, he fluidly slid one leg at a time over the last buttress, allowing his boots to make a slight rustle.

The guard whirled around, wide-eyed.

Steel swung the butt of his knife into the man's temple. The soldier slumped to the ground. Clenching his knife, Steel stared at the limp body. The guard looked young, maybe eighteen. A novice. Not an experienced soldier guarding a terrorist camp.

It cemented his distrust in the mission. Maybe the mission had nothing to do with terrorists. He swallowed. They would be out of here before the guard came to. The risk was that one of Danker's team would discover the man alive.

He picked up the guard's assault rifle, ran forward, and flung it away. Racing through the darkened forest, he slowed when the ranch-style stone building appeared, a lighter shape against the dark forest. Stopping behind a tree, he paused when he heard footsteps.

The friar broke from the surrounding trees in a run, his ankle-length habit flying out behind him as he yelled, "Intrusos! Intrusos!" The small man darted past the startled guards and into the building.

Steel was glad the friar had made it out of the forest without getting shot. He remained behind the tree—he was Danker's backup.

Machine gun fire erupted from several different locations.

Colonel Danker sprinted up beside a nearby tree. He dropped to one knee and sprayed a short burst at the two guards crouched in front of the building. Both men fell to the ground and Danker charged across the open clearing. A guard on the roof leaned over. Danker dove to the ground, rolling toward the building.

Steel stepped out from behind the tree and fired a spray of bullets to cover Danker, his shots much quieter than the staccato bursts coming from the guards around the compound.

The guard of the roof reeled backward.

Rising to his knees, Danker paused only a moment before he rose and ran through the door.

Steel followed at a dead run, adrenaline pumping his legs. More gunfire erupted in the forest. The other guards were fighting back, but he doubted it would help them. The radio silence from the Blackhood team confirmed it.

He rushed through the main entryway, past a large living room to the right. No civilians or soldiers. And none of the other Blackhood operatives were inside yet. A short hallway ran left. At the end of it stood Danker, facing a closed door. Steel kept his feet quiet on the stone floor as he ran forward, hoping the colonel didn't look back.

Danker kicked in the door and stepped into the room.

Steel ran harder, his hands like stone on his gun. He heard Danker's gun fire.

He stopped in the doorway just as the colonel swung his machine gun from one corner of the small darkened room toward the other. He glimpsed a desk and chair to the left. An interrupted line of bullet holes streaked across the wall behind the desk—it probably hid a corpse—most likely the target.

To the right, over the colonel's shoulder, he saw the friar—his small hands empty, his face hidden in the shadows. Steel snapped a kick into the side of Danker's left knee.

Danker grunted as his knee bent and his back twisted, but he remained upright. He tried to twist around, swinging his gun.

Steel jarred a knife hand into the side of Danker's neck and the colonel collapsed. Adrenaline flooded his limbs and his ears roared as he stared at Danker's crumpled body on the floor.

Glancing at the gaping friar, he motioned his gun to the waist-high open window.

The friar's eyes widened, but he ran to it and climbed through.

Steel crossed the room, keeping to the side of the window. He watched the friar disappear in the forest. Shots were fired almost immediately in the direction of the friar's flight. He grimaced. All of it for nothing. And there was nothing he could do for the other civilians. Now he had to worry about his own survival.

He barely whispered, "BB down, south wing."

Danker was unconscious, but a groan came from behind the desk. Simultaneously boots sounded on the stone floor down the hallway.

Steel fired a spray of bullets, aiming high into the forest. Pausing, he turned. A hooded Blackhood operative stood in the doorway, looking down at Danker.

"Let's get him out of here." Steel slung his weapon over his shoulder and hurried to Danker, helping to lift him to his feet. Steel grunted. Danker was heavy.

They half-dragged, half-carried the colonel, who mostly kept his eyes closed. On the way back they all took turns carrying Danker, but it still took an hour to return to the plane. After they loaded the colonel, Steel untied the line, pushed them away from the shoreline, and jumped aboard. The pilot started the engine, sending the smell of burned fuel into the air.

Sitting in a corner, Steel stared at Danker.

The colonel was stretched out on the floor between the others. His hood had been pulled back, revealing his thick black hair, eyebrows, and mustache. Opening his dark eyes briefly, he regarded Steel for a few moments before he closed them again.

There was no light in the plane, but in addition to the pain from a torn knee and screwed-up back, Steel thought he saw hate in Danker's eyes. He also wondered if the colonel sensed the out-of-control feeling sweeping his chest and locking his arms around his knees.

# CHAPTER 3

## Komodo: debriefing, 0800 hours

STEEL WANTED TO THROW Major Flaut into a wall. But he kept his emotion below the surface and allowed it to evaporate. What had happened on the mission had been shuffled into the background. Now he just wanted to go home to Carol.

He gave a quick upward glance, knowing Flaut would have those blue ice eyes on him, unwavering, cold as his bony face. The man stood over six feet and looked strong, wiry, with nothing that indicated compassion in his manner or words. Probably ex-Special Forces. He wore all black; jeans, turtleneck, and hard-soled shoes.

Flaut would have been assigned by the general running Komodo Op to replace Danker in debriefing. The man was as emotionless as the room they were in.

Steel looked at the bare table, rubbing his forehead with one hand and heaving a sigh, sure the blond-haired Flaut would take it as a sign of weariness. That much was true. He hadn't slept much, instead spending most of the flight preparing his story.

They had flown back to the U.S. in the DeHavilland, first landing briefly somewhere to refuel. Eventually they arrived at a small airfield where all the operatives were separated for debriefing. Steel had waited in the interrogation room for an hour before Flaut arrived. With no chance to shower, he needed fresh clothes and a shave. His uniform reeked.

"Let's go over it again, Major Steel, beginning after you killed the guard."

Steel looked up with a frown. "I ran behind a tree near the target site and saw Danker."

"Colonel Danker."

"Danker killed the two door guards. A guard appeared on the roof. I took him out and then followed Danker in."

"And?"

"I ran in, saw Danker lying in a doorway at the end of a hallway, and ran down. I glimpsed someone outside a window and ran to it." He paused, the image of the friar's face tightening his chest. "I fired, but the person escaped into the forest. Then we dragged Danker out."

"Colonel Danker."

"That's all."

"You didn't see anyone else in the building?"

"No."

"And you didn't see who attacked Colonel Danker?"

"Are you listening?" He glared at Flaut.

"What do you think happened to Colonel Danker?"

"It's obvious, isn't it?" He arched his eyebrows, sensing anticipation in Flaut's stance and his sharp-featured face. The man reveled in this.

Steel focused on Flaut's blue eyes and fair-skinned face. He intuited something else just below the surface. This man could be violent. It was written in his thin lips and taut lines.

"Tell me what's so obvious."

Steel looked down. "Someone in the building surprised Danker."

"Why wasn't Colonel Danker shot?"

He shrugged. "Ask Danker."

"How many other people were in the building?"

"A friar, a cook, a maid, a driver. Maybe a few others. People came and went and I did my reconnaissance at night." That wasn't true. He had used camouflage to observe daytime activities too.

Flaut crossed the small room and sat on a corner of the metal table. He stared from three feet away. Steel didn't look up, but he noted Flaut's smooth movements. Athletic.

Flaut continued. "The other men say that the cook and the maid were the only civilians."

Steel glanced at him. Flaut was lying. They had to know about the friar and the driver. It made him wonder how many others might have been inside the building. His gut tightened. "What happened to the cook and maid?"

"One of the other operatives killed them as they ran out the back door."

"Were they armed?" He locked eyes with Flaut. Tell me that, you SOB. He decided Flaut knew the Komodo Op was a hit squad, probably before he did.

Flaut gave a small smile. "I'm sure they were. You know the mandate for Blackhood missions."

"Covert Blackhood Ops approved by the president to terminate or kidnap terrorists on foreign soil for interrogation and closed trial for crimes committed or planned." He paused. "Noncombatants can be killed only if necessary for mission success, and only if they give primary support to terrorists." He watched Flaut for a reaction, but the major didn't give one.

Flaut pulled out a cigarette, lit it, and took a deep drag. He blew the smoke into Steel's face.

Steel sat back. "Do you mind? There's no smoking."

"Everyone on this Op seems to have a different story, Steel."

"Major Steel to you." He glared at Flaut. "Haven't you ever seen combat? Everyone always has a different story."

A flicker of anger slid through Flaut's eyes "We've been over your map. It looks like you were the closest man to Colonel

Danker. It would have made sense that you went in immediately behind him and would have seen his attacker." He blew another cloud of smoke.

Steel had expected this. It was the weakest part of his story. He decided to go on the offensive. "Danker's orders were for no one to leave the site alive." He looked at Flaut. "Those were Danker's orders, weren't they?"

"The mission statement for Blackhood Ops doesn't allow for that. I'm sure you're mistaken."

"Then it sounds like a lot of people might be mistaken about what they saw and heard."

Flaut gave a weak smile. "It was a very capable man who attacked Colonel Danker. There doesn't seem to be a likely candidate."

"How long am I going to be kept here?"

"A few more hours, if you cooperate. You will cooperate, won't you?"

"Sure, as long as you're civil." He gave a plastic smile when Flaut's face darkened. "Look, we're wasting time here, aren't we?" Bunching his shoulders, he leaned forward. "What motive could any of our men possibly have for disobeying orders and attacking a senior officer?"

He waited, knowing Flaut would have no answer, and that if Flaut did have an answer, he couldn't state it. He shook his head. "Had to be someone in the building, one of the target's guards." Sitting back, he waited, knowing he had stated his case as strongly as he could.

Flaut moved off the table and leaned against one of the walls. "Let's go over it a few more times. Maybe something will turn up."

# CHAPTER 4

S EVERAL HOURS LATER FLAUT was alone in a small office. He stared through the open door and down the hallway at Steel's receding back—imagining it exploding and spattering the walls in red.

He dialed a number on his phone and said, "You're not sedated?"

"I am but tell me anyway."

"Steel's story holds water. Barely. I'm wasting time at this point so I released him."

"But you think he's lying?"

"Sure."

"He doesn't know that you've been on Blackhood Ops before?"

"No chance."

"Good. I'll take it from here."

Flaut hung up and made another call. To Torr. He had a hunger and he wanted Torr to feed it.

\*\*\*

Danker put his phone down on the table next to the hospital bed. He bunched his big hands into fists on his white nightgown and clenched his jaw. The Komodo Op had been a complete failure and his reputation had been tarnished. Worse, he had always prized his healthy body, which was now a mess. A cripple for life.

Pillows supported his aching knee, which still had the surgery dressing wrapped around it. His neck felt like it had a spike rammed into it. But he would be out of here in a day or two. The most painful part was that he wanted to put a bullet into Steel—and couldn't. It wasn't legal stateside. Though he wouldn't have hesitated on the Op.

He believed in following the law. Even in the little things like not going over the speed limit. That frustrated people sometimes, but that was okay with him. A few friends were enough. His dad had drilled it into him that if people didn't follow the law, all you had left was chaos.

He had followed orders. And Steel was the only operative who had questioned his command to neutralize everyone at the compound. When Danker considered the assault positions of the other men on the Komodo Op, and the targets at the compound, only Steel would have been close enough to attack him. And only Steel had the ability to surprise him and take him down so fast.

That was part of the reason Steel was always desirable on Ops. He had an uncanny, nearly virtuoso skill set that few could match. The guy was also one messed up SOB.

Questions about Steel's decision-making skills had been raised a year ago in a previous Op, Hellfire, which had caused Danker to wonder about Steel's sense of priorities. At the time he had no proof, and Steel had been heroic. However, Komodo Op confirmed that the man would disobey orders in favor of his own set of values.

Time and planning would bring Steel to him. Being practical and methodical had always served him well. Patience. He would find a way to bring Steel down.

He looked at his aching knee. The doctor said it would never be the same again. He started moving his foot up and down—and gasped in pain.

For the first time in his life he considered breaking the law.

# CHAPTER 5

THE NAVIGATOR'S VOICE WOKE Steel when they landed at Langley Air Force Base. Rubbing his eyes, he grabbed his bag and hurried down the steps to the tarmac. The October sun was high and warm. He was glad for the heat. He had slept in his jeans and sweatshirt and looked forward to a shower and food.

In twenty minutes he pulled his black Jeep out of the parking ramp and began the three-hour ride home. Northwest from Hampton, skirting Richmond, north to Fredericksburg, then northwest on highways and county roads to Rappahannock County.

He drove the speed limit on the interstate until he was out of Fredericksburg and free of heavy traffic, still traveling northwest. Buildings and concrete were slowly replaced by open farmland. Eventually scattered forest took over. He drove faster.

On the way home his forehead remained creased. He replayed the interrogation with Flaut over and over in his mind, quickly exhausting it. Convinced they had nothing on him, and thus had been forced to release him, he still eyed his mirrors to see if he was being followed.

This was the first time he had stepped outside the chain of command. Through four years of Army, four in Special Forces, and seven in Delta Force—including tours in Afghanistan, where he earned the rank of major—he had always remained the obedient soldier. Yet on two Blackhood Ops he had strayed beyond orders. Maybe it was time to do something else.

His hands tightened on the steering wheel. Someone had gotten away with murder and used him to do it. It left him with an ugly feeling to have been a part of it. He wanted those responsible to pay.

*** 

The Jeep's tires crunched over the gravel of the half mile driveway of his property. Sugar and silver maples were scattered along the sides of the drive, along with dogwood, ash, and black oak.

The leaves had turned. Bright reds, yellows, and oranges splashed against the skyline. Usually that change brought a smile to his face and a light to his eyes. But today his chest tightened.

Song sparrows mobbed a red-tailed hawk flying across the driveway ahead of him. He rolled down his window. Carolina wrens flitted between bushes and a woodpecker's bill echoed off a tree trunk in the distance. The smell of fallen leaves filled the air. His eyes raced ahead.

Trees hid the two-story, four-bedroom rustic house at the end of the winding drive. The forest also gave him privacy from neighbors. County roads ran on three sides of his property, and to the west the foothills of the Blue Ridge Mountains loomed not far from his back door, isolating him further from prying eyes.

They had moved onto the square mile of woods ten years ago, when everything around them was forested. Now suburbia had nearly reached their door. Even the mountains couldn't escape the never-ending tide of people moving out of the cities.

His parents had left him everything in their will, which had allowed him to buy the place. He would rather have them back. He missed them. They had given him a mixed heritage of Cajun creole—Spanish, French, Native American, and Caribbean—leaving him with a light olive color skin. Born in Louisiana, he had moved to Virginia at age one—so his roots were here.

Near the house stood a giant sycamore. From one of its lower branches hung a tree swing. His gaze, as usual, paused on the swing as a lump formed in his throat. A flat stick with *Rachel* painted on it was stuck in the ground near the swing.

Carol's crimson BMW was in the circle near the house. His spirits sank further. But maybe things could be worked out. Maybe she would talk to him.

He pulled up behind her car, memories flashing through him. Carol humming in the kitchen. Laughter as she flicked water at him while washing the dishes. And the perfume she wore when she massaged his shoulders. All of it brought a frown to his face.

Exiting the Jeep, he gave a quick glance to the south side of the house. A large, rectangular red barn ran east-west. Rounded roof, steel siding, and no windows. The single steel house-sized door faced west and was closed.

He carried his bag to the house, opened the front door, and stopped immediately inside the spacious living room. Ten steps in front of him a stairway led up to an open second floor, the ceiling of the living room stretching up to it. The interior was rough-framed in cedar, with oak and mahogany blended in. It was designed to feel open, but that restful quality eluded him now.

Carol sat on the edge of a sofa, her tall, slender frame captive in a beige suit, keys in hand. An ebony pin held her shoulder-length auburn hair to the side. Dressed for a case. A successful defense attorney, she was normally straightforward and direct. Her hazel eyes focused on his chest, her sharp chin pulled sideways.

Spinner, their chocolate Labrador, lay at her feet, head on her paws. Usually the dog leapt up to greet him.

He sighed.      .

"They said you would be home today." Carol fumbled with her keys. "I have a trial that starts on Friday. I have to spend time with the client so I'm going to the apartment." She looked at him. "I didn't want to leave a note."

His throat tightened and he let the bag slip from his fingers. "You're not coming back?"

She shook her head.

"I was hoping we could talk."

She stared at her keys. "I've tried for a year to talk to you and you always put up roadblocks."

He swallowed, knowing she was right. "It was hard."

"It was hard for me too."

Desperation welled up inside him. "Isn't our marriage worth one more chance?"

"I'm tired of trying."

He searched for words to change her mind, to convince her they could make it work. "Let's take a trip, a break from all this."

She glanced up at him, her voice gentle. "I don't think going somewhere else will change anything for us."

"Is this final?" He didn't want to hear her answer.

"Things happen, Jack." She wiped her eyes. "Something's shifted. How I feel."

"Why? Over Rachel?" He choked on their daughter's name. "Just talk to me. Please."

"Every time you leave, I don't know where you are or if you're ever coming back."

"I'm thinking of quitting, getting out of the service."

"You said that a year ago. The missions are your escape. Even when you're here I've been alone. You just can't let Rachel go."

He winced, knowing she was right. "You never forgave me."

"You never forgave yourself."

Minute facial movements and a shift in the cadence and tone of her voice prompted him to ask, "What else?"

"You've been gone for a month." She got up with a frown, her forehead wrinkled. "I have a friend."

His stomach tightened. Jumbled words and images took over his thoughts. He couldn't speak.

"I needed someone to talk to." She wouldn't meet his eyes as she walked to the door, her perfume in the air between them. "I haven't slept with him. If it's any consolation, I'm taking a break from him too." Pausing at his shoulder, she whispered softly, "Now we can blame each other."

From the living room window he watched as she got into the BMW and drove off, a small trail of dust the only link left between them.

***

One year ago his daughter Rachel had gone missing while he was away on a mission.

They found her bicycle outside a vertical chute leading to a cave. A cut piece of rope was attached to her bike. A rescue team couldn't even go down the chute because recent rain had created a river at the bottom of the shaft.

Carol's accusations still haunted him. *Your daughter had to be a great explorer, to live up to her father's expectations. You trained her well. You should have been here.*

He got up and walked outside, striding to the barn. Spinner walked with him, her head hanging, her energy subdued. When Rachel went missing, the dog had lost some of her spirit. Carol leaving would add to that strain.

Retrieving a key from his pocket, he unlocked the deadbolt. Next he hit numbers on an electronic keypad to open the second lock. Pulling open the one-inch-thick steel door, he entered, sliding the one-by-four-inch deadbolt arm behind him.

He flicked a switch, lighting up a massive six-inch-high raised padded platform to his immediate right, a computer station on the far end of it. An exercise area with hanging ropes took up the middle of the barn, and a firing range filled the far end of the building.

He strode past the platform to a door on the left that led to a shower room, where he washed away the grime and pain that coated his body.

His own self-incriminations ran through him for the thousandth time. Despite his cautions to Rachel about safety, he had often recounted to her the times he went into caves alone as a child and came out unscathed—often after some minor problem. She had asked him to repeat those stories over and over. He never thought his smiling daughter would want to emulate his deeds.

Over the last year, as much as Carol had distanced herself from him, he had also isolated himself from her. His guilt had added to the ruination of their marriage.

They both used to go spelunking with Rachel, and he knew Carol must have asked herself if she had been too busy that day to go out with her daughter. He had never questioned her about it.

Eventually he became convinced that someone had kidnapped Rachel. He had no proof. He just didn't believe she would have risked the chute cave. And some weeks after she had disappeared, he had received a call consisting of three words: *Your daughter's okay.* Carol thought it was a prank call—maybe a religious zealot wanting to give them hope--and the FBI, police, and private investigators hadn't turned up anything. It had been determined the call might have come from a throw-away cell.

After working a list of potential enemies that hadn't turned up any leads, he had moved on to other possibilities.

He obtained the list of known sex offenders within a hundred miles, and visited all of them, aggressively questioning them—one placed a restraining order on him. When a police officer told him to let it go, he had punched the man. Only his military background had saved him jail time. The officer didn't press charges.

All of it had fatigued Carol.

In a way he wasn't surprised she had sought support wherever she could find it. Her decision to leave brought clarity to his eyes. All that mattered to him now was fighting for their marriage. He had failed Rachel. He didn't want to fail with Carol too. He couldn't survive another loss.

Walking out of the shower room, he turned off the lights and climbed into the nearby sensory deprivation tank. Spinner rested her head on her paws as he shut the tank door.

Darkness. The utter lack of stimulation seemed to damp down the pain that streaked back and forth behind his eyeballs like an electrical storm. He didn't want to see any light for some time to come.

# CHAPTER 6

WHO DOES TORR THINK he is?" The president tossed back a half glass of warm sherry, his eyes glittering. William Torr's name rolled around on his tongue like a small ball of acid.

Torr had struck at them like a coiled snake hidden under a lifted rock. Fast and unexpected. The president wanted him dead.

His gaze slid off the spotless, beige wall of the Oval Office, across the maroon carpet, and up to the emotionally-masked face of CIA Director Peter Hulm. Even in the dim light, all kinds of imperfections were visible on Hulm's puffy face. Deceit. Lies. Treachery. Cover-ups. And too much patience.

The president didn't believe Hulm was calm, at least not inside. At the moment he wanted to kick the short man, like you would kick a whiny little dog for tripping up your feet.

"I'm the one who ultimately is accountable for Blackhood Ops, so you don't care, do you?" The president flicked an imaginary crumb off his white shirt, where his acceptably-slight potbelly pushed out. "You think you're invulnerable? Do you? You think Torr won't dream up things for you to do too?"

He ground his perfect white teeth. All the years of work. Party servitude. Just to end up as another stooge for someone else. Hulm better answer soon, he thought, or his thrown glass might add to the other imperfections on the CIA Director's face.

Hulm seemed to sense it too. He barely shook his dark-haired head and leaned forward. His gray coat, which he hadn't bothered to remove, wrinkled like stiff laundry over his small frame. "We're safe. Komodo was a covert Op to get a drug lord who supports terrorists."

"We both know that's a lie." The president slammed his glass down hard on the English oak desk, leaving droplets beaded on its waxed surface. "Two generals and a friar."

Hulm shrugged. "We play it straight. We got misguided intelligence and signed off on it. It doesn't come back at us that way. We didn't know the truth. It's been done before. Blackhood takes the heat."

"We risked an international incident. Invaded a friendly country. Killed their citizens." The president's moist lips twisted as he leaned on his desk. "When a president assumes this office, he takes an oath from the Chief Justice of the Supreme Court. He swears to take care that laws are faithfully executed. To fail can be an impeachable offense."

The president paused and straightened his tall frame. "It could ruin me for the next election."

Hulm was silent.

The president strode to a window that overlooked the White House lawn. Lights shone down on every square foot that might otherwise have shadows. His shoulders tensed. He wanted to hit someone. Hulm.

It took three deep breaths to calm down. He ran a hand through his graying hair and a frown creased his face. "We better make sure no one else knows what Komodo was really about. Otherwise we're both finished. We'll go down in the history books as criminals."

Hulm shrugged. "Look at it this way, Komodo Op was a small payoff to Torr, that's all."

"I don't have to pay off anyone. I'm supposed to give orders, not take them!" The president's voice ended like the crack of a bullwhip.

"There wasn't any choice. At least it's over."

"Torr won't stop with this," snapped the president. "He's just getting started."

A spark showed in Hulm's eyes. "We'll have to think about that, won't we?"

The president didn't hear Hulm as he studied the shadows among the trees on the lawn and behind the shrubbery. "I'm the president," he said softly. "And I want Torr gone."

# CHAPTER 7

WILLIAM TORR, CEO OF MultiSec, liked his bulldog build. Rock solid, like his face. It made bald, short, and fifty feel better. He picked a piece of lint off his five-thousand-dollar gray vicuña suit, and then studied his manicured nails.

To the side of the room stood a large glass case. On the top shelf rested a first-place trophy from his college gymnastic rings competition. That trophy brought back images of several thousand cheering spectators. Torr liked to be reminded of that whenever he sensed a headache coming on. Like now.

He swiveled his chair, his gray eyes focusing on the paunchy four-star army general who sat in front of his glass-and-chrome desk. The general was number three on a long list of flunkies. "Well?"

General Sorenson was tall and dressed in uniform, complete with tie. He stirred and made a gurgling sound in his throat that slipped from quivering lips. His sunken eyes looked out of hooded caves, just over a bulbous nose.

"There's nothing we can do now." The general's voice was hushed, as if he spoke in a church.

"I don't accept failure," said Torr. "Tell me about PR. Point and recon, right?"

"He's a decorated soldier. One of our finest. He's been on all the Blackhood Ops."

"What is he, a renegade? A traitor to his country? Why would a man who's served his country so admirably disobey an order?"

"We don't know."

Torr sighed and stared at the pitiful man before him. "What do you know? How the hell did he blow the Op?"

"We think he attacked Colonel Danker."

"But you don't know that for sure either, do you?" He shook his head and rolled his eyes. "What a first-rate operation you fellows run. I hate to think that our national security is in your hands."

Sorenson's face reddened and his right hand formed a fist on his thigh.

"What's PR's name?"

Sorenson shook his head. "That's classified."

"I don't care," snapped Torr. "You don't have a choice."

Sorenson glared at him. "Major Steel."

"That wasn't so hard, was it?" Torr tented his hands. "I think Major Steel deserves punishment, don't you?"

Sorenson shook his head. "We have no proof, nothing. He could take it public. We can't do a thing." He looked at his black wingtips. "We did what we could. It's best if we let it go."

Torr frowned. "General, we'll let it go if, and only if, I say so." He smiled when Sorenson's face scrunched up. It showed off the general's wrinkles. "But you're right, it might be best if you're not involved. And I need some time to deliberate on General Vegas."

Sorenson shook his head again and his voice shook. "No more Ops on him." Both his hands formed fists.

"For now." Torr swiveled his chair one-hundred-eighty degrees so he could look out the windows of his forty-fifth-floor Manhattan office and view the city. "Run along, general. I'll call as soon as I'm ready to talk again."

Sorenson's reflection rose in the glass window in front of Torr. The general stared at Torr's back for a few moments. Then he stepped forward and picked up the baseball-sized paperweight on the desk.

Torr thought he could see the general's fingers turn white around the black stone. Holding his breath, he gripped the arms of his chair and set his feet flat on the floor, ready to push off.

Sorenson stood still, the paperweight held waist high. His eyes narrowed and his face tightened. Drawing back his arm, he twisted and threw the paperweight at the glass case, shattering it. The stone made a sizeable divot in the blue wall paint before it fell to the floor.

Sorenson straightened his suit and walked out.

Torr exhaled quietly. At least the wimp had missed his trophy. He didn't turn around until the door closed.

When he considered how much the botched effort of the combined strength of the CIA and a covert squad of highly trained Army personnel might cost him, he squinted. As if that could make the dollar amount become smaller.

His headache began and he knew who to blame for it. No matter. It would just require more effort. He would eventually get the job done. That much was certain. It would just take more planning.

But before that he had to satisfy two needs. First he had to find out what had really happened on the Komodo Op. He didn't like unknowns. They could come back to haunt you. And only one person could provide that information. Major Steel.

His second need would be easier to satisfy. Besides his belief in obedience, he also had a strong belief in punishment. It was a great motivator for flunkies and a great pain reliever to see opponents hurting. However he wanted something more permanent for Steel.

Even though he had numerous choices for both options, he decided to use the opportunity to punish Hulm, his number two flunky. The CIA Director hadn't bungled his part in the Komodo Op, but he was part of a failure, nonetheless.

From memory he dialed Peter Hulm's personal phone number to make his request. It brought a smile to his lips. Hulm would get one day to set it up, and one day to execute. He could wait two days to send Steel to his grave.

He opened his center desk drawer for his aspirin bottle.

Afterward he had to make another call. For insurance. Major Flaut.

# PART 2

## OP: PARAGON

# CHAPTER 8

O N THE FIRST DAY Steel woke up feeling like a windblown desert—barren, lifeless, and used up. And acutely aware that Carol wasn't present. He quickly buried all of it, before it buried him.

His security system hadn't sent any alerts to his phone. Still he grabbed the Glock 19, cautiously exiting the house back door to take the two dozen steps to the barn. Using the key and number code, he unlocked the door, deadbolting it behind him, and strode across the platform to the computer station.

The large padded platform served as a state-of-the-art virtual reality station. Sensors in the front corners of the barn allowed room-scale tracking, and he used a wireless motion-tracking controller. A full-body haptic suit simulated pain, temperature, uneven surfaces, and inclines. Boots, gloves, a head piece, weighted pistol, and goggles completed the sensory input.

Blackhood Ops had developed the VR program to train senior operatives. He had convinced them that it would elevate his performance if they supplied the program to him for home use. And it had. After buying the computer and peripherals, he had used the VR equipment obsessively to develop the razor-sharp skills that minimized his risk on Blackhood Ops.

The VR sessions were also an escape from the harsher realities of his life.

\*\*\*

*He stood in the forest. Four unarmed men appeared from behind trees and strode toward him from all sides. They attacked him simultaneously, all proficient with fighting techniques. He used a combination of Brazilian jiu-jitsu, kung fu, and Special Forces techniques to subdue them.*

After running scenarios like this for a year and a half it was too easy. He increased the number of attackers to six and increased their skill level to the maximum. He also tried several different surfaces, and the program provided different combinations of attacks. With six assailants he grunted a few times from blows—the suit's sensors gave him jolts. Still he put them all down. He tried one more simulation with eight attackers. This time he took some damage before it was over.

He changed the VR program to one he had developed by modifying the military program.

*He was floating with the current in an underground cavern, following the river around bends and into side caverns. It was completely dark, except for his headlamp.*

The real cave system was located a mile away on public land. It was where Rachel had supposedly drowned. He had mapped it with sonar sensors the day after she had gone missing. Kergan had been right. The cave floor he had discovered with Rachel months earlier had collapsed into a hidden river below it. It bothered him that he hadn't known about the water.

The VR program took him past a number of caves and side tunnels that he had checked out repeatedly using miniature SCUBA tanks while attached to ropes that were anchored topside.

*He continued to float along as far as he could before the tunnel narrowed to a small hole. Then he had to grip a rock projection on the ceiling to keep from bumping into the wall.*

He took off the wireless headset, staring at the computer.

Somehow it never felt real to him that Rachel was gone. For a long time he strongly believed she would still turn up someday. He didn't know if he was crazy—if it was just his obsessive nature that couldn't let go—or if his intuition sensed she was still alive.

Maybe it was just grief talking. And even though the hope of her return was beginning to fade, he wasn't ready to give up on her.

Images swam through him like ravenous sharks, scattering his focus. Rachel. Carol. The mission. His career. He knew where he had to start. He didn't have a choice. Before he could do anything, he needed proof. The sooner the better.

When considering his options, all of them carried risk.

Striding past the computer station, he stopped in front of a locked cabinet on the north wall, dug out another key, and opened it. Inside were shelves loaded with equipment. On one of the shelves were a half-dozen burner phones. He grabbed one, locked everything up, and got into the Jeep.

Detecting movement on the driveway, he leaned forward. A corn snake wound its way across the dirt.

He went for a drive, checking his mirrors to see if he was followed, and then headed to DC. After parking he found a small café on 15th Street and sat in a booth. The waitress took his order for coffee. He told her that would be all he would need. Then he used his phone to access the Internet.

He typed in *Venezuela* and *assassination*. Disappointment filled him when nothing came up. Either the results of the Blackhood Op were being blocked in public communications or he was wrong about the location. After Venezuela he tried El Salvador, then Honduras, Panama, and finally Nicaragua. He searched a few more South American countries with no luck.

Sifting through his memories of the jungle, he tried to remember any bird or animal calls that might be distinctive to a particular region. However, everything he recalled inhabited the tropical jungles of any number of countries in Central and South America.

He stared at the phone, wanting to put his fist through it. They could try him for treason for investigating the mission—for breaking his oath of secrecy to Blackhood Ops—and he had nothing.

A long shot, he typed in Belize. Nothing. Then Costa Rica.

He was startled by an article and quickly scanned it:

*...attempted assassination of General Garcia Vegas...Costa Rican special forces search jungle for attackers...six Costa Rican nationals killed...nine Mexican soldiers...Vegas, a candidate in the presidential election for Mexico...*

That the target site was in Costa Rica shocked him. Six citizens killed. Sanctioning a massacre that included two generals in a friendly country was beyond brazen. And getting involved in politics in Mexico, something the CIA had been infamous for in South America during the Cold War, seemed such an act of stupidity that he needed a moment to adjust to the idea.

Komodo Op was obviously a political hit, which disturbed him even more. But the target had survived, sending a surge of adrenaline through him. It also made him wonder about the friar.

He typed in Mexico and read the same news about Vegas. The news brief also stated, *...Vegas has a chance of winning the general election against the incumbent.*

General Garcia Vegas's website had a picture of Vegas standing alongside an even bigger man, General Rivera, whose arm was in a sling. Usually generals didn't gain popularity in Mexican elections, but maybe the voters wanted someone strong to get rid of the drug cartels.

Steel remembered seeing both men during reconnaissance for the Komodo Op. He was surprised the generals had managed to survive. Vegas must have gotten out first, and Rivera was the one Danker had shot in the room.

His eyes raced over the website. Vegas wanted to reform a number of areas of government to help the poor and middle class. The usual political drivel. No radical or terrorist language.

It didn't make sense.

A recent picture of the friar appeared, which straightened his shoulders. Francis Sotelo. No wonder he had sensed something familiar about the man.

A few years back Sotelo had gained fame among the U.S. environmental community. Steel had first read articles about the man in Audubon and a Greenpeace article online. He had been interested in Sotelo because of his affinity with wildlife and nature. However, in past photos Sotelo had a beard, moustache, and long hair, and had been an elementary teacher. Now he was clean shaven and a friar.

A small cheer stirred in his chest that Sotelo was alive. When he had first read about Sotelo, the teacher was relatively unknown, living in a small village in Mexico. Now people were comparing him to St. Francis of Assisi.

Sotelo talked almost exclusively about how environmental pollution and degradation affected poor people, wild animals, and nature in the same way. He wanted justice for the poor—education, reparation money, housing, and health care from the governments and corporations raiding their land—and justice for nature. The two themes were inseparable in his talks.

The friar's reputation had blossomed, especially with the multitude of looming environmental disasters. People were flocking to hear him speak. Sotelo was helping Vegas make a race of the election.

If the Komodo Op was politically motivated, maybe Vegas secretly supported terrorism and the U.S. saw him as a serious threat. Steel's mouth was dry. If that were true, it meant someone had decided to eliminate everyone with Vegas to protect the U.S. from recriminations from abroad should any survivors point fingers.

But it didn't make sense that Sotelo would align himself with a man who supported terrorism. Nothing fit.

He cleared the phone's browsing history, put on disposable gloves, wiped it clean of prints, and took it apart. On the way back to his car—after making sure no one followed him—he slipped its pieces into different trash bins along the sidewalk.

He used his other phone to call Carol's Washington apartment. Voice mail. He left a message. If his resolve held out, he wouldn't call her again for at least a few days.

No, deep down he knew he might call her again tonight. If the nightmare came. Where he watched her jump off a cliff with his daughter, and he was unable to grasp either of them. That usually woke him up in a sweat, gasping for air. Steel, he told himself, you're bent.

Anger over the Komodo Op welled up in his chest again. Whoever wanted Vegas and Sotelo dead would try to kill them again. He wanted to find the man behind the orders before that happened. There was no doubt now that they would come for him too—he was a liability and a dangerous loose end.

If the President was behind things, he didn't know what he could do.

When he thought about who he could go to for help, there was only Kergan. Another risk.

# CHAPTER 9

WHILE DRIVING HOME THE phone rang. Steel stared at it, answering on the second ring.

A woman's voice. It took his jumbled thoughts a few seconds to realize it wasn't Carol. He sank into the car seat.

"...Major Steel? Are you there? This is Christie Thorton. Jack Steel?"

He remembered Christie from a Pentagon function long ago. Part of the Pentagon's liaison personnel with Blackhood. An analyst. Used to be, at least. Sharp, quick, lots of energy. He almost hung up. "What can I do for you, Christie?"

"I'd like your advice on a scheduled Op in Afghanistan. Kergan referred me to you."

"I'd like to help you, but I don't have time."

"Kergan said you were the best choice, since it involves a cave system that you explored."

"I'm in the middle of something else." He tapped the steering wheel softly with his knuckles.

"Kergan says you're the best."

"This is a bad time."

"Isn't that the way it always is? Life's never quite right, is it? Can you squeeze me in? A few hours." There was a pause. "Please. It would help your country and possibly save soldiers' lives."

He didn't want to do it. His knuckles pushed against the wheel.

"Kergan said you would make time for me. He said you're a great guy and you would see me. I need to do it soon. Orders. Could you? Please?" She chuckled softly. "I'm begging, Major Steel."

His lips twisted. Kergan's endorsement backed him into a corner. "All right. Come out to my place tomorrow morning." The words grated over his teeth. He gave her his address.

"Great, see you then." She hung up.

He tossed the phone on the passenger seat, suddenly realizing the other thing he had felt for the last days. Anger. Anger that Carol had left. Anger she might leave him for someone else. Anger that she wouldn't work to save their marriage.

*You've got it all together now*, he thought. *What a pro.*

The second call was his choice. He punched a number and let it ring once and hung up. Dialing it again, he let it ring twice before he hung up. The third time it was answered on the third ring. There was no greeting on the other end and he said nothing.

Silence. He was glad.

***

They met in an hour on a quiet dirt road in the foothills of the Blue Ridge, northeast of where he lived, halfway for both of them. Dark clouds pillowed the sky and the air chilled his skin.

Steel parked his Jeep on the side of the road and got into Kergan's Mercedes. They went for a ride. Steel wore jeans and a gray pullover, Kergan a gray sweater and black slacks. Kergan had fifteen years on him and was fit, with wide shoulders. A head taller than Steel, he had thick silver hair and a commanding presence.

Kergan was like a father to Steel. Steel's mother had died in a car accident when he was sixteen, and his father—a sergeant major—had died two years later in combat. Kergan was a colonel at the time, and also a good friend of his father's, and had kept in contact with Steel because of it.

Over the years Steel often turned to Kergan for advice. He trusted and admired him. Kergan didn't say anything, his slate eyes looking forward, his strong hands on the wheel.

They had arranged this type of routine when Steel first enlisted in Blackhood Ops. It was a precaution, in case anything ever went wrong. Kergan was good at that, always seeing what might lie ahead and being prepared for it.

Kergan had overseen intelligence gathering units, including Steel's, in Afghanistan. He had a lot of connections, and at the time of his surprisingly early retirement he wielded a lot of power as a four-star general. Kergan was the only person Steel knew who might be privileged to inside information about Blackhood Ops.

Steel cleared his throat. "Carol left me."

Kergan kept his eyes on the road. "She called me."

He winced. Carol had probably called everyone but him.

"I don't want to be caught in the middle between you two," Kergan said softly. "I've told her the same thing. I value both your friendships."

The hills were painted with leaves that had turned color. Steel noticed a doe not far off the road. "Did you refer Christie Thorton to me for Op analysis?"

"Is it a problem?"

"No."

Kergan turned the car around. "I heard things didn't go well on the Komodo Op." His deep voice rumbled over the words.

Steel had no idea how Kergan would take a confession from him. He decided he couldn't give one. It might compromise Kergan with others, and it might compromise their friendship.

Kergan glanced at him. "I know how dirty things can get, and how quick."

"I want to know who we targeted and why." He didn't want to tell Kergan he really only needed the *why*.

Kergan eyed him. "You haven't been looking into it, have you?"

He didn't answer.

"They can put you in jail for life, Jack. What are you thinking?"

"Do you believe every order should be followed?"

"I'm talking with you, aren't I?" Kergan paused. "Let it go, Jack."

"I can't."

"You have to. There's nothing you can do."

"Maybe."

"It's over."

"Maybe not."

"I'm telling you, Jack, as your friend, don't do this. If not for yourself, then for Carol."

Steel's fingers tightened on his thighs. If he somehow put Carol in danger he would never forgive himself. Not after Rachel. He exhaled. This had nothing to do with Carol and she had moved out. She was safe. His hands relaxed. "Some things have to be answered for."

"Some things are better forgotten. Get on with your life."

"I don't have one."

Kergan eyed him. "And what do you get out of it?"

"My conscience."

"What good is that if you're in jail?"

"It's all I have."

"It was that bad?" Kergan sighed. "All right. General Sorenson ran the Op. I know he's not happy about it. I was led to believe you went to South America. Where exactly and for who, I have no idea."

"Could you find out?" They had lied to Kergan about the location so he doubted they would tell him the *why*.

"I'd have to be blunt and Sorenson would want to know why." He looked at Steel. "They know we're friends." He turned away. "If they come after you, you're finished."

"What about you?"

"Let them try."

"If it's no risk to you, I could use your help."

Kergan glanced at him. "I'll see what I can turn up."

"Thanks." He sighed. "How are things with you?"

"I'm getting over Mary's death. It was hard for a long time, but I'm finally remembering the great years we had. And there's someone else there now to share my life with."

"I'm happy for you." The pit of Steel's stomach tightened. He didn't want to think of needing someone else to share his life. He looked out the window. A flock of geese made a V in the sky.

Kergan pulled up even with his car. "Listen, if you get yourself into a situation, call me." He gripped Steel's hand. "Call me anyway."

"I will." He wondered how many times in the last ten years people had said that to him and he had promised to, but never called. He would this time.

He watched Kergan drive off. The steadiness and security of his friend's presence remained with him, but his eyes locked onto his mirrors all the way home.

# CHAPTER 10

MAJOR CHRISTIE THORTON TARGETED her green eyes like lasers on Steel's back as she chased his black sweat suit through the woods, weaving in and out of trees and running hard.

The crunch of leaves beneath her tennis shoes sounded a rhythm for her strides. The sun beat down on her forehead and she was glad whenever she had shade. The big friendly chocolate lab stayed beside her step for step, something she didn't understand. After all, the lab was Steel's dog.

She had arrived at eight-thirty a.m. Steel had expected her around ten and was about to begin his run. If she wanted to stay, he told her that she had to run with him. He didn't want her hanging around his property while he was away and he didn't want to skip the exercise. *Take it or leave it*, his eyes had said. Stubborn and weird. Annoyed, she had almost left.

But she wasn't sure he would allow her to come out again and figured it might be another way to connect with the paranoid guy. Her gym bag was always in the car and he had given her five minutes to change.

He had a gun beneath his sweatshirt. She could see its outline. Cautious. No. Prepared. For what? That unsettled her and planted a small seed of fear in her thoughts. Maybe he knew why she was really here. That stiffened her back.

She liked the colors and quiet in the forest, broken by birdsong. Normally it would have had a restful effect on her. All of it signaled Steel's preferences.

As they ran through a meadow, sharp whistles of northern cardinals broke the beat of their steady footsteps through the grass. A bright multicolored canopy of treetops stretched to the mountains in the distance. Above her, a red-shouldered hawk circled, and a light breeze blew, caressing her skin. She had to get out of the city more often.

They headed back into the woods. In another quarter mile Steel ran across a small arched wooden bridge built over a stream. He jumped over something as he crossed it and pointed to the right. Christie almost tripped as she followed his arm.

A small black bear stood far upstream, and she saw almost too late that she needed to jump over a six-foot rat snake curled up in the sun on the wood bridge. She landed off-balance, glancing back at the snake that hadn't moved.

Steel turned his head and smiled at her.

"Does he think he can scare us?" she asked the dog.

Spinner barked.

Steel led her on an obstacle course next. Log hurdles. Under obstructions. And up a rope that hung from a branch fifty-feet up, and then down a pulley cable. She was impressed with how fast Steel went up the rope.

Finished, they jogged back to the barn. Sweat ran down her face and beneath her green sweats.

Steel punched in the code and unlocked the barn door, opening it so sunlight splashed inside. Christie was surprised with his security. Deluxe paranoid.

He eyed her. "You're in great shape."

"Rules and regulations made by stiffs at the top." Smiling, she wiped sweat off her brow. She wanted to fling it at him, but instead studied his details. It was something she was proficient at, sizing someone up.

Brown curly hair, a little messy and kind of cute around a friendly face, eyes that seemed trusting, with something else beneath that. Light olive skin. Strong shoulders. Six inches taller than her toned, five-eight frame. One ninety pounds, fifty over her one forty. Thirty-five, five years over her thirty.

"Are we through?" She undid her ponytail, letting her brown and blond-streaked hair fall to her shoulders, framing her heart-shaped face.

He gazed at her, as if studying her. *Was he on to her?* "Look, Steel, you said do the workout and you would go over the Op. I have a busy day."

"That's fair." He led her inside.

She noted the computer station, the VR setup which Kergan had mentioned, the sensory deprivation tank, and the ropes and target range. Impressive.

He stopped next to the tank and pointed to a nearby door in the wall. "Sauna and shower are in there. Towels are in the closet. I'll get us something to drink."

She used the hot shower like a massage, letting the spray beat against her tanned skin, soothing the aches she felt all over. Steel had worked her hard.

She wasn't quite sure what to think of him. He had unique toys. That side of him fascinated her. Something else also drew her to him, something visceral that she couldn't easily identify. She could see pain beneath his sincerity, written on his eyes— which appeared to be searching for empathy. She had to watch that, feeling any sentiment.

\*\*\*

Steel walked to the house and filled two glasses with lemonade. He had expected Christie to leave when he demanded she run with him. When she agreed, he had been both surprised and disappointed.

But the run woke him up. Besides feeling a little foolish over his demand, he realized he was glad to have company.

He returned to the barn and set the glasses on a desk near the computer.

His desktop and phone beeped simultaneously. Lasers and cameras on the perimeters of his land triggered a text to his phone and an alarm on his computer if they were tripped. He sometimes wondered how—with all this security to protect his family—he had still managed to lose his wife and child.

He stepped up to the computer and hit a key. The large wall screen showed a live view of the end of his driveway and the county road. He pushed more keys, bringing up camera feeds from closer areas on the driveway. A black two-door Lexus appeared on the screen, driving past the cameras. A signal had also gone off from a laser on the south county road.

Hitting more keys, he brought up camera views along the county roads on the east and south side of his property. Nothing. No stored images for the last hour either. Could have been a deer that tripped the laser, and then jumped the camera. It had happened before.

Spinner lifted her head and watched the barn door intently, giving a low growl.

Drawing his Glock, Steel glanced at the shower room door. "Come on, girl." He strode out with Spinner, his gun level, pausing at the corner of the barn to peek around it.

The Lexus appeared, moving slowly, stopping twenty yards away. It had tinted windows, hiding the interior. The driver got out, smiling. In his thirties, the big man wore dark shades, jeans, a yellow polo shirt, and had short hair and a fat face.

Steel didn't trust the smile.

Spinner growled and spun around to face the forest.

Steel whirled and knelt, his gun facing the same direction. He fired two shots at a man aiming a pistol at him from behind a tree.

The man ducked behind the trunk, but a silenced bullet dusted the ground a few feet to the side of Steel.

"Drop the gun or the next bullets take you and the dog." The voice came from behind him.

Steel glanced at Spinner, and slowly put down his Glock. "Sit, Spinner."

The dog obeyed with a small whine.

Steel slowly straightened, watching the man behind the tree approach him. The guy had to have come in from the south county road, dropped off by the Lexus earlier, and had somehow bypassed his sensors and cameras. Pros. Expensive.

The driver of the Lexus was much closer. "We just want to talk."

Steel didn't believe that either.

# CHAPTER 11

THEY MADE HIM PUT Spinner in the shower room and close the door. He did it quickly, hoping Christie took long showers.

He thought of the two men as Yellow and Blue. Blue was dressed like Yellow, except for his shirt color, and had a moustache and hairy forearms. Yellow had fluid movements. Blue had more muscle mass but looked slower.

"Love dogs. Glad we didn't have to hurt her." Yellow pointed to the two glasses of lemonade by the computer. "The Jaguar outside—a woman's, right? In the shower?" He put his ear against the shower room door and smiled. "We'll have fun with her later."

"She doesn't know anything." Steel wanted to inflict pain on Yellow.

"But you do." Blue stood in front of Steel, his Smith & Wesson 9mm level.

Steel eyed him. "What do you want?"

"The truth." Blue smiled. "Then maybe we don't hurt the woman."

He knew the man was lying. "About?"

Yellow stepped away from the shower room door. "Shame on you."

Steel flicked his eyes to Blue. Ten feet away. Too far to attack.

Yellow clapped his hands together. "Turn around and face the wall."

Steel did. In seconds he collapsed to the floor.

*** 

The last time Steel remembered kneeling he was ten years old in church with his mother. This time his feet were pressed against the north wall of the barn, with his hands zip-tied behind his back. They had Tasered him, but now they held guns.

He looked up at fat-faced Yellow and mustached Blue. He was close to the sensory deprivation tank and the shower room door. The cement floor was uncomfortable beneath his knees. Frustration welled up inside him that with all his security and a gun in his hand, he had allowed them to capture him. He hadn't been focused. Distracted by Christie's presence.

He felt for the OTF knife in the belt-sheath—it wasn't there.

Blue smiled. "In case you're wondering, we found your knife. It's by the computer."

Yellow put away his gun, took a quick step, and kicked Steel in the stomach.

Gasping, Steel fell to the floor on his side. He had expected the kick and was ready for it.

"We've been told to keep this up until you talk," said Yellow. "Even a couple of days if we have to. And we don't mind. Do we?"

In answer, Blue put his gun away. He kicked Steel in the right thigh. "Yeah, we've got plenty of time."

Steel groaned. Spinner barked.

*** 

Christie heard the dog bark. It sounded too close. She opened the shower stall door, grabbed a towel from the wall handle, and wrapped it around her torso. Carefully she peeked into the short hallway leading out.

Spinner stood in front of the closed door leading into the barn, whining and glancing at her. The dog looked upset. There was no logical reason for Steel to shove the dog into the shower room.

That creased Christie's forehead. She hurried to dry off and put on her clothing.

***

Steel looked at their shoes. His stomach had taken the blow without much damage. His thigh hurt, but he put the pain into a small box and buried it deep in his consciousness.

With his cheek pressed into the cool cement, he gave Yellow and Blue a different picture with teary eyes and groans. He had replayed this situation hundreds of times in his VR simulator.

"Don't hurt the woman," he said hoarsely. "I'll tell you everything."

Yellow looked at Blue, and then shook his head. "I don't believe you."

Steel groaned softly. "You'll have everything you want in five minutes."

"Maybe we want to take our time," said Blue.

Steel's voice hardened slightly. "Maybe if you hit me again you'll never get anything."

Yellow spread his hands in a magnanimous gesture. "A show of good faith."

Steel kept his voice strained. "I need something to drink."

"Why not?" Yellow walked across the barn floor toward the lemonade resting by the computer station.

Blue drew his gun again.

Steel peeked at Blue's gun—pointed at his torso. He needed Blue on his knees, to shield him from Yellow. With one eye he watched Yellow until he was striding across the platform. Slumping his shoulders, he turned his forehead into the floor and counted to five. It would give Yellow enough time to reach the lemonade and pick up a glass.

Then he rapidly rolled away from the wall.

Blue tried to step out, firing the gun, the bullet pinging off the cement where Steel had been lying a moment ago. Steel felt his side burn, but he kicked out from the floor. Twice. He caught Blue hard between the legs and on the inside of one knee.

Groaning, Blue fell to his knees, dropping his gun and cupping his groin with his hands.

Steel had already swiveled to his butt, keeping Blue between himself and a charging Yellow. He quickly slid his hands beneath his butt and then his feet, using a quick, hard elbow motion to break the zip tie. Grabbing Blue's gun, he shifted to his knees behind Blue, using him for protection. He ignored the pain in his side.

Yellow ran for the door, his arm outstretched, firing his gun. As expected, he moved faster than Blue.

Steel shifted around Blue, firing three times at Yellow, the reverberations ringing in his ears.

Yellow staggered off the platform, his thigh and lower stomach red—Steel had aimed below any possible body armor the man might be wearing. The killer hit the concrete on his belly near the door and didn't move.

Spinner banged against the shower room door with barks and growls.

Steel let go of Blue, who collapsed to the floor and threw up. His side on fire, Steel slowly stood and backed up, watching both men. Yellow looked dead. He wanted to keep at least one of them alive for questioning. He leaned against the sensory deprivation tank.

Blue groaned and curled tightly onto his side, his back to Steel.

Steel was aware of Blue working at something on his lower leg. "Don't do it."

Blue abruptly rolled onto his back, a small gun in his hands.

Steel shot him in the head. Blue's arms fell to the concrete. Already on his feet, Yellow was opening the barn door. Steel fired but hit the closing door—the man was out.

He slid down to the floor, still eyeing the barn door. He doubted Yellow was coming back.

# CHAPTER 12

THE SHOWER ROOM DOOR cracked open. Christie stared at him. He saw the worry in her eyes. Probably for her own safety.

Spinner pushed past her and dashed to him.

"Hey." He rolled to all fours, gasping, as Spinner licked his face. "Christie, get my gun."

While Christie bolted for his Glock, which the killers had tossed on the platform, he stood and walked in a limping gait toward the outside door. Kneeling ten feet from the door, he painfully went prone and waited for Christie. "Open the door fast but stay behind it."

He held the gun in both hands and aimed at the doorway. "Lie down, Spinner." She did.

Christie flung the door open, her gun up, and Steel checked his trigger finger. Yellow lay outside in the grass, on his stomach again.

Steel rose and walked to the doorway with Christie. Yellow was missing part of his head. Without stepping out, he peered south into the woods. Spinner was beside him and showed no signs of agitation. He lowered his gun and looked at Christie. She didn't look happy.

He thought about options. Burying the bodies on his property wouldn't work. He couldn't trust Christie to keep it to herself.

"Do you want me to call the police?" She frowned at the body.

Blackhood Ops wouldn't allow the police to investigate one of their operatives so he said, "Military might not want that."

He didn't want to, but he had no choice but to call Colonel Danker, the only liaison he was permitted to call regarding Blackhood Ops concerns. Danker might suspect that he had attacked him on the Komodo Op, but it would look even more suspicious if he didn't call him now. He had Danker on speed dial and explained the situation.

"Hang on," said Danker. "I have to ask on this one." He came back in a minute. "They want us to handle it. Keep the police out of it. Army Criminal Investigation Command will be out ASAP."

Steel looked at Christie. "Let's wait in the house. CID is coming."

# CHAPTER 13

CHRISTIE OPENED ALL THE closed blinds until the spacious, oak-floor room with its high, rough-beamed ceiling shone with light. The wood furniture had cushions and was nicely spaced and casual.

It would have made a better impression on her at a different time. She sat on a sofa arm and looked out the front window, swinging her foot back and forth with her toe tapping against the wall, her lips pursed.

Steel's flesh wound was bandaged and he sat on the same sofa. He had refused to go to the Army hospital so the medic shrugged, made him sign a release, and let it go at that. The CID medical examiner took the two corpses that had no IDs. The car was stolen.

CID had taken their statements. Then Christie talked to them outside alone, out of Steel's sight. She wanted it that way. They soon left.

She cleared her throat. "What about the mess in the barn?"

Steel didn't look like he wanted to talk, nor move.

She left and searched for supplies in the laundry room. He said nothing as she trudged out of the house to the barn. She viewed the barn floor in distaste. Steel couldn't do it, and he wasn't going to hire a cleaning service after what had happened. Besides, it might make him view her more favorably if she helped him.

She cleaned up the dropped glass of lemonade on the platform first. Easy. While there, she spotted the automatic OTF knife near the computer—it had to be Steel's. She pocketed it.

The rest of the cleanup was obnoxious. Her knees felt sore on the cool cement as she scrubbed with arms and shoulders that already ached. She swore several times. The smell of bleach, iron, and puke filled her nostrils.

Still jittery over what had happened, she paused once. If she had been shot, someone might be cleaning up her mess now.

She returned to the house, a sudsy bucket of sloshing pink liquid in hand. Still on the living room sofa, Steel stared out the window at the driveway, one hand on Spinner, who sat beside him.

"I got most of it out." She walked past him. "At least it's sterile."

"Thanks." He didn't look at her.

She returned to the laundry room to empty and clean the pail and wash her gloves. Finished, she quickly checked the backdoor locks—standard key and deadbolt—and then walked into the kitchen to wash her hands.

The kitchen sink window gave a view of the side of the house. A bird feeder stood a dozen feet away. Grosbeaks and cedar waxwings picked at seed, while a red squirrel ate leftovers on the ground. A hummingbird feeder was attached to the house, and a pair of birding binoculars and a digital camera with a zoom lens rested on the counter.

She shook her head. Mr. Nature.

Quickly and quietly she opened all the cupboards and drawers. Steel had a lot of canned dog food and a dozen cereal boxes, but little else. A gallon glass jar stuffed with wrapped bubblegum sat on the counter, but the jar cover had dust on it.

When she returned to the living room, Steel still hadn't moved. She sat on the arm of the sofa again, already tired of him. Digging out his OTF knife, she tossed it onto the sofa. "You should have gone to the hospital, Steel."

He was stone silent. The guy was eerie. Her voice steeled and she gestured with a sharp wave. "What was that all about?"

He looked up at her with a drawn face and shrugged. "Loyalty."

"To what?"

"I don't know." He turned away.

"Hey, I could have been killed." He still didn't look at her. His eyes told her that he wouldn't say more. She wanted to yell at him for the danger he had put her in, but she forced those feelings down, keeping her voice soft. "Someone should be here with you, Steel. Where's your wife?"

He didn't answer.

His silence bothered her, but she decided on a different approach, asking a question for which she already knew the answer. "What are you doing with all the bubblegum?"

His face shadowed. "It was for my daughter."

"I heard about that. I'm sorry for your loss."

"We used to play a game to see how many bird species we saw in a day." He glanced at her. "I haven't given up on her. I'm still looking."

Christie didn't want to empathize but couldn't help it. The pain in his eyes softened her expression. The man lived in a nightmare. "I hope you find her."

"So do I." He sagged deeper into the sofa.

Somehow she knew better than to touch him. It looked like no one had for a long time.

He looked away. "I need a favor."

"What?"

"I want to know the identities of those two men. Can you follow the CID investigation?" He looked up at her. "If it doesn't put you in a compromising position."

She waved it off. "I have to ask my superiors and get back to you. On one condition."

"What?"

"I need you to go over the Afghan Op. Tomorrow."

"You want to meet with me again?" He lifted an eyebrow.

She wanted to shout, *No!* She already had enough of his emotional black hole, not to mention the risk of being a casualty of whatever he was mixed up in. However, she said, "You bet, Steel." Her buoyancy seemed out of place, even to herself. "Orders are orders."

"Are they?"

Picking up her workout bag, she moved to the door. Suddenly she had to get out. A threat loomed over her, one she couldn't identify. His voice stopped her at the door.

"The name's Jack."

She turned to him. His eyes resembled a lost puppy. Gripping the doorknob, she swung the door open. "I like Steel, if you don't mind." Less personal, and what she needed to stay objective. She couldn't walk any faster to her car.

She slammed the gas pedal of the Jaguar, throwing dust into the air as she spun down the driveway. As soon as she was out of sight of the house, she punched a number on her phone. It was answered on the third ring.

"What the hell have you gotten me into, Danker?" she yelled.

# CHAPTER 14

AFTER CHRISTIE LEFT, STEEL grabbed his Glock, OTF knife, and phone and took small steps out of the house, locking the door behind him. The searing pain in his side made him dizzy.

Spinner whimpered several times beside him. He tried to comfort her with gentle pats on her neck. "Stay here, girl." Spinner whined but lay down.

He drove the Jeep down his driveway, stopping fifty feet from the county road. Behind his vehicle, on either side of the driveway, were heavy metal gates that swung on six-inch-thick metal posts. It was painful, but he managed to pull both gates closed, then fastened and locked the sturdy chain and padlock. Bolt cutters wouldn't work, and a car couldn't drive through it or around it, forcing a stop and resultant camera shot.

He drove south on the county road to the next intersection, taking a right and driving along the south end of his property. He parked on the dirt shoulder. A car was coming from the east so he held his gun and waited, sliding down sideways as a precaution.

The sedan sped by and didn't stop.

Making sure there was no further traffic, he checked a few of the hidden perimeter cameras. He found one that had a device taped to it. He pulled it off, staring at a small camera with a photograph of the woods from his camera's perspective.

CID hadn't found any useful evidence of the shooter who had shot Yellow in the head. Steel figured the man had entered at the same point as Blue, explaining why there was no photo. The killer had waited in the woods, watching the barn door. To do what? Ensure Yellow and Blue did their job? Someone wanted to make sure there would be no mistakes.

He tossed the camera into the Jeep and kept driving down the road. When he reached the end of his property, he drove another half mile until he came to a wooded lot with a dirt driveway and locked metal fence. A sign read, *Private Property. Keep Out.*

Making sure no one was following him, he drove up, unlocked the fence, and drove in, locking it behind him. He drove another hundred yards to a large steel shed hidden from the road. Exiting the Jeep, he walked up to the keypad on the side of the garage, punched the combination, pulled the door up, and drove in.

To the side was a black and blue Yamaha SR400 motorcycle with a black helmet and black leather coat on the seat. The helmet had a tinted visor so no one could recognize the wearer.

He put the helmet and jacket on, wheeled the bike out, and locked the door. When he had purchased the house, he had also bought this lot from the owner, who had purchased it under an anonymous LLC so it couldn't be traced to him. No one could tie it to Steel either.

After locking the outer gate, he drove east to the next county road, taking it north to the highway. Then the highway west, back toward his property. No one followed him.

A half mile past his east county road, he pulled onto his land into a narrow dirt road with grass growing in it. Another sign read, *Private Property. Keep Out.* The road ended in fifty feet. A narrow path continued through the trees and foot-high grass. He followed the trail to a small shack with an exterior of dilapidated wood.

Parking the bike's kickstand on a flat rock, he opened the shack's wood door, revealing another keypad on a steel door. He punched the code, slid the thick door sideways, and quickly drove the bike inside. The cement floor was dry and bare, like the steel walls and ceiling. He left the helmet and jacket and locked up.

From there it was a slow, painful hike to the rear of his house. Glock in hand. Spinner was waiting for him, tail wagging, eager for his return. He patted her side. "Good girl."

He unlocked the barn door, deadbolting and locking it behind him. The door had two more deadbolt bars, both two inches wide and a half inch thick, one high and one low, and could only be released from the inside. He slid them across the door.

The whole barn had a thick steel interior shell inside of the steel siding. Someone would have to use an RPG to get in. Even that might not work.

Getting out his phone, he called Kergan and left a message: "Had some visitors. Out for a run. Please get a rain coat for Carol." Kergan would know it meant he had been attacked, was on the run and not at home, and to protect Carol.

He turned off his computer equipment and walked through the darkened barn, not needing light to guide him. Years of spelunking had given him almost a second sight in darkness.

At the far end of the barn he stopped by the last shooting target on the wall. He knelt next to the floor molding and pulled on a small section. It broke away on a hidden hinge, revealing a black button, which he pushed. He snapped the molding back in place and stood.

A four-by-six-foot section of the floor slid back, revealing a retractable stairway in the corner leading down. Spinner hopped down the steps behind him.

He pushed another switch when he reached the bottom. The flooring slid back to cover the opening again, the ladder pulling up beneath it.

The previous owner, an ex-military paranoid survivalist, had screened buyers, waiting for someone like Steel to show up. After talking to Steel for a while, and noting his interest, the owner had showed Steel the secret level he had built. It had sealed the deal for Steel.

The lower level had a small kitchen with a stove, refrigerator, pantry shelves full of enough canned and dried food to last for months, a deep freezer, microwave, and a large living room complete with a sofa and large TV. There was also another computer station and large screen, and a bedroom with a walk-in closet and bathroom.

The survivalist's rich wife had funded the previous owner's security system—maybe just to keep him happy. When she had died, the man had moved to an even more remote location with even more security.

Steel had never told anyone about the hidden level. Not even Carol. He figured if someone wanted to get to him, the less Carol knew the better. But maybe that was another way he had created distance between them. Isolating his life from hers.

From the refrigerator he grabbed a grapefruit-flavored water, washed down two aspirin, and sat on the sofa, exhausted, his side throbbing.

Yellow and Blue's attack had to be over the Komodo Op. It was also a message: *We know what you did and we are going to make you pay.*

The military might want to interrogate him further. Even try him in a closed hearing for a prison term if they believed they had enough evidence. But they wouldn't send two killers to murder him. It made him think someone outside of the government had ordered the Komodo Op. But who had that kind of power over the president?

It angered him that they had invaded his home and threatened him here. More upsetting—and another sign that he couldn't let go—was that he wanted to be here in case Rachel returned. What if she came back and no one was here? That idea seemed stuck in his brain. He missed her that much.

He called his current private investigator, Larry Nerstrand. Larry had cracked some long-standing cases that others had quit on. Steel couldn't deny a tiny seed of hope in his heart.

"Hi, Jack."

"Any news, Larry?"

"I found someone who has a record that passed through your area about the same time your daughter went missing."

Steel clenched the phone. "What kind of record?"

"Let me chase him down and talk to him, Jack."

The target had to be either a pedophile or involved in sex trafficking. He swallowed. "No one will admit to something like that."

"I know how to be persuasive."

Steel believed him. Nerstrand was big, ex-army, and tough.

"Look, Jack, you're a nice guy, and I want to find Rachel. But I'm done after I find this guy."

"I can get you more money." Though he would have to ask Carol and she would refuse. Maybe Kergan. He had some emergency money stashed too.

"That would be nice. But if this guy is a dead end, I think you have to accept she's gone. It's up to you, but I've done everything I can think of."

"Thanks." He hung up, wondering if he could ever let Rachel go.

He considered the attack again. Whoever was after him wouldn't just blow up his house. They wanted to know what he knew. Which meant they would come at him again. Next time he would ask the questions. He settled back, thinking of his next point of attack.

Christie.

# CHAPTER 15

FLAUT HAD FOLLOWED STEEL west but was forced to drive by him when he pulled over onto the shoulder. He didn't try to return later. Steel would spot him.

He felt sated, like he always did after a kill. As if he had plugged a hole in his head with a good drug. But the unfinished details surrounding Steel gnawed at him during the drive home. Not wanting to ruin the moment, he pushed those concerns aside.

In a half hour he pulled out his phone and called Torr. Torr was the first CEO he had ever worked for. He found that amusing. He wasn't sure how Torr had located him. Probably through someone in the CIA. Torr was one of the few people he had ever worked for that he respected. Like himself, the man had a sense of godliness in his attitude toward people.

Torr listened in silence as Flaut filled him in, and then said, "The two idiots blew it."

"Steel is good."

"Where is he now?"

"After CID left, he took off in his Jeep. He locked his driveway gate. He's on the run. It's what I would do."

"And you didn't follow him?"

Flaut's fingers tightened on his phone in response to Torr's condescending tone. He let it go. "I recognized a woman leaving Steel's. Christie Thorton. She's an analyst at the Pentagon. Counter-terrorism Ops. I think she works for Danker."

"Fine, just don't tell Danker anything." Torr paused. "Steel must be special. I'm sure we can give you a crack at him soon."

Flaut knew Torr was treating him like a dog, throwing him a juicy bone. His face tightened, but he said, "I'd like that."

*** 

Torr got off the phone with Flaut and immediately called his number two flunky. CIA Director Hulm. Torr couldn't wait to tell him of the failure. He was sure the two dead men weren't CIA. Hulm would have hired out through intermediaries. Still. Failure.

While Torr waited for Hulm to answer, he doodled on a pad of paper on the glass top of his desk. No one was dependable these days. Except Flaut. For some reason that idea made him scribble harder on the paper.

The other reason he wanted to call Hulm was to make sure the man was clear on what to do with Steel. He opened the file folder on Steel and scanned the information. There were lots of ways to make him pay.

He had a sense for things like this, how to time them perfectly. Whether in the boardroom or in a corporate takeover, instinct guided him. It got him to where he was today. Head of the flunkies.

Hulm answered curtly. "I'm aware. I'll take care of it. Whatever you do, don't send Flaut after Steel. If anything goes wrong, they'll trace Flaut back to you." He hung up without waiting for a response.

For some reason Torr didn't find Hulm's response trustworthy, but he did agree with not using Flaut. He called the head of his company security. They would find someone to do what he wanted.

*** 

This time Hulm was the one who wanted to punch someone—the president. But Hulm didn't allow his puffy face to show it.

The president smiled at him. "So now Torr has *you* jumping through hoops. How does it feel?"

"Torr wants Steel dead, but I have an idea."

***

When Flaut arrived home, his three-year-old golden retriever, Lacy, ran up and stopped just before him in the kitchen, her head bowed and her eyes averted.

"Good girl." He stroked her head until she finally lifted her gaze to his. Lacy had been an abused dog that he had adopted. Sometimes he still wanted to track down the abuser and make him pay, but the shelter had no information on the previous owner that had abandoned the dog.

He threw a frozen dinner in the microwave for himself and cooked a pound of lean hamburger on the stove for Lacy. They ate together. Afterward he sat on the couch in the living room and put in a porn DVD. One of his favorites. Lacy sat next to him while he stroked her back.

He took a shot of Jack Daniels. Then he slipped a thin silver case out of the coffee table drawer in front of him. With practiced care he opened the case, not wanting to jar it. It was filled with a layer of white powder. He took a credit card and cut three lines. Using a thin straw in the case, he took one line into a nostril, settled back, and waited for the rush to flood his limbs.

Steel.

The fact that Steel had allowed targets to live on the Komodo Op drove a needle of anxiety into his head. It left him with an unfinished feeling. As if he was seeing a beautiful sculpture ninety-five percent completed, but with all work on it stopped. Some part of him couldn't resolve itself with that, and Steel had caused this incompleteness.

Eventually he would have to go south to finish the Komodo Op, with or without Blackhood Ops. It bothered him that he was so enslaved to finishing things, but he reminded himself that it was perfection he sought. Like any great artist.

An image of his father swam into his eyes.

*You can't be great at anything unless you do it perfectly, said his father. You're going to swing that bat until you have a perfect swing. No dinner until you do. And no talking unless you're talked to. His father rapped his palm with a bat.*

Flaut blinked and the image disappeared. He didn't let it come back, instead choosing to ride the rush back to Steel.

Torr would eventually send him after Steel, but he didn't know if he could wait. He didn't mind that Torr had sent hired guns against Steel. If Steel hadn't been able to handle them, he wouldn't be worth the bother. And before today, Flaut didn't know how good Steel was.

Performance, even excellence, on pre-planned Blackhood Ops was different than performing in improvised situations. But now he knew Steel represented a challenge that made his heart race.

A solution came to him. Check out Steel's virtual reality operation. He had used the Blackhood Ops VR program many times in training and was well-versed in it. But he wanted to run something special on Steel's system. Look at it as a preview of things to come.

# CHAPTER 16

T HE NEXT MORNING STEEL'S side felt better.

He changed his security text alerts to a new phone he had ready for such an occasion. Taking the old one apart, he trashed it. Using another burner phone, he sent a text to Christie. He wasn't sure about her, but the fact that Kergan had recommended her meant something. And Yellow and Blue had planned to kill her.

If the people she reported to were behind this, they were keeping it from her. Letting her know he wasn't living at his house anymore would get the information to her superiors. If they were the ones involved, they wouldn't come to his place to look for him unless they were following her. He wanted to find out.

Christie returned his text with a call, and he said, "I'm not staying at the house anymore so we have to meet elsewhere. There's a truck stop a half hour east of my place on the highway. Noon sharp. Make sure your car doesn't have a tracker on it and you're not followed."

"You think I led those men to you?" Her voice held surprise.

"It's for your own safety." He hung up.

Another thing bothered him. Yellow and Blue had bypassed his perimeter too easily.

He went up to the first level. From a locked cabinet he selected a number of wireless pressure pads, minicameras, and motion sensors, and threw them all into a bag. Then he exited the ground-level door and walked with Spinner into the woods. His Glock traveled with him all the time now.

Anyone entering his property would eventually funnel into a few choke points that he could monitor. He didn't want to use booby traps, since bear, deer, or Spinner could set them off.

He hid a motion detector and camera on the bridge over the stream. Next he buried the pressure pads just under a film of dirt in two different places he felt an intruder might take if they were coming toward his home from the south or east.

Satisfied, he returned to the barn to make sure he could pick up the new feeds. After that he took Spinner to the lower level, said goodbye, and left. Spinner wasn't a barker, and the ceiling was sound-proofed anyway.

Taking a pair of binoculars, he hiked to the motorcycle shed west of the house, grabbed a spare helmet hanging on the wall, and rode the motorcycle east on the highway.

Thirty minutes later he pulled into the truck stop. Christie's green Jaguar was easy to spot. He rode around the lot. Nothing but a few pickups and truckers. No sedans. No SUVs. No one hanging out on the highway shoulders.

He pulled up beside Christie's Jaguar, keeping the helmet on, and curled a finger at her.

She powered her window down. Her thick gold-streaked hair lay on her shoulders. A bright picture. Sunshiny, except for the creases on her forehead. "Really, Steel? I don't like riding on bikes."

"I'll be careful."

"You better be." She wore light gray jeans and a long-sleeved white top that barely reached her pants, with a jean jacket over her top.

"Leave your phone here." It was unlikely anyone was tracking her by phone, but he wanted to be thorough.

She stared at him, but then put it into the glove compartment and exited the car, holding a thin folder. "Satisfied? And no tails, no trackers."

His gaze lingered a bit too long on her curves. He was glad the helmet hid his eyes. She put on the extra helmet, got on the bike, and put the folder between them, wrapping her arms around him—he liked that.

He drove around to see if anyone was following, and then he ran the county roads bordering his property to see if anyone was parked on any of them. Nothing. Returning to his driveway, he unlocked the gate, drove the bike through, and locked it again. In minutes he unlocked the barn door and let Christie in.

She entered, giving him a thin smile. "Good day to you too, Steel."

He dead-bolted the door, aware of the frustration behind her smile. "Sorry. Precautions."

She walked with him across the platform toward the computer. "Where's Spinner?"

"Safe."

"You must be worried to leave your house."

He shrugged. "I like low risk. Did you get the CID info?"

"After we work on the Op." She pulled out a flash drive and handed it to him, setting the folder to the side.

He sat down in front of the computer. She leaned on the back of his chair, her crossed arms touching his shoulder blades. Her perfume mimicked Frangipani, a tropical flower with a rich floral scent. Carol used to lean on his chair like this. It distracted him as he looked at the screen. He wondered if Carol remembered anything he used to do with her.

"Steel?" Her voice was soft.

He sighed. "All right, what are we looking at?"

"There's reason to believe a high-ranking ISIS splinter commander is hiding in the bunker you're about to see. It's in the Paktika Province bordering Pakistan. We want him, dead or alive, but the cave is extensive and deep. It's near a village in Pakistan so we can't risk using the GBU-43/B Massive Ordnance Air Blast—it might result in Pakistani casualties and we would lose an ally."

He opened the flash drive and pulled it up on the large screen. She told him to open a video which showed aerial shots from far out, slowly zooming in on a large cave entrance. It brought back memories of his time there. He was glad he was out.

He said, "A lot of the smaller caves are lined in steel, built by the CIA when we helped them against Russia. Later, bin Laden used the caves and expanded the tunnels connecting them."

"You recognize it?" She leaned closer.

"I do. I'd expect land mines outside the entrance and booby traps inside. Multiple escape exits."

"Give me your best-case scenario for going in."

He shook his head. "Don't. They'll hold the upper hand because they live in the caves, know them extensively, and don't mind dying."

"Let's say we're going in anyway. Then what?"

He spent an hour describing different possibilities, risks, likelihood of success, and what they would need for equipment. She asked insightful questions and he enjoyed the exchange of ideas. Afterward he closed down the computer and handed her the flash drive.

She motioned to the computer. "I'm glad I'm not in the field."

"Why?"

"Last month an Op targeted a Taliban leader in a village. One of our soldiers refused an order because he believed innocent women and children were going to die in the attack. The soldier is being court-martialed." She frowned. "It might seem weak, but I don't think I could risk killing women and children noncombatants to get one Taliban."

He winced, remembering the Komodo Op. "Without knowing the particulars, I can't comment on that. Maybe the soldier's assessment wasn't good. Or maybe it was and the Op should have been designed better."

She sighed and straightened. "I'll talk this through with my superiors. I might have a few more questions."

"Sure." He swiveled his chair and caught her by surprise, an inch of her exposed stomach in front of his face. Toned. His eyes and thoughts wandered. He told himself he just missed Carol.

She backed up as his face turned pink. They both tried to smile.

She handed him the folder. "The CID investigation and IDs on the two men who attacked us. I'd like to hear your opinion on them."

"I appreciate it." He noticed she included herself in the attack. She was there, but not a primary target.

He cleared his throat. "Something quick to eat while I look at it?" Her eyebrows raised, and he added, "Since I'm not living here, there's some fresh food I need to use up. I don't want to haul it out."

They ate a salad of greens with sandwiches of cheese, meat, and tomatoes. Steel opened the file Christie had given him and went through it. The IDs on Yellow and Blue revealed a Frank Getty and Peter Farsk. Both had rap sheets for assault and battery. Hired guns.

He had guessed as much but wanted to make sure. Hired by whom, was the question. And he still didn't know what they believed he knew.

He said truthfully, "I don't know these men or why they came after me." He had no information that was worth anything. But someone thought he did. The more he thought about it, he concluded again the attack had to be over the Op. Someone outside the government didn't like what he had done. He had to find out who.

"Could the attack have anything to do with your wife?" Christie frowned. "I've read about her in the paper. She defends some pretty high-profile criminal elements."

He considered that. "No, they were after me. Besides, she's not living here."

"For good?" She shook her head. "Sorry, it's none of my business."

"I don't know if she's coming back."

Christie's voice softened. "You've both been through a lot."

He looked at his plate and had to steady his voice. "When Rachel went missing it put something between us. Neither of us understood how to resolve it." He looked at her. "Have you ever been married?"

She shook her head.

"Ever get involved with a married man?" He wasn't sure why he asked that. Was he propositioning her? "Forget I asked."

She put down her sandwich, her face darkening. "It was a long time ago. I was much younger and naïve. He didn't tell me he was married."

Steel nodded and picked up his sandwich, avoiding her eyes. "It's different," he said softly, "being on the other side of things. The married one."

Later he drove her back to her car. She left, and he wondered if that would be the last time he would see her. It didn't look as if her superiors were tracking her to find him.

His thoughts turned to General Vegas. And Mexico. If someone outside the government had hijacked the Op, it wouldn't have been over terrorism. It had to be over money.

***

Christie was impressed by Steel's astute perceptions on the Paktika Op and had enjoyed working with him. What he didn't know was that they had already tried the Op and failed—for all the reasons he had stated. However she hadn't gotten any closer to her main objective, which was discovering whatever Steel was hiding.

Danker believed Steel had disobeyed orders on a classified Op, allowing a terrorist to escape, but they had no proof. She had made up the story about the soldier being court-martialed, to see how Steel would respond. Danker assumed Steel was into something illegal for money. Steel was in debt with his house, maxed out on credit cards, and the recent attack suggested shady connections.

She hadn't seen Steel's Jeep anywhere on the premises so he had to be living elsewhere. For him to risk meeting her suggested that he was checking her out. That made her wonder how much danger she was in just by associating with him.

Danker had told her to play along with whatever Steel wanted. Find out what he was hiding. Nothing else mattered.

Danker had made it sound like a test. *If you want a promotion, let's see what you can do.* This was her chance to prove herself and get out from under all the paper-pushing office work that she detested. Danker was sexist and using her because he thought Steel would slip up more easily around an attractive woman.

She didn't care. She wanted the promotion.

Then CIA Director Hulm had shocked her by contacting her privately on her phone. Hulm had stated he needed her for a job that was high priority, if she was interested. She would get paid for it. He stated it could lead to other work as well. Impressed that the CIA director would contact her personally, she had said yes immediately.

Hulm told her to continue getting close to Steel and give him any help he needed—but keep him clueless about CIA interest. When she had asked why he was interested in Steel, Hulm had replied, *He's a traitor*, adding, *Keep Danker in the dark.*

After the attack she found herself wary about reporting secretly to two men in two different agencies. Whatever Steel had done, it had to be big for CIA Director Hulm to get involved.

Her confusion came from her sense of people, which was usually accurate. Steel didn't seem like a threat. And his interest in making sure soldiers didn't die in the Paktika Op felt genuine. Still he had to be hiding something. Two men were dead because of him.

She would play it out a little longer. But if nothing else came up she was going to run out of excuses to see him.

Her personal question about Carol was to hook him deeper, even though it bothered him. His question had bothered her just as much. She was aware of the looks and glances he was giving her. She had found herself stealing glances at him too.

She had already deduced he was separated from his wife. At a gut level she found him attractive. And his lifestyle and skills were more appealing than those of any man she had met before. Escaping from two hired killers was impressive. But she wanted no part of his problems.

She called Danker first and said, "He's not living on his premises anymore. We met at a truck stop and he arrived on a motorcycle."

Danker replied, "Keep at it. He's dirty." He hung up.

Hulm had a different response; "He'll ask for help eventually. Make sure he gets it."

"Sir, do we have any idea who tried to kill him?"

"That's above your pay grade." Hulm hung up.

Frustrated, she wondered what Steel had done to convince two agencies he was a traitor. They were playing him, and her, and none of it felt good.

To protect her own back, she hadn't told Hulm or Danker that she had gone to Steel's home to analyze the Paktika Op. The CIA might be tracking her phone so she had less control where they were concerned—she was actually glad Steel had made her leave it in her car.

But if there was a leak inside the Army section running Steel's Ops, she wanted to minimize her chances of ending up on the wrong side of a gun again.

# CHAPTER 17

THEY MET IN LATE afternoon on the same road, pulled up close to each other, pointed in opposite directions. Kergan's window was down, his strong face cast in shadows as he talked.

Steel listened.

"Be careful, my friend. I have a bad feeling about things. General Sorenson's lips are sewed shut. I couldn't get him to say why they did the Komodo Op. I went at it softly, but he wouldn't comment. It's a dead end."

Disappointed, but not surprised, Steel digested that.

Kergan continued. "I made it clear that I was unhappy that someone tried to kill you. Brought it up casually, as if I was mentioning the time of day. Sorenson sympathized. I said if anything happened to you, I'd start a small war to find out who was behind it. I'm sure it'll get passed around. I don't think anyone inside had anything to do with it."

Steel believed him. "Who's watching Carol?"

"Someone experienced, twenty-four-seven." Kergan's eyebrows raised and his face tightened. "Has anyone threatened her?"

He shook his head. "Preventative. I'll pay." He didn't have any money to give to anyone.

Kergan waved a hand. "Don't worry about it. I know how much you've spent to find Rachel."

He swallowed. "Thanks."

"Do you know what this is about, why someone tried to kill you?"

"No."

"It has to be related to you looking into the Op. End it, Jack. Is this how you want to live?"

Though he valued Kergan's advice, he thought it was too late to back away. He didn't want to.

On the way home his phone beeped. He pulled over. A sensor had been tripped along the east county road. He pulled up camera feeds. A photo of one man. This time he was going to have a conversation.

He drove the bike to the shed and locked it up, and then hiked through the woods. Glock in hand. He planned to catch the intruder at the house. Remaining behind a tree, he surveyed his house with the binoculars. He received another text alert. A photo of the same guy exiting his property at the same point of entry.

He entered the back door of his house, locked it, and hustled down the basement steps. The basement was finished with wood paneling and lightly furnished. A built-in bookshelf took up the southeast corner.

He depressed a narrow panel on the wall near the floor in the southwest corner. It slid sideways, revealing a numeric pad. He punched in the code, heard a click, and closed the panel. One side of the bookshelf was ajar and he pulled it out, revealing a locked steel door. The door key was the same one for the locked cabinet in the barn's first level.

In moments he entered a dark tunnel. Turning, he pulled the bookshelf back to the wall until it clicked in, and then shut the door. The tunnel was braced with cement blocks, and he trailed a hand along one wall as he hurried through it.

At the far end he punched the code into another keypad, and then pushed the door open into the lower barn level. The door was hidden behind paneling, which he closed.

Just to be sure all the sensors were working, he checked the new camera placements on his computer. Nothing. Whoever had come in had left without reaching the chokepoints, much less the house or barn. What was the point? Maybe a trap of some kind. Explosives. Possibly on his running course.

He hurried to the upper level and walked outside. Keeping parallel to the driveway, he remained in the woods. Nearing the east county road, he kept himself hidden in the trees and walked south parallel to the road. At the triggered camera position the road was empty.

Hunting around yielded a partial boot imprint. And a speck of red. The tracks led faintly to the road, but there was no car.

Worried, he walked briskly into the woods and called for Spinner. She had been out running while he was gone, something he never worried about since she always remained on his land.

Once, some years ago, Spinner had been hurt by a coyote or bobcat. She came to the house door late in the night, whining until Rachel woke up and let her in. Rachel had held and stroked Spinner gently while Steel tended the dog's wounds.

The memory made his eyes moist. Rachel loved the dog. His stomach tight, he walked the inner training course, off to the side of it while checking for any disturbance in the soil. And kept calling for Spinner. Several times grouse flew up ahead of him. Once he saw a raccoon staring down at him from a hole in the trunk of a big oak tree.

He found her on the stream bridge, curled up, asleep in the last of the sun on the warm wood. His stomach finally righted and he heaved a deep sigh.

"What are you doing out here, Spinner?" His smile faded as he walked up to her. Her eyes remained closed and she didn't move. A patch of red marked her right flank. Going to one knee, he stroked her side. Spinner barely cracked her eyes but didn't lift her head.

He called a local vet. Gently lifting her, he carried her home as fast as he could.

When he had first brought Spinner home. Rachel was just five years old, chasing the crazy puppy round and round, because the puppy chased its own tail.

"She's spinning." Carol laughed with Rachel.

He had laughed too and said, "Spinner." The name stuck.

Spinner was another connection to Rachel. If his daughter ever came home, he wanted the dog waiting for her too.

***

"If you hadn't found her, she would be dead by now."

Steel swallowed. "Will she make it?"

"I think so." The vet shook his head. "Any reason why someone would shoot her?"

He kept his face calm and shrugged. "A stray bullet?"

"That's possible. I'll need to keep her for a while."

"Thanks." He stroked Spinner's head as she lay resting inside the vet's van, her eyes closed.

"I'll keep you posted." The vet drove off.

His actions had brought this to Spinner. The killer had come for him, but instead Spinner had surprised the intruder, giving him an injury that had forced him back to his car.

His fists clenched. The enemy was still coming at him and he had no clue who it was. He didn't want to tell CID. They would find out he was living at home.

Carol would want to know about Spinner so he left another message on her voicemail, suggesting they meet for dinner. Maybe she was just too busy for him or spending time in an affair. If he followed her for a day he might find out who the guy was, but he worried about what he might do if he knew.

Needing exercise and fresh air to think, he decided to make sure the sheds remained untouched. It was dark when he walked to the motorcycle shed, and then the LLC Jeep shed. Everything was fine. The air was cool. An owl hooted in the distance and brown bats flitted through the sky, devouring mosquitoes.

From the LLC shed he walked back halfway to the motorcycle shed and stopped. He stood in the darkened forest, spotting an old oak tree. Standing on its west side, he counted off ten steps, and knelt down. Stuffing the Glock into his belt, he dug his hands into the leaf litter, feeling for a handle. Finding one, he lifted it.

A round manhole cover came up, with four inches of leaves and sticks glued to its top. It opened to vertical on its hinges. He descended the rungs, closing the cover behind him, which left him in darkness.

At the bottom he found the pad and punched the code. The lock clicked, and he pushed the metal door inward, closing it behind him. The dark tunnel was also braced by cement blocks. It took minutes to reach the entrance to the lower barn level. Like the house tunnel, this exit was also hidden behind wall paneling.

His thoughts returned to the Komodo Op. He needed to explore the money angle. Using a secure browser, he went online and bounced his ISP around the world. He researched articles on the friar, Francis Sotelo. After some digging he found one that held his attention.

Sotelo supported Vegas because the general wanted to hold companies responsible for environmental degradation in Mexico, especially foreign corporations, and make them clean up land and water they had polluted. One major concern were hormone-mimicking chemicals that scientists worldwide were saying could cause cancer and reproductive problems for humans and wildlife.

Most of the pollution had been dumped in poverty-stricken areas. Steel's jaw tightened. Environmental issues had always concerned him and having a child made him even more concerned about the future of the planet.

The estimate for cleanup costs and related health care costs for affected Mexican citizens was in the billions. One of the U.S. companies listed was MultiSec. They had the most flagrant pollution infractions, resulting in thousands of citizen health complaints, and stood to lose the most financially if Vegas was elected.

In an article dissecting one of Francis Sotelo's speeches, the reporter stated that the friar had mentioned MultiSec's flagrant environmental pollution. But Steel couldn't see how a corporation like MultiSec could take over a Blackhood Op and order a hit on two generals and a friar.

He checked MultiSec's management list, advisors, trustees, and anything else he could find. No names registered. He stared at the photo of the CEO, William Torr. MultiSec could have bribed people, but it would have to go all the way up the line to the president, who signed off on Blackhood Ops missions. That seemed even more absurd.

It felt like a dead end.

There was one other point of attack. He looked up a list of MultiSec's subsidiaries. Another name caught his attention. Spirax. The smaller company had recently merged with MultiSec. An old friend worked at Spirax, one of many with whom he hadn't maintained contact.

Someone else he didn't know if he could trust.

# CHAPTER 18

S TEEL PUSHED THE CANDLE centerpiece aside. He had declined the server's offer to light it, even though Dixie's interior was dimly lit. He liked the shadows.

There were tables for two and four in the center of the bar restaurant. Booths along the walls. His back was to the wall in a corner booth, and the voices from nearby tables tumbled all around him. He listened attentively to John Grove, while consistently scanning the other tables and aisles. On the way to the table he had looked over everyone in the restaurant, but new people were arriving.

Grove was a retired Army captain. Overweight and overworked. A paper-pushing captain morphed into a paper-pushing CFO.

Grove wore a gray suit and had a shock of black hair, an energetic face, and was six-five with a paunch. He was also high up in the MultiSec food chain. Two years ago, when they last met, Grove was honest. But people changed.

Steel wondered if he would see shadows everywhere now, distrust everyone.

"What did you want to talk about?" Grove sipped his beer.

"What can you tell me about MultiSec?"

Grove's face went from relaxed and smiling to tight and frowning in the time it took the words to reach his ears. "Why MultiSec?"

"Why not?"

"It's against policy for me to talk in any detail about our company to an outsider. I just told you I'm the CFO at Spirax, which merged with MultiSec, and it could cost me my job."

"No one would have to know."

"Someone always knows."

Steel hesitated. "They might be involved with something illegal."

Grove sat back and ran a meaty hand through his hair. "In what capacity are you investigating them?"

"A concerned private citizen."

"You have no legal standing."

"So?" He didn't understand Grove's resistance.

Grove shook his head. "Can you tell me what it is they might have done?"

"It's better if I don't."

"You'll have to give me more than that, Jack."

"It would put you at risk."

"Talking to you puts me at risk."

Steel thought that could be true, but for different reasons. He didn't want to mention the three hired killers or the attack on Spinner. Grove would never talk then. "I'm asking as a friend."

Grove shook his head. "I'm sorry, Jack, I can't."

He hesitated but didn't see a choice. There was one last point of attack. He had known Grove on and off for ten years and had served under him at one time. "You owe me."

Grove's eyes narrowed. "What do you mean?"

"Afghanistan." Grove had botched planning an Op, which Steel had rescued from disaster. Afterward Grove had suffered a reprimand and had been relegated to office work.

Grove's face darkened. "You lowlife. To bring that up."

"I need help."

"Go to hell. I've paid my dues."

A few people looked their way. Grove didn't seem to realize how loud he was, or maybe he didn't care.

Steel lowered his voice. "You wouldn't have kept your career if I had told them what I knew at the time. Men died needlessly."

Grove started to get up.

Steel grabbed his wrist. "Do you want me to start telling that story to some of your old friends who lost buddies on that mission?"

Grove's chin tightened. Steel released him and sat back, resting his left arm on the table in case Grove took a swing. He remembered the man had quick hands for a big guy.

Grove teetered for a moment, his face contorted and his lips twisted, but he sat back down. His voice was hoarse. "I pay this debt, you don't call me again."

"Sure." He would add Grove to the list of people he never called.

Grove downed half his beer. It took a minute before he calmed enough to talk, and then he kept his eyes on the table. "A lot of MultiSec's holdings are diversified now, but they used to work almost exclusively on missiles, tracking systems, and auxiliary components for aircraft. Now they're also manufacturing paper products, synthetics, soap, plastics, and chemicals. Before the merger we performed due diligence to see if MultiSec had all the holdings it claimed existed. It was routine. Our lead information systems audit manager, Tom Bellue, headed the project. In some ways it was an enormous undertaking. Old defense contracts can be hard to audit."

"Why?"

"A lot of it, especially in the past, was black budget, meaning you didn't have an audit trail to follow on expenditures. In the past, half of the Army bill for tactical weapons research was black budget. Navy had a third of its tactical warfare black budget, and Air Force had almost all of its intelligence and communications research black. I lost track of all that long ago."

"What about MultiSec?"

Grove looked into his beer mug. "Tom Bellue had access to MultiSec's records while performing the due diligence. He went through ten years of data. Tom was excellent at his job and he enjoyed tracking down little mysteries. I'd call it an obsession with anything that was out of the ordinary." He paused. "Like you in that regard. At some point Tom detected something inconsistent and wanted to talk to me late on a Friday. But I was on the phone in the middle of another mess."

Grove sipped his beer. "I was busy so I never found out what it was or how trivial or important it was. Tom was like that. He came to me with a problem straight-faced, and for all I knew our company was going under or there was a five-dollar error somewhere."

Grove kept his head down, his voice weary. "Tom was killed the same night he wanted to talk to me. A month ago, on a Friday evening."

"Murdered?" Steel spotted a big guy by the bar eyeing them. The man looked like a pro wrestler in a suit, but he turned away.

"A burglary break-in. He surprised a thief. They haven't caught the killer and it doesn't look like they have much to go on."

"You suspect foul play due to the audit?"

Grove shook his head. "We didn't find anything on Tom's computer that showed any problems, and we continued the due diligence and didn't find anything out of the ordinary."

"Then?"

Grove finally looked up. "Tom's wife, Janet, is upset. She works as a floor manager at a department store. She doesn't believe the burglary explanation. But as far as connecting Bellue's death to what he wanted to talk to me about, that sounds farfetched. We have pretty tight security at Spirax. It's doubtful someone got in and wiped out a file he worked on."

"You've told the police this?"

Grove nodded. "They don't believe it was anything other than a burglary that ended in a shooting."

"And you don't either."

"What do you think?"

Steel considered Grove's words. "Could I talk to Bellue's wife?"

"When?"

"ASAP."

Grove stared at him for a few moments. Pulling out his phone, he stepped away from the table. He quickly returned and sat down. "She lives in Fredericksburg." His face tightened and his brow furrowed.

"There's something you're not telling me."

Grove glanced away for a moment. "Janet Bellue was with me the night her husband was killed." He paused. "She feels guilty. So do I. That's why she won't let this go. She wants the killer caught to make her feel better, I guess."

Steel looked down at the table, a sour feeling in his gut. He suddenly had less of an opinion of Grove. Grove also had motive. His earlier resistance to talk made sense. He wondered if Grove had told the police about his affair with Bellue's wife. They would have considered him a suspect.

Grove leaned forward, his face earnest. "Just try to reassure her, will you?"

Steel gave him a sharp glance. "About what?"

"That it's not her fault that Tom's dead."

He wondered if Grove wanted reassurance too. And now he had another reason to talk to Janet Bellue. She was going through the same thing he was, in a way. Like himself, she grieved the loss of a spouse. It was also a way to see Carol in Janet Bellue, stepping out on him. He wondered what the Groves of the world thought when they became third party to a marriage.

Grove's voice dropped to a whisper. "I owe her."

It occurred to him that Grove owed Tom Bellue something too, but that debt could never be repaid. Who was the thief in his marriage, stealing emotions that Carol kept hidden from him? What gave a deep ache to his chest was that he had kept his own emotions from her.

Steel nodded. "All right. I'll do what I can."

"Thanks." Grove kept his eyes lowered.

He wasn't doing this for Grove, but he kept silent about that too.

They left the restaurant. Steel waited to see if the big man at the bar would follow them. The man never came out. Scanning the streets, he watched Grove until he drove away. No one tailed him.

He staggered slightly to his Jeep, got out his keys, and fumbled with them. They slipped out of his hands, hit the edge of the curb, and dropped down to the street.

Kneeling down, he reached for them, quickly eyeing the bottom of the car for tracking devices. Standing, he stumbled to the front of the car and knelt down, reaching beneath the car, pretending to be looking for his keys again. Shifting around to the driver's side, he repeated the same charade.

Finally he stood, keys in hand, and opened his door. He quickly drove away, watching his six.

# CHAPTER 19

J ANET BELLUE AVERTED HER eyes, staring at the tan carpet which matched the soft pastels of drapes and furniture. The interior of the house suited the quiet suburb outside. Comfortable. Tidy. Ordinary. Janet Bellue seemed to belong here too.

She pressed her wrinkled yellow summer dress over her knees. "Pepperoni pizza and cookie-dough ice cream."

"What?" When Steel had arrived she was waiting for him, almost too quick to invite him in. It made him wonder what Grove had told her.

"Every Friday Tom bought pepperoni pizza and cookie-dough ice cream. He never missed a Friday. There wasn't any here the night he..." Her brown hair was in disarray, like her features. Wrinkles lined her high forehead, accenting her puffy eyelids and bloodshot brown eyes. She was small and petite, her attractive features twisted by her emotions.

"A door or window was forced?" he asked gently.

"The back door."

"What items were taken?"

She looked at her lap, tears on her cheeks, unable to answer.

*Just your husband, huh?*

"Money and jewelry," she finally said. "About five thousand dollars." She looked up at him. "Things were disturbed though."

"What do you mean?"

"Books were slightly pulled out on the shelves and papers were shuffled on Tom's desk." She wiped her eyes. "As if someone was looking for something."

"Do you have a safe?"

She nodded. "On the wall in our bedroom. That's where we kept the jewelry."

He wanted to know her feelings, get those on the table. But he asked, "Can I see Tom's office?"

She led him upstairs to a medium-sized room. Bookshelves lined the walls, filled with volumes of accounting manuals, novels, and children's books.

"You haven't touched anything?" He didn't see much out of place.

"No, but Tom was fastidious. Everything was perfectly straight and orderly in here all the time. The children's books were for the future," she added softly.

He and Carol had purchased children's books too, before Rachel was born. Avoiding her eyes, he looked at the computer station. "Was he in here a lot, working on anything special recently?"

"He came in here late at night sometimes." She moved closer to the desk, next to him. "I'm a sound sleeper so he didn't wake me up. If he did, I'd fall right back to sleep again."

"May I?" He gestured to the computer. She nodded, and he turned it on, looking at the files on the desktop. Bellue had home accounting and business files, miscellaneous files, and some games. And an icon for Steganos security software. Two flash drives were near the computer. He picked them up and turned to her. "Can I look at these?"

She nodded again, and he put one in. It had the Steganos program on it. He put the other flash drive in, but it only had personal photographs.

He turned to her, close enough to smell her sweat, her pain. His gut wrenched. He held up the first flash drive. "Can I keep this for a little while?"

"Of course."

He shut off the computer, needing to swallow before he asked the next question. "Did Tom seem worried in the last month or talk to you about anything in particular that was work related? Anything unusual?"

She shook her head and heaved a breath. "He was always excited about his job. He was happy. We were happy."

His eyes went back to hers in accusation. *And then it all fell apart. How? Did it disappear overnight? Or over months?*

"I should have been here." She turned to him, her eyes questioning, her mouth twisted down.

He shook his head. "You would have died too."

"Yes." She said it as if that would have been preferable.

He wondered if Carol carried that much pain over Rachel. Maybe. That idea gave him little satisfaction.

"I was with someone else." She moved closer to the bookshelves, her fingers running down the spines of Mother Goose and other books. "During the last hours of our marriage, I was in someone else's bed." She put her head into her hands and began to cry silently.

He didn't want to but couldn't help himself. Quietly he stepped closer and put a soft hand on her shaking shoulder. "I'm sorry for your loss." The next words almost choked him. "In time it will get better." A year of missing Rachel hadn't been enough for him.

Her head barely moved up and down.

He returned to the desk, using a pen and notepad to write down his burner phone number. He held it out to her. "If you think of anything else, call me. Any hour." He hesitated. "It doesn't matter why."

"Thank you," she whispered, taking the paper from him.

At the door of the study he paused, his own grief close by. "You loved him. Why did you step out?"

She didn't move. "I don't know. I just don't know."

He went down alone, not making a sound on the carpeted steps. Opening the front door, he set the lock.

Soft, quick footsteps from behind.

Janet gripped his hand on the doorknob, her face tight and red. "Will you find Tom's murderer, please?"

Her question demanded a promise, one he wasn't sure he could keep. Her teary eyes searched his and again he couldn't help himself. "Yes."

He left, needing to get out. He felt smothered.

# CHAPTER 20

JANET BELLUE'S HOUSE WAS at the end of a block, in a cul-de-sac, and there were no other cars parked nearby. He quickly went around his Jeep in a crouch, feeling beneath the chassis. Near the front he found a small oval GPS tracker attached to the frame. It hadn't been there at the restaurant.

He pulled it off and drove away. On the way home he punched a number on his burner phone.

"Steel, do you know what time it is?" Christie's voice held an edge, but he was still glad to hear it.

"Sorry, but I need another favor."

Her voice softened. "What?"

"I'd like the police and autopsy report on Tom Bellue. Died about a month ago in Fredericksburg."

"I'll have to ask my superiors."

"I think it might be tied to the men who attacked us, but I don't want CID involved just yet."

"What do I get for this?" Her words held a hint of humor.

"Whatever you want." He didn't see that he had much to give anyway.

"Remember that, Steel. Whatever I want." She hung up.

He wondered what she wanted. She hadn't earned his trust yet, but he was certain the attacks on him were coming from outside Blackhood Ops and the government. It wasn't much of a risk to go to her.

***

He headed west-northwest, making a series of turns for an hour and a half that led him up into the Blue Ridge Mountains. A car was following a good distance behind him. He wanted a secluded place. From his days of spelunking he knew all the roads and turnoffs.

He rolled the window down and cool air rolled in, fresh on his skin. As the vehicle climbed in elevation the scent of pine trees filled the air. It brought back memories of Rachel. Shared sandwiches. Excited conversations. Photos of rock formations, and hikes. He swallowed.

The place he was searching for appeared in his headlights. He took a quick right into a tourist lookout and turned off his lights. Trees hid his Jeep. Grabbing the tracker, he ran back into the shadows along the road.

Stopping, he tossed the tracker as far ahead as he could along the road and off the edge so it disappeared in the canyon. Then he squatted back off the road. He didn't have long to wait. A metallic blue Volvo swung around a turn below him, killing its lights as soon as they speared his parked Jeep.

The Volvo skidded to a stop.

Steel ran up to the passenger side of the car and shot one round into the window, past the startled driver. The gun report was loud in his ears and the glass was blown out on both sides of the car. The driver was the big guy from the bar.

Steel caught something glinting and ducked as two shots were fired at him through the window.

The car rocketed backward.

He knelt and aimed at the front windshield, putting holes in it. The echoes of his shots were drowned out by squealing tires as the Volvo turned and roared down the road.

Running to the Jeep, he made his own tires squeal as he turned around to follow. Even though it would be impossible for his Jeep to catch a Volvo, he accelerated in case he had put a bullet into the driver.

He never saw the car again.

# CHAPTER 21

H IS GAZE WAS STUCK in his rearview mirror all the way home.

He took a different county road as he neared his property so he could check on tails. After multiple stops he was convinced no one was following him. He pulled the Jeep into the shed on the LLC property and took the tunnel back to the lower barn level.

Using his computer, he checked stored images on the cameras along the driveway. No parked cars or hidden visitors. The outer gate had remained locked.

Thirsty, he got a glass of lemonade, his gun cleaning kit, and sat in the living room. He turned over a few Audubon magazines on the coffee table, covered them with newspaper and a heavy cloth, and pulled out the Glock.

Mechanically he ejected the magazine, checked the chamber, pulled off the slide, and took out the recoil spring and barrel. Working with a rag, solvent, patches, a bore brush, and oil, he scoured it, letting the night's events sift through him.

He wasn't followed to Dixie's. After the incident with Yellow and Blue, he had been careful. Thus the man must have followed Grove, knowing Grove would send him to Janet Bellue. Which meant they knew about Grove's affair with Janet and were worried Janet still posed a risk for something her husband knew. Or else the opposition believed he was on the run and they were trying to find out where he was living.

The phone rang. He finished reassembling the Glock and set it down, picking up on the third ring.

"I just remembered something else." There was a pause.

"Go ahead," he said softly.

Janet Bellue's voice broke. "Well, it's just that Tom didn't sleep well anymore. All last month he was often up in the middle of the night. I'd ask him why in the morning, and he would say he was listening to music and having ice cream. *Beatles and blitz at three*, he used to joke."

"His sleeping problems were unusual?"

"Yes, we always used to sleep in each other's arms until morning..." Her voice trailed off.

He knew she had the same thoughts occurring to him. And when did your relationship with Grove begin? Did your husband suspect it? Even unconsciously? When did you stop sleeping in each other's arms? What were the other signs?

He had never suspected Carol. Maybe he had just blocked it out as impossible, or perhaps he had missed the signs because he had put distance between them. He didn't like that he was also responsible for what had happened to them.

"Oh, no," she said. "I'm sorry." She hung up.

He understood the real reason she had called. She was desperate. If there was a gentle way to tell her that she wasn't the only one, he would have. For a moment he considered calling her back and warning her that she might be in danger. But what could she do? He felt like a fish with sharks circling closer and sensed he was running out of time.

# CHAPTER 22

TORR STEELED HIS EYES into Sorenson's to see how long the four-star general could hold his gaze. Sorenson lasted three seconds before he looked at his lap. Toady old general with a big nose. And a gun.

"What are we going to do about Steel?" asked Sorenson.

Torr smoothed his hand over the MultiSec logo engraved into the glass top of his desk. "What do you think we should do?" He sat back. The killer his security people had hired through intermediaries had failed, and Steel was on the run. He felt a headache coming on. "Maybe Bellue was more careful than we thought."

He slid open the center drawer on his desk. A Smith & Wesson .44 Magnum lay there. Shiny.

"Bellue was tortured," said Sorenson. "He was an accountant. He would have talked."

"Perhaps." Torr was seven when he had toured one of his father's many car dealerships. His dad had taken him aside and whispered rule number one in his ear; *Son, make sure you're always in control of the flunkies. Then you'll get it done right.*

Torr missed his father. "We'll wait and see." He shifted to a different stressor. "I've been considering our problem south of the border."

Sorenson's body stiffened.

Torr smiled. *Rule number two: Put pressure on the flunkies so you know what they're thinking.*

The general's pointy jaw stuck out. The old boy had some spunk left. Not totally worthless.

Torr nodded. "Maybe you're right. We don't need another Op. A lone assassin would be better. Tell Hulm. Get one of the cartels to hire someone. They can erase that friar along with General Vegas." He paused. "Actually I think the friar may prove to be more of a burden than Vegas."

Sorenson's forehead wrinkled and his white face became taut, but he said nothing. His hands were fists on his thighs.

Torr waited. Security had informed him that Sorenson had a weapon. He had ordered the guards to let the general through. He wanted to see if Sorenson had any real guts. *Rule number three: Never back down to a flunky.*

"This is the last request, and the last time we meet." Sorenson's voice trembled with anger.

"I'll decide that, general."

Sorenson slowly stood up, unbuttoning his uniform coat. A small revolver was stuck in his belt. "I've lived a long, honorable life, with only one regrettable mistake."

Torr rested his hand on the arm of his chair.

Sorenson thrust out his jaw. In slow motion he moved his hand to his revolver.

Torr's hand slid forward to the Magnum.

Sorenson gripped the handle of his gun and stood motionless.

Torr gripped the .44 in the drawer.

Sorenson drew his gun in a slow, methodical movement.

Torr lifted the Magnum, matching Sorenson's speed.

Sorenson extended his arm and aimed at Torr's head.

Torr was satisfied to aim his gun at the general's belly.

Sorenson's trigger finger tightened. "We're through with each other today or we can finish each other right now."

Torr tightened his own finger, staring into Sorenson's dark eyes. The old toady general had some guts after all. He held his breath.

Sweat beaded the general's forehead.

Torr exhaled. "I think we understand each other, general." He slowly turned his gun sideways, laid it in the drawer, and closed it.

Sorenson gave him a fierce stare. Lowering the pistol, he stuffed it behind his belt and buttoned his coat. Then he wheeled and left.

Torr had already dismissed the flunky. His father would have been proud. He swung his chair around to look out at his city. His world. Steel threatened that, but he had a new plan of attack to bring the great Steel into line. Steel could still be useful.

*** 

The president watched Hulm, hating the fact that the man never showed his emotions. He studied his nails, wondering what he could say to get to Hulm. He couldn't remember why he ever appointed him director of the CIA. At the time he must have been out of his mind. "So we know Steel is looking into things and Torr knows this as well. What next, admiral?"

Hulm shrugged. "We wait."

"Torr wants you to hire an assassin for the friar." The president smiled. "And of course you're going to do as you're told, aren't you?"

"I've finally got one of Torr's top financial advisors to play along."

"Swell. And if this mole doesn't know every little hidey-hole that Torr has, where does that leave us?" He sat back, his stomach lurching over where that would leave him. In prison. Impeached, at least. "I don't want you to do anything without consulting me first. Do you understand?"

Hulm just nodded.

# CHAPTER 23

THE NEXT MORNING STEEL called Grove. His mood soured at having to talk to the man, but he had no choice.

Grove's voice was hushed. "I'm in a meeting, Jack. Thanks for talking to Janet." His voice stumbled. "I owe you."

Steel wondered if Janet Bellue had called Grove after she had talked to him, and if she would continue her relationship with Grove. Disgust filled him and he had to clear it before he spoke again. "I need the phone number, user name, master password, and anything else required to gain full remote access to Spirax's data."

"Hang on."

Grove hurriedly talked to someone else, and then returned to the phone. "Why do you want to pursue this?"

"Why not?"

"We already checked Bellue's files."

"Bellue had security software. He might have encrypted a file." Steel paced in his barn.

"They can trace access back to your computer."

"I have software to prevent that." He paused. "I told Janet I'd look into it." Silence. He wondered if Grove was fuming again over being pressured or feeling indebted to his lover. Maybe both. He waited.

"Jack, you have to be careful. Just view things, don't make changes with anything. You understand?"

"Sure."

Grove gave a phone number, his username, two passwords, and an eight-character alphanumeric code. Steel memorized all five. "Are all the files Bellue worked on still listed in the system?"

"Just call up the MultiSec file." Grove paused. "Let me know if you find anything."

Steel hung up and stared at the phone. He had expected to be turned down, or at least face heavy resistance from Grove. Grove was almost too cooperative in letting him into Spirax's security. It tightened his stomach.

He got online and accessed Spirax's site, plugging in the user name, passwords, and alphanumeric code. The MultiSec folder held files of all MultiSec subsidiaries. Under each company name was a list of defense and civilian projects that the company had worked on over the last ten years.

He pulled up individual projects. Different data sets appeared, including audit files on each one. His little knowledge of accounting wasn't enough to dig too deeply into what was on the screen. He sat back in his chair. If Grove hadn't discovered anything in the audit statements, then he wouldn't either. Unless Grove was part of the problem and Spirax was hiding things for MultiSec.

MultiSec's holdings included a lot of diversity, worth billions. But none of it led anywhere. He loaded Bellue's security software and stared at it.

An idea came to him. Tom Bellue's slogan for his late-night snack—*Beatles and blitz at three*—might actually be a clue for a three a.m. login. He would have to wait.

He left the site and looked for any current information on General Vegas and Francis Sotelo. Nothing remarkable, other than political news. After the Komodo Op, Vegas's security would be ramped up even more. As a general, Vegas would have the army at his disposal.

An email with attachments came in from Christie. The police report on Tom Bellue.

Bellue was shot once in the forehead. The black and white photo showed a dead center wound. Striations revealed the bullet came from a Walther PPK/S. Bellue was found facedown in the front hallway of his house. Death was instantaneous. No other wounds were found on the body, except a slight bruising that might have occurred with the fall.

Next followed a list of the specific items that Janet Bellue had reported stolen. The police also noted her concerns that the house might have been searched.

He studied the black and white photo of Bellue's head. How many burglars carried a Walther PPK/S? A pocket gun, made of steel, it was very accurate. But polymer guns like the Glock were dominant now.

It was odd a burglar would carry a Walther. It wasn't out of the question. Still it bothered him, along with the dead-center shot in a darkened hallway. But maybe Bellue surprised the man, who then ordered him to close the door and shot him. Maybe.

The scene didn't fit a surprised burglar who took a shot in haste. Unless he was a real pro. But what the Bellues owned, though a temptation to the common house burglar, didn't seem enough for the type of pro Steel thought necessary. And if the killer was that calm, why not just tie up Bellue? Didn't want a description of himself given to the police? That would fit.

He put the file down. Tom Bellue's death reminded him of his own life. Nothing was certain.

The phone rang. He answered and his back stiffened

Danker.

# CHAPTER 24

H E CHECKED HIS SIX all the way to the Pentagon parking lot, finally able to release the anger that clenched his jaw. His parking permit gave him access. He left the helmet on the bike. His military ID got him into the Pentagon. A building pass was waiting for him.

Danker's small office had a desk, file cabinet, and a wastebasket. The colonel's injured leg was stretched to one side of the desk. Danker didn't stand to greet Steel, but he did hold out a large, hairy hand.

Steel took it and stared into Danker's dark eyes.

Danker wore his uniform and his thick, black hair was combed back, his moustache trimmed. His large frame hulked over his desk. He folded his hands on it and nodded.

Steel took a chair.

"You've been cleared of what happened on the Komodo Op." Danker leaned back and looked at him.

"Was everyone cleared?" He didn't show any surprise.

Danker nodded. "We think you were right, someone in the ranch house did me. I bungled it."

"How's the leg?"

Danker winced, his heavy brows hunched together. "The knee's screwed, literally. Lots of physical therapy, and I still might never have full use of it again."

"Sorry." He remembered how hard he had kicked Danker. He should have kicked him harder.

Danker waved a hand. "Not your problem. I called you in to see how you're doing."

"It's been rough."

Danker nodded, a hint of a smile on his wide face. "I heard your wife left you."

He didn't give Danker any satisfaction with a reaction. But he wondered if someone had put a poster near the front door of the Pentagon: *Steel's wife left him.*

Danker frowned. "I'm concerned about the two men who tried to murder you. Do you have any idea what that was all about?"

He shook his head. "Do you?"

"It's a mystery we're looking into, but nothing has come up so far. Are you worried about it?"

"Not much I can do."

Danker leaned forward. "Exactly. I called because we have another Op we want to run ASAP. We need you and want to know if we can count on you. This one's top priority."

Steel sat back. "I'm thinking of getting out."

"Bruised by the interrogation after the Komodo Op?"

"The missions have gotten too intense for me." He shrugged. "I'm older."

"Understandable. I won't be going on any more Ops. Too slow with this bum knee." Danker fixed his eyes on Steel. "One more Op, what do you say? This one's in hurry-up status and there's no one else with your credentials and experience that we can drag in right away." He paused. "We'll even brief you first on the target, what he's charged with and how we want to take him."

"Why brief me?"

"You'll be heading the Op. They were going to groom you for my position anyway."

He watched Danker carefully. Was this a bribe to keep him quiet about the Komodo Op?

Danker spread his hands flat on the desk. "You'll call all the shots. Even if you want out, how about taking this last Op, then deciding? The target's important and we're desperate for you, Steel. We'll listen to whatever you want."

He sat back and locked eyes with Danker. "Are we killing civilians?"

Danker gripped the arms of his chair. Then he nodded and relaxed. "I didn't feel good about that either, but I was following orders. I assumed those above me had a legitimate reason for that decision and that they acted for the good of the country."

"And if not?"

Danker frowned. "Do you think we can have every soldier on the battlefield ask that question and still have an army that functions?"

"We shouldn't have to ask."

"There has to be trust, Steel, in our leaders, our army, and our country—the way things operate. Otherwise there's just chaos."

"Trust can't be blind obedience."

"We're at war with terrorists and I want to keep our country safe as much as you do. That sometimes means doing things you or I don't like for the greater good."

"We may have to commit a small evil to prevent a greater evil from occurring."

Danker nodded. "That's right. It's not a perfect world. I wish it was."

He shifted his gaze off Danker as he considered the colonel's words. Danker was a good soldier, one of the best. That bothered him in ways and to a depth he couldn't quite understand. He looked up, curious about how much control they would give him. "Do I pick who goes with me?"

"General Morris does that, but you'll decide everything else."

"Morris?"

Danker lifted a few fingers. "General Sorenson is going to retire. Morris is his replacement. He has a career as distinguished as yours. Look it up. It's up to you, but your country needs you, whether you like it or not."

He didn't. "Give me a few days to consider it."

"That's all we have."

On the way out to the parking lot his private investigator, Larry Nerstrand, called. Steel held the phone tightly.

"Jack, I don't want to get your hopes up, but the guy I'm tracking has made a habit of picking up young girls and selling them into sex trafficking. I'm close to finding him."

His heart beat faster. "I can help. I can be anywhere you need me to be."

"I need calm and no violence, Jack. If I need help, you're the first person I'll call. Give me a few more days."

He almost began arguing that he should join him, but quickly decided against it. "Thanks, Larry."

His palms were sweating and blood rushed to his ears. If he found Rachel, no matter what she had been through, he would do whatever it took to get her healthy again. He wanted to scream.

# CHAPTER 25

H E MET CAROL IN Richmond at a cozy place called Rudie's—
she had sent a text. Small, tables for two, dimmed lights
and soft music. Before he joined her, he casually walked
through the restaurant, scanning the patrons. No one looked
suspicious. No one had followed him.

She had ordered soup and salad for them. It was waiting for
him on the table. In the past if she ordered their food before his
arrival it meant she had little time.

He sat down and watched her face for any sign of what was to
come. A man in a waist-length leather coat sat at a corner table,
eyeing them. Kergan's watcher.

Carol wore a deep blue suit, her auburn hair falling on her
shoulders, her sharp chin in her palm braced by an elbow on
the table. She looked beautiful. But who was she? His wife? A
stranger?

He wouldn't tell her about Larry Nerstrand's call. He had done
that too many times in the past, raising her hopes about finding
Rachel, only to dash them again.

"Jack," she said softly. Her hazel eyes settled on his plate. "I
hope it's all right."

"Spinner almost died. Someone shot her."

"Oh, Jack." Her eyes widened and she slid a warm hand over
his. "Why didn't you call me?"

He frowned. "I did."

"She'll be okay?"

"She'll be with the vet for a few days." He took a deep breath. "I miss you."

She removed her hand. "I don't like needing someone to chauffeur me around. What's going on?"

He detected anger and couldn't blame her. Guilt swept him. "I'm sorry. I don't know. I'm trying to find out."

She stared into his eyes for a few moments. "Jack, part of me wants to give us another chance."

His heart beat faster. "We can make it work. I'm different now."

"I don't want to live in fear and worry anymore. I need to know you're out of the military for good, and I need to feel you want to be part of my life too. Get more involved with my friends and social gatherings." She paused. "The reason I began talking to this other person is he makes me feel safe. I don't have to worry if he'll make it through another mission."

He swallowed. "I can do that. Get out and stay out. And you know I'll always protect you, Carol." He thought about the three men that had recently tried to kill him. She was right, his life wasn't safe. "Can you give me a few weeks to work things out?"

A long silence followed while she looked at the table, then up at him. "I want some time away from you, Jack. To think about all this. A month. No calls, no letters."

"Are you taking a break from him too?" He put his fork down and clutched his knee. She had decided this alone, without him. Not a partner. An acquaintance.

She looked down and said softly, "I'm deciding whether I want to be with him."

He dug his fingers into his thigh. "Is it a contest? Strongest man wins?"

She mechanically stirred her soup, her lips trembling.

"You didn't answer the question. Are you taking a break from him too?"

"I don't know," she whispered.

"Great. Maybe he'll help you decide." Blood rushed to his ears. "Glad you're so fair about this. I've been with you for ten years, and he for one, and I'm the one you need a break from."

"Please, Jack."

He got himself under control and kept his voice calm. "How will you decide? By having sex with him? Talk it out with him? I'm sure he's unbiased and will give me a fair shake."

"Jack." Tears sprang into her eyes. "I've never lied to you."

"Has he promised you a child to make up for my mistakes? Is that it? Or do you just want to punish me?"

"I don't know."

"We're both to blame for what happened in the past, but you're the only one to blame for what's happening now." He needed to get away from her. "I need some fresh air." She didn't answer, and he added gently, "Wait here, okay?"

"Sure, Jack."

His last image of her was her face hidden by her hand. He decided he was pathetic. And maybe they both needed to punish each other.

Outside he heaved a deep breath and leaned against the building near the door. Light traffic moved back and forth in front of him. Sunset was close and shadows interrupted the sidewalk.

A black SUV with tinted windows was parked halfway down the street to the left. Nothing of note to the right. The SUV had been there when he had arrived. He didn't think it meant anything. Still.

He walked back in, bypassed Carol's table—she glanced up at him in surprise—and approached Kergan's man. The watcher looked up at him, his eyes steady. A professional.

"I'm concerned about a black SUV parked out front. Maybe a spotter. You go out the front, as if you're checking things out, while I take her out the back. Then come back in as if to get her. Call her in fifteen and we'll meet."

The man nodded. "Sounds good."

Steel hesitated. "How were you going to take her out of here?"

"Out back. My car is parked on a side street."

"Okay." He returned to Carol's table.

She looked up at him questioningly. "What's wrong?"

"Maybe nothing. Come on." He gently prodded her elbow and she rose without resistance.

Leading her to the back of the restaurant, he waited for Kergan's man to exit the front door. Immediately he pushed through the employee door and hurried through the kitchen with her, past surprised cooks, busboys, and waitresses.

In his peripheral vision he spied someone in kitchen whites coming out of a stock room fast from the right side. He nearly pulled the Glock, but the man froze, a stack of pie tins in his hands.

"Evening." Steel ignored Carol's wide eyes and hurried to the back door, which was separated from the restaurant kitchen by a tiny entryway.

He pulled the Glock and quietly pushed the door open only an inch. An outside light above the door illuminated a shadow on the pavement. Peering out, he also saw a SUV to the right, facing away.

He stepped back a little and kicked the door open all the way. It banged into something, and he stepped out. A man was lying on the pavement, looking dazed, a gun lying near his hand.

The SUV's rear passenger door opened. Steel put two bullets into it as a warning. The vehicle took off, the door closing on the way.

He stomped the fallen man's hand and kicked him in the ribs. The man rolled over onto his side, groaning. Using his foot, he shoved the man's gun down the alley.

He grabbed Carol's hand. "Come on."

They ran in the opposite direction of the fleeing SUV. Once out of the alley they dashed across the street. His Jeep was fifty yards away, his Glock beside his leg. At the corner he looked toward Rudie's. The SUV was gone. So was Kergan's man.

Police sirens.

They reached his Jeep, and in seconds he pulled away. In the rearview mirror he watched the police pull up in front of the restaurant.

Carol wrapped her arms around herself. "Why not just talk to the police, Jack?"

"The guys that tried to grab you are long gone and the police can't keep you safe."

He called Kergan, who picked up on the second ring. "We were at Rudie's. Someone made a try for Carol."

"My man?" Kergan's voice was gruff.

"He'll call me in fifteen."

"I'll call him. Bring her to me, Jack. Same place. Make sure you're not followed."

"See you in forty." He hung up. His mouth was dry and his stomach churned. This was Rachel all over again. His actions had brought this to Carol.

She was curled up in her seat, her face ashen, her arms wrapped around her chest. "Are you going to tell me what this is about, Jack?"

"I honestly don't know." He didn't want to go into everything. And telling her about the Komodo Op wasn't possible. "I hope to have answers soon. Then this will all be over."

Her jaw hardened and she hit his shoulder several times with a loose fist, yelling, "You brought this into my life, Jack! You did this!"

He leaned away but didn't resist.

She pulled back, her lips pursed as she wiped tears from her eyes. "Damn you."

She was right. Nothing had changed. Secrets. Lies. Distance. He felt it himself.

In a little over a half hour they met Kergan on a deserted dirt road in the country. He was waiting by his car, another car parked behind his. Four men stood on the road with him, holding shotguns and FN P90s.

Carol got out of the Jeep in silence and rushed into Kergan's arms. Feeling small, Steel got out and waited in his headlights. He couldn't even protect his own family. In moments Kergan opened his rear car door and Carol got in. He strode to Steel, stopping in front of him.

Kergan's deep voice was hard. "Do you have any idea who sent them and why?"

"I might have a lead late tonight."

"I'll hide Carol where no one will be able to find her." He paused. "Find a way to end this, Jack."

"I'm sorry, Kergan. Without your help..." He didn't finish.

"That's what friends do, Jack." Kergan rested his palm on Steel's shoulder. "Make it end, whatever it is."

He watched Kergan drive Carol away, and sat in the Jeep, thinking. Carol had almost been kidnapped because of him. Whoever it was would most likely have killed her to get at him. Fury sparked his eyes. They had gone after his family.

They were going to pay.

# CHAPTER 26

STEEL REMEMBERED THEIR HONEYMOON.
*They sat on Seven Mile Beach on Grand Cayman Island watching the sunset, his arms wrapped around Carol. Warm air, lapping water, and soft sand beneath them.*

*"I know it may sound silly," he whispered. "But I'll never leave you. No matter what happens, I'll be there." His lips were close to her ear.*

*"It's not silly," she said. "I'm committed. No matter what. I won't go away."*

He had believed her. Carol used to be enthralled with his life in the military, but those sentiments had faded over the years. Living with the secrecy and constant unknowns was different than looking at it from the outside. It had worn thin. Especially over the last year when she needed his support after Rachel's disappearance. He couldn't blame her.

He was in his lower barn hideaway in thirty minutes. Tired. Impatient to do the Spirax login. He couldn't sleep. He did some light weights in the upper level of the barn to calm down.

At two-fifty-five a.m. he sat down at the computer station, ready to go.

At three sharp, Grove's passwords and access code got him into the system at Spirax. He brought up the MultiSec folder and the list of its subsidiaries. One by one he opened the subsidiary files. Nothing new. He stared at the computer.

Janet Bellue's words *Beatles and Blitz at three* floated back to him. Maybe it wasn't just a three-a.m. login. Maybe the whole sentence was a clue. A file search for *Beatles* found an audio file: *Beatles.wav.* He opened it and *A Hard Day's Night* played on his computer speakers.

He closed the file, loaded the Steganos security software from Bellue's flash drive, and applied it to the audio file. A password box appeared. He tried Janet and Tom Bellue's birthdays, their address, street name, Mother Goose, and others.

Stumped, he sat back, going over the sentence Janet had given him again. *Beatles and blitz at three.* It seemed too easy, but he typed in the word *blitz.* A file folder labeled Paragon appeared. He clicked it open. It looked like another audit. Complex. He stared at it with bleary eyes but couldn't sort it out. There were also old account payable files and some copies of records of incorporation. The document was fifty pages long.

It was three-thirty a.m.

He copied the file to two flash drives and his computer, and then printed one copy. The print copy was for a quick assessment from Grove. He wanted a thin leather briefcase that was in the house.

Pocketing the flash drives, he took the print copy and walked the lower tunnel into the house. The briefcase was on the second floor. He put the paper copy and one flash drive in it, stashed the case, and returned to the lower level of the barn.

It was three-forty-five a.m. He waited impatiently. At five a.m. he called Grove. He hoped Grove would have time to look at the report before he went to work.

Grove answered on the first ring. "Yes?"

"I need to talk to you right away."

Grove sounded annoyed. "Not possible. Do you know what time it is?"

"It's important."

Grove talked in a hushed voice. "I'm already pressed for time and I've got meetings all day, lunch with the board, and I'm booked all afternoon and early evening."

"Any time during the day?"

"Impossible."

Steel rubbed his eyes. "When?"

Grove hesitated. "It can't wait?"

"No."

"All right. Dixie's. At eight."

"Pick a new place."

Grove hesitated. "The Fish Shack on the highway strip just outside of Richmond. It's usually crowded so grab a table."

Exhausted, Steel turned in, feeling momentum on his side. He fell asleep immediately.

# CHAPTER 27

ANKER'S THROAT HAD BEEN parched for almost an hour, but he put off his thirst and called General Sorenson. He had thought it was a mistake to ask Steel to join the next Blackhood Op, but General Morris had ordered him to. And Sorenson had backed up Morris. It frustrated him.

The general answered in his tired voice. "Sorenson here."

"Colonel Danker here, reporting on Major Steel, sir." He paused, but Sorenson didn't respond. "I'm sure Steel researched the Komodo Op. He has to be dirty. There's no reason why two men would try to kill him if he wasn't. And he's not living at home anymore. He's on the run."

Sorenson's weary voice held only apathy. "Keep me updated, colonel."

Danker's eyebrows shot up. "That's it? This is a Blackhood operative we're talking about, sir. We should bring him in immediately for questioning. Arrest him before he disappears for good. For all we know he's a traitor. He shouldn't be involved in any more Ops until he's cleared." He imagined slamming his big fists into Steel's face during the arrest.

"That's not necessary, colonel." Sorenson's voice sounded like he barely had enough energy for those four words. "He's already been cleared on the Komodo Op, and General Morris wants him."

Danker's neck grew hot. Maybe Sorenson just didn't care anymore. Too washed out, ready to retire. He looked through his office door at the water cooler down the hallway. It was a mile away. His mouth was so dry he couldn't swallow.

"Sir," he continued, "I strongly recommend we take action. I can do the interrogation alone if you're too busy. I'm certain Steel will crack. His wife left him so he's probably a mess. It could work in our favor."

"Just keep him under surveillance for now."

Danker bunched his free hand into a fist. Sorenson was an idiot. "We have to proceed with the act of treason."

"What act of treason?"

Sorenson must be senile. "Steel has to be the one that attacked me on the Komodo Op. He needs to be held accountable."

"We have no proof. All in due time, colonel."

The line went dead.

Danker swore and slammed the receiver down. What a joke. If it was up to him, he would pull Steel in and tear him apart with a week of interrogation.

Christie was the key. Instinct and the desire for revenge told him to keep her around Steel. Steel was a ship with a hole in its side, and Danker wanted to add a little more cargo to sink him. If Sorenson didn't move on the treason charge against Steel, he would do it himself. Go over Sorenson's head. That calmed his racing pulse a little.

Steel was close to a court-martial and he didn't even know it. The great, careful Steel was acting sloppy enough to make a junior prosecutor smirk. He smiled. It made up for his limp, at least a little.

His thirst finally won out. He needed both of his arms to push out of the chair. Then it was an awkward hobble to the water cooler. He cursed the knee. He cursed Steel. At least his neck was better. The chiropractor had helped that, but he still moved like an old man with the injuries. Disabled.

He could see it coming. Put out to pasture with a pension. They just hadn't talked to him about it yet. Administration would wait a year and then bring it up casually, like it was a new idea. Budget cuts, they would say.

He limped back to his desk chair and sipped water, suddenly bleak about all the years he had followed orders. Just to end up like this. He believed in rigid obedience. The army demanded it. Needed it. But it had done nothing for him personally. He didn't even have any money to travel, to meet all the eligible women out there who wanted a healthy man his age.

The Army was his wife, mistress, and family. Thirty years. His marriage hadn't even survived that long. He had a kid in college in Florida, an elderly mother in Kansas, and an ex who took monthly checks from him. It seemed a grim summary for his life.

Someone wanted Steel dead. The most likely explanation was that Steel was involved with something illegal. Most crime involved money, and Steel had a lot of debt and was mortgaged up to his ears.

Maybe Steel was hiding something of value in his house. If there was something worthwhile there, Danker didn't want Christie finding it. She would report it. And it would be too much of a risk for him to go there.

He looked at his knee and fury welled up inside him. To hell with Steel and all of them. It was time to take care of himself.

# CHAPTER 28

STEEL PEERED OVER THE *cliff edge and watched Carol and Rachel fall. They didn't call for help and something about their calm expressions told him that maybe they were flying. Not falling. He watched, sensing he was going to fall too. And he knew he couldn't fly.*

When he woke from the nightmare, he sat upright. Late afternoon. It was dark in the lower level. He checked the cameras and sensors. All operating, nothing unusual.

His burner phone beeped. Christie texting him.

*I need you to analyze another Op in the Paktika caves.*

Meeting her at all could put her at risk. Just like Carol. He sent a text. *Not a good time.*

*We're running this Op soon and soldiers' lives are on the line. Your advice could minimize risk. We need your help.*

He hesitated.

*Did the Tom Bellue report help you?*

She was saying he owed her. And she was right. He also didn't want men dying because he hadn't looked at the Op ahead of time. Another thing he couldn't deny was that he wanted to see her. To have an affair? No. He didn't have an answer to it.

Meeting her at a café or her place, or anyplace other than his, posed more risk because he couldn't control the situation.

He sent her a text. *Same truck stop. Three p.m. Watch your six.*

He showered, pulled on black jeans and a dark blue cotton shirt, and exited via the forest tunnel. From there he walked to the LLC shed. A dark line of clouds was moving in and he didn't think Christie would want to get soaked on the motorcycle.

Flicker woodpeckers were hammering trees and cardinals were singing. It was times like these that he missed Rachel the most. She always loved to hike with him.

By the time he met Christie it was pouring. In forty minutes they ran into the barn.

Christie was bright-eyed, with damp hair and green jogging pants. She went into the shower room to get a towel to dry off her face and limbs. When she came out he was sitting at the computer station. She walked right up to him. Her blouse was damp, clinging to her body. He looked away.

"Everything okay, Steel?"

He glanced into her eyes, seeing sincerity behind the question. She wasn't probing for information. It felt good to have someone care. He took a deep breath. "Yeah. What can I do for you?"

She handed him a flash drive. "We're not going into the first cave system based on your recommendations. However, the target has moved and we have another cave system in Paktika we want you to evaluate. It has the same issues of close proximity to Pakistan, resulting in our inability to drop large bombs."

He swiveled his chair, pulled it up on the monitor, and began examining it. After an hour he gave her recommendations, as well as concluding they could successfully go after the target in the new location. She posed questions and ideas, always insightful, and again he found working with her enjoyable. He had never been able to share this part of his life with Carol.

He ran a VR simulation for her to see the proposed Op firsthand.

Afterward she said, "Love it. Good job."

"You helped."

"Coming from you that means something."

He checked his watch. "I'm going to have something quick to eat. Last meal here, if you're hungry."

"Sure, why not?" She smiled at him, looking slightly awkward.

He felt the same way. Again he wasn't sure why he was doing this. Maybe just to have some normal companionship, something other than death and violence.

Later in the kitchen he found himself gazing at her slender legs and toned arms. He hadn't had touch in a long time and he missed it. Missed having someone to share things with. Her back was to him at the counter, but she glanced over her shoulder and caught him.

He looked away, wondering if that was how it started with Carol and her friend. A look. One idea that caught her off guard. Or maybe it was more planned than that. More deliberate.

"Where's Spinner? Chasing rabbits?" She turned, a glass of water in her hand.

"She's at the vet. Someone shot her."

Her smile disappeared. "Someone tried to murder your dog?"

He shrugged. "A stray bullet. I was walking her somewhere else."

She walked up to him and rested a soft hand on his shoulder. "I'm sorry, Steel. I really am. She's a beautiful dog. A good friend. I hope she'll be okay."

"The vet said she would recover. Spinner meant a lot to Rachel and I want her here in case..." He didn't finish.

"You love your daughter very much, Jack, and that's the best thing a father can do."

He looked at the table. "I didn't keep her safe."

"No one can keep anyone safe twenty-four-seven. You're too hard on yourself."

Her empathy touched him. And in two sentences she had given him more absolution and understanding than Carol had done in a year's time.

"Look, Steel, you lost your daughter and wife, someone is after you, and your dog was shot. That would be a nightmare scenario for anyone. Are you in some kind of trouble?"

"Maybe."

Her voice softened. "I'll help if I can."

"Right now it's handled. Thanks for the offer though." He didn't want her targeted like Carol. And he doubted there was anything she could do for him anyway.

Her hand slid off his shoulder and she set down her glass and turned to leave. He followed her out.

At the door she turned. He almost bumped into her. Her eyes were inches from his, her thighs against his. She looked into his eyes a few moments, and then leaned up to kiss him. He found himself wanting that kiss, yearning for it.

At the last moment he backed up, his hand between them.

She tried to smile, saying softly, "Oh, well."

He couldn't even try to smile. If he kissed her, he was no better than Carol—still married and looking for something outside. If he was still married. He felt a deep ache inside.

He drove her back to the truck stop and watched her leave, making sure no one followed her. Christie reminded him of Carol. She wouldn't want to hear that. But she was stronger in ways that appealed to him. Maybe he should have asked her to stay.

It was still raining so he drove the Jeep to his front gate, locked it after he drove past, and parked in front of his house. He was tired of hiding. Kergan was right. He didn't want to live like this. Someone was going to pay for all this hell.

# CHAPTER 29

C HRISTIE'S LIPS PURSED AND her jaw tightened. Based on Danker's description of the situation, she had expected that everything with Steel would be simple and straightforward. But Danker didn't know what was going on if the CIA was involved too.

She called Danker, telling him that someone had shot Steel's dog. "I doubt they came for his dog. There might be a body buried somewhere on his property or elsewhere."

"Excellent," said Danker. "Excellent."

"How much longer do you need me to work Steel?"

"He's dirty. Stay on him. We need a confession."

"What Op was he on when he disobeyed orders?"

"Classified."

"Then give me something else to work with."

"I told you, he botched a classified Op and allowed a terrorist to go free, which cost taxpayers a fortune." Danker hung up.

The music on the radio distracted her and she turned it off. The problem was, in-between wanting to expose Steel, she felt empathy for him. She had noticed the marker for his daughter near the rope swing in front of the house.

She called Hulm. After briefing him, she asked the same questions she had asked Danker.

Silence. Then, "Keep assisting Steel's efforts. He's close to breaking." Hulm hung up.

Her hands tightened on the wheel. Hulm and Danker were both hiding things.

Her thoughts returned to Steel. He had sounded like a little boy when he told her that someone had shot his dog. It had taken all she had not to hug him.

Yet during all her years in the armed services she had remained professional with men. She didn't want to change that with Steel. She had to keep her feelings out of it.

Yet Steel's values resonated with her. His loyalty to his daughter. His concern for his dog. Even his misplaced loyalty to his absent wife. He seemed dependable and trustworthy, and that touched a part of her that had given up on ever finding a great relationship. She knew her attraction to Steel was in part influenced by the fact that she hadn't been interested in a man in a long time.

Still something else tugged at her when she was around him. She searched for what that was but couldn't find it, and decided it wasn't important. Do the job, get a confession, and let Steel hang himself, if that's what it came to. She wasn't responsible for his sins or his sorrow. And she didn't want his problems to become hers.

She wanted the promotion. Lieutenant colonel. It was the carrot that kept her around Steel.

When she had tried to kiss him, she had told herself she was doing it to make it easier for him to confide in her. Yet part of her had desired that kiss. She felt letdown when he rejected it. That made no sense to her. The last thing she wanted was to cozy up to someone on the rebound. And Steel was hiding things too.

It all came down to trust.

The way Steel tried to hang onto his wife suggested he considered himself one of the True Blue. Someone who lived out promises—made and kept them forever. But in the real world even people close to you sometimes betrayed you. Her mouth turned down when she realized she would be the one to teach him that lesson again.

Her eyes flicked to the rearview mirror. She opened her glove compartment and pulled out her SIG Sauer P320 compact, setting it on the passenger seat.

Steel had somehow brought hell into his life and she didn't want it in hers.

# CHAPTER 30

F LAUT COULDN'T DISTINGUISH REALITY from his dreams. And wasn't sure what he enjoyed more. He drifted in and out of a shallow sleep. The TV showed blue on the video channel.

It was mid-afternoon, but he had stayed up late the night before. The ringing phone wouldn't let him drift away again. He grunted and sat up. His naked, pale skin was cool. He reached over and answered. It was Torr.

"Someone got access to the Spirax system last night."

"So?" Flaut knew what was coming.

"I'm concerned that Janet Bellue told Steel something useful."

"You want me to talk to her."

"Tonight. In your special way."

"What about Steel?" Flaut allowed an edge to his voice.

"Patience."

"I'm tired of waiting. I want him."

"I know you do."

"You owe me that and promised it. I take promises seriously."

"Of course. Don't worry. You'll have your chance."

*** 

Torr hung up and stared at the phone. Flaut reminded him of a bulldog who wouldn't let go. He had a terrible headache that had begun when he learned the men he had sent after Steel's wife had failed. Not one of his better decisions. It was time to let others handle Steel.

He put in a call to Hulm, who answered on the first ring. "There's been a security break at Spirax." He paused. "There was a download."

"I'll take care of it." Hulm's voice had a rare edge to it. "You're making a mess of things."

Torr pressed his palms harder into the edge of his desk. Hulm must have found out about the attempted kidnapping of Steel's wife. He doubted Hulm knew about the botched hired killer too. Still the CIA hadn't done any better. "I hope you can finally put an end to all of this." It was as much of an apology as he would give Hulm. "How are you going to find Steel?"

"We know where he's going to be."

"Flaut wants Steel." Torr wondered what would happen when Flaut discovered that someone else would be handling Steel.

"You know you're going to have to do something about Flaut eventually, don't you?"

Torr hung up. It was probably for the best, in that respect. Flaut would do what he was best at, and so would Hulm. But he couldn't take his eyes off the phone. He decided bulldog wasn't an accurate description. Flaut seemed more like an unpredictable, rabid dog that could turn on him at any moment. A dangerous flunky.

Hulm was right. Eventually something would have to be done. But in the meantime, Flaut was useful. Like all good flunkies.

# CHAPTER 31

RACHEL STOOD IN FRONT of him, a wide grin on her freckled face. Her red hair was in the beam of his flashlight. Steel's throat tightened. They were in a cave, one of the first he had explored with her.

"Come on, Dad!"

He moved forward. Rachel waved, urging him on. They went around a corner and the darkened tunnel narrowed and sloped down. His eager daughter's flashlight led him along another smaller tunnel.

Rachel lowered to her knees and turned to smile at him, blowing a bubble with her gum. "We can do it, Dad. We can do it."

***

He ripped the VR goggles off his head and took deep breaths. Two years ago he had taken the video of Rachel in the cave, and then downloaded it into the program for her.

He didn't understand why he had done this to himself. Maybe he needed a reminder of the pain, afraid that without it he would forget Rachel. Or perhaps he wanted to break free of the past, see it in a fresh light. What he really needed, and what the computer couldn't give him, was to hold his daughter again.

He put the equipment away, turned off the system, and used the lower level tunnel to return to the house, hustling upstairs to his bedroom walk-in closet.

In front of him shirts were hanging from a head-high hangar pole. He parted them and ducked beneath the rod, standing on the other side of it. On the rear wall a horizontal pole at waist-level had ties and belts hanging from it. This rod was four feet wide.

He stretched his arms, pushed in on both ends of the pole, and heard a click. With both hands he lifted the pole up. Half the wall slid with it, revealing a three-foot-by-four steel safe. The previous owner had installed it. A similar one was installed in the bedroom closet in the lower level of the barn.

He parted the ties and belts and punched four numbers on a keypad, grabbed the handle, and lifted it. The door slid up, revealing a large cavity with weapons, money, passports, and other gear, along with the briefcase with the Paragon file.

He took out a silencer for the Glock, a second Glock which he put inside the briefcase, and night vision goggles. Debating on a fixed blade, he decided the OTF knife was enough.

Closing the safe, he moved the clothing back, and stuffed the silenced Glock beneath his shirt into a custom leather belt holster. He took the flash drive out of the briefcase, deciding to hide it in the house.

Once in the Jeep he put on the goggles and started the engine, keeping the lights off. He drove north into the darkened woods, through a narrow stretch he had marked years ago with tiny fluorescent paint dots on trees.

Whenever necessary, he cleared brush from the path. The rough trail ran half a mile north of his driveway entrance, and then turned east toward the county road. He drove slowly and carefully, not wanting to risk a flat tire.

Moths flitted by in front of him and he rolled down the window and listened. Crickets chirped. An owl hooted. He put the window back up to keep out the mosquitoes.

Minutes later he neared the gully before the county road and slowed down. Stopping, he made sure the courtesy lights were switched off before he opened the door. He ran up to the road, looking north and south with the night goggles.

No cars. To the south, the county road curved so that anyone south of it wouldn't see him. He ran back to the Jeep. Edging the vehicle up onto the road shoulder, he turned and headed north, still going slow to reduce engine noise. Keeping his lights off, he checked his rearview mirror frequently.

Just before the highway, which ran east-west, he parked on the shoulder of the road, ran up to the intersection, looked in both directions, and ran back to the Jeep. When no traffic approached from the west, he made the turn east. After five miles he was convinced no one had followed him. The night goggles came off and the headlights came on.

He punched the gas pedal.

# CHAPTER 32

D ANKER HAD NEVER BEEN dishonest in his life in anything that really mattered so he wasn't sure what to think of himself now. It helped when he angrily reminded himself that Steel had screwed up his body and career.

He stood behind a big oak tree near the county road, just north of the curve past Steel's driveway. Using night vision binoculars, he had risked one quick look—enough to see Steel drive away in his Jeep. He figured the guy might be parking his Jeep in the woods and sleeping in his house. He had almost missed him coming out of the woods. It didn't surprise him. He expected something bizarre from Steel.

Limping back along the county road, he hurried to his Taurus, parked just south of the driveway. If Steel had seen his parked car, he had planned to say he had come out to talk to him about the Op again. Lame. But he didn't care. He knew he needed some luck, and now he had it.

Inside his car he pulled a black hood over his face, night goggles over the mask. He drove slowly down the county road, lights off.

Before the second curve, he parked, got out, and walked along the road until he could just barely view north. He glimpsed the Jeep stopped before the highway, and he stopped, backing up a few steps to keep out of sight. Steel had to be using night vision too, driving with his lights off.

Danker waited ten seconds and took another peek just in time to see Steel make a right onto the highway, heading east. Walking back to his car, he spun it around and drove back to where Steel had exited the forest. He parked on the county road.

Christie had told him that Steel would have his driveway gate locked. And it would take him too much time to limp in and out from the county road. The only option was to drive in.

He was sweating. It was a risk. If he had a flat tire or didn't see the path clearly, his car would be stuck on Steel's property. He would have to call a cab or friend.

He knew from CID that Steel would get a security alert for an intruder. He waited forty-five minutes. Long enough to make Steel think twice about returning—and enough time for what he had planned even if Steel did come back.

He drove off the county road into the woods, his meaty hands clenching the wheel. Immediately he spotted the tiny fluorescent dots on the trees and used them to follow the path. In minutes the driveway turnaround appeared.

Stopping in the woods, he grabbed his Glock and hobbled to the edge of the trees. And stared. It shocked him to see how nice Steel's place was. Steel's lawyer wife pulled a big paycheck or Steel swam in dirt.

He cursed. It was either the house or the barn. There wasn't time to search both.

He limped through the forest until he was across from the side of the house. Gritting his teeth, he quickly strode the dozen steps to the house in a normal gait, rounding the corner and heading to the back door. There he pulled a pair of latex gloves from his pocket and put them on. His knee hurt like hell, but at least Steel wouldn't catch him limping on camera.

Christie had told him about the locks on the back door. Standard. According to Christie, Steel trusted her. He snorted in derision. The great Steel, driven to ground by a woman.

Danker had made keys at a locksmith job for four years in high school, and often had been sent to open doors when people had locked themselves out. Easy. From his pocket he pulled out his tools and was inside in seconds, shutting the door behind him. He saw the stairs leading up to the second level.

"Hell," he muttered.

He gave several more curses while climbing them. Working fast, he went through the master bedroom and found the safe, which soured him. Even a sledgehammer wouldn't help.

He stared at it, hoping it was meant to mislead thieves so they would stop searching elsewhere. It probably held Steel's guns and other weapons. Steel wouldn't want them loose in the house with a child running around. He hoped it wasn't his only hiding place.

Pulling the pole back down to hide the safe, he put the clothes back in place. He quickly went through the other rooms, careful to leave everything just as he found it. The kid's room was set up like a shrine and still held the girl's things. It looked like Steel expected his daughter to come back from the dead.

He returned to the ground level. He was running out of time. Standing in the living room, he tried to picture Steel in his house, hiding something. It would be someplace unusual. That would suit Steel.

Cursing the knee on every step, he hobbled into the kitchen. The freezer and refrigerator yielded nothing. He went through the cupboards one by one, the upper level first. Nada.

Growling, he slapped the counter with his hand. His watch said he had to get out in ten minutes, fifteen at most, to be safe.

The lower cupboards were all that were left. It was harder because he couldn't squat due to the knee and was forced to sit on the floor. He jerked open one narrow cupboard, which held rows of vegetable cans.

He almost slammed the door shut, but something looked off. Sticking his arm in, he touched the back, noting how far in his limb went. Sliding his butt over the wood floor to the adjacent cupboard, he quickly stuck his arm into that one. It went in three inches farther.

Working fast, he pulled the canned goods out of the narrow cupboard. Next he pressed his fingers against the wood at the back. When he reached the top, the wood depressed under his pressure and a board toppled down, clattering against the bottom shelf.

He pulled out a large leather pouch from the hidden cavity. It was zippered and held a flash drive, a SIG Sauer P320, and a stack of hundred-dollar bills banded together. About twenty grand.

Steel was in the Army, supposedly loyal as the founding fathers, and he still planned for things going bad—which they had. He shook his head. This had to be related to the two men who tried to kill Steel. Steel had to be dirty. Maybe the flash drive held the evidence he needed to prove it.

He stared at the money. A down payment from Steel for ruining his knee. It wasn't really stealing, he reasoned, if he took it from someone who had crossed the line. He shoved the pouch and gun back into the cubby, his fingers racing to stack the clinking cans back into the cupboard.

He quickly backtracked through the forest to his car. Sweat poured down his chest as he peered through the rear window while backing out. His knuckles hurt because he gripped the wheel so hard.

It wasn't until he was on the county road that he heaved a deep breath. In a minute he was on the highway, headed east. He wasn't followed. Still his throat tightened. He didn't know what he was getting into.

His actions might blow Christie's cover. He smirked. Too bad for her. His days were numbered and he didn't owe her anything. And if he was lucky, the flash drive would be payback for all the hard years of busting his butt.

When he got home he put the flash drive into his computer and scanned the solitary file on it, his thick fingers punching keys fast.

Long ago he had taken some accounting courses. He quickly realized Steel had discovered that someone was playing with the numbers at a corporation called MultiSec. Steel must have been blackmailing them and they decided to take him out. Most likely a separate issue from the Komodo Op. He would have to do some research.

He grinned. This might be an extra pension plan he was looking at. He liked that idea a lot.

# CHAPTER 33

TWO-THIRDS OF THE WAY in to see Grove, Steel received text alerts of an intruder on his property.

While driving he pulled up photos of a car entering his secret exit, and the intruder entering his house. Even after enlarging the photos he couldn't identify the man because he wore night vision goggles and a hood.

Someone had watched him leave. Perhaps they knew about the Spirax download.

He had a choice; keep the meeting with Grove or turn around. Grove could help him go to the police. If he returned to his house he might not get anything out of it besides another dead body or injuries—or lose the copies of the file he had with him now. Or the man might be gone, or there might be a dozen intruders if this man was just the point person.

He kept driving.

He reached the restaurant and sat in a rear corner booth again. The Fish Shack was crowded as Grove predicted. A younger couple sat at a nearby table. Steel watched their smiles and bright eyes. That kind of connection seemed lost to him. He and Carol didn't have it anymore.

Grove was already a half hour late. Steel grew impatient. Maybe Grove had alerted whoever was searching his house now.

He was about to leave when Grove walked in. The big man joined him in a hurry, grabbing a beer on the way to the table.

His brown suit was wrinkled, his black hair in disarray, and his usually energetic face looked sweaty and fatigued.

"Sorry I'm late," he said. "Busier than expected." He didn't offer his hand.

Steel tried to gauge Grove's expression. All the way over he wondered if Grove had used him to find the Paragon file, because Grove wasn't able to. Even though he had called Grove, maybe Grove realized the convenience of helping him. Maybe Grove knew about Carol's kidnapping, and maybe he intended Carol to be leverage if Steel found something.

"Beatles and blitz at three." He watched Grove for a reaction.

Grove looked at him with bloodshot eyes. "What are you talking about?"

"The month before he died, Tom Bellue often got up during the middle of the night. Janet said he joked about getting a late-night snack by saying *Beatles and blitz at three*."

"Some type of code?" Grove's forehead wrinkled.

"He encrypted a carrier audio file to hide a copy of his audit, then programmed it so that it was only accessible after three a.m., probably for an hour." He paused. "Bellue was worried to take precautions like that."

Grove's shoulders hunched. "You actually found a file?"

"Paragon. Ring any bells?"

Grove sat back in his chair, his eyes wide. "Paragon was a weapons missile project MultiSec worked on for the DOD ten years ago. It never made it to the third milestone for full-scale production and deployment. Cost close to a hundred million before the project was killed." Grove took a sip of beer. "Where's the file?"

"In my briefcase." He kicked it under the table. "Do you want it?" He watched Grove carefully.

"We have to look at it, don't we?"

"Bellue was murdered for this report."

"Are you kidding?" Grove swung his gaze around the restaurant, then back at Steel. His voice lowered. "How can you be sure?"

"The way he was killed was a little too neat and the weapon used was not your standard burglar's gun. My guess is he was tortured first."

"Why didn't he crack? Tom wasn't a soldier. He was an information systems audit manager."

"If he was tortured he probably knew he would be killed. My guess is he held out." Steel gave a thin smile. "Even information systems audit managers can be brave in the face of death."

"You know what you're saying?" Grove leaned over the table, his voice hushed. "This means someone in MultiSec or Spirax killed Bellue. We've got a mole."

"Maybe. Any ideas?"

Grove finished his beer. A server came and he waved him off. "We have to go to the police."

Steel believed Grove was sincere. "First you should have a look at the audit. I'm not an accountant and I can't make sense of it."

"Sure, sure." Grove again swung his gaze around the restaurant.

"I was followed the night I saw Janet Bellue."

Grove's face tightened.

"At the time I thought it might not be connected, but now I think it is. Whoever tailed me might have followed you the first time we met."

Grove's eyes widened. "Why didn't you tell me? What if I was followed here tonight? I'm not into this cloak and dagger stuff like you are, Steel. I don't want to die. I—"

"My guess is they haven't touched you because they don't want more scrutiny. Which means if we act quickly we'll be all right."

Grove wiped his forehead. "Still, it puts me at risk and—"

"They tried to kidnap Carol."

Grove sat back, gaping at him, and then nodded. "All right. What do we do?"

"We look at the audit, see what's there, then we go to the police."

"You take the file. I didn't come with a briefcase and I shouldn't leave with one."

Steel finished off the lemon mineral water he had ordered. "I didn't have a tail on me tonight. Let's guess that you might have."

"What'll we do?" Grove wiped his forehead. "I've got a wife and kids."

Steel looked at him hard. "Is that what you told Janet?"

Grove's face reddened. "It's none of your damn business what happened between me and Janet. I told you that just so you would understand. If you don't, that's tough."

"You're right, I don't."

"Are we through here?" Grove's fist bunched on the table.

"We'll take my Jeep. It's in the back lot." Steel threw money on the table. He didn't look forward to spending more time with Grove, and he was angry at himself for his comment about Janet Bellue.

Grove stood up. "Where are we going?"

He grabbed the briefcase. "Straight to the police. Can you look at the information while I drive?"

"Yes."

They exited the restaurant and Steel surveyed the front. The parking lot wrapped around the building, and he had parked in the rear overflow lot. Cars were pulling in and out of the front lot and pedestrians strolled past them. Nightclubs bracketed either side of the Fish Shack.

Steel led Grove toward the rear lot. There were fewer pedestrians, but he kept alert. Grove glanced everywhere, his forehead creased.

When they reached the back lot, Steel heard footsteps behind them. It could be anyone, but the hairs on the back of his neck stood up. He nudged Grove to take a right past a line of parked cars. As they turned, he glimpsed a stocky man wearing a short coat.

"Don't turn around," Steel said quietly.

Grove stiffened.

After a half-dozen yards, he stopped Grove with his hand and faced him. He pulled the silenced Glock, keeping it hidden next to his thigh.

Grove's eyes widened. "What are we going to do?" he whispered.

The man behind them rounded the car at the end of the row and reached beneath his jacket. He pulled out a gun but kept it down beside his leg too. Amateur. Steel didn't wait for him to raise it. He twisted and shot him in the stomach. The man went down.

Grove gasped.

Behind the fallen man, a black Cadillac with dark-tinted windows slowly rolled toward them. The driver might be looking for a parking space, but Steel doubted it.

A tall man stood up behind the trunk of a nearby parked car, aiming a gun at them.

Steel pulled Grove down in a crouch between the two closest cars and scrambled between them, toward the next row of cars. He stopped when he glimpsed two men at the end of the far row, hidden behind cars, one of them the tall man. Steel took a shot at each of them, and they ducked down.

"Don't make us shoot," said the tall man, remaining hidden. "Just put your gun down."

Steel was surprised they were willing to risk a gun battle in public. He crouched to shoot beneath the cars at their feet but twisted when an engine roared.

The black Cadillac screeched to a stop at the end of the row and a black man with a silenced FN P90 leaned out the passenger window. He released a spray of bullets, blowing out the car windows on either side of them.

Steel dropped to his knees, pulling Grove down too, as glass pattered against their backs.

When the shooting stopped, he was aware of the other two men standing and aiming guns at them. He placed his on the pavement.

The man holding the P90 said, "Into the car, fast, or we do you now." He leaned over the front seat and pushed open the rear passenger door of the car.

The two gunmen behind them motioned toward the open door of the Cadillac.

Grove went first.

Steel noted Grove's trembling hand. He didn't consider swinging the briefcase. Three guns were still aimed at him and the men behind him kept their distance. He heard sirens. Too far away to help.

A brown sedan pulled up behind the Cadillac. The man Steel had shot was lifted into it by two men. The third gunman jumped into the same car.

Steel followed Grove into the back seat of the Cadillac, two guns trained on him from the front seat, neither close enough to grab unless he lunged forward. They were being very careful. The driver had wide shoulders, a wide head, and thick forearms. The front passenger had a thick neck and wore a silver grill on his front teeth that sparkled with tiny diamonds—his P90 was trained on Steel.

Steel was also aware of the tall man outside the car, aiming his gun at him through the open door from five feet away. The man was kneeling between two cars so his gun wouldn't be easily visible to anyone else in the parking lot.

The gunmen weren't worried about Grove.

Fighting scenarios flashed through him. He could maybe take the two in front, but he had no way to shut the door and avoid a bullet from the tall man. All three of his captors had clear eyes and easy, practiced movements. They would react quickly to anything he tried.

The driver pointed a pistol at Steel and tossed a black hood onto his lap. "Put the brief on the seat. Now. Then hands in your lap."

Steel complied.

The driver kept talking. "See the handcuffs by your feet? Put them on your left ankle and right wrist, then pull on the hood and sit on your left hand. Keep your head between your knees."

Steel leaned over his knees and saw that the handcuffs were attached to a very short, thick chain bolted into the flooring. He put them on his wrist and ankle, and then pulled on the hood and sat on his left hand. The short chain forced him to remain bent over. He was aware of the tall man getting in and felt the man's pistol pushed into his ribs.

The Cadillac took off. The whole thing took ten seconds. When they exited the lot, Steel sensed the Cadillac taking a left, heading back to Richmond.

"Please, we don't know anything." Grove sounded panicked. "Take the briefcase. I haven't even seen the file yet. Then you can let us go. Please."

The driver said, "Get the brief up here."

Steel was aware of the tall man passing it up front, and heard it click open.

"Hey, bonus," said Charlie.

Steel knew Charlie had found his spare Glock.

"Quit playing around," said the driver.

"Hey, Rusack, mellow out," said Charlie. "We got it, don't we?"

"I have a wife and kids," said Grove.

"Ain't that sweet," said Charlie.

"Shut up and get ready," said Rusack.

"For what?" Grove sounded hoarse.

Charlie said, "Hey, Rusack, should I tell him what we're going to do?"

"What are you going to do?" Grove's voice broke.

"We're going to let you go." Charlie sounded happy.

Rusack made a few turns, and then stopped the Cadillac. "Just so you know, Steel. I will shoot you if I so much as see you move a millimeter."

The tall man pushed his pistol harder into Steel's side.

Steel heard the front passenger door open, and in a few moments the rear passenger door was opened.

"Get out," said Charlie.

Steel felt the weight on the seat shift as Grove complied. He heard some grunts—Grove was being hit.

Two silenced shots were fired. His Glock.

The gun reports echoed in Steel's ears as he heard Grove collapse to the pavement. A terrible sadness and despair filled him. He had brought Grove into this. Grove's death was his responsibility.

Charlie jumped back in the front seat and shut the door. "Should we do Steel next, Rusack? Pow!" Charlie laughed. "You're the lucky one. Ain't he, Rusack?"

Steel's arms tensed. But not out of fear. Fury. They weren't ready to kill him yet. When they released his handcuffs he would act.

The Cadillac raced away.

Steel couldn't help wonder who would be sadder, Grove's wife or Janet Bellue. He didn't think anyone would miss Jack Steel.

# CHAPTER 34

S TEEL WONDERED IF HE would see Rachel soon, a possibility that gave him some comfort. His head was down between his knees for the rest of the drive.

When the car stopped, the tall man exited the vehicle. Steel prepared himself. Somehow the chain was released from the floor, with the handcuffs still on his wrist and ankle.

Rusack said, "Get out, Steel. To your left. Slow."

He slid over the seat, able to sit up a little more, his wrist still attached to his ankle. Carefully he swiveled and exited the car, hunched over, standing on two feet. The car pulled away. With the hood on he couldn't see much. He guessed two guns were aimed at him. It smelled musty and the floor was cement.

A garage door was lowering. Footsteps approached from the left. He was pushed hard and fell onto his side.

"Take off the hood," said Rusack.

He used his left hand to pull it off. Rusack and the others stood ten feet away, their guns aimed at him. The garage was huge. Maybe a converted first floor of a building. One small bulb provided dim light. Yellowed scraps of paper and stains covered the floor. Stained plasterboard formed the walls.

Rusack tossed a small key in front of Steel's face. "Unlock the cuffs and get on your knees."

Steel followed directions.

"Now crawl straight ahead."

He crawled. Five feet ahead of him the ceiling had two-by-six wooden beams running across it. From one beam hung two ropes six feet apart with slipknots in the ends. The ropes ran through holes drilled in the beam and the slipknots were a foot off the floor. There were also two ropes lying on the floor, also with slipknots on the ends, running from large eyebolts set eight feet apart in the concrete.

He considered strategies. None felt winnable.

They motioned him forward to the hanging ropes with three guns on him, still from ten feet away. Rusack told him to slide the floor slipknots over his feet. Charlie and the tall man snugged them tight around his ankles, pulling his legs four feet apart.

Next, Rusack told him to place his wrists into the hanging slipknots. When he did, they pulled the ends tight through the floor eyebolts, pulling him off the floor to a standing position. He gripped the ropes so they didn't wrench his shoulders. When he stood, his arms and legs were spread wide and he couldn't move.

Patting him down, they found the flash drive.

Charlie sat in the shadows on a stack of wooden pallets, the Glock and P90 in his hands. The tall man stood behind Steel, near the garage door, smoking, his pistol cradled in his crossed arms.

The driver, Rusack, went to the far end of the garage, talking on a phone.

Steel couldn't hear what he said. It didn't matter. He knew what they were going to do, and he knew why they were waiting. He tried to loosen the ropes that bit into his wrists and ankles, but they didn't budge. His legs and shoulders ached from the tension on the lines.

As he stood there, feeling vulnerable, he tried to summarize his life. Encapsulate it into a meaningful image or a few words. At one time it would have been easy. Now it seemed impossible. A failed marriage, a missing daughter, and a ruined career came to mind.

He felt empty. But he didn't want to die.

Rusack got off the phone and walked over, looking at Charlie. "Burn it."

Charlie put down the guns and sauntered closer. Steel noticed his greasy sweatshirt and jeans. None of it matched the sparkling grill, but maybe Charlie had dressed for work tonight.

Charlie picked up the copy of the Paragon file that sat in Steel's open briefcase and allowed the papers to slide into it in a scattered loose collection. He grinned at Steel. Pulling out a lighter, he touched the tiny flame to the pile. It went up in a blaze of red.

Rusack walked in front of Steel, his wide face calm. "We have someone searching your house for copies of the file. You could save yourself some pain if you tell us where they are."

Steel guessed that the man his security cameras had picked up on his way to meet Grove was the point person for a larger force that was now on his property. "I made another copy."

Rusack's expression didn't change so he kept talking. "If they want to know where it is, I'll give it to them for a trade."

Rusack crossed his arms. "What do you want?"

"My life. Without the file I've got nothing on anyone. They won't find it. And I can promise that if I die, it'll turn up where they don't want it to."

Rusack looked at him, hesitated, and then walked back down to the end of the room to make another call. Steel could hear him talking, but again couldn't make out the words. He doubted his ploy would work. He also doubted that the copy of the file would elude them. If they looked hard enough, they would find his cubbyhole.

Charlie gazed at him with a twisted smile of glitter, flicking the cigarette lighter on and off rhythmically.

All that was left of the Paragon file was a small pile of smoldering ashes. A cloud of smoke lingered in the air above the embers, drifting to Steel's nostrils.

Rusack appeared in front of him again. "They can't find a hardcopy or digital copy in your house." He looked at his clean fingernails. "Maybe you're lying."

Steel kept the surprise off his face. "I mailed it."

"They think maybe there is no copy. They don't believe you sent a copy anywhere or gave it to anyone."

"I did."

"Point is, you're definitely not getting out of this alive. That's what the man says. You get to either go quick or with lots of pain. Your choice."

Steel stared at Rusack. Despair started to well up in his chest. Abruptly he stopped it. *Stay calm, assess options, look for a solution.*

Rusack lifted his chin. "Charlie, come over here."

Charlie shuffled over, flicking his lighter on and off.

"The man thinks he can take whatever we dish out," said Rusack. "You believe that, Charlie?"

Charlie grinned and stepped closer, leaving the lighter on.

Steel retreated into himself and cut off his surroundings and the burning in his shoulders and ankles. He took his mind into its own little room. From there he could watch and observe, and minimize any reaction to the pain that was coming.

Kobayashi Maru. He would find a way to escape and kill all of them.

# CHAPTER 35

A FTER A DOZEN BURNS, Steel babbled that he had copied the Paragon file to his barn computer. He hoped they would accept that as his final copy. He had endured enough pain to make his admission believable. He also gave the combination to the keypad on his barn door.

Rusack delivered a number of hard punches to see if he was holding out. After the first three Steel closed his eyes and went limp, pretending to be unconscious, which stopped the onslaught. His head hanging down, he barely cracked his eyes.

Rusack and the tall man kept their guns on him from a distance. Charlie slipped another rope over one of Steel's feet, released the floor rope, and then tied his ankles together. There was no chance to fight back so he kept his limbs slack, his body hanging from the ceiling ropes. His shoulders burned from his weight.

Charlie released the ceiling ropes and Steel collapsed to the floor in a heap. Willing himself to stay limp, he fought the urge from his nervous system to curl up like a fetus on the cold, dirty floor. Charlie tied his wrists together. Steel continued his pretense of having blacked out.

Snatches of words drifted in and out of his awareness as his senses fought to escape the pain. He held on to the one idea that made him suffer through it without a scream: the pain was temporary, one way or another.

They picked him up. Car doors opened and they shoved him headfirst onto a bench seat and rolled him onto the floor. Had to be between the front and rear seats. He tasted carpet and smelled the leather upholstery. They sat on either end of him, their shoes on his calves and head. A sack of painful trash to be taken to the dump.

The car moved, the wheels humming.

*Hang on*, he told himself feverishly. He howled inside. Images of Carol came to him. He sought those that would keep him alive and hopeful. But instead Grove's face replaced Carol's and guilt shifted to despair. He pushed it away.

It seemed like a long while before they stopped and dragged him out, feet first. He kept himself slack even as his head banged hard on the car frame and then the ground. He forced down a cry in his throat. The night air was cool on his skin.

Rough hands carried him. A car door clicked open. He was lifted and positioned so that he sat upright. A hand against his chest held him up, while his head sagged to the side. Fingers removed the bindings on his hands and ankles.

He wanted to open his eyes. *A little longer.* He tried to gather his energy, but he had nothing left. So instead he gathered his rage, focusing the screaming insistence of the burns on his chest and arms into his desire for revenge. Each wave of agony he turned into an image of violence against the men who had tortured him. He visualized what he was going to do.

An engine started.

He cracked his eyes, and then opened them all the way. The lit dashboard of his Jeep was in front of him, its headlights spearing empty darkness ahead. The Jeep door was open. Someone was standing beside him, leaning into the vehicle, the back of the man's head near his chest.

He flung his pent-up fury into his limbs. Right hand to the shift lever, while he wrapped the other around the neck of the man in front of him.

Shifting into reverse, he jammed the gas pedal. The engine whined and the Jeep shot back while the man struggled against his arm. Steel couldn't hold him. The man's upper body and head slid off his lap and banged against the Jeep door frame before disappearing into the darkness.

He slammed on the brakes, rammed the shift into drive, and aimed the Jeep at the man rising off the ground in his headlights. Charlie.

Charlie dove to the side, but the Jeep hit him in midair, sending his body sideways where it bounced off a pile of rocks.

Dull pops sounded on the door. Steel ducked down as glass ruptured into the interior from the passenger side window, spattering pieces all around him. He reversed the vehicle again, the tires spitting gravel and dirt as he floored it.

He lifted his head for one quick look. Rusack stood with the tall man beside a parked car, framed in the Jeep's headlights, guns pointed his way. The tall man ran toward him, firing his pistol.

Steel hammered the brakes again, put the shift in drive, and floored the accelerator. The engine roared. He kept his eyes just above the dash.

The tall man ran to the right.

Steel followed him and the fender caught him in the hips. The man banged over the hood and thumped against the windshield, still hanging onto his gun. Swinging the Jeep in a sharp right, Steel braked hard and the body rolled off the hood.

The other car started, tires screeching.

Steel drove over the tall man and stopped. Ramming the shift into park, he crawled over glass on the passenger seat. He opened the door, fell out of the Jeep, and hit the ground in a confusion of limbs. Dirt and stones bit into his burns and he gasped.

It took him some fumbling to find the tall man's body in the darkness and pry the handgun from the man's clenched fingers. He stood up, leaned on the Jeep's hood with both arms, and fired once out of anger at the disappearing Cadillac.

The gunshot echoed in the darkness.

Pain numbed his senses. He slumped over the hood. Groaning, he slid around to the driver's door, using the vehicle to stay upright.

He stumbled to Charlie, who lay on his back, eyes closed. Steel found his Glock in the man's belt and took it. The silenced Glock was gone. He wiped the tall man's gun down with his shirt and dropped it.

Janet Bellue.

His enemies would have sent someone to kill her at the same time they were killing Grove.

Still. His fingers fumbled in his empty pockets and his worry escalated. His phone had either been taken or lost when he tumbled out of the Jeep. He couldn't go to her house. It might be a setup, with the police on their way. Worse, it would take him an hour.

He searched Charlie's jeans and found a phone. He punched Janet's number. No answer. Without hesitation he called the police, saying he was a neighbor and heard something like a door getting kicked in and a scream. He gave Janet Bellue's address and hung up.

The police would be there in three minutes. Wiping the phone free of his prints, he tossed it near the body.

It took another major effort to get in and drive. He decided to go home. Whoever had searched his property had to be long gone.

It didn't take long to figure out that he was in the Blue Ridge Mountains, northwest of where he lived. He tried to sort out what to do, his thoughts interrupted by spurts of intense pain. John Grove had been shot with his Glock. He guessed the Paragon file in Spirax's system would be erased. They would have figured that out by now.

A number of times he swerved onto the shoulder or into the other lane. The burns made him shout as he clutched the steering wheel. The pain came in waves. Since he was more alert now, the agony was more acute, more unbearable.

A half hour later he entered the LLC driveway and parked the Jeep in the shed. Gripping the handgun, he staggered into the woods, leaves crunching beneath his feet. The eerie muted trill of a male screech owl made him pause once.

It took him five minutes to find the tunnel entrance. Five more to reach the lower barn level. He remembered his promise to Janet to find her husband's murderer. The same person would have been sent to kill her, and he had brought the killer to her by downloading the Paragon file. He swallowed on a dry mouth.

When he checked, he found the Paragon copy deleted from his computer. And Grove's passwords no longer gave him access to Spirax's data.

He had no proof for the police. And any police report he made would trigger involvement by the military—they would move quickly to get any Blackhood operative out of police scrutiny. And then they might follow the trail from Grove to MultiSec to General Vegas and the friar Sotelo—and discover that he had broken his Blackhood Op oath of secrecy.

Tom Bellue's murder was already classified as a burglary. His wife's death would make it appear that the same man had returned because he knew a woman would be alone in the house. Grove's death would look like a robbery.

His torture wasn't as easily explainable, but it wasn't enough evidence for the police to act on. And if the men he had left in the Blue Ridge were dead, and his phone was found there, he would be implicated.

He checked the cameras and sensors. All photographs of any intruders had been erased. From the cabinet he retrieved another phone and synced it with his computer so he would get text alerts.

There was no evidence of a break-in. He wondered how they had managed to get the other deadbolt bars open on the barn door. Maybe a powerful magnet. Someone had to have told them. Christie. He didn't want to believe that, but who else was there?

The security access to Spirax's system must have been monitored without Grove's knowledge. A possibility. The only one that made sense.

He still had no idea how the Paragon file was connected to the Komodo Op, and who in Spirax or MultiSec was making life and death decisions. MultiSec's CEO, Torr, most likely. But he had no proof. Whoever was behind all this had money and power.

He needed allies on his side or things would be maneuvered against him. Shivering with pain, he bent over for a few minutes. Everyone had a breaking point. It felt like his was near.

# CHAPTER 36

FLAUT WAS WALKING ON the ceiling by the time Torr called him. He had already chased two lines of white heaven and now sprawled naked on his couch. A taped *Best of Breed* dog show played. Lacy rested nearby.

"Did it go all right with Janet Bellue?" Torr's voice was flat.

"Perfect." Flaut doubted Torr wanted to hear the particulars of how he had persuaded the woman to talk.

"What did she tell Steel?"

Flaut stroked Lacy's neck. "Some vague suspicions, and *Beatles and blitz at three.*"

"A file and access code. Bellue hid a copy of his audit in the system."

"What Tom Bellue handled in terms of pain to hide that is a record in my book."

"Good job. Money's on its way."

"Steel?"

Torr paused. "He's on the run. Leave him alone for now. I'll call you."

The connection ended and Flaut hung up. A cold glass of whiskey rested on his stomach and droplets of water dribbled down his hard muscles. He made a decision, sat up, and got dressed.

# CHAPTER 37

S TEEL TOOK THE TUNNEL to the house.

Nothing looked disturbed. Whoever had searched the house had assumed he would be dead and didn't want to give the police any reason for suspicion. It gave him some comfort that his home wasn't torn apart.

He sat in front of the kitchen cabinet that had the cubbyhole. Pulling out the vegetable cans sent tremors through his torso. He removed the board and grabbed the leather pouch. Empty. Except for the SIG Sauer. The flash drive and twenty thousand in run money were gone.

More confusion. Why would whoever had found the flash drive lie to Rusack? Maybe to see if he would come up with another copy elsewhere. And he had. The barn computer.

Or maybe the lone masked intruder had been on his own and found it. His head throbbed because of his clenched jaw, which was in reaction to the pain that still wracked his body. It was hard work going upstairs.

The safe in the closet was intact. He opened it up. Nothing had been touched. Either they didn't find it or had opened it and left the contents alone.

He walked to the bathroom and slowly pulled off his tattered shirt. A dozen red, raw burns marked his stomach, chest, and upper arms. He took aspirin. After one rough night the pain would be substantially reduced. Wincing at every touch, he put cream on the burns, followed by taped nonstick gauze and a soft cotton shirt.

Going down the stairs was easier and he sat in the dark in the living room, trying to untangle the night's events. He called Kergan. No answer. And his voice mail was turned off. He left his new number.

He needed to hear another voice. Debating on how wise that was, his emotions finally won out and he called Christie. Voice mail. It made him feel acutely alone that on a planet of over seven billion people he had no one to talk to.

His throat was parched. The effort to get off his chair seemed monumental. Walking hunched over, Glock in hand, he limped into the kitchen and downed a glass of water.

His phone beeped. Text alert. Someone was walking in from the front gate. The camera showed Rusack.

Rusack wouldn't know he wasn't living here. It must have taken him a while to find his address and drive out. Maybe he had cleaned up the bodies of his friends.

Steel thought about it, went to the back door, and unlocked it. Then he backed up against the wall behind the door. In a few minutes the knob turned and the door slowly opened. A gun appeared. Then Rusack.

Steel shoved his gun into the man's ribs. "Drop the gun."

Rusack complied.

"Step forward."

Rusack did, and Steel kicked him between the legs. Rusack fell to his knees. Steel followed with a hand strike to the neck, which sent Rusack unconscious to the floor.

Hurting Rusack felt good, but the pain caused by his actions made him woozy. He kicked Rusack's gun—a S&W 9mm— farther inside. It slid across the living room floor.

He waited for Rusack to come to, and then forced him to crawl on all fours. "Try to get up," he said softly from behind, "and I'll shoot you between the legs for starters."

Rusack groaned and crawled to the barn. At the door Steel made him stop so he could unlock it and punch the key code.

Once inside, he ordered Rusack to crawl past the VR platform to a four-by-four post and sit with his back against it. Steel got strands of rope from a wall hook and tossed them to him. "Tie your ankles together, tight. Then your knees."

Rusack obeyed, and Steel said, "Hands behind the pole." He put a zip tie around his wrists, and then tied the man's hands together. Lastly he wound rope around the man's thick chest and the post a half-dozen times.

Satisfied, he dragged a chair over and sat down in front of Rusack. It hurt too much to stand. He stared in silence at Rusack.

"What do you want?" asked Rusack.

Giving a crooked smile, Steel walked to a cabinet near the computer station, where he retrieved an extension cord and a pocket knife. Rusack watched him return to the chair. Using the knife, he cut off one end of the cord, peeling back the plastic insulation. He held it in his hands, staring at Rusack.

"What do you want?" repeated Rusack.

Leaving the wire on the chair, he plugged the other end of the cord into a wall socket. He picked up the live end of the wire and dragged the chair closer to Rusack and sat down.

"Tell me what you want!" Rusack blinked at the wire.

Steel rolled the cord back and forth between his thumb and finger. "I want to hear you scream." Slowly he extended the wire toward Rusack's face.

Rusack jerked his head away. "I'll tell you anything you want!" he said frantically.

Stopping a half-inch from Rusack's averted face, he said softly, "I'm going to ask you some questions. Keep in mind that if you lie, and I don't make it back, there might not be anyone in this barn for weeks. You'll die a slow death."

Rusack's eyes widened. "What do you want to know?"

"Who hired you?"

"Quenton."

"Where were you supposed to go tonight after you finished the job?"

"King's Bar in Richmond."

"What time?"

"Soon as I was done."

"Then what?"

"Nothing. I sit and wait."

"Where can I find Quenton?"

"You can't. He's never in the same place twice."

"How do you get in contact with him?"

"I don't. I finish the job and get paid by messenger."

"Why did you come back here?"

"You don't do a job right for Quenton, you're good as dead anyway."

"What else do you know?"

"Nothing." Rusack stared wide-eyed at the live wire next to his face.

Steel didn't believe him. "Where's my silenced Glock?"

"Gone. I made a hand-off to someone in a car before I came here. Didn't see them. Don't know who."

Steel set the wire on the floor next to Rusack's leg. "If I don't like your answers, we'll play some more."

Rusack looked up at him with a drawn face. "What happens if you don't come back?"

"You better hope I do."

Using his phone, he found the address for King's Bar, locked the barn door, and walked back to the house. Putting on a light jacket, he stuffed the Glock in his belt in front and Rusack's S&W in back.

From the kitchen he got a butter knife and walked into his study. Wincing, he knelt and lifted up a rug. With the knife he pried up one of the four-inch-wide oak floorboards. It squeaked and popped up, revealing a narrow, rectangular combination floor safe.

Spinning the dial, he opened the safe and lifted out ten grand. It wouldn't be enough for what he needed, but fifty grand probably wouldn't be enough either. He put it into his jacket pocket. Another twenty was in the safe, as well as a silencer for the Glock. Staring at the silencer, he decided to leave it. It would make the Glock harder to conceal.

After tapping the board back in place, he replaced the rug. He was going to take the tunnels but decided that would take too long. The opposition wouldn't be organized yet. He held the advantage and time mattered.

It took another painful walk through the woods to return to his Jeep in the LLC garage. On impulse, he checked beneath the front passenger seat, and found his phone. He would have to trash it. Then he had a long drive. It would take a few more shouts out of him.

# CHAPTER 38

FLAUT PARKED HIS CAR just west of the south stretch of Steel's place. He strode into the woods with Lacy at his side, walking north a good distance before turning east.

Coming in from the west would be safer for him. After the two men tried to kill him, Steel had enough sense to have set up security at obvious choke points. Flaut didn't want to trip those, and he also didn't want Lacy to get hurt.

He had floated down from the ceiling an hour ago, and now it felt like only two feet of air separated his feet from the ground. The Walther PPK/S rested in his pocket, but he didn't think he would need it. Steel wasn't living on his property anymore.

The night was warm and he wore all black. Tennis shoes, jeans, gloves, and a sweatshirt. Not wanting his pale skin to show in the moonlight, or in a camera, he also had a black stocking mask pulled down over his head. A sling bag held a laptop, among other things.

Lacy remained at his side. He was glad she could be in the woods. He would have to remember to brush her later. That reminded him of donations he needed to send to the Humane Society and PETA.

An old incident came to him, one he remembered often.

*"You stupid, dumb kid." The bearded, overweight man backhanded the blond-haired boy stuck to his leg and yanked the*

*whining puppy on the leash. The puppy slid across the cracked linoleum to the man's feet.*

*"I'll train him, he'll learn," the boy said. Blood trickled from his lip as he sprawled on the floor, wide-eyed.*

*"He's made the last mess of his life." The man disappeared into the dark of the backyard, leaving the door half-open.*

*"Mom!" The boy turned to the woman who stood by a sink full of dirty dishes. She wore an old nightgown, her face lined with wrinkles and framed by messy blond hair. She held a whiskey glass and took another drink. Her bloodshot eyes didn't seem to see anything.*

*The boy heard a sharp yelp, then silence.*

His face burned as the image weakened. If his father was still alive, he would keep him in a chair for months before he was through with him. But the image held no promise so he let it fade.

At one point the clouds cleared and Lacy stopped. So did Flaut. To their left, fifty feet away, a deer stared at them. Illuminated in moonlight, the doe's eyes shone like bright dots before the creature turned away and darkness claimed it again. Flaut loved the dark for what it hid.

His fingers clenched and unclenched rhythmically. When Torr had paused on the phone, he perceived something. All his years of persuading, and detecting lies, left him with a sense of what people tried to hide beneath their spoken words. Torr had lied to him about sending him after Steel and his teeth grated over that.

He scanned ahead. Even a half hour of fresh air didn't stop the white heaven from making him feel lighter than his two-hundred pounds. He could respond almost as well like this as when his mind was clear. But with someone like Steel it was a risk.

The darker image of the house appeared. He stopped, took a leash from his pocket, and tied Lacy to a small tree. Stroking her neck, he whispered, "Lie down, girl."

She complied and he stroked her a few more times.

He strode to the house, stood by its southwest corner, and listened and watched. The driveway was empty. The swing was nearby. Walking to it, he pushed it lightly, sending it back and forth. He noted the stake with *Rachel* carved into it.

He walked to the barn door. Heavy steel and double locked. From his sling bag he pulled out a set of specially designed pins, two of which he inserted into the deadbolt lock.

In his teens and twenties he had spent a lot of time breaking into places and getting past locks. Steel had an above-average deadbolt lock so it took him ten minutes.

Finished, he pulled out a canister of invisible UV powder and sprayed it on the keypad. A portable, battery-charged black light showed the fingerprints on the keys. Six keys had been used. He had a good sense for these things too. It only took him a dozen attempts before he had the door open.

He entered and pulled the door closed behind him, rendering the barn pitch black inside. Gun in hand, he ran his palms along the wall until he found the light switch. Turning it on, he saw the computer station, which lit up his eyes, and a man tied up against a post. The man wasn't blindfolded or gagged and stared over his shoulder at Flaut.

"I can guarantee ten grand if you get me out of this," said Rusack.

Flaut slid the three door deadbolts, and then went to the computer console. He took the covers off the equipment, impressed by what he saw.

"Look, I'll make it fifteen grand, you untie me right now," Rusack pleaded.

Flaut didn't look at him. "Where's Steel?"

"He left an hour ago. Went into Richmond. Be at least two hours before he's back. Help me kill him and I'll give you fifty grand. We have time to get ready."

Flaut turned on the VR equipment and ran his hands over the peripherals. Bringing out his laptop, he plugged it into the computer. When he was younger he had spent years hacking computers. He was past Steel's passwords and onto his desktop in minutes.

He booted the VR program. While it came up, he opened a file on his laptop and transferred it to Steel's computer, and then used the VR program to access it.

Rusack stared at the monitor.

Flaut put on the VR goggles and sat in the computer chair, waiting.

*** 

*The Taliban soldier's baggy clothing was ragged and he sat on a wooden chair in a dimly lit room with stone walls and a dirt floor. A scraggly turban covered his head and his sandals were worn and dusty. His gaunt, bearded face held sunken eyes and his hands were tied behind his back, his legs tied to the chair. In the shadows, two Afghan soldiers flanked the prisoner.*

*Flaut strode up to the bare feet of the prisoner.*

*A table of implements stood to the side. A gun, for the end, rested on the table. The floor and walls were otherwise bare so the prisoner had nothing to focus on, except Flaut.*

*Flaut smiled at the two Afghan guards, who stood at loose attention behind the prisoner. They smiled back.*

*He nodded. The guards tied one of the prisoner's hands to his thigh. Flaut stepped to the table and picked up a thin sliver of a knife. Then he walked up to the trembling prisoner and stared down at him.*

*** 

A half hour later Flaut sat, unable to move, satisfied as if he had eaten a good meal. He took off the goggles and retrieved the flash drive from the computer. The video was one of several in a collection, all rendered from videos he had taken of prisoners in various places. For this one he had positioned the camera on a shelf in the room. The memories were priceless to him.

He wondered what else Steel had to play with.

A weighted pistol and haptic suit lay near the computer. He had noted the VR programs on the computer. The equipment was easy enough to put on, and he selected a program for planet Bok, a laser, a thousand aliens, and a chase. It was complete carnage.

***

After he took off the VR suit and goggles, he finally floated down from his white heaven surge.

Rusack stared at him, wide-eyed.

The live wire near Rusack's leg made Flaut smile with sudden inspiration. Something to add to his collection.

# CHAPTER 39

HALFWAY INTO RICHMOND, STEEL got text alerts from his western border. Not long after, alerts arrived from his barn and house cameras.

The intruder was alone and had a different build than the other man who had entered his land. This intruder went straight to his barn. Maybe Rusack had a partner. There was nothing in the barn that mattered. And even if freed, Rusack wouldn't contact Quenton to tell him he had botched the job and given up contact information.

Steel felt his plan was still viable.

He reached King's Bar parking lot and sat in the Jeep, watching the patrons come and go for a few minutes. Satisfied, he went inside. The interior was dimly lit, the tables shadowed. Muffled voices created an ebb and flow of sound.

Ignoring stares from a few patrons, he walked up to the bar. The bartender was husky, about fifty, with a scruffy beard and nearly bald.

Steel took out a hundred-dollar bill and slid it across the counter. "Bourbon, and a message for Quenton from Rusack."

The bartender stared at him, then at the hundred. Slipping the hundred into the pocket of his dirty apron, he poured the bourbon and walked away.

Steel picked a corner booth and slid into the curved seat with his back to the wall. He stared into the eyes around him until they looked away. His drink sat untouched.

In a quarter hour a thin man in his mid-twenties entered the bar and approached the bartender at the far end of the counter. The bartender said a few words and the man nodded.

The young man walked directly from the bar to Steel's table. He had short hair and was dressed in a red sport shirt, black slacks, and black shoes. Sitting across from Steel, his eyes seemed too bright even in the dim light.

"What does Rusack have to say?" asked the man.

Steel lifted his chin. "Rusack says Quenton might like a hundred thousand to tell me a name."

The thin man's bright eyes gave no reaction. "Quenton doesn't talk to anyone."

Steel pulled out a wad of bills. "Here's five thousand. A small down payment." He smiled. "Don't cheat Quenton. Word might get back to him and he might get upset." He paused. "The offer's only good tonight. I'll wait here a half hour, no more. I want to meet with Quenton in person."

The man took the five thousand and left.

Steel took a sip of the bourbon. It warmed his throat and gave him a little diversion from his pain. He rarely drank, but he finished the glass. Leaving the table, he strode to the restroom.

It was dirty inside, the floors and walls grungy, the stall messy. The paper-littered floor smelled of urine and feces. He took out the Glock and set it inside the waste bin, under some paper towels. Then he moved the S&W revolver into the front of his belt.

He returned to the bar and ordered another drink. The alcohol had settled him down and helped with the pain. The second drink he left alone on the table.

It took the whole half hour, but the young man returned. Along with a bigger companion with a smashed nose and barely open dull eyes. They slid into the booth on either side of him.

"Your piece," whispered the young man.

Steel lifted up his shirt. The big man grabbed the S&W and stuffed it into his own belt. The young man patted Steel's jacket pockets but left the other five thousand on him. Next he ran his hands down Steel's back, his hands sliding along both of his legs to his ankles. He missed the OTF knife in the belt-sheath.

The big man just stared at Steel without blinking.

Sitting up again, the young man wore a passive expression. "Quenton will meet you, but not here."

Steel nodded. "Wherever."

All three of them slid out of the booth, but Steel strode from them to the restroom. The two men stared after him, and the younger one said, "We're leaving now."

Steel paused, turning to them. "I sat for thirty minutes waiting for you. It will just take a minute. You're free to join me." He turned without waiting for a response.

He went into the restroom, pulled the Glock from the trash, and stuck it in his belt in front. The most obvious place. He flushed the toilet with his foot and went out. The two men stood at the bar, staring at him as he walked past them.

A black Cadillac was parked in front of King's, the evening warm and humid. The big man motioned to the car.

Steel got into the back, sliding over the leather seat. The men sat on either side of him. The driver had an afro and didn't look at him. They drove in silence. Steel noted the turns.

They stopped a few miles later, and he exited the car with the two men. The driver remained with the car.

They entered a warehouse that showed signs of fire, with hollow black openings for windows and doors. Steel walked behind the younger man, the big one behind him. A short entryway led into a large room with cinder block walls and a cement floor littered with trash.

A hundred feet in, a single light bulb hung from a wire. Beneath the bulb was a huge black man with a calm face standing behind a dusty metal desk. The man wore a purple jogging suit, had short wavy hair, and a gold earring in one ear. His gaze focused on Steel.

Fifteen feet from the desk, the big man grabbed Steel's shoulder, stopping him. Steel noted the steel strength in that grip. Removing his hand, the man stayed just behind him to the right. The younger man leaned against a post several yards to his left, his eyes still bright.

Steel kept his hands at his sides, his weight shifting to the balls of his feet. He ran through a quick scenario in his mind of what he was going to do. Something he had played out many times in VR simulations.

He assumed the young man would be fast, the big one slower but more dangerous because he could absorb blows. The man he wanted alive was in front of him.

"You want a name." Quenton had a scratchy voice. "A hundred grand. Must be an important name."

"Who hired you to kill me? I recorded Rusack saying you hired him. That recording is somewhere that will prove inconvenient for you if I go missing. After tonight you better believe I've taken precautions."

Quenton's eyes narrowed. "That's blackmail." He frowned, but then burst out laughing, looking first at the young man and then the big one. He turned serious. "A hundred? Sounds fair. Where's the money?"

Steel pulled out the other five thousand.

The big man grabbed his arm, his other palm extended. Steel placed the cash in his hand, and the man walked forward, placed it on the desk, and returned to his position behind Steel.

Quenton picked it up and looked at it, his eyes sliding back to Steel. "This is what, another five?"

Steel nodded. "You give me the name, you get the other ninety."

"Sure, sure." Quenton paused for a few seconds. "You killed what, four of my men tonight? Very impressive, especially after what they put you through." He placed his palms on the desk. "Explain to me how that's supposed to make me trust you."

"Rusack's alive."

Quenton's eye glittered. "I don't believe you."

Steel considered that. "I can arrange a phone call."

"If that's true, Rusack failed me anyway. Kill him and save me the trouble."

Steel tried another tack. "Whoever hired you, government or private sector, doesn't like loose ends. Look how aggressively they're coming after me."

"And?"

"You're a loose end too. You screwed up."

"Have I?" Quenton straightened and shrugged. "They don't know where I am. I'm the rat who knows the maze."

"You won't be hard to find." Steel lifted his chin. "Once they learn I have a recording from Rusack admitting that you hired him to kill me, they'll come after you. Give me a name and you walk away with a lot of money and you won't have to worry about them."

"You weave a good story, Steel. And I think you're right. I will have to be careful. How do I know you'll pay me?"

"I don't want to be looking over my shoulder all the time."

Quenton nodded. "When and where?"

"Tonight. Your two men can come with me."

"Very enticing." Quenton looked thoughtful. "I think two more things, Steel. One, you're lying about the money—word is you're broke. Two, you're dangerous." His eyes shifted to the right of him.

Steel dropped to his right knee and brought his right elbow back hard in an arc, hitting the big man in the groin.

There was movement to the left. Steel lifted the bottom of his coat, pulled the Glock from his waist, and threw himself forward onto his side on the floor.

The young man was swinging a revolver at him.

Steel shot him in the chest, the sound ringing in his ears. Rolling to his back, he saw the strong man still on his knees, struggling to pull the S&W. Steel shot him, and rolled once more to his belly, twisting toward Quenton. The big man held a shotgun.

Continuing to roll, Steel extended his arms as the shotgun fired. Pellets struck the floor and followed him as he fired the Glock while rolling. Two of his shots caught Quenton in the chest and throat, sending him crashing to the floor.

His burns on fire, he scrambled up and hurried around the desk. Quenton was dead. Not what he wanted. A quick search of his pockets revealed nothing. He grabbed his money, stuffing it down his shirt. Watching the doorway, he searched the other two men and found nothing. He took the S&W.

Jogging toward the entryway, he expected the driver to be waiting. Instead a face appeared in one of the broken windows along the front wall. Ducking down as he ran to the door, he expected a shot that never came. At the doorway he knelt and looked out.

Footsteps retreated as a shadow slipped down the street.

The Cadillac was still parked in front of the building. He took it. It took him twenty minutes to find King's Bar. Relief swept over him that his Jeep was still there. After wiping his prints from the Caddy with his shirt, he drove off in his Jeep.

It wasn't until he was on the freeway going home that he relaxed again. His burns were on fire.

# CHAPTER 40

STEEL PARKED THE JEEP in the LLC shed and took the tunnel to the lower level. Text alerts showed that the unknown intruder had left, alone. Maybe sent to kill Rusack? But Quenton had thought Rusack had already been killed.

He took the stairs to the upper level. The barn was dark and he walked quietly along the wall to the platform, gun in hand.

He searched for the dark shape that Rusack should have made against the four-by-four on the other side of the barn. The pole was bare. Freed by the intruder? Maybe still here.

The computer screen glowed brightly, displaying one of the VR programs. He gripped his gun and sidled along the wall. After a silent inspection, he knelt and turned on the light. His gaze swept the barn, his gun following. Nothing.

However the VR waterproof helmet was missing from the computer station.

He walked to the sensory deprivation tank. The tank door was locked from the outside. Unlatching the door, he flung it open, pointing the Glock. It wasn't necessary. Rusack was face down in the water, wearing the VR helmet.

His first thought was to run. That this was a setup for a murder charge. He threw the other deadbolts on the door and rechecked the camera shots of the last intruder, the man's face hidden by a black mask. Cameras around the house showed the intruder arriving an hour after he had left for Richmond and departing nearly two hours later.

It made him feel creepy that the man had been here that long. The man was a pro to get past both barn door locks. He hadn't set the other deadbolts, figuring no one was going to come back this soon. Sloppy.

He returned to the lower level and took the tunnel to the house. The house was secure. He was about to leave when his landline rang. The line was for Rachel—he didn't want her to have a smartphone at age ten. He had often wondered if a phone would have saved her life.

He answered and put it on speaker.

"We have your silenced Glock, Steel—the one that was used to kill Grove. You go to anyone about any of this and your gun goes to the police. Then we'll kill anyone you talk to. You'll always have to look over your shoulder. So will your wife. Remember that. You have nothing. We have what we want. Let's both leave it alone."

The line went dead. He checked his watch. Three-thirty a.m. He grabbed the S&W and returned to the barn. He clenched his fist over the phone threat, and the idea that whoever had engineered the Komodo Op would get away with it.

The lone individual that had been here had played with the VR system, unafraid of being discovered. It made him feel queasy that someone had been bold enough to come onto his property, hack into and play with his computer program, and sadistically kill a man. Almost as if the killer had no fear of being discovered.

Rusack might have told the intruder where he was going, and the killer could have estimated the time it would take to get to King's and back. That fit. Still. It left him wary. An unknown adversary was watching, monitoring, and stalking him. He couldn't think of anything to do to change that for the time being.

He had to talk himself into pulling Rusack out of the tank. Rusack's ankles, knees, and thighs were tied together, his hands tied behind his back and then bound to his feet. Rusack could have kept his face out of the water only by using his neck muscles. In time he would have tired. The killer had tied him up, then lifted and placed him in the tank. That took strength.

He stared at the body. He couldn't go to the police and tell them he had kept Rusack hostage, and that someone had murdered him while he was away. Nor did he have an alibi. Unless he wanted to say he had killed Quenton and two of his men.

Returning to the LLC shed, he drove his Jeep to the barn and put a plastic sheet on the floor by the tank. He put on disposable gloves, and lifted Rusack out. Some of the salt water dribbled off the corpse onto his shirt. The salt hit the burns and his skin screamed.

He placed the body on the plastic, wiped clean the S&W, and rolled the plastic up around both. After tying it, he loaded it into the back of the Jeep.

He quickly drove out to the east county road that bordered his property, and south along it, toward the only parked car. It had to be Rusack's, because no one else was around and no one left cars parked along county roads. The car keys were in Rusack's pocket, and he put them in the ignition. Then he dragged the body into the trunk of the car, and called a fixer he knew.

Standing beside his Jeep, which he parked fifty feet north of the sedan, he waited.

In thirty minutes a pickup truck appeared south of him on the county road. It slowly drove closer, finally parking a quarter mile behind Rusack's car. It flashed its lights twice.

Steel walked back to the sedan, tossed the ten thousand onto the driver's seat, and then returned to his Jeep and got in. In his rearview mirror he watched the pickup pull up beside Rusack's car. A man exited the passenger side of the pickup and entered the car. Both vehicles quickly turned around and left.

He drove home, spent hours cleaning up, and then returned to the lower level, where he stripped off his clothing and changed his bandages. By the time he was done it was early morning. On the way to his bedroom he had to use the wall to keep himself upright. He was exhausted.

He sat on the edge of his bed, thinking.

Something about Rusack's murder stirred other memories. Whoever was responsible wanted to torture the man and had been leisurely about it. The time spent with the VR and the tank, and the way Rusack was tied up, indicated an unhurried person who could operate with little time and remain relaxed about it.

He believed it was the same person that had killed Yellow. Someone was still playing tag with someone else. And he still had no idea who it might be. Again he concluded MultiSec's CEO Torr would be a best guess as to who was behind the killer.

A ragged breath made him shudder and he wished he wasn't alone right now. Tossing his gun to the side, he lay down to sleep.

# PART 3

## OP: SERPENT

# CHAPTER 41

STEEL CHASED SHADOWS, OR *they chased him, down dark corridors and around sharp corners, where he sensed a threat waiting for him like a raised knife. He ran faster and faster to find the door out of the maze. Then he was out, through a black opening that led to a steep slope, running down it headlong, nearly out of control.*

*Carol and Rachel, their faces upturned, were falling over the cliff below him. Unable to grasp their outstretched hands, or stop himself, he fell over the edge with them.*

He woke with a gasp, his pillow and sheets drenched in sweat. His arms and chest were sore, his skin tight. The pain had lessened, but the burns still hurt every time he moved.

His brain told him the phone rang, but his ears heard nothing. Then it returned. Two rings. Silence. He swung his legs out of bed as the burner phone rang again. Three rings. He picked it up. Silence. He hung up and ran.

*** 

They met on the same dirt road. This time Steel pulled up behind Kergan's Mercedes.

Kergan got in, and Steel pulled away.

"How's Carol?" Steel noted a deer not far from the road.

"She's upset. It'll pass." Kergan turned to him. "Talk to me."

"It's over." Images of Grove, Janet Bellue, Carol, and Spinner rose up before his eyes. His responsibility.

"Are you sure?"

"Yes."

"I think that's smart." Kergan looked at him. "You don't look very healthy, my friend." He glanced at the glass on the floorboard. "Neither does your Jeep."

"We're alive."

"I've been asked to talk to you."

"Who?" His grip tightened on the wheel.

"General Morris. He's solid. I had a look at the Serpent Op. It's important and straightforward. Connections to expected future terrorist acts." Kergan paused. "They know I'm close to you and they know you trust me. They said they need you on this one."

"What do you think?"

Kergan continued. "You would have a few days before it's a go. And since you would be team leader you'll be briefed first and can take a look at the other operatives."

Kergan crossed his arms and sat back. The wind ruffled his mane of gray hair. "When I got out it was the same way. One day I was in, the next it was all too much. Emotionally more than physically." He glanced at Steel. "I understand. Do what you have to, my friend."

Steel drove a little farther and then turned the Jeep around. "Do you think it's a setup?"

"Not with Morris on board. He's beyond reproach. Since Danker is out, they can't do this one if you're not on board. The target will move again soon and he's hard to locate. They've got good information and it's the first time in a year they've had anything specific on advanced whereabouts with him."

Steel felt all used up, a mattress with a hundred thousand nights of wear. Weak and limp.

"Go to the briefing. Then decide."

"You'll keep watch over Carol."

"My word on it. For now it's better if you don't know where she is. Let's see if things really settle down." Kergan paused. "I'll talk to her. It'll be all right, Jack. She still loves you."

"She does?"

"I'll get her to call you."

Hope filled Steel's chest.

Kergan's face was taut. "I'm glad you let this go, Jack. I don't want this violence to spill over into my life, my friends. You understand?"

***

He called Christie and left a message for her.

Then he went online and checked the local Fredericksburg news. An article discussed Janet Bellue's murder. It mentioned the police got an anonymous phone call and responded right away. They found her already dead. It made him swallow. He had hoped he was wrong about them killing her.

Christie called and he was glad to hear her voice.

"How are you, Steel?"

A rush of conflicted emotion filled his chest. "Who do you report to?" He waited, realizing he should have done this in person. This was sloppy too.

"Do you want to meet, Steel?" Her voice was quiet, soft. "I have plans, but I can break them."

Her response caught him off guard. Emotion versus intellect. His voice hardened. "You didn't answer my question."

"That's because you're being silly, Steel. You're acting as if I'm spying on you. You did a great job of analysis. We're through with that, but I'll still make time for you if you want me to."

Maybe he had it all wrong. There were other ways the enemy could have gotten information about him and his security without using her. The idea of her ending up like Janet Bellue sent a chill down his spine.

Gripping the arm of the couch, he said, "Look, someone tried to take Carol. She's all right, but I don't know who's after me. Watch your back."

There was silence, and then, "I appreciate the heads-up. You have no idea why?"

"It's related to a mission I can't discuss. I've reached a dead-end on the why." He paused. "You don't have any information, do you?"

"If I did, I'd tell you."

"I appreciate it."

"You don't sound good, Steel. Are you all right?"

"Thanks for asking. I'll talk to you when I can."

"I'm not going anywhere, Steel. Are you going somewhere?"

"I'm not sure."

She sighed. "Take care, Steel." She hung up.

He remembered similar talks with Carol and the bitterness of her responses over the last year due to his vague answers. He wanted a private life that was open and honest, uncorrupted by work.

Christie and Carol were both strong women. However, Christie was more invasive, more direct than Carol in some ways. He wasn't sure why he wanted to save his marriage with Carol. Maybe nine years of emotional investment. And trust. Which at one time he believed he had with her. He missed that.

He called Larry Nerstrand, dreading what he would hear from the PI.

"I can't talk, Jack. I'm following the guy. I think he's got a stable of girls working somewhere. I'll let you know. Hang in there."

"Where are you?"

"California. I'll call you as soon as I have something."

The line went dead. He dared to hope. His hands were jittery as he imagined finding Rachel alive after all this time. Holding her, talking to her... he quickly let those thoughts go, not wanting to suffer through another deep disappointment like those of the last year.

He searched for news about General Vegas and Francis Sotelo. A religious fanatic had tried to shoot the friar at a speaking engagement, accusing him of abusing his religious duties by equating the plight of animals with humans. Sotelo escaped unhurt.

His chest tightened over headlines about another attempt on the friar's life in a small coastal village. A bomb had gone off at a speaking engagement. Generals Rivera and Vegas had survived it, as did Francis Sotelo. There was speculation that the drug lord Gustavo Alvarez was behind it.

He thought about the friar, who was taking a stand against the powers that ran society to try to bring about a major shift in viewpoint for the poor and nature. The friar struck him as courageous. He wanted to help him. It gave him a feeling of impotence that he could do no more than observe.

MultiSec had most likely tried—and perhaps was still trying—to kill this man and what he stood for with no fear of repercussions. Whoever was behind everything was no better than well-funded assassins or terrorists.

And whoever had commandeered the Komodo Op had collaborated with or forced someone inside Blackhood Ops to go along with it. He wanted both parties dead.

# CHAPTER 42

## Serpent: briefing

STEEL FOCUSED ON THE details. Danker disgusted him, but he shoved that down.

Danker pointed to a photo. "That's Gustavo Alvarez."

Steel stiffened over hearing Alvarez's name—the man thought to be targeting the friar, Francis Sotelo. He studied the image on the monitor, noting the half-moon facial scar.

"Don't let his size fool you." Danker motioned. "Alvarez has killed as many men with his hands as he has with guns. He personally supervised the torture and killing of a DEA agent his men caught."

"How do you know that?"

"Informant. Thing of it is, there's no proof. Colombian judges tend to die when they have any, and on paper Alvarez is a law-abiding Colombian."

"How was the DEA agent caught?"

"Pretended to be a buyer and they smelled him out."

Danker talked his way through a number of photos of Alvarez's jungle compound, and of Alvarez's woman, Marita Lopez.

Danker shut off the computer and leaned back in his chair. "DEA intel is that someone hired Alvarez to kill General Vegas, one of the candidates in the Mexican election."

Steel wondered if the target was Vegas or the friar. It could be the general. Vegas wouldn't be someone Alvarez could intimidate or bribe so the drug lord might have his own reasons to get rid of him.

Danker added, "DEA also learned that after the failed attempt to kill Vegas, Alvarez was asked to kidnap the friar Francis Sotelo to force the general to withdraw from the election. However we want Alvarez for different reasons. We have intel that Alvarez is supporting terrorists with money and logistics. Maybe he's already planned an attack. His brother was killed by a DEA agent and he wants revenge against the U.S.

"His compound is in the Choco jungle in northwest Colombia. You would have one day to reconnoiter the place. We have to move fast." Danker paused. "We want him alive, to get the names of his terrorist contacts here."

Steel didn't see that he had a choice now. It was a chance to stop terrorists and to help the friar. If Alvarez kidnapped Francis Sotelo, the Choco hideout would be a likely place to hold him. If he hadn't yet kidnapped the friar, capturing Alvarez would help protect the friar. "Any chance he knows we're coming?"

"I've been told none. The man has a huge ego and thinks he's invulnerable." Danker looked at him. "What's your decision?"

"Let's go over assignments."

"I take it this means you're going."

Steel avoided his eyes and grunted. "Let's get started."

# CHAPTER 43

AFTER TWO DAYS OF healing he did mild exercises in the barn. It felt good. He pushed himself just enough to keep an edge to his senses, an edge which he had lost over the last days. The following day he ran far inside the perimeter of his land, still wary. He missed running with Spinner but didn't want to bring her home until he was sure things were safe.

The solitary cawing of a large crow stopped him. The vocalizations changed to a chuckling caw before the bird finally flew away. Crows were as smart as chimpanzees. He wondered what the bird was saying.

Carol called his burner phone at six p.m.

"I'm sorry," he said.

"Kergan explained things." There was a pause. "I'm still upset with you, Jack."

He held his breath in the long silence that followed.

"I loved you before we lost Rachel, Jack. I've thought about that more and more this week, but I don't know what it means. I don't know what the emptiness inside me means."

"We both have it." He swallowed. "We could help each other heal." There was only silence. "Does it matter to you that I'm getting out of the Army?"

"Kergan said you're doing another mission." She sounded accusatory.

"The last one." He realized even as he said it how many times he had promised similar things to her.

"You told me you were done." Her voice had an edge.

"This is it. Kergan thought I should do it too." He regretted using his friend's advice like this, but he felt desperate to convince her.

"I'm just not sure. I need more time."

"All right." He couldn't deny the surge of energy in his chest. "I love you, Carol."

"I love you too. Take care, Jack."

***

Several days later he drove to Langley Air Force Base to take the first of two flights which would eventually drop him into the jungles of Colombia, a hundred miles northwest of Medellin.

Buckling himself into the seat of the Army plane, his thoughts turned to Carol. He wondered how long he could give her to make a decision. They had spent ten years together. A few more months were either worth the wait or what they had shared didn't matter that much to begin with.

He wanted to give their marriage every possible chance before he abandoned it. What made him swallow hard was that Carol wasn't doing the same.

# CHAPTER 44

D ANKER WONDERED IF HE would ever be able to dance again. He enjoyed waltzes and it was the easiest way he knew to meet eligible women.

The cab stopped. Using the door to brace his body, he slid his good leg out and planted his foot. As he pulled and pushed to his feet, loud chants assaulted his ears.

He paid the cabby and hobbled along the sidewalk with his cane. A crowd of protestors marched in front of MultiSec's tower, one of the tallest and most expensive buildings in Manhattan. Danker smiled over that as he headed toward the demonstrators.

They were draped in black rags and carried posters that read: *MultiSec Creates Death Row*; *Multi Ways to Destroy*; and *Ban MultiSec from Defense Contracts*. A husky man with short hair, wearing a brown sport coat and sunglasses, directed their chants while also handing out leaflets to passersby.

Danker limped up beside him. "Environmental group?"

The man nodded. "A coalition. Half a dozen organizations." He handed him a leaflet.

Danker glanced at it and slipped it into his briefcase.

"We want MultiSec to clean up the dozen Superfund sites they've created in the last ten years," said the man. "And we want them to stop creating more of them. They're guilty and irresponsible."

Danker extended his hand, which the man shook firmly.

"Rich Plugh. I'm the coalition's lawyer."

"Colonel Danker." He grinned. "Looks like you have a fight on your hands."

"I know it."

Danker clapped Plugh's shoulder. "Good luck."

He found the floor directory inside and looked up William Torr. Forty-fifth floor. He got in the elevator and smoothed down his black hair and moustache. It took effort to keep the grin off his face.

\*\*\*

Torr remembered when he was a child and used to stomp on ants. From the office windows he was unable to see the demonstrators, but security had told him they were down there. Like pesky bugs. He wanted them swept away.

No matter. They would rant and rave, the press would get a headline, and a day later the public would forget about it. He smirked. Getting press in this country no longer meant anything. News was mostly sensationalism anyway. Entertainment for the masses.

MultiSec's bank of lawyers would go to work tying up the molasses-slow wheels of justice until it was decades before they would have to do anything about any Superfund sites. Eventually the environmental groups might be able to claim some minor victory that the public would see in a small paragraph on an inside page. Big deal.

By then MultiSec would find legal loopholes in responsibility with regard to any lawsuit claims against them or point to ambiguity about many Superfund sites. And since work on defense contracts had produced some of the problems, the government also held some responsibility.

He shook his head. The environmentalists just didn't get it. They had already lost.

Colonel Danker was shown in.

Torr turned and sat down. Gripping the arms of his chair, he studied Danker intently. He was surprised the colonel wore civilian clothes. Loafers, khaki slacks, and a short-sleeved tan shirt.

When Danker had called for the appointment, Torr called General Sorenson. But Sorenson didn't know any more than he did. Torr had told Sorenson not to interfere. He preferred that Danker keep the appointment. It was the best way to find out what the colonel wanted, and what he knew.

Torr's neck tightened. Danker shouldn't even know who he was. He felt a headache coming on.

Danker sat down. "You have a few problems out there, huh?"

He immediately disliked Danker. Cretin. Big and oafish. The man sounded slow and stupid, his heavy brows and wide face confirming it. "What can I do for you, colonel?"

"It's what I can do for you that matters." Danker smiled and gazed around the office. "It looks like MultiSec is doing well. I can ensure that its string of successes continue."

Torr said nothing.

Danker leaned forward. "Aren't you even a little interested in how I can help MultiSec?"

Torr looked at his watch. "In two minutes I have another meeting."

Danker nodded and reached into his leather briefcase. He pulled out an inch-thick manila folder, which he tossed onto Torr's desk. "It wasn't hard to figure things out once I saw MultiSec's name in the report. I did some research. I assumed the guy at the top would be running the show."

Torr went rigid, his eyes on the folder. He knew what it was. A copy of the Paragon file that Steel said he had made, which Hulm insisted didn't exist. And Danker was the lone intruder that Hulm's people had seen on Steel's security system.

His heels pressed into the floor over Hulm's mistake—the stupid flunky. His eyes turned cold on Danker, who he now knew wasn't as stupid as he looked. He didn't even bother to open the folder. A sharp spike of pain struck behind his eyeballs and he squinted. "How much do you want?"

"First let's set some ground rules." Danker sat back. "I know you already sent men after Steel so I have to take you seriously. I want to make sure you take me seriously too. I've made a dozen copies of the file and sent them all over, sealed with instructions."

Danker nodded at the folder. "You can keep that one. The copies will turn up in the news should you decide to take action against me. I wouldn't advise it, or from what I've read in that file, MultiSec might have a few problems, don't you think? I'm guessing one of those problems might involve jail time for you."

Torr returned Danker's icy smile. "You're interfering with some pretty big players, colonel. Do you feel safe?"

"Do you?" Danker got up. "I want you to think on that file going public. What it's worth to you. I've looked up MultiSec's assets and they're impressive. Billions. Lots and lots of reasons to run a clean ship. A ship that a lot of people would like to sink. Some of them right outside your window." He winked. "Think about it. I'll contact you in a few days. Maybe you can come up with a favor you would like from me to make it square." He smiled again. "Whatever."

"How much do you want?"

"How much can I have?"

# CHAPTER 45

**Serpent: midnight, first day**

STEEL LIFTED THE NIGHT vision monocular and looked at the Alvarez compound. A light rain fell and mosquitoes buzzed around the black hood covering his face. The humid air carried the rich scent of the green vegetation surrounding him.

He was fifty feet up in a wimba tree, a hundred meters south of the C-shaped compound building. Tree limbs blocked his view of parts of the garage, barracks, and main building. However, he saw enough.

The main building was dark green, covered with camouflage webbing that stretched to the surrounding trees. It had no windows and only one locked steel door on the west side. Spotlights shone from the roofs of all the buildings and lit the center of the compound. Only a few shadowed areas escaped the light.

The compound was on a small plateau that rose twenty-five feet above the surrounding jungle. The hill made any assault on the compound more difficult.

Earlier he had watched Alvarez arrive with his woman, Marita Lopez, in a black SUV with tinted windows, accompanied by an identical black SUV. Both vehicles had pulled up close to the building door. Alvarez and Marita had immediately gone inside and remained out of sight.

The friar Francis Sotelo wasn't visible. Steel doubted he was at the compound. Sotelo's best chance was to have Alvarez out of the picture. He resolved to make that happen.

Nine guards were spread out in the compound, armed with sheathed knives, grenades hanging on their vests, and AK-47s slung over their shoulders. Steel estimated six guards inside with Alvarez, another dozen in a small barracks across from the main building. The guards split the night shifts. Half slept, half stayed awake. Only three guards walked German shepherds on leashes.

Danker's information about perimeter defenses was accurate. Fencing was absent. Steel had watched the guards take dogs for walks past the perimeter in a number of places, indicating it wasn't mined or booby-trapped.

He put the monocular in a pocket and used his gloved hands to slide down one of the wet lianas, which he had scaled an hour ago. What he planned was dangerous, but he didn't see a viable alternative.

Once on the ground he ran into the forest deep enough so tree cover would make it difficult to spot him with night vision binoculars. From another pocket in his dark green camouflage fatigues he retrieved a small, silver tube.

Putting the dog whistle to his mouth, he gave a few short blows. He slid behind a tree trunk.

All three dogs turned his way and barked, moving uncertainly on their leashes. Cradling their machine guns, the guards peered into the forest. Some used night vision binoculars. Guards from the north side of the compound joined the guards on the south side.

One of the guards went into the barracks. Soon the rest of the guards tumbled out, still getting dressed, weapons in hand. No guards came out of the compound building.

Steel gave another long blast on the whistle. The dogs strained on their leashes, barking with more intensity. Guards took up defensive positions behind walls and corners of buildings.

Steel blew the whistle one last time, then put it away.

The dogs gave frantic howls and jumped against their leashes. Several guards conferred with each other, and one unhooked his dog's leash. The animal bounded down the hill and into the forest. Three guards followed with their weapons raised.

Steel grabbed the HK416 assault rifle lying at his feet and ran south along a planned route. When he neared a tree he had scouted earlier, he jumped over one of its five-foot-high buttresses so he was hidden on both sides. The ground was moist and soft, the humus smelling of rich decay.

He sat with his legs spread and his back pressed against the tree trunk. Drawing two Ka-Bar knives, he kept them against his chest. He couldn't risk silenced shots for fear the guards would hear them. Adrenaline filled his limbs and sweat coated his skin.

Paws made soft pats on the jungle litter.

A blur of exposed canines, glinting eyes, and open jaws came at him. He shoved both knives up into the animal's lower jaw and neck and the dog dropped dead on his legs. Grabbing the animal's fur, he pushed with his heels against the soft ground, pulling the animal closer. He drew his gun.

Low voices whispered less than ten yards away.

Silence.

Steel held the silenced Glock barrel vertical near the side of his face. Footfalls approached. Narrow beams of light lanced into the trees on both sides of his position. His hand tightened on the gun.

The footfalls stopped. He could hear the guard breathing. A dozen meters to the right a voice called out. Next a whistle. Then low voices again.

"...fue un jaguar..."

"...probablemente...."

"...perro estupido..."

The guards suspected nothing more than a big cat. It also meant they might not respond to a repeat reaction from the dogs the following night.

The guards retreated, their voices fading.

Steel allowed himself a slow exhalation and sat still for another half hour. A night monkey twittered. The insect noise increased, and an occasional squeal in the distance signaled predators and prey at work.

Pushing the dog aside, he holstered the Glock. He looked at the lifeless animal. It reminded him of Spinner and he looked away, regret sweeping through him. Swearing silently, he suddenly didn't like what he had become—someone who traded small evils for the greater good. The evils didn't feel small anymore.

Slinging the dog over his shoulder, he told himself he had no choice. He had to know how the guards might respond. It also meant one less dog to deal with on the following night. It didn't make him feel any better.

Slipping off his hood, he walked north. He planned to hike two miles before he buried the dog, in case Alvarez decided to send out men at daylight to search the jungle. Two miles was enough to discourage the guards, even if the dogs picked up his scent. Then he would get rations and water from his sling bag.

During the daylight hours he would find a safe place to sleep. He hoped Alvarez wouldn't leave the following day. It would render all his work useless. While he walked, he retreated inward. The last weeks were a jumble of pain, death, and confusion that he didn't know if he would ever be able to sort out.

Though a part of him couldn't let it go. John Grove and Janet Bellue wouldn't allow him to let it go. But under the circumstances, for once in his life he felt stumped by an immovable object. This situation was unlike any he had overcome in the past.

Perhaps his sense of commitment was overzealous, always taking things to extreme degrees, not knowing when to back off. With Rachel, retelling his spelunking stories had that flavor. His zeal had also kept him chasing the Paragon mystery, even going after Quenton when maybe he should have called the police. Maybe obsessive behavior drove him to try to make things work with Carol, which perhaps might be a mistake too.

A twittering in the distance made him look to the side. Sweat and rain dripped off his face. He couldn't wait to sleep.

# CHAPTER 46

## Serpent: 2330 hours, second day

STEEL SQUATTED JUST INSIDE the tree line of the small clearing, waiting for the Black Hawks, his hood pulled down over his face.

He had reconnoitered the compound again. Alvarez and his woman, Marita, were still inside, their vehicles in the garage. All sides of the Black Hawk landing site were safe too. Free of Alvarez's men.

Long ago he had dreamed of being in this position—Op leader—but the reality brought a furrow to his brow. He didn't understand how he had arrived so far from where he had started in his career. Danker's attitude on command structure was clear—it was the military's. But now he resented following orders at any level.

The Komodo Op had tainted everything for him. He had no trust in a blind chain of command anymore. And he didn't want to ask those beneath him to trust in it either. But there was something deeper bothering him that he couldn't quite understand.

At least he was helping the friar.

From his sling bag he retrieved, and then activated, the GPS tracking device, which displayed his location. He ran his gaze over the area once more. Loggers had clear-cut a road into the jungle some time ago, so the bigger trees were gone in a fifty-yard-wide stretch that ran several miles out of the jungle. Smaller bushes and growth had filled it in, but there was still a visible swath cut through the forest, ending where he waited behind a tree.

At 12:09 he heard the whirring blades of the Black Hawks. He could see their dark shapes approaching. Remaining behind a tree, he stood up. The choppers flew fifty feet off the ground. But when they neared the landing site they rose up sharply.

He tensed. Before he could move, a bright red and white flame hissed out of the jungle from the east side of the clearing. The closest helicopter exploded in a loud shower of flame, the wreckage dropping into the jungle in a jarring crash.

The other Black Hawk immediately responded with two missiles and machine gun fire, strafing the other side of the clearing. The helicopter's rockets exploded amid the trees, and the Black Hawk rose high and fast.

Stunned, Steel watched another ground rocket chase it, but there was no explosion.

He tossed his HK416 assault rifle into the clearing and quickly climbed the tree. Stretching his arms around the trunk, he curled his feet in to give him leverage. Digging his fingertips into the gnarled bark, he heaved himself upward. His boots made soft scraping sounds against the trunk.

When he was twenty feet up, a bright light from the clearing flared past the sides of the tree. Adrenaline flooded his chest. He held the trunk tightly as sweat poured down his skin. Numb over the downed Black Hawk and dead soldiers, he tried to focus. Alvarez had found out they were coming—the only question was how.

Footfalls approached from the forest behind him. What he had expected.

Shouts and engine whines came from the far side of the clearing. The enemy must have been far enough from the landing area to avoid forward-looking infrared detection from the helicopters. Those who fired the RPGs had hid behind trees or in pits. They would come at him in force now. His ankles and shoulders burned.

Vegetation rustled. Shadowy figures holding rifles moved below him in a line that entered the clearing. In moments he heard their energized voices when they found his HK416. They would assume he had crawled farther into the field.

He climbed down. The slight scrapes of his boots against the tree furrowed his brow. When his feet were on the ground, he drew the silenced Glock and backed away from the tree one step at a time. Voices reached him from the field.

He quickly moved deeper into the trees. Dogs barked from the clearing. He whirled and ran.

Shouts followed, spurring his feet faster. Beams of light chased him into the forest and the automatic fire of AK-47s tore up the quiet. Hundreds of bullets chewed up bark, lianas, and dirt all around him. He bent over, keeping low to present a smaller target.

Pain bit his calf and his leg convulsed. He stumbled, tripped on a vine, and flew headlong toward a tree. He twisted to protect his head, but his shoulder hit the trunk hard in a crunch of bone against bark. His body crashed into the ground and his hand slapped something hard. The Glock flew from his grasp.

He wanted to get up and run but his limbs wouldn't respond. The firing stopped, but the barking drew closer.

Gasping, he pushed to his knees. His right shoulder ached, his right hand numb. Crawling, he swept the ground frantically with both hands. And then he saw it. The metal of the Glock glinted a few feet ahead of him.

Soft pats on the forest floor fit a pattern he recognized.

No time.

Ignoring the gun, he pushed himself to his feet with a groan. He had practiced VR sims with dog attacks a thousand times. He drew one of his knives.

They came at him fast—dark, silent shapes from front and back.

He launched himself backward, while he struck out at the neck of the dog leaping for his throat. Missed. Burying one hand in its fur, he tried to hold off eager jaws.

He grunted as he fell atop the animal behind him. It yelped and scrambled out from under his weight. Struggling with the growling animal on top of him, he buried the blade in the dog's neck. The animal collapsed. Reversing the knife, he swung his arm back without looking. A vise of teeth gripped his forearm.

He cried out and rolled to his side.

Shouts approached his position.

He struggled to his knees. Sweeping his free hand, he searched for the Glock, the shiny eyes of the dog on his. The animal dug in its feet and pulled hard on his arm until he fell forward. His free hand struck the Glock, fumbled with it, and finally found the grip.

The dog released his arm and lunged with bared teeth. Steel twisted and shot it twice. It fell beside him.

The whole action had taken seconds, but the voices were closer. Spears of light flashed through the darkness. Sharp stabs of pain burned his shoulder, arm, and calf.

Scrambling to his feet, he ran, his eyes barely discerning trees, brush, and roots. He fell twice in the first fifty yards and got up so fast he hardly noticed he had fallen. Brush whipped his face and chest. A tangle of lianas caught him and he suppressed a shout, whipping his arms viciously to get free. He stumbled ahead, careened into a tree trunk, bit his lip, and ran on automatic.

A survival run. Pain, bruises, and injuries didn't register—all were kept buried.

Stopping abruptly behind a tree, he listened for his pursuers. His wounds doubled him over and he regretted stopping. Soft voices approached his position.

Silence.

Bullets ripped into the trees and ground around him. The staccato of three, maybe four machine guns surrounded him, spraying in wide arcs.

Quiet.

Taking shallow breaths, he slowly lowered himself to his knees, and then his belly, remaining behind the tree. He took a quick peek around the trunk, and then crawled on his stomach toward the guards. In twenty feet he stopped. Two shadowy figures appeared on either side of him, both ten yards from his position.

Quietly turning onto his left side, he fired two shots at the figure to the left. The man collapsed. Rolling right, he shot the other guard who still hadn't spotted him.

Soft voices. Two more men at least.

Hastily crawling to the body of the first man he had shot, he turned it over. He tore off the vest—it held two spare magazines and two grenades—and put it on, and then grabbed the guard's AK-47. More voices. He crawled on all fours behind a tree.

Taking a deep, quiet breath, he stood and walked out from the tree, the gun level and aimed ahead of him. Five steps out he could make out three shadows huddled over the other dead soldier.

He fired for three seconds, the gunfire filling the forest. The men fell without a cry among them. Avoiding looking at their faces, he grabbed magazines and grenades, and fled south. Shouts chased him.

His calf was on fire. He couldn't even acknowledge the pain or he would fall, and maybe pass out. A fierce ache settled in his shoulder. Running harder, the pain made him feel deranged—wide-eyed and out of control.

Abruptly he realized how much noise he was making crashing through the thick jungle. Slowing, he walked at a quick pace. Quieter. If he stopped again to listen, he worried he wouldn't be able to continue. Deep breathing finally calmed his racing pulse. Pain, not exertion, had caused his lungs to heave.

Straining to hear anything beyond the sounds of insects, nothing alarmed him and his limbs finally relaxed. Without the dogs they would be as blind as he was, and maybe even frightened—at least wary—to pursue him. That made him feel good. He slung the carry strap of the AK-47 over his head.

Continuing south, he tried to keep a straight bearing, a plan already forming in his mind. It was risky, but he didn't see any other choice.

His jaw clenched over what had happened. But nothing was clear about that either. Perhaps the DEA informant had sold them out or had been tortured. Or this was all a setup by Alvarez from the beginning to gain revenge.

He paused and ran his fingers over his calf. A jagged bullet furrow still bled. The dog wound on his arm was almost as serious. He let it bleed too. The throbbing shoulder didn't feel dislocated or broken. Lucky. He barked a short, bitter laugh.

When he considered the next day, what he would have to do, and how much farther he needed to walk, an involuntary shudder swept his body.

# CHAPTER 47

## Serpent: 0300 hours, second day

H E LEANED AGAINST THE tree trunk. Pain and fatigue made him wish he didn't have to move again. It was still two hours until dawn. The climb up the tree had been hell. Cicadas sang like chainsaws in the forest.

From his vantage point in the tree he could see the center of the compound, the barracks, the garage, and the road gate. Six men were on duty, leaving four to six in the building, another fifteen in the barracks.

Alvarez's desire for safety might prompt the drug lord to flee. Then again, the man's desire for revenge might sway him to remain and see if his men could track him.

During the night he had walked four miles west, then a large circle south, and lastly southeast. His compass was cracked and the GPS unit battered. Thus he had wandered a little before finding Alvarez's stronghold. The compound's lights had eventually guided him.

He had bandaged his wounds and curled up between the buttresses of a tree to rest for an hour. Pain and tension made sleep impossible. While he rested he grasped at the image of Carol, and some type of future life with her, to give him hope. It seemed pathetic that a failing marriage was the best he could do for inspiration. Still, as he thought of her, their past years together, he yearned for her love and nurturance.

To some degree he understood the desire for nurturance was a direct result of his current wounds. But he also couldn't quit on Carol any more than he could give up on Rachel.

His plan was dangerous. But his chances of survival anywhere else in Colombia were lower than what he had decided to do. Alvarez would have informants everywhere. And going to the authorities would necessitate revealing who he was and why he was here. The U.S. government would deny any claims he made about Blackhood Ops and the Colombian government might send him to prison. A prison term in Colombia would equal a death sentence.

More importantly, he wanted to protect the friar. Alvarez had to be shut down, one way or another.

Even with the nightly rain he feared they might be able to follow his trail and find him. If Alvarez's men left the compound in the morning to track him, he planned to create a diversion to lead them southeast—in the opposite direction of the planned Black Hawk extraction in the evening.

That line of reasoning had led him to his current position. It might give him better odds to avoid facing a large group of armed men at the exfil point.

The emergency pickup was his last chance and he couldn't afford to miss it. He wasn't sure the Black Hawk would come. If he had been betrayed, a rescue would be doubtful. And if Alvarez already knew about the exit plan, there was nothing he could do to save himself.

The only part of his plan that he had no answer for was how he was going to get Alvarez.

Movement and engine noise in the compound caught his attention. He focused his bleary eyes through the night scope. Guards were backing the two SUVs out of the garage. Other guards carried fuel cans, while two more cleaned the windshields.

He made a decision and climbed down, groaning with the effort.

Walking south until he was sure he couldn't be heard, he ran west, past the compound, and then north again. It took him an excruciating half hour to find the winding muddy road that led away from the compound and down the hilly countryside.

Standing in the tree line, he listened, taking deep breaths to calm the pain in his leg. No engine noise. He walked out onto the narrow road and jogged west on it, away from the compound, the pain constant.

Two miles later he found what he needed. A sharp turn in the road and good tree cover. He reconsidered. If he was too close to the compound, whoever was left there would be on him quickly. He kept jogging.

In forty-five minutes he came upon another sharp turn and stopped in the middle of the road again. Still no engine noise. He hunched over, exhausted, unable to move. Another idea came to him, but he didn't have the energy for it. It took him a minute to get his feet moving.

Walking around the turn, he quickly began hauling branches and short logs out of the forest to build a barricade across half the road. He figured he had until sunrise—less than an hour away—because they wouldn't want to drive this road in the dark.

Dragging the debris across the ground aggravated his calf, arm, and shoulder injuries. He often gasped in pain. But in the end he was satisfied.

Walking back up the road a short distance, he chose a spot behind a tree, sat, and waited. Before he allowed himself to sleep, he visualized how he would handle the two SUVs, replaying it over and over in his mind until he was confident. When he finished he immediately fell asleep.

Engine noise saved him.

He woke with blurry eyes and hurriedly rubbed the sleep from them. Predawn light filtered through the forest and shadows still covered the road. Pulling down his hood, he scrambled to his feet, the AK-47 in his hands.

From around a curve two SUVs approached his position, already starting to slow for the sharp curve ahead. He pulled the pin on a grenade.

When the SUVs were twenty feet away, he rolled the grenade into the middle of the road. Stepping out with the AK-47 leveled, he sprayed the front tire of the lead SUV. Immediately he stepped back behind the tree and covered his ears.

The grenade exploded, sending a rush of pressure into the air.

His gun leveled, he stepped out from behind the tree again.

The lead vehicle swerved to the left, teetering, and then fell onto its side, sliding down the road, its metal grating over the small rocks. Instead of slowing, the rear SUV swerved and accelerated around the lead vehicle. A window slid down with a gun barrel protruding from it.

Steel ducked behind the tree as bullets chewed up vegetation, thumping the trunk he hid behind for a few seconds. Rounding the other side of the tree, he walked onto the road, watching the toppled SUV.

Doors swung up into the air and two guards rose out of the vehicle. He sprayed bullets at their heads and they dropped back inside. Running toward the SUV, he pulled the pin on a second grenade and tossed it through the open door.

Muffled shouts erupted in the vehicle.

Without waiting, he turned and ran across the road into the jungle, toward the downhill side of the turn ahead. A *whomp!* sounded behind him. He couldn't afford to turn around.

Ahead, he could see the lead SUV. It had skidded to a stop sideways in the road, right up against the log pile.

Steel ran out onto the road, firing at the front windshield. Divots and cracks appeared on the glass, but it didn't shatter. Pulling out a grenade, he pulled the pin and held it high, waiting.

Both front doors opened.

Cautiously he walked sideways toward the driver side. Gun barrels appeared. He tossed the grenade just beyond the passenger side into the pile of debris, and ran right, firing beneath the SUV driver's door. The driver slumped to the road with leg injuries, and then died as Steel shot him again.

The grenade exploded just as Steel threw himself into the ditch. Ears ringing, he rose to his feet and quickly loaded another magazine into the AK-47. The front passenger was dead, the side windows blown out.

Steel said loudly, "You can live or die. You've got one second to get out."

The passenger door on the driver's side opened and a raised empty hand appeared.

Alvarez.

Steel moved sideways, then strode up to the SUV. Alvarez had an average build, a trimmed beard and moustache, and wore all white clothing—pants, vest, shirt, sport jacket—except for brown boots.

Marita Lopez was huddled over her knees. She sat up when Steel approached the door. A simple blue satin shift covered her voluptuous body and shiny dark skin. Long black hair fell to her shoulders and high cheekbones gave her an intelligent appearance.

A gun rested on the seat next to Alvarez. Steel motioned them out of the vehicle.

"Ir a la mierda," Alvarez said as he climbed out. His right arm was covered in blood.

Steel pushed him against the SUV to frisk him. Twisting, the drug lord tried to elbow him. Steel swung the stock of the AK-47 at his head and the man dropped in a heap.

Steel recognized the half-moon scar on the right side of Alvarez's face. It looked more prominent now in the dim light than it had in Danker's photographs.

It would be easier to kill Alvarez, but the man might provide bargaining insurance should the drug lord's men track them. More unlikely, maybe he could still bring Alvarez back alive so they could stop any terrorist action he had backed.

Marita got out of the SUV. She had small cuts on her bare lower legs. Steel motioned with the gun and she backed up a few steps, her expression frozen.

He quickly patted down Alvarez. No other weapons.

"I'm on your side," said Marita. "Take me with you. I witnessed the DEA agent's death. I'm the informant."

He struggled with that. If she was honest, she deserved a chance to get out. The guards would kill her, even mutilate her if they suspected betrayal. She could also testify against Alvarez for a murder charge. But if she was lying, she would wait for the first available chance to help Alvarez.

"Did he call the compound?" he asked.

She shook her head. "I pretended to be scared and knocked his phone to the floor."

Stepping closer to the SUV, he saw a phone lying on the floor. He glanced up the road. Even if she was telling the truth, the men from the compound would be here soon, alerted by the grenades and guns. Minutes.

But he was counting on the lead guard vehicle from the compound running into the brush pile too. It would buy them a little more time.

"Help me with him," he said, motioning to Marita.

They lifted Alvarez into the back of the SUV. Steel ripped off part of the man's shirt and tied his hands behind his back. He grabbed the phone and gun and tossed both into the jungle. Quickly they pulled the two bodies away from the SUV.

He nodded to Marita. "Get in."

She climbed in the front passenger side, and he drove, jockeying the vehicle past the debris. He accelerated once they were clear.

A few miles later he spotted more level ground and stopped the SUV. Turning the vehicle wide, he accelerated off the south side of the road into the vegetation, going as fast as he could to get as far from the road as possible.

Fifty yards in, the vehicle crunched to a stop, the wheels spinning. Trees and thick growth hemmed them in. He quickly got out and shook Alvarez alert, motioning him out of the SUV. The drug lord glowered as he clambered out.

Steel shoved him hard, hurrying him back toward the road. "If you call out, I'll kill you."

At the side of the road he heard engine noise in the distance. He pushed Alvarez across, and told Marita to use brush to erase the tire tracks and their footprints. She seemed willing and thorough.

Alvarez's SUV wouldn't be easily spotted from the road. Even if it was, Steel hoped Alvarez's men would think they had headed south. It might be enough to buy them some time. He prodded Alvarez into the forest, heading north.

The engine whines increased. Steel pushed Alvarez to the ground, motioning Marita down beside the drug lord. Shoving his knee into Alvarez's back, he put the gun muzzle into the man's cheek and covered his mouth with his other hand.

Through the vegetation he glimpsed several Jeeps and a small truck speed by on the road. They must have assumed Alvarez's SUV had escaped—as he hoped—and were looking for it on the road. Thus they missed spotting it in the jungle.

Steel pulled Alvarez up and kept moving. A hundred yards into the tree line he told them both to kneel. He untied Alvarez and had him take off his jacket and vest.

Using one of the fixed blade knives, he cut the clothing into strips, which he used to secure Alvarez's hands even tighter behind his back, and then Marita's. She looked at him wordlessly while he tied her up. He avoided her eyes and gagged both of them. The bindings were marginal but would hinder any quick actions.

They stumbled through the jungle single file, heading northwest, Marita ahead of Alvarez, Steel behind both of them.

"If you run," he told them, "I'll shoot out your knees first."

# CHAPTER 48

**Serpent: 0900 hours, second day**

FOR HOURS THEY HEARD nothing but the sounds of the forest. Steel found it difficult to stay awake. Marita was docile and flashed secretive glances at him whenever they changed directions. Alvarez trudged along in silence.

He stopped them to get his bearings. Alvarez was breathing hard so he took off their gags.

Bending over to catch his breath, Alvarez looked up at Steel. "The DEA agent we caught a few months ago was brave for a while too. You want to hear how he died? We carried him into the jungle and staked him to the ground in the path of army ants. They can strip a horse to bone in no time at all. The man was screaming when we returned."

The drug lord chuckled. "My men didn't like having to rescue him from the ants, but I wanted to see what he would tell us. You know what he told us? Nothing we didn't already know. We brought him back to the ants."

Steel frowned. "Sit down."

They complied, and he used his knife to cut strips from the rest of Alvarez's vest. While he worked he said, "You're trying to interfere with the Mexican presidential election."

Alvarez smiled. "Many people want General Vegas dead."

"You're trying to kill Francis Sotelo."

"The friar is a fool who thinks he can change things." He lifted his chin. "Untie us. We'll forget about all of this and go our separate ways."

Steel ignored him.

Alvarez straightened and said, "Tu eres hombre muerto, y tu familia tambien."

"If I'm a dead man, then so are you." He kicked the drug lord's wounded arm and the man gasped. He gagged them both again.

***

Steel was concerned he would miss the extraction point since he didn't have a compass or GPS. And the high canopy made it difficult to use the sun for direction.

Instead he counted paces. It was a crude estimate but would yield approximate distances. When he felt they were close, he would conduct a simple search pattern.

The emergency coordinates, in case the mission was blown, was another abandoned lumber road farther north from where the Black Hawks were attacked. If he found the first failed drop site, he should be able to find the emergency pickup. Under normal conditions he would trust his abilities to do this, but fatigue, pain, and lack of sleep affected his accuracy.

His worst fear was that Alvarez's men would discover the SUV south of the road and assume he might use the same northern extraction point.

An hour later he stumbled within eyesight of the abandoned logging road. Emotion choked his throat. He wanted to cheer.

Remaining within the tree line, he followed it. His whole body sagged in relief when he reached the end of it and found it quiet, free of Alvarez's men. Pushing Alvarez, he continued northeast.

Trudging behind his captives, he replayed the events of the last day. Even though necessary for survival, and part of the mission, the violence numbed his sensibilities. Ever since the Komodo Op he realized he had begun divorcing himself from this life. None of it felt tolerable anymore.

The heat spurred waves of sweat beneath his clothing and often he wiped moisture from his eyes. Marita and Alvarez were just as drenched and their torn clothes clung to their bodies. Marita's long dark hair was strewn around her shoulders in tangles, and Alvarez's hair lay limp on his head. The drug lord seemed weaker, slowing and stumbling more as the day progressed.

Steel's limbs hung at his sides. He had gone through his water and felt dehydrated. Maps he had studied before coming had shown a river to the west, and possible streams, but with his captives he decided it best to focus on the exfil site. He just had to last a dozen hours. Often his weary feet stumbled over vegetation. Able to find a few vines, he cut them with his knife. They dribbled sips of water, though he didn't offer any to Marita or Alvarez.

Howler monkeys sent their unique, loud bellows across the forest. Insects droned everywhere. Iridescent blue morpho butterflies floated across their path, and the whistling of a black-cheeked woodpecker cut through the humid air. A hermit hummingbird sipped at a red passionflower they passed.

Steel found all of it at odds to guns and killing, but it soothed him, and reminded him of Rachel and the friar.

By early afternoon they trudged a distance that seemed adequate. It took him an hour in a quadrant search before he found the backup exfil site. It was more overgrown than the first, but recognizable.

The plans called for a quick in-and-out at midnight. With or without a signal. He had planned for every contingency. He decided to tie Marita and Alvarez together in the middle of the extraction site. If they were prone, in the open, it would be read as safe. He would stand beside them.

They had nearly half a day to wait. He cut lianas and had Marita and Alvarez sit against a large tree. He tied them as securely as he could, while Alvarez stared at him with hardened eyes.

Marita glanced at him questioningly.

Exhausted, he put down the rifle, drew his knife, and stood facing Alvarez. For a while he rolled the knife handle over and over in his hand. Eventually he sat against a tree a few yards away, staring at the drug lord.

A boa constrictor crawled across a nearby tree branch.

Steel considered Alvarez. Colombian drug lords were vengeful. Alvarez was helping terrorists out of revenge against the DEA for killing his brother. This man would do anything to gain retribution. The man might someday send a hit man after him or Carol. Or kill anyone else close to him.

Almost nodding off, he jerked his head upright.

Marita and Alvarez were still there, tied to the tree.

He brought his jumbled considerations back to his predicament. Alvarez would be tried in the U.S. for murder charges if Marita would testify—and if she was telling the truth about being a DEA informant. Then Alvarez would sit in prison for the rest of his life. But he still might be able to send out any orders he wanted.

Alvarez lifted his chin to him, as if he wanted to talk.

Steel ignored him for a while. But eventually he rose and slipped off the man's gag.

Alvarez stared at him. "Jack Steel, if I die my family will seek retribution against you and yours."

He gaped at the drug lord. "Who gave you my name?"

Alvarez shrugged. "An informant, through a long line of informants. Someone wants you dead."

He clenched his hands. It confirmed that someone had set him up and had been willing to sacrifice the other soldiers and the helicopters too.

Alvarez's threat ate away at him and worry for Carol sent his thoughts spinning. He struggled to keep his eyes open. Sweat poured over his skin and he nearly fainted.

He picked up a stick and rubbed it between his fingers. Thoughts whirled in his mind until he concluded there was only one solution. He would have to kill Alvarez to protect Carol and the friar. He couldn't worry about Alvarez's threat—the drug lord would come after him anyway if he let him live.

His decision didn't bother him as much as he felt it should have. Maybe he just wanted an easy way out, though it seemed justified.

"We're not all leaving here, are we?" asked Alvarez.

Steel stared at him. "Don't worry about it."

"You're a coward."

Marita's eyes widened.

"Se ha terminado," said Alvarez.

Steel said nothing as he repositioned the man's gag. But Alvarez was right. It was finished. He sat down again, his head resting against the tree trunk. Alvarez and Marita stared at him. The forest's humid air lulled his eyelids shut repeatedly.

He shook himself alert and finally decided it was time. Deep shadows filled the rainforest. Drawing his knife, he cut Alvarez's and Marita's bonds.

Alvarez rose, nodding to him. "Good choice, amigo."

Thinking of the soldiers Alvarez had killed, Steel swung the stock of the AK-47 at the man's head. Alvarez fell to the ground and Steel stomped one of his knees. Alvarez crawled away, slowly rising to his feet, barely able to limp away.

Marita stood with her back to the trunk, her face drawn and her arms trembling as she watched.

With his finger on the trigger, Steel stood in front of her. Shadows covered her face. She pressed herself against the tree, her eyes wide. If she wasn't the informant and he brought her back, she could betray him later to the cartel. He wondered who else besides Gustavo had his name. He needed to question her more.

"I'm innocent." Her voice wavered.

"Can you prove it?"

"How?"

Noises came from nearby. Alvarez.

"Wait here," he said gruffly.

"Will you take me with you?"

"I want to talk to you first."

He pulled the gun down and lurched to the right, following the sounds.

Hunting.

***

At midnight a lone rope ladder dropped down to him. He grabbed it and an automatic winch hauled him up in the light rain that was falling. His wide eyes mirrored the copilot's. Crawling into the back of the otherwise empty Black Hawk, he sat with his head in his hands.

Guilt filled him over Marita, but there was nothing he could do. He didn't say a single word to anyone until much later.

# CHAPTER 49

## Serpent: debriefing

THE OTHER FOUR MEN stared at Steel, while he looked at his fingers, the clock on the wall, the grain of wood on the table, and their clothing. Anything but their eyes.

He wore khaki trousers, a tan shirt, and brown loafers. His shoulder was sore, and his side, calf, and arm were bandaged. Due to his wounds and the tension in the room, he sat stiffly.

Generals Morris and Sorenson sat at the other end of the oval table, Major Flaut and Colonel Danker on either side of them. The generals and Danker wore uniforms. Flaut was less formal with a black, short-sleeved cotton shirt, trousers, and wingtips.

Morris was tall and slender, with ebony skin, graying hair, and glasses. Sorenson looked like a ghost of a man, weary and worn out.

They were in a conference room in the Pentagon.

"You're saying the landing area was secure." Danker stared at Steel.

Steel's throat tightened. "I observed no hostiles. But when the Black Hawks arrived they must have seen Alvarez's men on infrared. By then it was too late."

"And you ran." Danker shook his head.

Steel glared at him. "There were too many to fight."

"Go on," said Morris.

"I ran east."

Danker waved a hand with a flourish. "You were surrounded by a small army of men and yet you escaped. Is that right?"

Steel kept his voice level as he described his run through the woods and his capture of Alvarez. Only Flaut interrupted him a number of times to clarify the methods he used in fighting and escape.

"Alvarez described in detail how the DEA agent was tortured and killed," said Steel.

"How?" Flaut leaned forward.

Steel repeated Alvarez's story.

Flaut's eyes flickered and he sat back in silence.

Steel continued the story up to the second Black Hawk pickup.

"You say Alvarez came at you with a knife?" asked Sorenson.

He nodded. "It was hidden in his boot, a small shiv. A few hours before exfil I needed to stop for sleep. Alvarez cut Marita free and came at me with the knife. I shot Alvarez, and Marita ran off into the jungle. It was dark and I didn't have time to follow her."

"You know absolutely nothing about how the Op was compromised?" asked Sorenson.

He shook his head. "Does CIA or DEA have any clues?"

"You're sure you weren't observed before the Black Hawk was shot down?" asked Morris.

Steel grimaced. "No. But they knew I was there. They waited for me to bait the Black Hawks."

Danker sat back. "You're asking us to believe that you escaped Alvarez's small army without a hitch, but were surprised by a seriously wounded Alvarez and forced to kill him?"

"I went through hell because someone betrayed me. Alvarez had my name."

Danker scoffed. "How could he get your name on a highly classified secret mission?"

Wondering the same thing, Steel stared at the generals.

"You have to realize how this looks, major," said Sorenson. "Your story verges on the incredible."

"It's the truth."

Flaut stared at him intently.

Steel averted his eyes and wiped his sweaty palms on his knees. "I have no reason to lie about why I had to kill Alvarez. If I could have produced him at the extraction, his presence would have validated my story."

"Why didn't you bring Alvarez's body back?" asked Flaut.

"I didn't think the U.S. would want to be embarrassed with the body of a man who wasn't yet convicted of a crime, but only charged with one. That would be committing murder on foreign soil, sanctioned by the U.S."

"It still is," said Flaut.

"What's worse, Major Steel, is that this is the second mission you've been on that has been compromised in some way." Sorenson held up a hand before Steel could react. "I'm not saying you had any responsibility for what happened on the Komodo Op. Everyone was cleared on that mission. But it still is a fact."

"Why would I make up a story?" He couldn't keep his voice calm. "Why wouldn't I just say hostiles got the Black Hawk, I ran for it, and eventually made the extraction point? I could leave out all mention of Alvarez. Look at my record. I'm as loyal as any of you." He glared at each of them in turn.

"This isn't a question of loyalty, but one of understanding the truth." Danker spread his big hands. "Maybe you were spotted by Alvarez's men and they followed you to the Black Hawk. Maybe you're too scared to admit it and are trying to come in with a story to vindicate your sloppiness."

Steel ignored Danker. "Can DEA or CIA confirm that Alvarez is dead?"

"The man is in hiding so much it might take a while to learn the truth," said Morris.

"I've told you the truth. What would I have to gain in compromising the Black Hawks?"

"Money." Danker swiveled on his chair. "If your wife goes for a divorce you're going to lose your place. You're in debt big time. People do lots of things for money. Maybe Alvarez got to you before the Op or during it and made you a proposition. Or maybe you approached him."

Steel clenched his fists on top of the table. "That's absurd. I'd be risking my life going to an animal like Alvarez with a deal for money."

Silence held the room.

Morris sighed. "Colonel Danker's allegations do seem far-fetched, but we had to air them to see your response, to assure ourselves of our own concerns. Because otherwise we have to assume the CIA or DEA were compromised by their informant or one of their own people."

Morris paused. "Marita Lopez's body was found outside the U.S. embassy in Bogotá late last night. DEA confirmed that she was their informant."

A ball of pain formed in Steel's gut, which he kept off his face. "How was she killed?" he asked quietly.

"She was tortured extensively," said Sorenson. "She died from her wounds."

Keeping his eyes lowered, Steel clasped his hands together.

"Why would Marita run away from you?" asked Flaut.

"I don't know."

"You were considering retirement before this Op, weren't you, Major Steel?" asked Sorenson.

"That's right."

Sorenson nodded. "Maybe that would be for the best."

# PART 4

## OP: DRAGON

# CHAPTER 50

A S STEEL DROVE HOME his mood sank into the black hole that seemed to represent his life.

The Jeep's window had been repaired while he was away. Both windows were rolled down and he drank in the fresh air. The relief that he imagined would wash over him at this moment was nonexistent. He had left the service in disgrace, with mutual distrust.

And he had nothing at home to return to. His only satisfaction lay in the fact that Alvarez couldn't support terrorists or hurt Francis Sotelo.

He parked the Jeep in the LLC shed and took the tunnel to the lower level. Cameras and sensors showed no intruders had come while he was away. The absence of a familiar voice greeting him on his return did nothing to buoy him up. He checked the upper barn level next, but found it trouble-free, like the house.

Wanting a distraction, he turned on the VR station and put on the goggles and suit peripherals. He selected a chase, six men, and a SIG.

*The pedestrians flowed by on the sidewalk. He pointed his gun at the back of a woman. Sweat ran down his forehead. It took all his will to pull the trigger. The woman went down in a splash of blood on the pavement. People screamed, running from him in all directions.*

*He turned. Across the street on the sidewalk stood six men. All drew firearms. Lowering his gun, he backed up against the building.*

*The men moved in front of him like a firing squad, their bullets tearing into him.*

Afterward he had to go into the tank to escape. The warm water enveloped him and the darkness helped him hide from his emotions.

***

Later, while sitting at the computer station, he called Larry Nerstrand. The PI answered on the first ring.

"We got the guy and freed all of his kidnapped girls, Jack. All young. He and another man were running them out of a building in a low-rent district in L.A."

He clenched his jaw, fearing the worst.

Nerstrand continued. "Rachel wasn't among them, and I don't think he ever took her. The police offered the creeps a deal if they talked about every one of their girls, and they did. The guy I followed, who brought them in, never picked up anyone in Virginia. Didn't even know where your area of the state was. His partner didn't recognize Rachel's photo. They both passed lie detector tests."

Nerstrand paused. "I'm sorry, Jack. If you want a referral, I can give you one. Send me two thousand when you can."

"Okay, thanks, Larry." He hung up, feeling lost. He needed air.

Stepping out of the barn, he gazed down his driveway at the trees on his land. More leaves were falling and the trees had taken on a skeletal appearance. He wasn't sure what he felt about living here anymore. It seemed as though he had been gone for months.

He wondered how long he would have to worry about his security. Maybe he should move. Carol wouldn't leave her job to go elsewhere. At one time he would have understood and agreed with that. His own career mattered that much to him once, even more than the wishes of a spouse to move. Not any longer. He understood what mattered now.

Belatedly, he was surprised he could think about leaving without closure for Rachel.

Another idea about MultiSec occurred to him. One last avenue to find answers. It also gave him an excuse to call Kergan—the only friend he had.

They met on the same road. Kergan got into Steel's Jeep.

"Is Carol safe?" asked Steel.

"Do I need to worry?" Kergan looked at him.

He paused. "Can you find out if Sorenson or Morris ever participated in oversight on any of MultiSec's weapons projects in the last decade?"

"Talk to me, Jack." Kergan's eyes were steady on his.

He hesitated, not wanting to put his friend at more risk. On the other hand, if he didn't tell Kergan something, his friend might not know when to watch his back. "I was betrayed on the last Op."

"Why would Sorenson or Morris risk that?" Kergan's eyes narrowed. "I've been patient, Jack, but if you want me more involved, I need to know everything."

Steel swallowed. What if Kergan's life was turned upside down or he was killed? He couldn't do that to his best friend.

Kergan's voice softened. "It's my choice, Jack. It's what friends do."

He took a deep breath and told him everything, from the Komodo Op to MultiSec and Torr, to Grove, Paragon, Janet Bellue, Rusack, Quenton, and the Serpent Op. Finished, he added, "After Grove was killed they threatened to kill anyone I talked to."

Kergan gave him a sharp look after he finished. "You should have told me sooner. Is all of this worth it?"

"Carol won't be safe until this is over, and neither will I."

"All right. Don't talk to anyone else. No one. I'll get what I can and I'll call you."

*** 

He kept to his routines for two days. Eating healthy. Taking walks inside his property. Watching his back. And another face joined his nightmares—Marita's, an add-on to Carol and Rachel.

The third day the phone rang once, twice, and a third time. Steel met Kergan in the early evening. They walked this time.

Kergan talked. "Sorenson was on the review committee for the Paragon missile project that MultiSec ran over a decade ago. Morris was never involved with any of MultiSec's projects."

Steel's fists clenched. "I'm guessing Sorenson and Torr ran the Komodo and Serpent Ops for their own agendas. And Sorenson could have betrayed me to Alvarez on the Serpent Op without Morris' knowledge. Whatever Sorenson and Torr are hiding, it had to be why John Grove and Tom and Janet Bellue were murdered."

"Sorenson's dirty," said Kergan. "I did some checking. He has too much money for a general's salary, but not enough to attract suspicion. My guess is he has offshore accounts too."

"Sorenson and Torr have to pay." He wanted to put bullets into both of them.

"I agree. Let me do some more checking. I have strong connections."

He felt hopeful with Kergan on his side. A retired four-star general had the kind of clout they would need.

Kergan shook his keys out of his leather pouch. "Under one condition."

"Name it."

"We're both on the line now and we have to be careful. We can't talk to anyone about any of this until we get proof, agreed?"

"Agreed." He paused. "Can you ask Carol to call me?"

He drove home, knowing Kergan was now at risk. But he needed his help. More than help, he needed redemption for Grove, Janet Bellue, and Marita.

***

On the fourth day, in the afternoon, the burner phone rang. Steel was watching TV on the sofa in the lower level of the barn, his fingers sweaty on the phone as he picked it up.

"Jack?"

The familiar voice brought him to his feet. "Carol."

"How are you?"

"Things have been rough." There was a pause. He knew she didn't want to hear about his troubles. He lowered his head and hunched his shoulders.

"Jack, I want to be fair to you. I know you've waited…"

"What?"

Silence. Then quietly, "I'm going to ask for a divorce."

He sat down. The TV faded from view and his eyes turned inward. "You don't love me."

She was silent for a few moments. "I do. Just not like that anymore."

"Who is he?" His hand tightened on the phone.

"It doesn't matter, Jack. He's not the reason I'm leaving you." She paused. "I still want to be friends."

"Who is he?" he shouted.

She hung up.

While the TV provided medication for his numbness, he did a search on a laptop for Francis Sotelo and General Vegas. Sotelo was going to Honolulu, Hawaii for the International Environmental Summit. Generals Vegas and Rivera would remain in Mexico to campaign. A TV news report about the friar would be aired later that evening.

He sank into the sofa and considered things. He didn't know how long he could wait for Kergan to investigate Sorenson and Torr before he acted.

Later he called Christie. Voice mail. He left a message. "Steel," he said softly. "Jack Steel."

When she returned his call in the early evening, he was still on the sofa.

"Steel, do you want to meet?"

"Please."

# CHAPTER 51

C HRISTIE HAD STEEL WHERE she wanted him. Broken and needy.

Danker had told her Steel had been forced to retire, and that on his last Op—she didn't know what that was—he might have compromised his loyalty again. That gave her enough motivation to try to get what she could from him.

Still she saw nothing to celebrate as she pulled her green Jaguar into Steel's driveway. She was surprised the gate was open and he wasn't meeting her at the truck stop. She had made sure no one followed her. Some part of her didn't feel good about trying to bring him down. She didn't know why, since her promotion to lieutenant colonel was in sight.

The barn door was closed and locked so she went to the front door of the house and rapped the window pane with her knuckles. No answer. She tried the door and found it unlocked. Surprised, she went in.

To her right, Steel sat on the living room sofa in jeans and a pullover, barefoot, his curly hair in disarray. He didn't look at her. The edges of bandages were visible on his arm and calf. He had taken some damage on his last mission. Needed a shave too. Dead man walking.

His Glock rested on the sofa beside him.

Cranking up her dwindling enthusiasm, she dropped her car keys on the coffee table and stood in front of the TV, blocking his view. She wore blue shorts, a white blouse, gold bracelet, and a nice tan. She doubted he noticed. "She left you, didn't she?"

He stared at her, pain evident in his eyes. Lost.

*Get a grip. She isn't the only woman in Virginia.* But a hint of something else was awry in his eyes. It didn't matter what it was. She didn't care. She wanted to leave him too. Now.

Instead she surprised herself and put out her hand, waiting until his was firmly in hers. "Come on, Steel."

She led him up the stairs to his bedroom. He followed her like a little boy.

After telling him to lie down on his stomach on his bed, she sat next to him and stroked his back. He didn't move. She didn't understand why she was doing this. It felt wrong.

He turned over and his palm slid up her arm.

"Steel?"

Looking into her eyes, he sat up. His lips brushed against hers. She didn't resist. Some part of her wanted to yell, *Stop!* But a deeper part of her couldn't move. His hands pulled her tightly into him, his lips finding hers again. She clutched his back. Emotions and thoughts swirled inside her.

Pulling away a few inches, he whispered, "Do you think love is possible?"

Her lips parted, but she couldn't answer. Didn't want to. Her hands fell away from him.

Releasing her, he rolled off the other side of the bed and walked away. She fell back onto the bed, put her hands over her face, and gave a loud groan. Danker could get his own dirt. She was tired of Steel. But she decided to wait him out.

He didn't return.

She found him on the sofa again. A sarcastic remark formed on her lips, but it was cut off by his fixed gaze on the TV.

A reporter on CNN was talking about a Franciscan friar, Francis Sotelo. The friar was attending the International Environmental Summit in Honolulu in several days at the Hawaii Convention

Center. The reporter talked about the controversy surrounding Sotelo, including his supposed miracles, past attempts on his life, and that he had taken a stand for the poor and nature, demanding governments support both. Support for Sotelo's message was building worldwide.

The report said the friar was going to Maui before the conference for a much-needed rest for a few days. Sotelo was also scheduled for a public discussion with a few business leaders to try and reach a settlement regarding pollution their corporations had caused in Mexico.

Steel murmured something, but she didn't quite catch the words.

"What?" she asked.

He got up and shut off the TV, turning to her, his features weary but decided about something. "I'm going to Hawaii," he said softly. "Want to come?"

She frowned. She had missed something. "Look, Steel, one minute you're passionate, the next you're cool and distant, and the next you're asking me to go to Hawaii. Why?"

"I'm not sure."

"That's not good enough. You said you would give me whatever I wanted if I got the Tom Bellue file for you. Well, what I want is the truth. All of it."

"I'll tell you in Hawaii."

She regarded him. "You get me to Hawaii and then say, 'Sorry, changed my mind.'"

He shook his head. "I keep my word." He hesitated. "Maybe you shouldn't come."

"I didn't say I didn't want to." She felt backed into a corner. Like he had planned to do this to her. She wanted to kick him.

"I'd like you to come. It's up to you." He paused. "I'm not sure what will happen."

It didn't feel safe. Him not telling her what this was about, and him possibly dirty and involved with something dangerous.

She wanted to say *No,* and report back to Danker that it was a dead end.

But duty, a promotion, and something else she couldn't identify pushed her forward. "Why not. I've always wanted to see the islands anyway. You're paying?"

"Sure."

"A weekend?"

He shrugged. "A week."

She bit her lip. "In what capacity am I going?"

"A friend?"

"Sure." She felt his eyes following her until she was out of sight. She called Danker and told him about Steel's interest in the friar, Francis Sotelo.

"Good. Play along with him. Have a fun trip. See what he's up to."

Danker's casual tone made her wary. It didn't sound like he cared what she learned about Steel. "What does the friar have to do with anything?"

"Classified. But I can promise you one thing. Your promotion goes through when you return."

"What am I walking into? Is it dangerous? Is Steel dangerous?"

"You'll be fine. You think I'd hang you out on a limb?"

She hung up. Danker and Steel were both using her and she didn't trust either of them. Danker was a sexist creep and Steel had his own secrets.

She called Hulm next, but the CIA director said curtly, "We won't be needing your services anymore with Steel. We'll send a check."

The line went dead. Frustration made her want to yell at someone.

Pulling to the side of the road, she used her phone to look up Francis Sotelo. That led to an article on the assassination attempt on General Garcia Vegas, and other attacks on him, Sotelo, and General Ramon Rivera.

But she came up empty as to how they were connected to Steel. It had to be related to one of his Ops, but Danker and Steel wouldn't tell her how. Still, Sotelo had to be why Steel was going to Hawaii.

Other things bothered her at a deeper, personal level. That Steel had rejected her, holding fast to some code he lived by, unsettled her. It bothered her even more that her heart had skipped a beat when kissing him, and that she felt pain over his rejection.

It all seemed absurd. She didn't consider herself desperate or lonely so she couldn't identify what drew her to Steel.

Yet as she drove she knew his question unsettled her the most. The man lived in fairyland. They had spent a few training days together, sharing sweat and some words. But Steel believed they had shared more. The guy must have been royally confused to ask a question like that. Or maybe just desperate to want someone to lie to him about love.

She hadn't been able to do it, say it to his face. Reel off an answer like she could have with almost any other question he might have asked her.

In a sense he had found her out and exposed a vulnerability. And she suddenly knew why his question—*Do you think love is possible?*—had brought such a deep ache to her chest. It had struck some part of her that hadn't been touched for a long time. And the answer she had wanted to give him, confusingly, was *Yes*.

# CHAPTER 52

DANKER HAD NEVER UNDERSTOOD how to win the big games of money, power, and status in life. But for the first time he had a chance. It meant that he would have to trudge farther down the road of illicit acts, but after the first few it wasn't as hard as he expected.

Looking back over his life, he realized a number of times he could have, and should have, broken rules. It would have made life easier. He also understood the danger involved now. Still, he had considered all the options and prepared himself as he did for any Blackhood Op.

He was ready.

The demonstrators in front of MultiSec's main entrance brought a smile to his face. Their leader, the blond Rich Plugh, was still at work with chants and leaflets. Danker limped past the demonstrators with his cane, toward the main doors. He nodded to Plugh.

"Hey, you're not on their side, are you?" Plugh took off his sunglasses.

Danker grinned over his shoulder. "We're on the same side, you can count on it."

Two minutes later he was ushered into William Torr's office. He winked at Torr's beautiful receptionist. Giving him a cool smile, she shut the door behind him.

He limped to the chair in front of Torr's desk. The CEO of MultiSec sat in his plush swivel chair, staring out the windows behind his desk.

Danker had known men like Torr in the military, who believed they were omnipotent. And he knew Torr didn't like him. The man had good reason to hate him.

But even so, Torr would never have liked him anyway. He didn't fit the mold that Torr wanted for his social connections. For that reason it satisfied him even more to have leverage on the man.

"The protestors are still out there." Danker spoke as if he had just dropped by to pass the time. Two could play at this game. "You're working hard to look green, aren't you? I mean, being one of the sponsors of the International Environmental Summit—I've seen your commercials."

Torr turned in his chair, hands tented, his face neutral. His bald head was shiny under the bright overhead light. "You don't understand it, do you?"

Danker shook his head, annoyed that Torr was talking to him like a child. "Why don't you explain it to me?"

"Any real environmental reform has to involve the large corporations. Ever since the first international conference in Rio, it was decided future conferences needed to be more inclusive. Allow corporations to be part of the process. We present economic priorities to the representatives of underdeveloped countries. The heads of state just need a package of ideas to take back to their people. The promise of jobs, a few more pollution controls, and the problem is solved."

"Bribing the politicos, huh?"

Torr's eyes iced over. "The politicians get campaign money, the stockholders see profits, and the consumers see lower prices. Isn't capitalism what you're fighting to defend?"

"I bet you're going to be there in Hawaii center stage, huh?"

"I take it you've settled on an amount?"

"I figured out what the Komodo Op was all about."

Torr didn't respond.

Danker smiled. "You saw General Vegas headed to a presidential victory and you wouldn't be able to bribe him. He actually has values. Kind of rare these days, isn't it? With Vegas in power, MultiSec would take a hit of several billion in cleanup work. That might bother the shareholders a little, huh?"

Torr's face darkened further, but Danker didn't lose his smile as he continued. "And your lawyers wouldn't be able to play games with the law south of the border like they can here. So you decided to use the Komodo Op as a preemptive strike before Vegas had too much security around him."

"Did you deduce that all on your own, colonel, or did you need help?"

He chuckled. "That's still a real problem for you, isn't it?"

Torr's fingers drummed the arms of his chair. "You could rectify that for me. The friar will be in Hawaii in two days. Enough people have called him a heretic to justify it, I should think."

"Why, Mr. Torr, are you asking me to break the law?" Danker enjoyed seeing the man wince over his feigned ignorance. Spreading his hands, he gave a mock frown. "I'll have to ask General Sorenson what he thinks about this, won't I?"

"Leave him out of it. You don't have to worry about him."

"Somehow I figured that. We'll have to bend some rules, you know."

"I'm sure your tremendous intellect can handle it."

Danker's neck grew hot. He gathered himself. "Forgetting about the Mexican general?"

Tor grimaced. "Why not? General Vegas' campaign will fall overnight. He'll fade to obscurity without the friar at his side. The election is still months away. Voters have short memories. They'll forget about Sotelo. And Vegas won't get anything positive out of reminding them about a deceased friar. We have friends on *El Universal* and *La Prensa* who will continue to raise questions about the possibility that the friar was engaged in devil worship."

"Nothing like good journalism." Danker winked at Torr.

"Ninety percent of all journalism is biased, minimally in subject matter, often in substance. It should muddy the waters enough. It's handled."

Danker smiled. "You might have more than just that problem."

"What?" Torr turned rigid.

"Steel's going to Hawaii with Christie Thorton. Wants to check out the friar too."

"So? Your people have some extra work. How many will you send?"

Danker thought about that. "Two."

Torr grimaced. "Make it four. And do it all in Hawaii. Sotelo is going to be in Maui a few days before the IES. I agreed to talk with him there, which should make your job easier. I don't want him to make it to the conference. I saw what the CIA did with Steel. I hope your people won't prove as embarrassing."

Torr paused. "Does Ms. Thorton know what's going on?"

Danker shrugged. "She's bright."

"You better take care of her too." Torr gave an icy smile. "Do you mind?"

He laughed. "Mind? You're paying me to act out a fantasy." He heaved a contented sigh. "Ten million."

Torr didn't even blink. "Two in any account you want, tomorrow, as a sign of good faith. Call me tonight after it's set up. You get the rest when the business in Hawaii is over and I have all copies of the Paragon file on my desk." He gripped the arms of his chair.

Danker sat back, deliberating. Two million was enough. It wouldn't pay to get too greedy. He nodded. "Sounds fine. I'll call you tonight."

"What's it going to be called?"

He paused. "How does Dragon sound? Yeah, Dragon."

When he didn't get up to leave, Torr asked, "Well?"

Danker smiled. "I brought an account number with me. I thought I'd give it to you now."

# CHAPTER 53

S TEEL COULD FEEL DANGER closing in on him. He didn't
know from what direction, or from whom, but he sensed
his enemies' footsteps deep in the reaches of his mind. He
wanted to see their faces.

Kergan met with him early in the morning on the same road.
Kergan drove. His silver hair blew in the wind from his open
window.

Steel told him about the IES conference in Hawaii.

Kergan's face tightened. "I'll keep digging. See who else is
involved and what we can do about it. You need to call me from
Hawaii if anything goes wrong. I want to be kept involved, is that
understood?"

Steel nodded. "I'll call you from Hawaii."

"We're tapping the shoulders of powerful people. You know
that, don't you?"

"Yes." He looked out his window. The hills were covered with
trees barren of leaves. "Carol wants a divorce."

"She told me. I'm sorry."

The silver Mercedes stopped. Kergan turned to him. "I have
your word that I'm in all the way on this?"

"All the way."

***

He took out the rest of the stash money. Along with a money belt, a Glock and disposable silencer, his gun permit and military ID, the OTF knife, a gun case with a combination lock and exterior padlock, and one small suitcase.

Ready, he sat in the dark and wondered why he had invited Christie.

The invitation was out of instinct. Despite his concerns, intuition said do it. When he had kissed her, he knew it wasn't right. Not now. Not yet. Maybe never. But at the time he had shoved that perception down. Thought it didn't matter. Wanted to believe it didn't. He wanted nurturance, someone there for him. Wanted to believe he had what Carol had—someone else.

And then he had asked the question.

The surprise on her face had embarrassed him as much as it had moved him away from her. His question had erupted out of self-protection. He understood rebounding. Yet he wasn't sure if what he and Carol had shared over the last year was anything to rebound from. It hadn't been much of a marriage during any of that time.

All he knew was that he wanted Christie to come. He was glad she said yes, even if he didn't know why.

# CHAPTER 54

D ANKER KNEW THIS WAS the most important mission he had ever organized. And the easiest. He spent some time on the computer going through operatives, a cold beer in one hand, the mouse in the other.

He didn't trust Torr. Luckily he had the man under the stack of his Paragon copies, so to speak. Torr couldn't touch him. Still, he was going to guarantee that.

All he had to do was make sure he had men he could trust to execute this Op. Out of two dozen options, he only had to find four good Blackhood operatives who understood how to obey orders without questioning them. They all had to be freelancers so that if they screwed up, or if Steel nailed them, there would be no ties to him or his office.

One of the men on the Komodo Op would work. And there was a Hawaiian who fit the bill. Four calls, he chortled to himself, and he would be home free with two million, minus expenses. What was beautiful was that the only person who might know his connection to Torr was Sorenson—and it sounded as if Torr was cutting his ties to the general anyway.

In an hour Danker made his first call. He recognized the voice and immediately said, "Blackhood." He followed with, "First targets in Maui, Hawaii before the IES conference: Jack Steel, Christie Thorton, and Francis Sotelo. Secondary target also in Maui, Hawaii, William Torr. Four operatives. Contact in Hawaii permitted as necessary. Rendezvous at the Grand Wailea, Maui. Op name: Dragon. Immediate delivery. All targets final. Photos follow."

He broke off the call, then placed photos of Steel, Thorton, Sotelo, and Torr in a secure online drop box for the operative. He smiled to himself. This was what Torr felt like. God.

*** 

When Flaut got Danker's call, he listened to the first part of it with a racing pulse. He had just taken a line of white heaven and his favorite porn video played. Danker's orders made it all seem sharper, more vivid. His adrenaline flowed as he considered Steel.

Danker continued. "There's something extra special I'd like you to do."

Flaut closed his eyes. He wanted to concentrate on Danker's voice. "Out of line, isn't it?"

"Are you interested?" asked Danker.

"How out of line is it?"

"Two hundred and fifty thousand dollars' worth."

Flaut smiled. He was going to enjoy this. "I'm listening."

*** 

A half hour later Flaut got another call. From Torr. He could guess what he wanted. It was one of his best nights in a long time.

# CHAPTER 55

HULM WATCHED THE PRESIDENT pace the Oval Office like a caged polar bear. Every so often the man gazed at him, while he sat rock-steady in the chair in front of the president's desk. He wore the same trench coat. He didn't take it off because keeping it on irritated the president.

The president scowled and swung to him. "I'm supposed to be at the IES conference, you know."

Hulm hid his frown. He wasn't stupid, even if the president thought so. "You can fly to it for the second day."

The president ran a nervous hand through his thinning gray hair and looked out at the well-lit White House lawn.

Hulm added, "I think we'll be ready in time."

"You think?" The president whirled with a glare. "What are you, crazy? If that mole you've recruited isn't one hundred percent accurate, one hundred percent, we're finished."

"I'm sure." He regretted his choice of words. "I'm sure we'll be ready in time."

"Is this all set up?" The president stepped forward, bracing his hands flat on his desk, his face pale. "We shouldn't move forward until we have what we need."

"We can't do it that way." Hulm felt as if he was talking to a child. "You know that."

"You're the Director of the CIA. I'm the president. We can do it whatever way we want."

Hulm didn't say anything. The president turned around and walked back to the window. He looked like a prisoner.

"Doing it in our own backyard like this, is that smart?" asked the president.

Hulm suppressed a sigh. The president had asked that same question for days. His eyes glazed over.

"Isn't that too obvious?" the president persisted.

It was precisely because it was too obvious that Hulm believed it was such a good idea. "When it's over, we'll leak to the press there was evidence that a radical Catholic was responsible." He shrugged. "With all the controversy in Mexico over the friar, it'll fly."

The president turned to him with disgust on his features. "It'll fly?"

"No one will ever know what was really intended. It will end up being described as a madman with a loose rifle."

"I want you to wait for my approval before you give final instructions to your man. Is that understood?"

"Yes." What Hulm didn't say was that he had already given final instructions to his man. There was no turning back.

# CHAPTER 56

STEEL WAS OUT OF touch with trying to explore someone. After ten years of marriage it felt foreign. He never thought he would need to do it again. It felt like high school.

As a result, on the plane he spent much of the time holding magazines. He just looked at the pictures. Christie shifted in her seat, and something prompted him to look up from the magazine. She stared back at him.

"Steel," she said, "I don't think we're ever going to get anywhere until we get past a few things."

He looked at her without comprehension.

"Why don't you tell me about your wife and kid." She sat back and closed her eyes. "I'll listen."

He glanced at her. Strong cheekbones framed by brown and gold hair. Her calm relaxed him and emotion abruptly flooded his chest. There had been no one to talk to during the whole last year and suddenly he felt like a sealed kettle that had gathered too much steam.

Leaning back, he closed his eyes and took a deep breath. Softly he began to talk about nine years of marriage, and one year of hell.

\*\*\*

Christie listened to Steel with more attention than she had intended. His emotions kept her alert.

She heard his devotion to his wife and daughter, along with the pain, commitment, and confusion. He blamed himself for losing his daughter and wife. He didn't say it, but Carol Steel had been one cold woman to her husband during the last year.

The other thing she realized, somewhat to her confusion, was that Steel seemed like a normal person. Like any other individual who had trusted someone to build a life with, made plans and dreams, and relied on that someone to help carry them out. He had failed. As did many who tried.

She couldn't help but hear his love for his daughter, and the guilt he still carried. At one point his arm nudged hers on the armrest and his fingers brushed against hers. She cringed. He wanted to draw her into his circle, his pain, and his failure.

But she surprised herself again and opened her hand. His fingers intertwined with hers. She shivered. *Christie Thorton, you idiot, get a grip.*

# CHAPTER 57

THE LAST TIME DANKER remembered feeling like this was when he was ten, on his golden birthday, standing in front of a huge pile of gifts.

He lounged in his favorite easy chair, drinking a cold beer and watching a basketball game. But the game didn't interest him. What did were the dozen travel brochures on his lap for the Riviera, Mediterranean, Caribbean, and South Pacific. He would visit them all, find the most beautiful women alive, and live a life of true bliss.

He didn't need fancy cars, a big house, or expensive clothing. He would live simply, like he always had. Which meant the money would last forever. Interest on one million alone would support the kind of lifestyle he wanted. And if he met a beautiful woman who fit his lifestyle, who was the love of his life—he grinned—maybe he would even settle down.

His rental duplex doorbell rang and he tossed the brochures onto the footstool that propped up his injured knee. With a grunt he grabbed his cane, got up, and hobbled to the door.

He looked through the peephole, and then relaxed. It was Flaut, dressed in his usual black garb.

Danker opened the door, surprised to see the man since he had just talked to him a few hours earlier. It was dark outside and he was glad his overhead stoop light had burned out months ago. He didn't want anyone to see Flaut here.

Flaut just stood there.

"Get in here!" barked Danker.

Flaut stepped in and walked to the couch. He had to move a pile of papers to sit down.

"The place is a mess." Danker motioned. "I wasn't expecting guests."

Plopping into his easy chair, he again propped his leg up on the footstool. "Why are you here?" He studied Flaut. The man's eyes revealed concern. He had never seen Flaut worried so he began to worry. "Well, speak up, man!"

"William Torr called me." Flaut paused. "He wanted to hire me to do you."

Danker's eyebrows shot up. His hands tightened on the chair armrests. He measured the distance to Flaut with his eyes. He was a long way from his bedroom, where he kept his Browning 9mm. "How does Torr know you?"

Flaut said innocently, "I've done some work for him. I've worked for the CIA in the past and they were kind enough to refer me."

Danker tried to keep his voice steady. "What did you say to Torr?"

Flaut shook his head and looked at his black shoes. "I told him sure." He raised his eyes. "I came right over here to tell you, to ask you what I should do."

"That lowlife." He relaxed his bunched shoulders a little. He couldn't believe Torr would risk a copy of the Paragon file going public. It didn't make sense. He studied Flaut. "I'll pay you to do Torr first, before the other special I ordered. You can do him before Hawaii. Any time you like, after tomorrow."

Flaut's face brightened. "That sounds good. How much?"

He hesitated. "When did Torr want you to do me?"

Flaut shrugged. "It's flexible."

He settled back into the chair. By tomorrow he would have the two million from Torr deposited. He would verify that first thing in the morning. It could work. He was already paying Flaut two-fifty big ones. If he doubled it, he would still have another mill and a half left. And he would send the copies of the Paragon file all over the planet. Torr and his friends would all pay a price.

He looked up. "I'll double what I was going to pay you."

Flaut nodded as if he was considering it. He picked a piece of lint off his black jeans. "Torr offered more for you."

Tension returned to Danker's shoulders. Flaut was squeezing him. A small pit of fear entered his loins, but he refused to give in to it. "All right. I'll triple what I was going to pay you."

"Torr was going to give more."

"How much do you want?"

Flaut gave an innocent smile. "Well, whoever pays top dollar should be my priority customer."

Danker removed his leg from the stool, lowered his foot to the carpet, and pretended to massage his knee. He hung his head a little as if he was tired. The cane rested against the chair, but he wanted to use his hands on Flaut. He tried to keep his voice calm. "How much is Torr paying you?"

"Three million."

Danker's eyes narrowed as he looked up. "For me? Bull! Torr wouldn't pay that much."

"The two million he was going to pay you and another million that I have to work for. I negotiated, since you've been a steady customer and I'd hate to lose you." Flaut paused. "But the real question is, can you outbid Torr?"

Danker felt the color flee from his face and he tensed his arms for his one shot. Leaning forward, he shook his head and looked at his shoe. "Well, I might be able to..." He flung himself off the chair at Flaut.

Flaut stood and twisted to the side.

Because of his knee, Danker couldn't turn fast enough to grab him, and his momentum carried him forward. Something rigid struck the back of his neck and the couch loomed up at him. He was senseless by the time he fell against it and bounced to the floor.

# CHAPTER 58

WHEN DANKER CAME TO, his body was sluggish and his senses foggy. He couldn't understand if he was dreaming, conscious, or hallucinating. His face was flushed, his head full of pressure, and his jaw hard to move. Chair legs and upside-down black shoes were a short distance in front of his eyes. Everything was blurry, with no focus.

It took several breaths for him to understand that it was he who was upside down. His back, chest, legs, and arms were tied to something that held him vertical.

Flaut. He remembered lunging, and Flaut moving surprisingly fast to avoid his hands.

"The tranquilizer will wear off shortly," said Flaut. "We had a long drive and I wanted you to be comfortable. We're in Steel's barn, but I don't think he'll mind."

"You can still get out of this clean," said Danker. "You work for the United States Government, mister." The words came out as if he spoke through a wad of tissues. His lips were puffy, clumsy. "I've kept files, I've—" A searing line of fire shot through his feet, down his back, and into his skull. He gasped and stiffened.

"Just testing it," said Flaut. "It's an alligator clip attached to your big toe. Every time you talk without permission, I throw the switch. Every time you lie or don't give me a truthful answer, I throw the switch. Do you understand?"

Danker's eyelids were stretched, his mouth clamped tight, his entire body rigid. It took a minute before his limbs began to relax and sink down again. He stared at Flaut's ankles and realized how mad the man was. And he understood Flaut intended to kill him.

The only thing left to him was how much pain he could avoid. And he wanted some way to get revenge on Torr, if Torr managed to survive the Dragon Op. He shouted as pain ripped through his torso again.

"I asked you a question," said Flaut. "Please answer. Do you understand when you should talk?"

He gave a muffled reply as he tried to recover from the last surge of electricity. The pain almost brought tears to his eyes, but he held it off, not wanting to give Flaut the satisfaction.

"What?" asked Flaut.

With a superhuman effort, Danker gave a wide-eyed, slurred, "Unnerstand."

"Good. I want the location of all copies of the Paragon file. Who has them, what their instructions are, when they're supposed to act on those instructions, and how you maintain contact with them."

"Go to hell." He blacked out this time.

When he was able, he babbled the information to Flaut as fast as he could.

***

They went over the details several times, and then Flaut called Torr. After he read off Danker's list, Torr chuckled on the other end of the line.

"The man's a cretin," said Torr. "Friends, a lawyer, and the rest hidden in his apartment. I didn't think he had any imagination. My people should be able to check this out within an hour. I'll call you." He paused. "Give my regards to Danker."

Flaut turned on Steel's VR station and carried the wireless VR goggles to where Danker was still tied upside down. After fitting the goggles over the colonel's head, he returned to the computer and selected a dinosaur pursuit program. He turned it on and sat in the chair near Danker.

Danker's body tightened in reaction to the VR program.

Flaut picked up his digital camera, which rested on the floor, and focused it on Danker's body. He hit the electric switch again. As Danker's body stiffened he snapped off a picture. He thought it was perfect and turned on the video.

\*\*\*

In an hour Torr called back. "We found eleven print copies, a copy he saved to his computer, and the original flash drive. He said he made twelve copies, and he gave me one already. That should do it."

Flaut was silent.

"The money will be deposited tomorrow morning." Torr hung up.

Flaut walked back to Danker, who hung without the goggles on. "Were there just twelve copies?"

Danker moved his head.

The colonel was too dazed to talk, but Flaut believed he understood. He bent over, near Danker's ear. "If it's any consolation to you, I still intend to honor our contract too." He smiled. "It's just going to be cheaper than you thought."

\*\*\*

An hour later Flaut dropped Danker's body off at his duplex, laying him out on his back in his living room. He pulled out a small bag of white heaven and sprinkled it like powdered sugar over the man's torso. Someone would assume this was a revenge hit over the Alvarez Serpent Op.

Minimally it would create suspicion and confusion.

Next he drove another hour to a pricey neighborhood in Maryland. Finding the address he was looking for, he walked up to the front door and rang the doorbell.

General Sorenson was in his pajamas when he opened the oak door. The general held a revolver, but it was pointed down. Flaut thought the general's bulbous nose looked even larger in the shadowed light of the hallway.

Flaut didn't wait for an invitation. He swung the silenced Glock from behind his leg until it was level. "Danker sends his regards," he said quietly.

Backing Sorenson into the house, he closed the door with a foot.

Sorenson tried to raise his pistol, but Flaut stepped to the side and hit him in the head with the butt of his gun. The general gasped and fell to the floor onto his back, releasing his weapon. Flaut straddled the dazed man and drew a knife. He cut Sorenson's right carotid, and then sprinkled white heaven over the general's prone body. He left hurriedly.

He had a red-eye to catch.

# CHAPTER 59

STEEL BECAME ALERT THE moment they landed at Kahului Airport in Maui. The enemy could already be here, waiting for them.

He collected his gun case. Christie had checked a gun too. He didn't mind. It couldn't hurt to have her armed.

After picking up the rental Jeep, they were soon driving the Mokulele Highway south, toward Wailea. Traffic was heavy and slow.

To either side of the road volcanoes reared up in the distance. Pu'u Kukui to the west, and Haleakala farther to the southeast. Ferns, watermelon palms, and wiliwili trees filled the landscape, and red and yellow hibiscus lined the road. The land rolled gently to the higher elevations leading to the volcanoes.

A cattle egret floated over the road in the distance and the air was warm and humid. All of it did nothing to ease the tension in Steel's shoulders.

He was quiet and couldn't think of anything to say to Christie. The talk on the plane had helped relieve some of his pain—for the first time in a year his guilt over Rachel's death began to slip away. Telling Christie things that he loved about Rachel also made his remorse fade a little. Christie had done that for him.

But she gave no empathy, nor expressed any understanding. Though she had squeezed his hand every so often when he had a difficult time continuing his story.

He glanced at her. The open air of the Jeep swept her hair off her face. She wore purple sunglasses, khaki shorts, sandals, and a blouse, her gaze focused on the mountains in the distance. A picture of beauty.

However that wasn't what he wanted right now. He wanted something of substance, and substance took time to build. But ten years with Carol hadn't produced it. That brought a frown to his face.

"Steel, do you mind if I make a personal observation?"

His hands tightened on the steering wheel.

"You're into guilt and self-punishment a bit much, don't you think?"

He stared at her.

"Here you are in paradise with a beautiful woman, surrounded by warm air and sunshine, and you still beat yourself to death over Carol and Rachel and whatever else that's bothering you." She looked away. "Are you sure you even want me here?"

"Yes."

"Good. Then act like it." She turned and smiled at him.

He managed a crooked smile. "Do you have family?"

"My parents and three brothers."

She kept talking, and he settled back and heaved a sigh. Stealing a look at her, he wondered what she would say if she learned what had happened on the Serpent Op. That was one burden he might have to carry alone.

# CHAPTER 60

S TEEL BOOKED TWO ADJOINING rooms in the Four Seasons Resort, each with an ocean view. He paid for five days in advance. Christie's eyes widened with the hotel clerk's when he laid out eight thousand in cash.

In his room he changed out of his jeans and pullover into white cargo shorts and a short-sleeved blue print shirt, which he kept untucked.

The Glock went into his belt at his back, beneath the shirt, the disposable silencer into a pocket, and a spare magazine on his belt. A money belt held his credit cards and ID. He slid the OTF knife into the belt-sheath.

Christie stood on their shared balcony, gazing out at the ocean. He watched her while he put a call in to Kergan. Voice mail. He left his hotel room and burner phone number, and joined Christie.

The light-brown sand beach was speckled with people. A few windsurfers raced back and forth in the blue-and-turquoise water and bathers basked knee-deep in the surf. Farther out, sailboats rocked in the waves. Sunshine sparkled on the water and gave a bright glow to everything in sight. A green gecko clung to the balcony railing. It all seemed like a different world to him, free of worry.

"You ever just want to take off, Steel, and be a beach bum?"

"I saw some of the world while spelunking. Over the last years I used to believe I had enough to do in Virginia."

"I wouldn't mind seeing more."

"I have to go out for a short while."

She glanced at him. "You're stranding me already?"

He was silent.

"What are we doing here, Steel?"

He put on a pair of black sunglasses. Part of him wanted to tell her, but he was impatient. "When I come back I'll tell you everything."

"That's a promise?"

He frowned. "I keep my word."

She smiled and playfully hit his shoulder. "I'm a big girl. I'll sit and read a book or take a walk on the beach. How long will you be gone?"

"Back for a late lunch, if not sooner. I left the Jeep keys on the table in case you want to go out."

"Bye."

In minutes he walked along the beach, heading north toward the Grand Wailea. His canvas loafers pushed against the shifting sand. Sea gulls stood on the beach, scattered among the people, and a few black noddies flew above the surf. He didn't have far to go, but on the way he kept a wary eye to see if anyone followed him.

His thoughts turned to Francis Sotelo. The friar was at risk.

The only good that had come out of his part in the Komodo Op, and all the pain and death since then, was that he had saved Sotelo. MultiSec and Torr still had a vested interest in the friar's death. And here Sotelo was exposed. It would be far easier to kill the friar here than at the Honolulu Conference Center, where security would be ramped up for the president and foreign dignitaries attending the summit.

He wanted to make sure Sotelo stayed safe. It had to end here. Even if it meant putting a bullet into Torr.

# CHAPTER 61

WATCHING STEEL WALK ALONG the beach, Christie used her phone to access a secure, members-only website. She logged in and left a message for Danker.

After slipping the SIG Sauer into a waist holster beneath her loose blouse, she grabbed her purse, her small umbrella, the Jeep keys, and hurried out to follow Steel. He was easy to spot. She hung back in the trees paralleling the beach, wondering what Danker had gotten her into. No, what she had gotten herself into.

She was glad she had a gun. She didn't ask Steel why he needed his. He wouldn't tell her anyway, and she didn't want to give him a reason to ask about hers.

Her stunbrella gave her another option. If she pressed a button on the thick handle, eighty-thousand volts shot out of its tip—enough to knock a big man down and keep him dazed long enough to either run or attack. It gave her extra security. And an umbrella on the islands was a natural since it often rained during some part of the day this time of year.

While she walked she considered Steel. She had enjoyed their talk on the drive south from the airport. He had listened to her and asked questions that showed interest. It wasn't as if she had told him anything significant about herself, but at least she had talked to him without any ulterior motives.

Maybe she would find the dirt he was hiding and they could end the charade. It would be a relief. And it would end the emergence of other feelings that she knew had no place in her assignment.

She had surprised herself by admitting to him that she wouldn't mind doing some traveling. That sentiment contradicted a decade she had spent climbing the career promotion ladder. Deep down she was weary of that struggle.

Some of the men on the beach gave her brazen gazes. Steel never looked at her that way. It occurred to her that she might not mind a look like that from him. That idea was also amusing because he seemed too straight to pull it off.

Regardless of her feelings, her doubts and suspicions continued. As expected, he had told her nothing about what he was doing here. She decided not to press him further. He might be more suspicious of her if she did, and she wanted him to be relaxed where she was concerned.

Too bad he had to be taken down, but if he was dirty, as Danker believed, then she couldn't waste time on regrets. Steel had dug his own hole to jump into, without any help from her.

# CHAPTER 62

STEEL WATCHED THE SUNBATHERS, walkers, swimmers, and gawkers. An impossible setting to keep anyone safe in, especially if the individual was targeted by a professional.

He wandered into the Grand Wailea lobby. Flowers gave off fragrance. The large water fountains and pools—along with the large openings in the ceiling and walls—made it feel spacious and relaxing.

There were posters in the lobby about the public talk between Sotelo, a small panel of environmentalists, and three CEOs of corporations that Sotelo wanted to pay for pollution cleanup and reparations in Mexico. The talk would take place the following day in the Grand Wailea's outdoor Molokini Garden, which could seat twenty-five-hundred people. People had to sign up for seating ahead of time and it was already fully booked. Steel assumed it was because of Sotelo's fame.

He found a cleaning attendant. For two hundred dollars, and the story that he was a reporter looking for an interview, he learned what room Francis Sotelo was staying in.

After studying the resort layout, he walked back outside along the inner south hotel wing. He was surprised to see the friar sitting on his balcony. The sight of Sotelo brought back memories of the Komodo Op and his attack on Danker. The danger seemed real again.

Casually glancing around the swimming pools and grounds, he looked for someone out of place. Someone who pretended to be there for the sunshine, but who in fact might also be watching the friar. He did it out of habit, not out of any expectation that he would find anything.

The friar remained at his table for a half hour. Steel felt a sudden urge to talk to him. He struggled with that idea, and then gave in to his instincts and went inside.

# CHAPTER 63

I T WAS DIFFICULT FOR Christie to locate a vantage point from which to observe Steel and not be seen by him. She wondered if he knew she was following him—but concluded he didn't. He went into the Grand Wailea, while she waited behind some trees.

About ready to follow him inside, she paused when he came out again, walking along one of the paths as if he was just enjoying the sunshine. She wasn't sure what he was doing.

When he turned around and went into the hotel a second time, she gave him a few minutes, and then followed. If he saw her, she would just say she wanted to see what the Grand Wailea was like. It would also give her more of a reason to ask him why he was here.

The fragrant flowers and pool of water off the lobby made her yearn for something pleasant in her life. Returning here for some R&R when this was over sounded nice.

She noted the posters about Francis Sotelo's talk on the following day with MultiSec's CEO, William Torr. But Steel was nowhere in sight. The lobby of the hotel was filled with people so she looked through a few of the lounge areas, but still didn't see him.

Hurrying to the main desk, she showed her military security ID, first to a clerk, then the manager, and asked if Francis Sotelo was a guest. They confirmed he was, and she obtained his room number.

She didn't understand how Steel knew Sotelo. Or how that played into Danker's accusations against him. But it was all she had at the moment. She debated between waiting in the lobby for Steel to reappear or heading upstairs.

If Steel met with the friar, they might leave through one of the side exits. She decided to go up to the second floor. The fire exit stairway was empty and she bounded up the steps.

# CHAPTER 64

STEEL WAITED IN THE main lobby only a minute to ensure no one followed him.

Convinced he was alone, he took the main stairs to the second floor and walked down the hallway of the south wing. The wing was nearly deserted. Few people would remain in their rooms during a sunny afternoon on one of the more popular beaches in Maui.

The hotel room numbers he was interested in were to the right. Fifty feet down the hallway a Hawaiian cleaning attendant stood at a door, approximately where the friar's room should be.

Steel stopped and faced a door on the opposite side of the hallway, pretending to get his keycard out. He didn't want anyone else present when he met the friar. It was enough of a risk just to talk to the man, and he didn't know how the friar would react.

The door in front of the hotel attendant opened and the man pushed the cleaning cart into the room.

Steel strode down the hallway, quickly verifying the room was Sotelo's. Something taunted him at the edge of his thoughts. He focused on what nagged him until it came to him. The cleaning attendant wore sandals, not shoes. Maybe it was a problem, maybe not.

He stepped up to the door and knocked hard.

Silence.

He gave one more solid knock. No response.

Glancing down both sides of the hallway to make sure it was clear, he drew his gun. After quickly attaching the silencer, he kicked the door in. In front of him was the attendant's cart.

To the left two men lay on the floor, shot in the chest. Francis' guards. To the far left he saw the bathroom door—closed. He knelt low near the edge of the open door and peered around it to look right.

Bed. Desk. Sofa. Balcony door open. He panicked that Francis was dead on the balcony.

The bathroom door opened a crack. Francis peeked out.

"Get down!" Steel swung his gun right.

The Hawaiian had his gun just over the back of the sofa, firing at the same time Steel did. Steel's bullets dug holes in the top edge of the sofa, while the Hawaiian's hit the bathroom door.

Steel scrambled behind the cart and fired two more shots.

Retreating footsteps.

He risked a glance around the cart. The Hawaiian had fled and he gave chase, stopping at the balcony. The killer had bolted over the railing and was hurriedly walking away on the grass below. Fast, agile, and good.

Steel retreated inside. Hurrying to the closed bathroom door, he jerked it open. The friar lay on the floor on his stomach, the hood of his robe partially hiding his head. No blood. Steel bent over to touch the small man's shoulder. "Are you alright?"

The friar jerked his head up, his eyes and mouth wide. "Yes."

"Francis Sotelo, my name is Jack Steel. We have to leave."

"I understand." The friar pushed himself to his feet, the color returning to his face and his limbs seeming to relax. "You saved my life. I would be a fool not to listen to you."

# CHAPTER 65

STEEL'S CALF INJURY BURNED from his exertions, but he shoved the pain aside. Certain the Hawaiian would have an accomplice, he opened the outer room door an inch.

The hallway was nearly empty, except for a few tourists fifty yards away, walking away from them. The safest course of action for Francis was to get out of the hotel while they held an advantage.

He sidled out of the room, his gun pressed to his outer right thigh. Francis moved to his right side. The friar's robe helped to hide Steel's weapon. They walked to the left, but Steel paused and turned almost immediately upon hearing a soft sound.

Twenty yards behind them a stairwell door opened just a crack, and then closed. Simultaneously a man exited a room ten yards beyond the stairwell door and walked toward them. The man wore a dark blue suit, his head buried in an open brochure. Stocky, with a clean-cut beard and mustache.

Steel continued to lead Sotelo down the hallway, away from the man, keeping Francis between him and the wall. He forced himself to not look over his shoulder, but he didn't want a bullet in his back either.

After counting to five, he stopped and gently pushed Francis with his left hand against the wall. Bringing his right hand up, he stuck the gun under his left arm to keep it hidden. It looked like his arms were crossed and he was engaging Francis in a serious discussion.

"Talk, Francis, say anything."

"I have faith you will keep me safe," Francis said softly. "God has sent you to me. I am glad you are here, my friend."

"Me too." Steel unobtrusively watched the bearded man walk toward them. The man still had his head down.

The bearded man passed the exit stairwell door.

Steel saw the door creep open again. Maybe the person in the stairwell was the Hawaiian's accomplice and planned to use the bearded man as cover. It might have been a bad plan to stop in the middle of the hallway, but now he was committed. He kept his right arm loose, ready.

When the bearded man was twenty feet away from them, the stairwell door opened farther.

"Christie," whispered Steel.

Wide-eyed, she looked at him from the stairway door. No gun in her hand. Surprised to see her, Steel pushed aside rising emotions of betrayal and disappointment, and focused.

The bearded man stopped, half-facing the wall, appearing intent on something in the brochure. He glanced sideways at Christie. His eyes narrowed and his lips tightened.

The brochure seemed to hover for a millisecond in front of the man, and then floated down with a soft rustling as he pulled a silenced gun out from under his suit coat. Dropping to his knee, he twisted toward Christie.

Steel shoved Francis behind him with his left hand, swinging his right to take aim at the bearded man's back.

Voices burst into the hallway as another door opened. Four chatting women exited a room across from the stairwell door.

Twisting away from the women, the kneeling gunman picked up his brochure—using it to hide his gun—and kept his back to the four women who walked toward him.

Dropping his gun hand, Steel partially turned to hide his own weapon.

Christie pushed open the stairwell door and hurriedly followed the women, remaining close to them as they walked through the hallway.

Standing up, the bearded man held his brochure and brushed off his pants, his gun put away. Like the Hawaiian, smooth and quick. The bearded man ignored Christie and strode away in the opposite direction, quickly entering the room he had previously exited. It all took seconds.

Steel waited for the women to walk by before he tucked his gun under his shirt. Christie was at his shoulder, but he gave her only a cursory glance. Gripping Francis' elbow, he hurried him along.

Christie followed.

# CHAPTER 66

CHRISTIE FELT LIKE A dog trailing its master as she followed Steel out of the Grand Wailea and back to the Four Seasons' parking lot. She remained beside the friar, often looking over her shoulder and ahead.

Steel did the same thing. Though his face was calm and his brow relaxed. Every few steps he gave an assured look over his shoulder at Francis. The friar glanced everywhere.

Part of Christie wanted to bolt. Make a call to Danker and get out. And part of her said she might be in worse danger if she left Steel's side.

When the bearded gunman in the hallway saw her, a look of recognition had swept his face. It meant something, but she wasn't sure what. It tightened her throat. The man would have killed her if given the chance. She didn't know if she should thank Steel for his help or scream in his face.

Stopping at their parked rental Jeep, Steel turned to her with his hand out. Feeling like an underage teenager handing over contraband, she dug the keys out of her purse and handed them over.

Steel unlocked the doors and got in behind the wheel. Francis climbed into the back seat.

Christie stood next to the front passenger door. She wanted to put her hand on the door handle and get in, but she didn't know if she needed permission. Or if she wanted it. Steel had control over the situation and she still had no idea what the situation involved. Damn him.

Powering down the window, Steel looked at her, his face neutral. "They're after you too. You can go to the police, but I don't think it will make you safe. You're on your own."

He started to power the window up, and she blurted, "Wait!"

She looked in at him and shivered, not sure if she believed him, not wanting to. Questions were on her tongue, but he wouldn't answer any of them now. "Whoever is after you and the friar want me dead too, Steel. We're in this together."

"Who do you report to?" His voice was hard.

"Danker, but he obviously sold me out. If he's involved with those men, he's been lying to me." His eyes showed he didn't care so she added, "You can have my phone. I'm an extra gun and I know how to use it. I just want to stay alive." He still didn't look convinced, and she continued, "Do you know how many people are after you?"

He started the car, backed up two feet, and then stopped. "Get in."

She got in and slammed the door, and then passed her phone to him. He pocketed it.

He drove through the lot and parallel parked in front of the Four Season's lobby entrance. Keeping the Jeep running, he put it in park. "I'll be right back." He left and entered the hotel.

Christie pulled out her SIG Sauer and rested it on her thigh as she inspected the lot, watching pedestrians and drivers of nearby cars. She looked for the bearded man. Five-ten, two-hundred-fifty pounds, early thirties, well-muscled, square jaw, neatly trimmed black hair, beard, and mustache.

Steel quickly returned, both gun cases in hand. He handed hers over, and she set it on the floor between her legs. She holstered her gun.

"Where are we going, Steel?" He didn't answer so she said with force, "What was that all about at the hotel? You said you were going to tell me everything."

He remained silent. His eyes said *Take it or leave it.* As he drove he glanced ahead and out the side windows.

Christie assessed the friar in the back seat. Five-foot-three, one-hundred-ten pounds, mid-forties, a small narrow face under a bowl haircut. She sensed emotional strength in his diminutive body. He sat with his small hands folded together in his lap, his dark eyes intent on her.

"I am afraid too," he said quietly.

Surprised, she faced forward. The three of them sat in silence. They were soon on the Mokulele Highway, headed toward Kahului. A few white clouds drifted across the sky ahead of them.

Christie's jaw clenched. She considered asking Steel to let her out, but his statement that unknown killers were targeting her kept her silent. She couldn't come up with any reason why anyone would want her dead, except by association with Steel. Her thoughts returned to Danker. Instinctively she knew the man had sold her out somehow. The who and why could only be explained by Steel, and his eyes showed he didn't trust her.

Halfway to Kahului, Francis said politely, "I have a very important public talk tomorrow in the late afternoon at the Grand Wailea that I cannot miss."

Steel glanced in the rearview mirror. "I'll get you there."

"Gracias."

They arrived at the airport in less than an hour. Christie wondered what Steel had in mind. He parked the Jeep and they got out. Steel kept his door open and faced inside the vehicle.

She watched him pull the silencer off the Glock and place it under the front driver's seat. He then pulled out his gun case, opened it, and emptied the gun's ammo into a small plastic box. Placing the gun and ammo inside, he put the OTF knife in too, locked the case, and looked at her.

While he watched, Christie placed her gun and ammo into her gun case, locked it, took the case in hand, and locked the Jeep door. She walked with him and Francis into the terminal, up to the ticket counter of Hawaiian Airlines.

"The next flight to Kauai," said Steel.

"Number of tickets?"

Steel turned to Christie.

She shoved her hands in her pockets and wouldn't meet his eyes. "Three," she said.

"Two items to check." He declared their guns and showed his permit.

Christie showed the airline clerk her permit too.

Steel paid for the tickets. Turning to them, he gave them their boarding passes. "Go to the gate." Then he strode away.

Christie glared at his back, but then walked with the friar to the gate. She couldn't understand how the friar could remain so calm after an attack on his life. "What happened at the hotel, Francis? I saw bullet holes in the door."

"A man shot my two guards. Steel saved me." He paused. "The killer escaped."

"So two men are after us."

"Jack is a friend of yours?" asked Francis.

"Francis, do you know what's going on? Why those men want to kill you?" Her shoulders tightened. Without Steel beside them she felt exposed and unprotected.

Francis shook his head and his face paled. "No. I'm waiting for your friend to tell me."

She pursed her lips. They both were.

# CHAPTER 67

STEEL MADE HIMSELF VISIBLE, leisurely walking through the terminal. The Hawaiian and the bearded man didn't appear.

Still it would be easy enough for someone to figure out where he, Christie, and Francis were going. And the killers could use another interisland flight service or even charter a private plane to Kauai.

For an hour he sat in silence with Francis and Christie, waiting for their flight. He wanted to go somewhere free of crowds. The killers didn't want publicity and he wanted to make them feel safe, even bold. He also wanted to take their pursuers to an area of his choosing, one he knew from a previous trip to Hawaii.

When considering who had sent the killers, he believed it had to be Sorenson and Torr. He decided to kill the general and CEO as soon as possible.

They finally boarded the plane. There was still no sign of their pursuers. He didn't expect any.

A number of times during the flight his attention strayed to Christie, who sat rigidly across the aisle from him. Her appearance on the second floor of the Grand Wailea could only signify one thing—she had followed him. And that could only mean she had been playing him from the very beginning, using the Paktika Ops as an excuse to get close to him. Danker must have directed her to find evidence to prosecute him for blowing the Komodo Op.

Disappointment and feelings of betrayal remained, but some part of him had known all along he couldn't completely trust Christie. Unable to admit that to himself before, he still couldn't deny how hard it was to meet her eyes now.

A few times he studied her, seeing the corners of her mouth pulled down. None of that swayed his judgment. He knew her betrayal cut deeper because of what had happened with Carol. If he wasn't careful his emotions would take him to a place he wasn't sure he could recover from. Losing Rachel, Carol, and his career had left him with little to hang on to. Christie had kept him afloat.

Yet he was glad Christie's charade was exposed. He wanted his life free of deception and hidden agendas, conditions he had operated under during the last year with Carol while serving in Blackhood Ops.

Even though it appeared that Christie was also a target of the killers, he wouldn't confide in her any more than necessary. Francis needed to survive. Steel felt it was his debt to the friar and he was willing to pay it. He wouldn't let Christie jeopardize Francis.

If at any point her presence endangered them or posed more risk, or if she tried to make contact with anyone, he would leave her behind. If it came down to it, Steel realized that Francis was worth dying for. His integrity was the one thing he had left.

They landed at the Lihue Airport and picked up their gun cases. He made a quick call to Kergan. Voice mail. After joining Christie and Francis at the car rental, he chose a Honda Civic. He dawdled for a while before he picked it up.

Christie stared at him, but he gave her no explanation. An hour later he was satisfied. They left the Lihue Airport and drove north along the east coast on the Kuhio Highway.

Evening approached. Ominous clouds covered the upper reaches of the inland Waialeale mountain range and the ocean turned dark blue. The sky ahead of them on the north coast was overcast.

It was typical that the north coast of the island received more rain, even if the rest of the island was sunny. There was a good chance the sunshine would be gone by the time they reached their destination. Steel hoped for rain.

He gave a quick glance at the friar. Francis trusted him with his life. The friar also trusted his silence for the time being. Steel was glad for that, for there was little he could give in the way of comforting words.

Their choices were to go to the police or act on their own. Going to the police would delay things, but it wouldn't give any long-term safety. And Steel feared the friar would be much more vulnerable the next day at his public talk if the killers remained at large.

A thin line of traffic trailed them. A number of those cars had followed them from the airport. He had no idea if the killers were in one of them, but his instincts told him they were.

When he reached a long stretch of road with no visible turnoffs, he abruptly pulled off the road onto the shoulder. He checked his rearview mirror. A quarter mile back a green minivan also pulled over to the side.

He waited five minutes before driving back into traffic, not surprised when the minivan did too.

Christie had watched her sideview mirror, and she turned to him. "They're following us. I hope you know what you're doing, Steel."

# CHAPTER 68

STEEL WANTED TO CHEER when the first raindrops pattered against the windshield, even if it was just a sprinkle. The Kuhio highway eventually turned west with the island's coastline.

At one point the road curved slightly inland, through Hanalei Valley, where they observed bison chewing grass, their massive shaggy heads bent down. By then a steady drizzle forced Steel to turn on the lights and windshield wipers. As he drove, Steel visualized his plan, going over variations of it until he settled on what felt like the best course of action.

The road followed the edge of the coast all the way to Ke'e State Beach Park, where it dead-ended at the beach and the hilly tree line of the northern Na Pali Coast. The ocean was gray, covered by three-foot waves tipped with froth.

Steel pulled the car into the parking lot and took a quick look around. The beach was empty, save for a pair of white-bodied Laysan albatrosses standing in the rain. Only one car was in the parking lot.

From the trailhead three hikers exited the Kalalau Trail, which paralleled the Na Pali Coast. Steel guessed they were the last of the day hikers. No one would start up the trail this late in the day. And those who wanted to hike to the Hanakapi'ai beach, two miles up the path, would have started much earlier.

After the hikers left in their car, Steel brought out his gun and tucked it into his shorts. Christie holstered hers. Steel exited the car, Francis and Christie followed.

Christie wrapped her arms around her chest. Like Steel, she wore shorts and a short-sleeved top. She held an umbrella in one hand but didn't open it.

Francis looked warmer in his ankle-length robe, and he pulled up his hood.

Steel led them to the four-foot-wide dirt trail. Scrub grasses and tall ferns were interrupted by low straggly palms and hala trees.

Farther inland the forest was thicker and lush, the skyline broken by high palms, wispy kiawe trees with thin curving trunks, tall clumps of thin bamboo, and sturdier eucalyptus trees with their long, narrow leaves.

At the trailhead Steel motioned to Francis. "Go as fast as you can and don't stop. We'll follow."

Francis glanced at both of them, his face wet with rain, and then hurriedly trudged up the hill.

"What's the plan?" asked Christie.

Steel turned away from her to view the parking lot. "Set an ambush farther along the trail. Stay with Francis. I'll catch up."

She looked at him, lips pursed, and then at the rocky path which cut through high mounds of plants, leading upward and quickly winding out of sight. Rivulets of water ran over the muddy ground. Francis was already out of sight.

Steel knew none of it looked inviting.

She turned and left, walking fast.

Backing up twenty yards into the tree line, he squatted. While he waited, his gaze wandered to the small bay beyond the white sand beach. Rachel and Carol had snorkeled at the coral reef there several years ago. Afterward, Rachel talked for hours about the brightly colored reef fish. The image brought a lump to his throat, but for once he was glad for the memory.

Ten minutes later the green minivan pulled up. The Hawaiian, the stocky bearded man, and another taller man got out.

The third man surprised Steel. He had expected two. Rising, he started up the trail at a slow run so he wouldn't trip and fall. The running brought stabs of pain to his calf on every stride. Christie was out of sight.

It would only be minutes before the three men surmised their targets weren't on the beach or following the shoreline along the coast. The absence of tracks and places to hide would ensure that.

That would leave only the trail. Maybe if they were lucky they would have a five-minute head start. It would have to do. If he was healthy and alone, he would have headed off-trail. But since he was injured and protecting Francis and Christie, everything became more complex, tightening his stomach. Yet his plan felt solid and workable.

The cloudy sky would bring an early nightfall. Yet they had enough time to make it to the stream he had in mind. The Hawaiian and the bearded man were good so he assumed the third man would be equally competent. He needed something to give himself an edge. The stream would have to do.

He knew these men would come for them without hesitation. It seemed a perfect situation for their pursuers. No witnesses, nobody within hearing distance, and no obstacles—except to catch them on the trail. He counted on all of it to make the killers a little careless and overeager. It was the central piece of his plan. They would expect a trap but come anyway. It's what he would do.

In minutes he spotted Christie and Francis a half mile farther along the path. He waited for Christie to look back, and then gave a quick wave.

They both paused and turned, their faces taut. Francis' dark hair was plastered on his head and his soggy habit hung from his small shoulders, its lower fringe muddied.

Christie held her gun against her leg, her hair limp on her shoulders. Her soaked clothing clung to her body. She had the umbrella open and tried to shield herself and Francis with it. They both had muddy feet.

He caught up to them and looked at Francis. "Can you run in your sandals?"

The friar looked at the wet trail that led up and around the next hill. "I can try."

"Do it," he said. "Don't risk a fall, but don't slow down."

Francis turned and jogged up the trail.

"How many, Steel?" Christie closed the umbrella.

"Three." He grimaced. "There's a stream you'll come to eventually. Cross it and wait in the trees on the other side. We'll be safe there."

"What about you?"

"I'm going to buy us some time."

"Wonderful." She didn't wait for a reply, and instead ran at a careful pace up the path.

Francis had already reached the top of the hill.

Steel wiped moisture off his face and looked back along the trail. From the trailhead the path wound back and forth through the trees and ferns like a snake. The section closest to him swung inland a quarter mile around a small, narrow ravine that cut like a sliver between the rugged cliffs that sloped down to the ocean.

He glanced up the path that Christie had just summited. From that position he could look directly down the trail, as planned. He would also be able to see the men as they moved across the far side of the ravine. It should be relatively easy to get rid of one or two of them. Whoever was left he would eliminate at the stream with ease.

He jogged up the hill, slipping several times in the mud. To his immediate left a small vertical cliff bordered the trail. To the right was the ravine.

The cool air chilled his skin. It was nearly winter, the temperature in the low sixties. Even in the tropics exposure to wind and rain could be deadly. None of them could stay out in this weather too long or hypothermia might be a problem.

Cresting the trail, he saw that it quickly led downhill again. At the bottom of the decline there was a turn, and Francis and Christie were already around it, out of sight.

The rugged cliffs of the coastline stretched east and west from his vantage point. At the top of the trail, on its inner edge, he selected a large boulder to squat behind, setting the Glock on his knee.

He scanned the trail across the ravine and waited.

# CHAPTER 69

C HRISTIE WAS SEVERAL STEPS behind Francis and paced herself to his speed. The friar had a difficult time running with his habit, but at least he looked warm. A shiver ran through her. She would have to keep moving to keep her body heat up and wished she was dressed better. She also regretted staying with Steel.

When they had started up the trail she realized that this was the last place she wanted to be—in the rain and underdressed—with three killers chasing them. There had to be a better way to handle the situation. She berated herself for giving in to Steel's macho silent crap so easily. This was another Army exercise for him.

She had read Steel's file long ago, before she first met him. He seemed to thrive in extreme challenges. Something even his training routines reflected. In a perverse way he probably enjoyed this. Though his eyes had held obvious worry over the number of killers pursuing them.

What she hadn't considered soon enough was that Steel probably had a narrow view of alternatives, given his training. All he could envision was some type of military tactic. To her it seemed absurd that she had played along with him.

The only thing that gave her any hope at all was Danker's grudging admission that—among Blackhood operatives—*Steel's the best there is.*

Her fingers tightened on her gun as she thought about Danker. She was equally upset at Steel for not confiding in her. Another deep ache inside kept her mood downcast. She didn't want to admit there was more at stake with Steel than just her blown cover.

She looked ahead. They were jogging downhill again and coming to a sharp turn along a steep cliff.

Francis stumbled on the trail and did a skip. His arms swung out as he tried to keep his balance on the slippery trail.

Christie ran faster, dropping the umbrella so she could grab his robe from behind before he fell. She made the mistake of trying to brace her feet on the trail to slow Francis' momentum. Her sandals slid on the mud and she went by the friar.

Francis toppled backwards.

Losing her balance, Christie was forced to release his robe so he didn't pull her down with him. A small wisp of a tree to her right appeared and she flailed her hand at it. She hit her wrist hard and her fingers opened, her gun flying off to the side.

Catching a different branch with her left hand, her momentum swung her past the tree. She was forced to let go to avoid sliding off the side of the cliff. Wide-eyed, she glimpsed the view twenty feet ahead. A drop-off of jutting rock covered by low vegetation.

Her right foot slammed into a rock and she cried out. Her knees bent and she fell forward onto her stomach, sliding with her hands in front of her. Gasping, she tried to slow her momentum with her palms. Stones cut her skin as her fingernails pushed through pebbles and dirt. Trying to dig her feet in behind her, a stab of pain in her right ankle made her cry out. Rocks clattered down the incline with her fall.

With her left hand she grabbed a rock that held, and finally stopped her slide with her eyes peering over the edge of the cliff. Resting her head on her arm, she took deep breaths. Needles of pain burned her arms and stomach, and her ankle throbbed.

A hand gripped her left ankle. She looked back. Francis. His narrow, brown face was pale as he dragged her a few feet away from the edge.

Rolling to her back, she painfully sat up and looked at her aching ankle. Lifting her blouse, she saw fine scratches across her stomach, matching those on her forearms. Mud caked the front of her torso and legs.

"Help me to my feet, Francis," she said.

The friar didn't respond. She looked up.

He was doubled over, breathing fast, his face flushed. She thought he had been injured in the fall. But after a few moments she understood. Panic attack. It was a minute before his breathing normalized and he could stand upright again.

"I am sorry." He put a gentle hand on her shoulder. "They began after the first time they tried to kill me."

He put both hands under one of her arms, and she used her good foot to brace herself upright. She put a little weight on the injured leg and gasped.

"My ankle is sprained or broken." She shoved down her fear. "I can't walk."

He handed her the umbrella. "Lean on me."

"Find my gun first."

He hurried away. She watched him search near the tree, cautiously inching up to the cliff edge.

When he returned he shook his head. "I am sorry. There is no sign of it."

She bit her lip. "Let's get out of here."

He helped her hobble back to the trail and then down it, their progress slow. The dark clouds above mirrored her thoughts. Worse than not having a gun, now she couldn't even run and hide.

# CHAPTER 70

S TEEL KNEW THEY WERE in serious trouble almost immediately. He had underestimated his opponents.

The Hawaiian appeared first, on the far side of the ravine. His dark-skinned body blended with the shadows on the trail and he moved fast, running at a steady pace.

Steel kept his head low and looked for the others. They weren't visible on the trail behind the Hawaiian. Lowering to his stomach, he squirmed to the far side of the rock, out onto the trail so he could see farther behind the Hawaiian.

The bearded man was partially visible behind a tree across the ravine, his gun pointed at Steel's position. Steel searched until he found the third man, running in the trees, ten yards in from the trail and parallel to the Hawaiian. Soon the tall man would be above the cliff bordering the trail and out of sight.

Steel didn't think they could see him, but he understood the three men were executing a precise military maneuver. The bearded man would make sure no one would surprise the Hawaiian from the top of the hill. The ravine ran thirty yards across. Even adding in the hill's elevation, the bearded man would have a good line-of-sight to Steel.

He crawled backward. When the rock provided cover, he moved to the other side of it and sat down. Pulling up his knees, he rested his gun on them and sighted down the path.

He wouldn't see the Hawaiian until the man was halfway up the hill, but at least he would remain out of sight of the bearded man. In addition, the tall man in the trees would have an obstructed view of him.

As he waited, he concluded that Danker or Sorenson had probably set up a Blackhood Op to target him, Francis, and Christie. The men chasing them were not just hired killers, but professional Army elite. It would explain the killers' skill sets. And they wouldn't stop until they fulfilled their contract. It verified Christie's story that Danker had sold her out—she was a loose end he wanted gone. It didn't make him feel any differently about her.

The Hawaiian rounded the bottom curve in the trail and disappeared out of sight. In a minute he appeared running up the path. Abruptly he stopped, gun in hand, staring up the hill.

Steel squeezed the trigger just as the Hawaiian jumped to the side of the trail. He missed the shot.

A bullet whined off the rock he sat behind. That shot had to come from the bearded man. Steel glanced down the trail. The Hawaiian must have his back pressed against the hill along the path, remaining out of sight.

The tall man might run inland and try to get ahead of him on the trail. He had to get out.

After squeezing off two quick shots at the trail near the hidden Hawaiian—to hold him at bay—Steel twisted onto his belly and rapidly crawled away from the rock farther along the trail. Two more shots struck the muddy path in dull plops two feet to his side, startling him. The bearded man must have moved forward for a better angle.

The Hawaiian might be running up the hill, yet Steel couldn't risk getting up until he was sure he was out of sight. He hadn't planned this badly. These men were just that good.

He crawled to the safety of another large rock, got to his knees, and risked a crouch. A shot pinged off the rock. Remaining low, he ran for it. He rounded a bend and left the trail to head inland.

Sunset was closing in, creating dark shadows among the trees.

A hint of pale skin appeared some fifty yards ahead of Steel. The tall man. That startled him. If the Hawaiian caught up to him while he was in the woods, they would have him in a crossfire. He ran faster through the waist-high ferns, lush grass, and young eucalyptus trees with narrow trunks, trying to close the distance before the killer became aware of him.

The tall man disappeared for a few moments.

Wary, Steel slowed his speed until he spotted the shoulder of the man behind a tree. Dropping to one knee, he took aim.

A warning shout erupted behind him. The Hawaiian.

Steel squeezed the trigger twice.

He thought he missed, but the tall man stumbled out from behind the tree, toward the trail, firing at him. The killer had a bloody shoulder and made wild shots.

Steel was still trapped by the man's position. He shot him twice more.

The man fell forward, face down.

Steel ran for the trail. Glancing back, he saw a flash of the Hawaiian's blue shirt. Pausing, he took one shot at the man to make him worry, and then sprinted.

Some fifty yards farther down, he ran out of the woods onto the path, running as fast as the muddy trail would allow.

# CHAPTER 71

HOPPING ON ONE FOOT, wet and chilled, Christie felt as if all the energy was expelled from her body. Like a pricked balloon. All that kept her moving was her will to live. The exertion exhausted Francis too, but he didn't complain and supported as much of her weight as possible. His shoulders slumped beneath her arm on every step.

The path became more treacherous. With the arrival of sunset and the constant rain it became difficult to see where the ground was solid, instead of just coated with a deceptive layer of mud.

Her sandal kept slipping off. Eventually she just left it behind in the mud. They couldn't waste time every few steps for her to put it back on. Her bare foot paid the price—whenever she hopped onto a sharp stone she winced. Soon several small cuts marred the sole of her foot, leaving tiny dark markers along the trail that the rain washed away.

Often she glanced over her shoulder, expecting the killers to gun them down. It kept her back stiff.

She tried to focus on their goal. The stream. She didn't know how much farther they had to go. Even if they made it to the stream ahead of their pursuers, they had no weapons to stop the killers from crossing.

Fifty more yards of trudging brought the sound of rushing water to her ears, barely audible over the rain that pattered against the foliage around them. They were walking along a level stretch five hundred feet above the sea.

When it ended she could see the dark stream far below. They would have to navigate their way through a series of switchbacks to reach the bottom.

After glancing back again, she clutched Francis' arm and they began their descent.

# CHAPTER 72

STEEL RAN AS HARD as he could. His calf injury made him wince, but he knew the other two men were close behind so he couldn't slow down.

He strained to hear sounds over the noise of his own squishing feet and the rain, imagining he heard their pounding steps. The image of a gun aimed at his back spurred him on.

On any stretch that allowed an unobstructed view for over twenty yards, he looked back to make sure he wasn't in their gun sights. He had managed to stay ahead of them. Perhaps they were following him with more caution because of his previous ambush.

He ran to the top of another small hill and stopped to peer ahead. Christie and Francis were a good distance farther along the path, but they had just begun the final descent down to the stream. Alarmed, he watched them disappear behind a hill. Moving at that pace they would never get across the stream before their pursuers caught up with them. That part was crucial.

Looking back, he spotted the Hawaiian running down the trail a quarter mile behind him. The bearded man wasn't in sight.

Standing behind a tree, he took two quick shots, sliding back behind the tree as bullets bit into the trunk. The bearded man was still covering the Hawaiian. He peeked out past the other side of the tree trunk. The Hawaiian had disappeared. They were being cautious. Slowly he backed away from the tree, and then turned and ran.

He continued running, knowing he had to make a decision. If he delayed their pursuers again he would lose whatever lead he had, and thus might not make it across the stream. And in a standoff he doubted he would be as lucky against the remaining two men as he had been the first time.

At the bottom of a hill he came to a gully. He heard a distinct slap against a nearby tree and glanced over his shoulder.

The Hawaiian stood on the path sixty yards back, taking aim at him.

He pumped his legs harder, running off the path but paralleling it. There was little chance the killer would hit him at this distance, especially in the dusk with the rain and surrounding vegetation.

Abruptly he tumbled head over heels, landing in a heap against a log. His head struck it hard and his outstretched hand slapped against the wet wood. He managed to hang on to his gun.

His numbed limbs barely responded, but he pushed himself up. Dazed and confused about what had happened, he looked down. Blood on his right thigh. His leg began to burn, as if it had just discovered the gunshot wound. He ignored it and ran. If he waited any longer he wouldn't be able to.

Stumbling along the trail, he glanced back. The Hawaiian still stood on the hill. Thick ferns and trees grew on either side of the path near him so maybe his pursuers weren't sure if he was hit or had just dove for cover.

As soon as he broke out of the vegetation, the two men ran down the path after him. He was relieved they couldn't see his leg wound. Stopping, he fired two shots at the killers. They ducked into the vegetation and he kept running.

His chest tightened with ragged breaths. His pursuers brought back memories of another chase, through another rainforest. There wasn't any choice about trying to delay the killers now.

He had to make it to the stream.

# CHAPTER 73

CHRISTIE STOOD WITH FRANCIS at the edge of the stream and stared at the dark swirling eddies in front of them. Under different circumstances it would be the perfect place for an ambush. She gave Steel that much credit anyway.

But what he had called a stream looked deep and swollen with rain. She quickly concluded that it would be too risky for her to try to cross.

The rushing current had stretched to thirty feet wide, covering a dozen large, flat-topped rocks that formed a path from bank to bank. Six inches of gushing water flowed over the stones. Other rocks poked up from the surface along the stream's course as it ran to the ocean. She couldn't imagine hopping across the rocks with her injured ankle.

Two thick cables ran four feet above the stream, stretching from a large tree on the near bank to another large tree on the opposite bank. The far bank rose six feet above the water's surface to a sparse tree line.

"Go," she said.

Francis looked at her calmly. "I'll help you."

"We can't go together. It's not wide enough." She turned to him. "I can't make it. You're our only chance. If you get across in time, they'll think we're both over. I don't know about Steel, but we have to assume we're on our own. Don't waste any more time arguing."

She hopped to the side of the trail and pointed up the hill to a clump of rocks. "I'll hide myself up there." Without looking back, she painfully eased herself to all fours and began climbing.

After a minute she turned, relieved to see Francis clinging to the cables and stepping across the stones. The lines sagged beneath his weight.

She continued her crawl upward, dragging her injured leg. On every movement her knees scraped against the rocky ground. Searching for solid handholds to pull herself up, she pushed with her good foot. The slippery ground felt like it had a coating of grease. Rocks skittered down behind her.

Images of gunmen running down the trail and shooting her in the back made her efforts more frenzied. The climb took whatever strength she had left and her whole body was shaking by the time she reached her destination.

She drew herself behind the low pile of rocks, put down the umbrella, and pulled a few hand-sized rocks to her side. Taking ragged breaths, she lifted her head to watch Francis finish the crossing and climb the bank. He waved once, and then withdrew into the trees.

Footsteps slapped the ground not far away. With her eyes riveted on the trail, she picked up a rock and waited. She quickly reconsidered and lowered herself out of sight.

For a moment she thought about her parents and brothers, wishing she had called them over the past month for one last talk.

# CHAPTER 74

S TEEL FELT HALF DEAD as he pounded down the last switchback to the stream, barely able to see the smaller rocks he needed to avoid on the trail. His leg burned and he felt nauseous and weak.

The empty trail ahead contradicted his expectations. Christie and Francis had crossed the water. That gave him hope. They would have two guns between them and thus a better chance against the killers.

He stopped at the stream, whirled, and saw shadowy figures at the top of the hill. To buy himself a minute, he fired twice at the killers, forcing them to duck into cover off the trail. Ejecting his empty magazine, he reached for his spare—and didn't find it.

The fall. He must have lost it then.

Shoving the gun inside his belt, he held the cables and stepped out onto the first rock, then the second. On the fourth his injured leg wobbled and his foot slid off the stone. The hissing stream caught it and threw him off balance. Water quickly churned around his knees as he hung onto the cables.

Twisting around, he saw two dark shapes descending the slope. That image kept him still for one moment, then like a madman he pulled himself hand over hand to the next rock.

\*\*\*

Christie bit her lip as she peeked over the rocks at Steel. She remembered how fast he went up the rope in the woods on their first run. He moved almost that fast now. But he was dragging one of his legs. She hoped he had his gun.

Turning, she saw two men running down the hill. Steel must have killed one of them. She wanted to shout a warning, but knew she was finished if she did. It felt like she was watching a movie with a front row view of the climactic death scene.

Steel pulled himself furiously toward the far bank. But the two men were fast approaching the corner where they would have a clear view of him.

As afraid as she was of being seen, she realized she was even more afraid of Steel dying. That concern clutched her heart like a vise.

Without waiting, she hoisted a rock and tossed it as far as she could downstream from the men, along the bank. It made a distinct thud and the two killers dove to their bellies just before the turn, their guns and eyes pointed downstream.

Steel dragged himself over the far bank, out of sight.

Christie sagged to the ground, eyes closed, umbrella in hand, waiting for the two men to figure it out.

# CHAPTER 75

STEEL EXPECTED BULLETS IN his back over the last few yards, so he practically flung himself up and over the bank. It surprised him that the two men didn't fire at him. He was even more stunned when he rolled back a distance, stood, and saw only Francis.

"She couldn't cross," Francis said softly. "Her ankle."

Those words felt like a punch to the stomach. He swallowed. "Does she have her gun?"

Francis shook his head.

Turning, he stared across the stream. He shouldn't have crossed. He was on the wrong side. Everything was wrong. He should have been over there, not Christie.

It reminded him of Rachel's death, and his wanting to take her place. Even though Christie had betrayed him, he didn't want her to die. That concern overwhelmed him for a moment and he had to push it down to focus.

His only advantage was that the two pursuers didn't know where Christie was. He limped to the tree that the cables were wrapped around. The two killers were hidden in the trees back from the stream. Sliding to the other side of the tree, he peered across the water, scanning the hill near the trail. He was certain where Christie was hiding.

He looked beyond Francis. The path ran a dozen yards through thick vegetation before the forest obscured it. From where he stood, a gentle slope led to the ocean, a hundred yards distant. He could hear the surf rhythmically lapping at the shoreline.

Francis walked closer to him, careful to keep the tree as a protective shield between himself and the men on the opposite side. "They want to kill me," he whispered. "If I go to them, they'll leave."

Steel shook his head. "They want all of us." He eyed the friar, wanting to get him out of reach of the killers' guns. "Run down to the beach. Let them see you and make some noise. Stay there."

Francis hesitated, and then stepped out from the tree and ran into the vegetation, crashing through it, his sandals slapping against the wet ground.

Steel watched the friar run into the thick growth, his sounds carrying to him even after he disappeared. At least Francis was safely out of the way. Though the friar was dead if the men made it across the stream.

He peeked around the tree again, watching the two men approach the opposite side.

The bearded man put his gun in his belt and started across the rocks. To cover his partner, the Hawaiian used the tree bracing the bridge cables for partial cover, while holding his gun in two hands with a wide stance. aiming at the opposite bank.

Leaning his back against the trunk, Steel closed his eyes. An impossible situation. No. His mind raced through strategies, none of which seemed winnable. He thought about the OTF knife but decided to leave it for close quarters. Instead he picked up two baseball-sized stones.

Then it came to him. Get the gun from the bearded man on the bridge and use it to kill the Hawaiian.

Holding the rocks in tight fists, he waited. The Hawaiian would target the tree he was hiding behind, so even if he hit the bearded man, he would take a bullet.

He couldn't believe that he had let it come to this. It seemed absurd that their lives depended on two rocks in his hands.

# CHAPTER 76

CHRISTIE WAS SURPRISED STEEL hadn't shot the bearded man. His gun had to be jammed or empty.

She heard Francis run off, guessing the risk Steel was going to take. If his gun was operational, he would have kept Francis with him. Sending the friar off signaled he was in trouble. Without a gun Steel would be left with either his knife or rocks. Even if he hit the man crossing the stream, the Hawaiian would shoot him.

She hefted another rock in her hands and quietly pulled herself to a sitting position. Even though she was visible, she doubted the Hawaiian would turn around to check. It surprised her that they hadn't figured it out the first time. This time it would be obvious.

Focusing on the tree on the far bank, she waited for Steel to make his move, knowing she had to anticipate him.

Then she realized her reaction would never be faster than the Hawaiian's trigger finger. Steel would have to act on her cue.

Struggling to stand up without making any noise, she balanced on her healthy leg, and took aim at the Hawaiian. She froze for a moment, and then threw the rock at his back, yelling as loud as she could.

\*\*\*

When Christie yelled, Steel looked around the side of the tree and glimpsed a flash of red clothing behind the pile of rocks. The

Hawaiian was already whirling to fire at her; her thrown rock had missed him.

Stepping out, Steel threw the two stones at the bearded man on the crossing. One missed the killer as he ducked, and splashed into the water, but the other struck the man's chest.

The bearded man grunted and shouted to his partner. The Hawaiian twisted to fire at Steel.

Steel jumped behind the tree as several shots chewed into the tree's bark with dull thuds. He peered out again on the other side of the trunk.

The Hawaiian was slowly backing up the hill. However, the tree anchoring the cables was blocking more of the killer's view of Steel's side of the stream.

The bearded man hung onto one of the cables with one hand, his gun in the other. But he lost his balance when water washed over his ankles. That forced him to tuck his gun back into his belt so he could grip both cables. He had ten feet to go to reach the other side.

The Hawaiian was still moving up the hill, walking backward.

Heaving a breath, Steel rounded the tree and jumped down the embankment. His leg burned and he wanted to scream. He shoved down the pain and leapt for the cables. By the time the bearded man saw him, he was already hurtling himself hand over hand across the cables. His move was too unexpected—and by then the bearded man partly shielded him from the Hawaiian's line of sight.

The bearded man stopped and reached for his gun, his face a pale specter in the dusk.

Putting all his weight on the cables, Steel swung both feet at the man, kicking him in the stomach. His injured leg was on fire.

Gasping, the killer teetered on the rock, the gun still in his hand, his arm swinging out. The bearded man tried to keep himself upright, his left hand clutching the cable.

Steel jumped to the next stone, clawing at the man's gun arm as it swung toward him.

# CHAPTER 77

CHRISTIE WATCHED STEEL THROUGH a crack in the rocks, while listening to the Hawaiian scramble up the hill toward her. The Hawaiian must have decided to get her first, and then worry about Steel. He was using his partner to buy him time.

She picked up another rock, keeping her back pressed against the ground. The scent of mud and sweat filled her nostrils. Inch by inch she edged herself sideways until she was parallel to the rocks hiding her.

If she extended her right arm up it would be the first thing the killer would see. Gripping the stunbrella, her eyes remained glued to the edge of rock above her.

It all depended on how close the killer moved to the edge. If he stood close enough, she could stretch over the rocks and strike his legs with the umbrella. But even if she stunned the man, if she didn't get to him quickly he might recover and shoot her anyway.

Her lips trembled. Shoes scraped on rock. Grit and sharp stones jammed into her back. Rain pattered against her face. She wanted to shiver but held herself steady. Just a little longer.

The sounds became louder. She resisted the urge to sit up. Eighteen inches long, the stunbrella gave her a four-foot reach. But since the rocks rose a foot and a half above her, even if the man stood a foot away from them she might not be able to angle her arm to strike him.

A whimper was trapped in her throat. She didn't want to die like this. In the middle of the woods, cold, wet, dirty. Injured like a sick animal. Not even knowing why. All alone.

The noise stopped.

She sensed he was close. From her earlier glimpse she guessed five-foot-eight, one-seventy pounds, mid-forties. Small for a Hawaiian. He might be easy to knock down.

Her choice was to either sit up and try to strike him or remain motionless for him to come closer. Unable to guess which was better, she didn't move.

Her lips twisted when the man's dark-skinned face appeared above the rocks near her feet. Too far from her motionless arm. As he looked down at her, the barrel of his gun swung into view.

# CHAPTER 78

STEEL GRABBED THE BEARDED man's gun hand, closing around it so the man couldn't let go. Aware of what was happening across the rush of water on the other side, his lungs held a stifled cry.

In one savage motion he brought the bearded man's gun hand past him, overhead. Holding the killer's gun in both hands, he forced the man's arm down, aimed the gun at the Hawaiian, and squeezed the man's trigger finger.

The gun fired.

The bearded man regained his balance on the rock, let go of the cable, and tried to club Steel in the face with his free hand. They both toppled into the surging water.

\*\*\*

The bullet ricocheted with a loud zing off the rocks. The Hawaiian jerked his head around, his gun still pointed at Christie.

She sat up and jabbed the stunbrella against the man's naked forearm, squeezing the trigger.

The man cried out and fell back.

Simultaneously a white, jagged line streaked down the wet surface of the umbrella to Christie's hand. Her body stiffened with eighty-thousand volts of raw charge. It felt as if someone had pressed a thousand needles into her skin all at once.

Numb, she fell back. Lying there, she stared up at the gray clouds, her hands trembling at her sides. Part of her brain struggled with the knowledge that she should get up and go for the gun or try to get away. Do something. Anything. But her limbs felt as distant as the sky above her and wouldn't obey any orders she gave them.

It took only moments for her whole system to emerge from the vacuum that engulfed her, but it seemed like an eternity. She wiggled her fingers and struggled to push herself upright.

Halfway up, her trembling arms wouldn't support her weight. As if she was trying to push energy and commands through neural synapses that were permanently shut down. She fell back to the ground with a gasp.

She wanted to rest for a few more breaths but panicked over the idea of the man recovering before she did. She pushed against the ground. This time she sat up and leaned forward. A groan escaped her pursed lips and she shivered violently as stinging sensations swept her body. Nauseous, she couldn't see the man.

Her legs wobbly, she painfully rose to her knees, her injured ankle burning.

The Hawaiian's foot was trapped between two rocks and he rested on his back, aimed downhill like an arrow with outstretched arms, his head on a stone, his eyes closed. He looked peaceful. But the blood on the rock beneath his head told her that he might be dead.

Her gaze shifted to the bridge. Empty.

She picked up the umbrella and slid down the rocks as best she could, toward the Hawaiian's gun. A Glock.

# CHAPTER 79

THE AIR WAS PUNCHED out of Steel's lungs when he struck the water, mainly because he landed on the bearded man's knee. Water flowed into his mouth. He tried to push himself off the killer, but instead got entangled with the man's limbs and sank. Water buffeted him on all sides. Cold liquid covered his face as he clawed for the surface.

A break appeared in the muddy water that was smothering him.

Surfacing, he coughed, choked on water, and was sucked under again. The killer's body became trapped beneath him like some macabre air cushion, which he rode along a furious hundred feet over rocks, quickly ending up in a small bay.

The other body drifted away.

Surf pounded him when he lifted his head up. Choking on salt water, its scent strong in the air, he tried to float on his back. After a few frog strokes, strong hands pulled him to shore. There he coughed up water for an agonizing minute.

Lying on the stony beach, he looked up into the friar's face, and then stared out at the water.

"You're the only one I saw," said Francis.

"We have to move. Christie..." Steel couldn't finish. He felt numb inside. He didn't want to face the fact that he had missed the Hawaiian with his shot. The Hawaiian would have killed Christie, and then come for them.

Oddly, Francis was smiling.

The friar touched Steel's shoulder, his voice calm. "Christie called our names."

# CHAPTER 80

CHRISTIE LEANED AGAINST A sapling, balanced on one foot while gripping the Hawaiian's silenced Glock. Her voice was hoarse from yelling their names over and over.

There was no way for her to cross the stream and hobble down to the beach. Maybe Steel was dead or dying. Francis would have no way to bring him up from the beach.

Frustrated, she didn't know what to do. She was soaked and muddy, her hair wrapped around her neck, her eyes filled with the constant drizzle. Exhausted. She couldn't leave so she waited, expecting the worst.

It seemed to take forever before the two men appeared on the opposite bank. While Francis and Steel climbed down to the ropes, she wanted to shout in triumph. Instead she pursed her lips and watched them cross the stream.

She saw the dark stain on Steel's shorts. The wound was an ugly gouge on his outer thigh. A film of red trickled over his skin, which the rain kept washing away.

Francis made it across first. She hobbled up to him and waited. He hugged her without hesitation. Tears filled her eyes, running with the rain down her cheeks. He pulled back from her, smiled, and they waited for Steel.

Steel crossed, stopping to glance up the hill at the dead Hawaiian. Francis allowed him to lean on his shoulder.

Christie kept her distance. A yard away. She looked into Steel's eyes. All her years of being aggressive, of taking the initiative, evaporated. Unable to act. Instead she waited for some sign or signal from him.

He looked at her, and for a moment she thought something had shifted between them. A hint of relief showed in his eyes. "How?"

She lifted the umbrella a few inches. "Eighty-thousand volts."

He lifted an eyebrow, and then said softly, "Thanks." Turning, he hobbled up the path, Francis beside him.

Standing still, Christie focused her watery eyes on the trail beneath her feet.

As if remembering something, Steel stopped and looked back at her. He held out an arm. In two quick hops she was beside him, and he looped his arm under hers and around to her shoulder. The three of them began up the hill. She realized this was as much as she might ever get from Steel.

It took them the better part of an hour and a half to return to the car. Along the way Christie recovered her sandal and Steel found his spare magazine.

The rain stopped, but they were exhausted, wet, and shivering. Steel dug out his keys, started the Civic, and blasted the heater.

Christie ripped off a piece of the lower part of her top and tied it around Steel's leg wound. Just the fact that he accepted her help signaled how weary he was. She knew he had lost a lot of blood. His pale face showed it.

Without a word he flicked on the headlights, turned out of the lot, and drove.

She sat in the front seat, her right foot extended, her left pushed against the floorboard. Francis rested in back. The friar seemed strangely calm after the deaths of three men. Christie still didn't understand why the killers had chased them. She was even more dismayed by the rush of emotion she had experienced over seeing Steel alive at the stream.

She couldn't remember how long it had been since she had experienced that kind of relief, joy, and happiness over anything. Maybe in college. One of her close friends had asked her to be part of her wedding. Something that simple had seemed extraordinary. She had felt special. Included. How strange and sad that she had to go through something like this to feel that way again.

It was easier now to admit that she cared about Steel. That love was possible. Too little too late. She had missed her chance. He wouldn't want to hear it now.

She glanced at him. Maybe he would never trust her again. Leaning her head back, she closed her eyes.

# CHAPTER 81

CHRISTIE VOLUNTEERED TO LIMP into the Kauai International Hostel, just south of Kapa'a, to see if she could get a room. Francis looked too conspicuous and Steel's leg wound too suspicious.

Smiling at the tired night clerk, she said she had a flat tire and had sprained her foot on a hiking trail. She explained she needed a private room for three.

The hesitant clerk agreed to move an extra mattress into a room with a queen-sized bed, but only after she offered double the room price. A communal kitchenette was available for cooking. Steel wanted the kitchen for breakfast.

She paid with Steel's cash and signed in as Mrs. Johnson. She asked for change to launder their clothing, and a first aid kit—which the clerk gave her for a hundred-dollar deposit.

The clean room seemed like an oasis compared to the rain, mud, and cold. They were all trembling, but Steel looked the worst off. Christie objected, but Steel insisted the friar take a shower first, then her, before he hobbled into the bathroom for his turn. She told him to toss his clothing out, which he did with the door cracked open.

While Steel showered, Francis rested. Christie bandaged her left foot, which had minor cuts. She wrapped her sprained ankle with some gauze which helped ease the pain.

Grabbing aspirin from the first aid kit, she gathered all their clothing, and limped to the laundry room with a towel wrapped around her. Cupping her hand beneath a washtub faucet, she downed the aspirin with some water. She remained there until their clothing was dry.

When she returned, Francis was lying on the spare mattress, covered with a sheet and blanket, which left the queen to her and Steel. She dropped the friar's robe beside him.

Francis smiled up at her. "Gracias."

Smiling briefly, she dumped the rest of the clothing on the foot of the bed. Keeping the bath towel around her, she got under the covers and sat in silence, her back against the wall at the top of the bed. The aspirin had kicked in, easing the ankle pain.

Steel came out of the bath wrapped in a towel too. His upper body surprised her. White, faded scars marked his torso and arms, and a large claw scar streaked across his upper back. It was another example of how little she knew about him.

"Here." She swung her legs out of the bed and opened the first aid kit.

He glanced at her, and then limped over, pulling back enough of the towel to expose the wounds. Her cloth bandage still covered the bullet wound.

She untied it, dried the area with the towel, and put bacitracin over the leg wound, followed by nonstick gauze pads. She wrapped self-adherent gauze around his leg to keep the pads in place. Glad to help, she didn't meet his eyes.

Finished, she handed him several aspirin. "I'll get you some water."

"Thanks," he said softly.

She returned in a minute with a cup of water, which he downed with the pills.

He limped to the opposite side of the bed, sat down, and gingerly swung his legs up. Leaning against the wall, he pulled the blanket up to his stomach. He took a deep breath, clasped his hands on his lap, and began talking. He explained the Komodo

Op in detail to them. His pursuit of MultiSec, the Paragon file, the shooting of his dog, the murders of Grove and the Bellues, the attempted kidnapping of his wife, Rusack, Quenton, and the Serpent Op.

Christie hugged her knees as her perceptions changed. Steel had the guts to take on the military on a covert Op, and Danker had twisted the facts about him to fit his own agenda. She believed Steel was telling the truth. She also understood how Danker had sounded so credible.

It was true, Steel had betrayed the Op. His values mattered more to him than his orders. That realization struck a raw nerve in her, because sometimes she had ignored her own values in favor of following orders.

Francis confirmed Steel's story with several nods, and said quietly, "I sensed it was you today at the hotel. There is some affinity between us, I think." He gave a gentle smile.

Steel nodded. "I felt it too, when you took your walks in the jungle. I kept thinking there was something familiar about you. I've followed articles about you for a number of years."

"Perhaps you also sense in me the same thing that God's creatures are drawn to," said Francis, his eyes shining. "Perhaps it is the same bond that connects all of us, which we could all sense if we were open to it."

Steel looked at Francis. "It's still dangerous for you to participate in the talk tomorrow."

Francis nodded. "I grew up in a poor area where a company dumped chemicals into our water and land, and many died of cancer. I have lived with danger all my life, as many poor people do. Tomorrow I have something very important to say, which must be said while the world is watching. I'm afraid at the Honolulu conference my voice will be buried. But tomorrow the press will focus on my message. And I will have you to protect me. Sometimes you must take chances in life." He glanced from Steel to Christie.

Christie blurted, "Danker ordered me to watch you. He said you were a traitor."

Steel didn't respond.

She kept talking. "CIA Director Hulm ordered me to give you access to any information you wanted. He also said not to trust you, that you were on the wrong side of things. I believed them." She saw no empathy in his eyes and added, "Hulm kept the CID away from you after you were attacked the first time. They wanted you to feel free to act."

Steel looked at her. "They wanted me to find Tom Bellue's hidden Paragon file. I'm guessing they also hoped I would give them a way to bring down MultiSec's CEO, Torr. Torr must have something over Hulm and the president. And I'm guessing Torr had Danker or Sorenson send these men to kill us."

She barely met his eyes. "The first Paktika Op you assessed had already been run and was a mess. The second one we ran with your suggestions and it was a success." He didn't respond and she kept talking. "I care about my country and doing what's right as much as you do. I trusted Danker and the CIA director— what would you have done?"

"You could have been honest with me about Danker and Hulm. I wouldn't have gone on the Serpent Op if you had."

She wanted to say more but didn't know if he cared to hear it. She wouldn't go back to Danker or Hulm with any of his story. Maybe Steel already knew that. That decision would compromise her orders, but she didn't care. The promotion wasn't important now. For the first time in years her career didn't matter as much as other things.

The shadows in the room hid Steel's eyes from her. She slid beneath the sheets and turned to face the wall. She didn't know how to bridge the distance between them, and she doubted he wanted her to try.

# CHAPTER 82

STEEL STAYED AWAKE UNTIL the others were fast asleep. Weary, his leg still throbbing, he considered what had happened. They were reasonably secure from any law enforcement investigation, but he had deeper concerns about those who had hired the killers.

It was probably safe to return to Maui the next day, but it wasn't a given. There was no way to be certain that the three men were the only ones targeting them, nor what might happen when it was learned they were dead.

His gun had been purchased off the grid but could be tied to the man he shot. He wasn't worried about the police charging him with murder. He just didn't want them holding him for questioning while Francis was vulnerable. After some deliberation he let it go, satisfied he could do nothing except shadow Francis tomorrow.

His eyes drifted to Christie's darkened form. She slept on her side, her back to him. The absence of light hid the colors of her hair and skin.

He wondered if he had known from the beginning that she wanted more than Paktika Op assessments. If he ignored the signals. Ignored them because at the time he swam in so much pain and wanted support from anyone. Like a lone survivor in a lost war, he had reached for her hand and hadn't wanted to let go.

Curiously he felt less emotional response toward the demise of his marriage than he had even a day ago. Perhaps the last day had driven him someplace more objective. Worrying about staying alive, and keeping Francis alive, had somehow put a year-dead marriage in perspective.

When he had walked with Francis up from the ocean, returning to the stream, just hearing Christie's shouts had made his eyes moist. Seeing her leaning against the tree, unharmed, had allowed the knot in his stomach to finally unwind.

Under different circumstances he might have given a relationship with her a chance. That seemed impossible now. He had minimized his response to her since crossing the stream. Her betrayal had taken them too far in one direction to change, and there wasn't anything he could do about that.

He downed two more aspirin and eventually fell asleep, but the aching pain in his leg woke him before the others. Late morning sunshine crept in past the sides of the closed blinds.

He rebandaged his wounds, pulled on his clothing, and limped out of the room. His thigh burned, but his stride improved a little as he limped along.

The clerk glanced at his leg but gave him directions to the nearest convenience store. He drove there to get food and stronger painkillers. Later he went shopping at a clothing store. He bought a pair of sandals for Christie and jeans for himself, which he slipped on at the store.

When he returned the others were awake. Without a word he left the sandals and food on the table, and then walked to the office to use a phone. Their phones had been ruined in the water.

He dialed Kergan's number. Kergan answered on the first ring.

"Everything's busted wide open, Jack. I'm waiting for you at the Four Seasons."

Steel sagged inwardly. "There were three of them here. It's been messy."

"We'll clean it up. It's been unbelievable stateside. Don't worry. I brought a lot of help. We'll wait for you. Just get over here, my friend. We have work to do. It's not over."

He hung up, feeling better with Kergan here. When he returned to the room, Christie and Francis were in the communal kitchen, cooking breakfast.

"We have help," he said. "It's time to go back."

Francis beamed at him, but Christie kept her eyes on the bacon sizzling in the pan.

# CHAPTER 83

BY PROTECTING FRANCIS, STEEL finally felt absolved from what had happened on the Komodo Op. Redemption for other things was possible too, he told himself.

They caught an early afternoon flight back to Kahului, Maui, and he drove the rental Jeep along the Mokulele Highway toward Wailea. The sun shone brightly.

Francis and Christie looked rested. Christie favored her foot, but from the look of things it wasn't broken, just badly bruised. The painkillers helped her, and also reduced his leg pain to a manageable degree. No one had been talkative in the morning, but Francis beamed in the back seat.

"This is a big moment in my life," said the friar. "For a long time I saw myself as a martyr to some cause, even ready to die for it. My friend Rivera told me I invited death. I think he was right. Now I'll finally realize the beginning of my mission and be able to give my message to the whole world. Thank you, Jack Steel, for allowing me to fulfill my hopes." He patted Steel's shoulder.

"I owed you." Steel took a deep breath and glanced over at Christie. Her head was turned away as she looked west at the rising peak of Pu'u Kukui.

The two of them hadn't exchanged more than five words all morning, each of them talking to Francis more than each other. He hadn't asked her, but he was sure she planned to leave upon their return to the hotel. It would be awkward if she remained the whole week.

Other feelings stirred below the surface, but he decided they were best let go. It was time for both of them to move on, past whatever they might have shared. He remained quiet.

They pulled into the Four Seasons and walked to his room. He put the key in the door, but it was unlocked. Christie pulled out the Glock. Francis backed up. Pulling his silenced Glock, Steel toed the door open.

Kergan sat on a chair on the balcony. He wore a gray shirt and white slacks, his gray mane of hair neatly combed. As always, his gray eyes were steady, secure. He quickly got up with a smile and crossed the room, his arms outstretched.

Steel put away his gun and grasped his friend tightly. He hadn't hugged anyone in a long time. He introduced Francis and Christie, and then asked, "Well?"

"A moment." Kergan returned to the balcony and pulled a chair in, then slid the door shut and closed the drapes. His gaze swung from Francis, who stood politely by the door, to Steel.

"I've told him everything," said Steel.

Kergan nodded and turned to Francis. "Our government owes you an apology, but I'm afraid you'll never get it. The president will never admit he authorized the Komodo Op, but we can tell you that the men responsible will be dealt with. They abused the power of their offices and will pay the price."

Francis nodded. "I understand. Corruption is not unique to the United States. Mexico is well acquainted with it." He looked to Steel and Christie. "Muchas gracias, amigos." He smiled.

Christie hugged the friar, as did Steel.

Francis left.

Kergan sat in the chair near the patio door, across from the side of the bed. He motioned to it.

Christie sat by the pillow, Steel at the foot of the bed. He didn't look at her.

Kergan studied them. "You both look a mess."

"What happened stateside?" asked Steel.

"Sorenson and Danker were murdered." Kergan shook his head before Steel could ask a question. "We don't know who did it. It was made to look like a Colombian revenge hit, but no one is buying it."

"Who, then?" asked Christie.

Kergan shrugged.

"It had to be Torr," said Steel. "How can you be sure the operatives targeting Francis are all secured?"

"I didn't want to alarm Francis, but we're not. I've got men watching him now. The Grand Wailea is swarming with our people."

Steel stiffened. "I need to be there for his talk."

Kergan raised an eyebrow. "I know, Jack, but we've got another problem." On the floor against the wall rested a thin, black briefcase, which he lifted to his lap and opened. "I want to show you something, to see if you recognize it."

"The Paragon file?" he asked.

"Not quite." Kergan closed the briefcase, a silenced Browning HP in his hand.

Steel felt like he had taken a punch to the chest.

"Don't look so shocked, Jack. You always were naive about people, weren't you? Too trusting. Pull out your guns, with two fingers, and throw them over."

# CHAPTER 84

S TEEL PULLED THE GLOCK from his back and tossed it.
Christie opened her purse under Kergan's watchful eyes and
brought out the Glock she had taken from the Hawaiian,
dropping it to the floor.

"The knife, Jack."

He reached behind his back and drew the OTF knife, tossing
it to the floor.

Kergan lifted his chin. "I tried to keep you out of this, Jack,
but you just wouldn't let it go. Sorenson wanted someone on the
inside so he approached Danker to ask Christie to run the Paktika
Ops by you. My referral of her was to make it feel legit."

Kergan glanced at Christie. "I thought it was a bad idea, but I
had no choice. I also knew Torr tried to kidnap Carol—to get to
you, Jack. He didn't like it that Hulm was letting you run free and
guessed they were using you to try to bring him down."

Steel couldn't speak at first. "Money?" he asked softly.

"Of course. The Paragon project shouldn't have lasted even two
years. However, two key people on the Senate Armed Services
Committee, and two individuals on the Pentagon's Defense
Acquisition Board, insured the project won continued support."

Steel's eyes narrowed. "Paid off by MultiSec."

Kergan moved his gun imperceptibly. "I'll shoot you before you
take one step, Jack."

Steel had to clear his throat. "Tom Bellue figured it out."

Kergan nodded. "Bellue did spot checks on warehouses where MultiSec claimed they had certain assets. One warehouse had eight million dollars in leftover parts missing from the Paragon project. Normally eight million would have been brushed aside, mentioned and written off with a multibillion dollar company like MultiSec. But in a way Bellue was like you. He just couldn't let go.

"I also think Bellue intended to be a whistleblower and try to get a percentage of the money that was taken. He looked at accounts payable and discovered millions went to dummy corporations whose records of incorporation showed they were filed under the maiden names of the wives of the four individuals who kept the Paragon project alive."

"You were one of the four people." Steel's mind raced through ways to attack Kergan.

"Sorenson was the other general."

"Who were the senators?" asked Christie.

Kergan smiled. "The current president and CIA Director Hulm."

"Hulm had Bellue and Grove killed." Steel didn't see how Hulm or the president could be brought to justice.

"I wasn't involved with the details." Kergan leaned back.

Steel's hands formed fists on his thighs, trying to stall for time. "You were like a father to me."

Kergan grimaced, lifting his gun slightly. "That's why I'm working myself up to this."

Steel seethed inside but kept his face neutral. "What went wrong?"

"When William Torr was vice president at MultiSec, he secretly recorded conversations between Sorenson, the president, Hulm, and myself when we talked to MultiSec's CEO and a few of their lead people to keep the Paragon project going. Torr blackmailed his superiors and took over MultiSec, and then threatened to use the recordings against us. I retired early so he couldn't use me. But he blackmailed the other three to run the Komodo Op, intending to kill General Vegas and the friar."

Kergan paused. "I've watched Torr jerk the others around and waited for them to pick each other off. I put in my two cents occasionally and was kept updated by Sorenson and a friend in the CIA. I'm certain Torr had Danker and Sorenson killed."

Steel realized then that Danker had been the lone person entering his property when he went to see Grove. Danker must have found the Paragon file copy and blackmailed Torr. "You're going to kill Torr."

"It's either him or us." Kergan's eyes and gun didn't waver from Steel. "Torr thought he was being clever, insisting that the discussion with Francis Sotelo be held in the Grand Wailea Molokini Garden, open to spectators and the press. His goal was to make Sotelo an easier target, but instead he set himself up perfectly for us. Sotelo agreed to the public talk because of the press Torr promised for the event. Everyone will assume the target is Francis Sotelo, and Torr's death will be viewed as an accident—he just happened to be in the wrong place at the wrong time. I'm waiting for the call that it's finished."

Steel stiffened.

Kergan smiled. "Afterward Hulm plans to confiscate all of Torr's holdings as a matter of national security. They'll get the recordings Torr used to blackmail everyone and we'll finally all be free of any leverage he had on us."

Steel clenched his jaw. "Who set me up on the Serpent Op?"

Kergan lifted his chin. "Hulm leaked information to Alvarez, including your name. He also fed the DEA the lie that Alvarez was going to kidnap the friar. They passed it along to Danker so he would tell you, motivating you to go. Sorenson almost had a heart attack when you came back on the Black Hawk."

"You're nothing more than a traitor and a killer," said Steel.

Kergan leaned against the wall. "I'd kill you just for the danger you put Carol in."

Steel's head snapped back and he looked carefully at Kergan. His chest went numb. "You're her secret friend."

"My new wife will be Carol Steel. You put her through endless misery this last year." He shrugged. "I was there to provide the comfort she needed, which you couldn't seem to give her."

"Is that what friends do?" Steel understood why they weren't dead already. Kergan had felt the need to tell him about Carol. His eyes clouded over. He felt adrenaline and momentum build in his head and shoulders. Vaguely he heard Kergan give a warning. He didn't care.

He hung his head and stared at his shoes, visualizing what he wanted to do next, knowing he had little chance of success. His shoulders slumped and he slowly bent over, lowering his head into his hands and inching his feet back beneath his knees. His whole body said, *I'm broken, Kergan, put me out of my misery.*

"Really, Jack, the signs were there over the last year. But you felt so sorry for yourself over Rachel's death that you didn't give Carol an ounce of attention. She was dying in your marriage. I helped bring her back to life. She's a beautiful woman and we've made some wonderful plans for the next years. To be fair, she didn't end up with me to spite you. It just happened. But I don't suppose that..."

Steel felt the weight on the bed change—Christie.

He glimpsed Kergan swinging his gun at her. Without hesitating he rolled to the floor toward Kergan's legs. Five feet separated them.

Kergan swung the gun back and fired, missing.

Steel came out of the roll on his knees and clawed for Kergan's extended gun arm, striking at Kergan's neck with his right hand.

Kergan blocked his strike and kicked him in the side from the chair. The gun fired again. Steel was aware of blood on his left arm—he fell to the floor, clutching Kergan's wrist with one hand, his other finding the OTF knife and clicking out the blade.

Christie reached for her Glock. Kergan shifted forward and snapped a toe kick into her chin. She cried out and fell back.

Kergan stood and kicked Steel in the ribs, trying to jerk the gun free. Steel stabbed at his thigh, missing but scoring the muscle. Kergan gasped and kicked his arm—Steel lost his grip on the knife, which flew across the room.

Christie jumped to her feet and punched Kergan in the head twice. He elbowed her, slamming her into the wall.

Letting go of Kergan's arm, Steel swept a leg sideways into his knee.

Kergan stumbled toward the bed as Steel scrambled over the floor.

Kergan turned with the gun.

Christie pushed his arm up and kneed him in the thigh. Kergan swore and swung his elbow, hitting her face and sending her to the floor.

Steel was on his feet, rage filling his limbs. He palmed Kergan in the sternum, which dulled his eyes, and then speared a stiff hand into the front of his neck, barreled a fist to his heart, and lastly palmed his nose.

Kergan collapsed to the floor, dead.

Steel stood over him, breathing hard, his hands clenched. The sense of betrayal still numbed him. He glanced at Christie.

She wiped a smear of blood from her lips and used the bed to pull herself upright.

There was a flesh wound on his triceps. The burning sensation on his arm was as intense as the betrayal he felt.

Christie ripped part of the bed sheet.

Yanking off his shirt with one hand, he watched as she silently tied a tight bandage around his arm. His eyes met hers, but he didn't know what to say.

He pulled on a clean shirt, a windbreaker over that, and then loaded a fresh magazine into the Glock which he shoved into his belt. He cleaned and sheathed the OTF knife.

Christie put the Hawaiian's Glock in her purse, and toed
Kergan's Browning beneath the bed. She left the stunbrella on
the floor.

Steel headed for the door.

Christie followed.

# CHAPTER 85

S TEEL ENTERED THE GRAND Wailea still reeling from Kergan's admissions, a tarnished image of Carol just beneath that. He pushed it all aside, frantic to find Francis.

To one side in the main lobby he saw Francis and Torr near a wall, chatting behind a line of photographers and news reporters. He stared at the man responsible for so much violence, but he couldn't waste time on the fury that clenched his jaw. It made him wonder how civil Francis was feeling, talking to the man who had sent killers after him.

The lobby was a security nightmare, but Steel didn't believe a shooter would risk capture here. Scores of people stood behind the news media, and Torr's security detail maintained a perimeter around both men. Two uniformed police officers stood apart from the photoshoot, eyeing the crowd.

He approached the hotel concierge and quickly found out that the lobby photoshoot and media Q&A would last another thirty minutes. Then Torr and Francis would head outside to the Molokini Garden for the main event. His forehead creased as he quickly scanned the crowd. He was glad Christie was beside him, also checking the spectators.

He considered the sniper. To make Torr's death look accidental, and have a reasonable chance of escape, the killer would need Torr and Francis standing next to each other.

The outdoor stage in the garden would present all kinds of problems for line-of-sight, given the trees and other obstructions on the perimeter. It would also make the shooter visible and escape difficult. A shot from a bobbing boat on the ocean would be too risky for the accuracy needed for the desired outcome. He discounted both scenarios, deciding the best position was to kill Torr while he was walking to the event with Francis.

A hotel room would be safest and require a certain angle.

When he considered the Grand Wailea's layout, he decided the killer would have to be in the southern Molokini wing. Most likely in one of the rooms overlooking the ocean so they would have a clear view of the path leading to the garden. They would have to be on one of the upper floors.

He glanced at Francis again. The friar would never agree to leave. Steel didn't want him to. He believed in the friar's ability to change the world and knew silencing Francis' message had been the goal of the Komodo Op and Torr from the beginning.

He whispered to Christie. "I'm going to check the rooms of the upper floors at the end of the Molokini wing. I think they'll try to shoot Torr and Francis on the way to the garden. If I'm wrong, keep him off the stage. Tell them we have proof of a hired killer, a bomb, whatever it takes. While I'm checking out the rooms, shadow Francis and scan the crowd for anyone that looks suspicious."

The irony wasn't lost on him that by protecting Francis, he would also be saving Torr.

Christie didn't say a word and barely nodded.

Hurrying away, he pushed aside any emotional response to her pain. He couldn't afford to be distracted now.

*** 

Christie hoped Steel's assumption was right. She tried not to consider what danger that might put him in. Blood still trickled in her mouth from a cut in her inner cheek, caused by Kergan's elbow. But that was the least of her wounds.

There was a heaviness in her chest. It was hard to be around Steel anymore. She wanted this to be over, and to be on the next flight home. She needed to be around family. She hadn't felt this hurt since she was dumped by a boyfriend in high school.

Clutching her purse with both hands, she looked for anyone that might pose a threat. It was an impossible task. She glanced at Torr. Five-foot-seven, one-hundred-sixty pounds, early fifties, and hard eyes that matched his emotionless face. Despicable.

She scanned the rest of the lobby.

Two individuals appeared just beyond the security perimeter. Even though they wore Hawaiian shirts and sunglasses, she recognized them immediately.

General Vegas was bull-framed, six-feet, two-twenty pounds, mid-fifties, an ample friendly face and chin, and short black hair. General Rivera was leaner, six-two, two-fifty pounds, about fifty, a pockmarked, brutal-looking face, and dark hair with a few gray strands. His right arm was in a sling.

It gave her some comfort knowing the two generals were watching over the friar too.

***

Steel took the elevator up to the fifth floor and ran down the hallway, smiling at the few people he passed so he wouldn't draw attention. He checked his watch. He had time.

The end of the wing ended in three or four rooms, depending on the floor. He walked to the middle of the three rooms on this floor and knocked on the door. An older man answered.

Steel looked over the man's shoulder and saw several people inside chatting and laughing. "Hotel security. Sorry. Wrong room."

Hurrying to the next door, he banged on it. No answer. He banged again. No answer. He tried the knob, then kicked the door in. He walked in on a couple in their thirties on a couch holding each other, wearing lingerie and underwear. They gaped at him.

"Sorry. Hotel security. Wrong room." He ran out and knocked on the last door. No answer. He knocked again, harder.

"Who is it?" A young woman's voice.

"Hotel security. We're checking rooms for safety."

The door opened. A teenage girl in a tee and shorts looked up at him. Biting her lip. She looked nervous.

He looked past her. "Everything all right, miss?"

She blushed. "Yeah, no one else is here. My parents are down by the pool. I didn't want to go."

"I have to check your room, miss." He pushed past her.

A shirtless teenage boy came out of a bedroom and gawked at him.

Steel walked past the blushing youth and looked out the balcony window. Three hundred feet away, several thousand people were either sitting in chairs or milling about in the Molokini Garden. The path leading to it from the hotel was mostly empty.

He spotted security people spaced along it and assumed they were Torr's. One police officer stood at the end of the path where it reached the garden. Glad to see the security, he didn't like the angle to the path from this height. The shooter had to be higher.

He ran from the room and raced up the stairs to the eighth floor.

\*\*\*

While Christie eyed the small crowd, Torr spent a few minutes talking about the need for corporations to reform their environmental practices and help the poor. Applause interrupted him several times.

Christie didn't believe anything Torr said. The CEO was cleverly preempting any attack Francis might bring in his speech against corporations.

Torr finished.

One reporter immediately raised a hand, asking, "Do you plan on making restitution to Mexico for MultiSec's pollution record there?"

"We will do the right thing." Torr smiled, patting Francis on the back and stepping back.

Francis smiled as the small crowd quieted. "Corporations are the new feudal lords, who answer to no one since they control all the politicians. Thus Mexico must take over the corporations that have hurt our land and caused massive health problems. Our government should seize corporate assets and hold them hostage until all reparations are made for the environmental cleanup, and health costs are paid to our poor. Then and only then will justice be served."

The audience applauded and cheered even louder than they had for Torr—who amazingly kept smiling. There were a few more questions. While Francis answered them, Christie scanned the crowd again.

In a few minutes Torr's security team enclosed the two men and they walked out of the lobby. They were heading for the garden sooner than Steel had anticipated. Christie didn't have a way to slow them down or tell Steel.

Remaining behind the small entourage following Torr and Francis, she ended up a few people away from Rivera and Vegas. Rivera eyed her briefly, and she avoiding looking at him again.

***

On the eighth floor Steel pounded on the first door to the left. Nothing. He pounded again.

A big man with a beer belly answered, unshaven and bald, in his forties.

Steel looked past the man and saw a woman on a couch. "Sorry. Hotel security. Wrong room."

At the adjacent door he knocked—no answer. After a second try he drew his gun and kicked the door open. A middle-aged couple were sitting on a sofa facing the outer balcony, their backs to him and their heads leaning against each other.

He was about to apologize when he noted the couple hadn't responded to him. Slowly he walked forward until he could see them better. Both of them had upper chest bullet wounds. The gunshots looked recent. Eyes closed.

Walking across the room toward the empty balcony, he aimed his gun at the bedroom to his left—empty. The room was a suite and a closed door to the right led to another room. He put his hand on the knob and quietly tried to turn it. Locked.

He debated kicking it in, but if the shooter was here he would be targeting this door after hearing Steel kick in the hallway door. Thus he continued to the balcony.

Christie had followed the others on the path but decided she didn't like her position. If someone came at Francis from the sides or front, she would have no chance to protect him. And if Steel didn't appear, it would be up to her to keep Francis off the stage.

She decided before Torr and Francis reached the garden she would scream, *Gun!* and point at the beach. It would be enough to prompt Torr's security detail to pull the two men back inside the hotel.

Veering off the path at a thirty-degree angle, she walked fast, striding through the palm trees while scanning the area. When abreast of Francis, she changed course again, paralleling the security detail. One of Torr's men eyed her briefly, his moving gaze showing he had decided she wasn't a threat.

She glanced back, and saw Vegas watching her. Rivera was eyeing the other side of the path.

Someone in the crowd behind Torr and Francis yelled for a photo. Torr stopped on the path, gripping Francis' arm to get him to stop too. They both turned and smiled.

*** 

When Steel reached the sliding doors, he slowly slid one of them open. Leaning forward a few inches, he eyed the next balcony to the right. Empty.

He stepped out, his gun aimed at the adjacent balcony—its door was open. When he reached the outer railing, he could see the end of a rifle silencer just inside the far balcony door. In that same instant he gave a shout and fired three times at the silencer.

A muffled shot came from the rifle. Then another.

***

Christie gaped as Francis seemed to be punched in the chest, collapsing beside William Torr, who seemed to react with less horror than one might expect. The next shot ripped into Torr's head.

The security detail froze, shouting to each other while eyeing the woods. Some pointed their guns up at the hotel's upper floors, others scrambled to reach Torr. Screams and shouts erupted from the crowd on the path, most of whom fled back toward the hotel. The cop drew his gun but didn't seem to know where to point it.

Christie's limbs were stiff as she ran toward Francis. She was kneeling beside him in moments.

Torr was beyond help, but his security detail still hovered around him, guns drawn. Christie didn't look twice.

Francis lay on his back, blood spattered all over his face and body, a bullet hole above his heart. The sight tightened her throat and she had to steel herself to all the blood. Frantically she tried to rip his habit free to see the wound and to convince herself he was really dead. She had heard of incredible rescues and maybe it could happen to Francis.

Her resolve crumbled as she pulled on the robe, unable to tear it. Frustration made her cry out.

A hand on her shoulder gently pushed her to the side. Vegas straddled over Francis, his wide face carrying a deep frown. The Mexican grabbed the center of Francis' habit with two big hands and tore it apart like paper.

Christie's eyes filled with tears when she saw the bullet had penetrated Francis' Kevlar vest. Vegas pulled the vest off, revealing a bullet wound in Francis' upper shoulder. Christie gathered the fabric of Francis' habit and pushed it against the wound, applying firm pressure.

Vegas put two fingers on Francis' neck, knelt, and began CPR.

Christie watched the friar's face for any sign of life. *Please, please, don't let this man die.*

# CHAPTER 86

S TEEL'S THROAT CHOKED AS he looked down. People were running everywhere, shouting. No one had control over the situation. Chaos. He ignored all of it except what he saw on the path.

Francis and Torr were both stretched out on their backs, blood on the ground. They were covered in it.

He wanted to scream. An ice-cold feeling hit his spine.

He ran back into the room to the door between the suites and kicked it hard. Gun up in both hands, he cautiously eased into the room. The rifle—a silenced H&K G28—was on the floor, the shooter gone. The G28 signified ex-military to Steel.

He ran to the hall door, peeked out, and looked down the hallway. Empty. Racing to the exit door, he took the stairs down three at a time, then five.

By the time he burst out the north side of the hotel he was in a state of frenzy. Beyond the fiery pain in his side, leg, and arm, he was barely able to hold off the grief building just behind his eyeballs.

The Glock was in his hand as he ran along the hotel's outer wall, then around it and south. To the west he was aware of the crowd and police presence where the bodies lay on the path. He remembered the hotel layout. The public beach parking lot would provide an easy exit for someone in a hurry.

A few tourists in lounge chairs saw his gun and gave startled gasps. Spotted doves and common mynah flew up from the manicured grass as he ran across it. He was oblivious to all of it, his eyes focused only on the parking area ahead, his legs like wooden spikes on the grass.

There was only the image of Francis lying in blood, Francis lying in blood, Francis lying in blood.

A man appeared ahead of him. Fifty yards away. Wearing a colorful Hawaiian shirt and shorts. He could have been just another average-looking tourist—except that he was running.

Steel brought the Glock up to his chest and ran harder.

The man glanced back, saw Steel, and ran into the parking lot. Trees hid him.

Heedless of the injury, Steel pushed his leg, wanting the pain to deaden the loss he felt. Extending the Glock as he ran, he took aim at a Camry whose tires were already screeching on the pavement. Shouts erupted from his mouth and his eyes blurred. He wasn't aware of what he said, not caring.

A man burst through the trees a dozen yards west of Steel, also with a gun extended toward the killer, his right arm in a sling. General Rivera.

Steel fired at the Camry, and continued to fire. He and Rivera shot out the Camry's two side windows. The car accelerated and flew through the parking lot.

Steel ran, shouted, and emptied the Glock into the rear window, aware that Rivera was matching his strides.

The Camry veered with whining tires, hit the curb, clipped a tree, and tipped onto its side, sliding across pavement. People strolling up from the beach jumped out of its way. The car slid forward in a shower of sparks across the pavement. A SUV entered the lot and clipped the Camry's trunk, spinning it once until it came to a rest—still on its side.

The front passenger door of the Camry opened and the killer attempted to climb out, gun in hand.

Another gunshot sounded as Rivera targeted the killer, sending him sinking back into his car. The general aimed at the Camry's gas tank next and it exploded. Flames engulfed the car.

Steel didn't register anything for long moments.

Fire and pain coaxed him back. He lowered his gun and turned to the powerfully built man beside him. Rivera's face was pockmarked and somewhat harsh. But what Steel focused on were the tears that ran down the man's cheeks, like his own.

# CHAPTER 87

VEGAS KEPT WORKING ON Francis, while Christie maintained pressure on the wound.

Torr's security had formed a perimeter around the bodies.

"Francis," whispered Christie.

A minute later the friar exhibited a heartbeat. In another thirty seconds he was breathing. Francis blinked and stared up at them with dazed, open eyes.

Christie gently stroked his forehead and sat back, blood on her hands. She used the back of her wrist to wipe tears off her cheek.

Police were suddenly everywhere, and EMTs took over.

Vegas rocked back on his heels. He sighed and looked at an agate in his palm. "When the three of us were orphans on the street, with nothing, Francis found this stone on a beach and said to me, 'Now you'll always have something beautiful in your life.' I knew then what I had was a beautiful friend." He looked at her. "But he's stubborn. We had to fight to make him wear the vest."

Christie concluded Steel must have interrupted the shooter's aim—the only reason Francis was still alive. She shook her head, noting the hole the bullet had made above Francis' heart in the Kevlar vest.

"Even friars need backup," she said.

A warm glow filled her that Francis would live. She wanted to celebrate that with one other person. Having heard the shots and explosion farther south, she worried about Steel. But she couldn't find out just yet.

As Vegas talked to a police officer, she did the same, showing her military ID and explaining what she had observed. The officer motioned her off the path, away from the crowd.

While the policeman talked to her, she looked for Steel, worried he might have been shot, or worse. She bit her lip when she saw him pushing his way through people on the path. General Rivera strode beside him.

Steel was safe.

Part of her wanted to hug him, talk to him, and share her relief—the relief he would feel when he learned Francis was alive. But that part of her, she decided, wasn't in touch with reality so she didn't try to get his attention.

*** 

Steel wanted to cheer when he saw Francis alive. He watched as General Rivera knelt near the friar. Vegas squatted near Francis' feet, resting a big hand on Rivera's shoulder. Steel wasn't sure what had happened until he saw the Kevlar. The shooter hadn't made the shot he intended or the friar would be dead. He'd done his job.

He glanced sideways.

Police were quietly approaching while staring at him from a hundred feet away on the path, guns drawn. Steel touched Rivera's elbow and asked if he had a phone he could borrow. The general saw the police and handed his to him.

From memory Steel dialed a secure number for Blackhood, gave a code number, and was patched through to whoever would replace Danker for the time being. General Morris.

He explained the situation briefly, and Morris told him to hand the phone to the police, who were now shouting at him to kneel, and then lie on his stomach, hands on his head—along with Rivera. He complied and held the phone up with one hand.

The officer in charge took it and listened, while another officer took Steel's gun.

In a minute the officer in charge gruffly asked Steel for his ID. Steel told him what pocket to search, and they pulled it out.

\*\*\*

Christie saw them detain Steel. After the police interviewed her, and took her contact information, she quietly left, blending back through the crowd.

Limping away from the path, across the grass and parking lots, she made her way to the Four Seasons. If she was going to make an exit, better to do it now. She didn't want any awkward goodbyes with Steel.

It seemed odd and painful how things had worked out. She was aware of a shift inside her, of refocused priorities in her life. Steel was the reason for most of it. It was because of the honesty and trust he was capable of that her emotions were always tugged around him. From the very first she had recognized sincerity in his eyes. She never knew how much that had affected her until she had lost his trust. Lost him.

The life and death experiences they had gone through in the last few days had somehow brought clarity to that loss. Suddenly she wanted out of her career. At least a long break from the never-ending attempts to climb higher. She wanted to explore things, the world, herself. Have trust and sincerity in all areas of her life. Find out what made her happy.

She choked on a breath, already knowing what might make her happy. Steel. But he would never consider her good enough for him now. She was tainted goods. Someone who had betrayed him. Her chance was gone.

She reached the hotel, found her room, and unlocked the door and went in.

Someone pushed her from behind with considerable force, propelling her across the floor and onto the bed, face down. A knee on her back kept her immobile. She barely felt the sting of the needle in her arm.

# CHAPTER 88

I N THIRTY MINUTES, AFTER General Morris had contacted police superiors, they let Steel go—with his gun. Rivera was still being questioned.

General Morris called Steel back and told him to wait at his hotel for further instructions. Steel guessed they wanted someone from Blackhood to pick him up for questioning. He wasn't sure who that would be.

Before he left, he scanned the crowd for Christie. It seemed odd that she wasn't present. He didn't know what the urgency inside him was, but he wanted to see her, say something.

Instinctively he headed toward the Four Seasons, suddenly realizing what was happening. He slowed to give her time. It was for the best and he guessed by now they both knew it. He wasn't sure how much of the grief he still held was due to the betrayals by her and Kergan, or due to everything else that had happened since the Komodo Op. It all spilled together.

Since the CIA director and the president were part of the opposition, he needed a heavyweight behind him to go anywhere with his story. And, he realized dully, he might not be able to go anywhere with anything. He doubted the president and Hulm would leave him alone once they found out Kergan was dead.

Limping along, head down, his mind felt numb. His leg wounds burned and his arm throbbed. It might be good to disappear into the islands or head somewhere far away. He didn't have anything left to give.

But the last few days had at least clarified something for him, which had been building inside ever since the Komodo Op. Witnessing a hired killer shoot a friar for profit distilled the complexity of it for him.

It came down to following orders.

Everyone was following, marching behind the plans of leaders, who often had their own interests at stake, and little else. The masses lurched forward out of habit. Steel now viewed the Komodo Op as a microcosm of the problems which that momentum caused at many levels in society.

He used to believe following orders gave structure to things, to his life. Now he understood that leading and following allowed for the worst kinds of evil and chaos to occur. In the future, whatever he did had to be on his own terms, and not under the thumb of anyone else.

When he considered what it had taken to bring about his change in perception, he wasn't sure the price was worth it. Lives had been lost and unbelievable pain endured. And it wasn't over.

Walking down the hotel hallway, he saw his door was ajar.

He pulled out the Glock, even though it was empty, and his OTF knife, and toed the door open. Shadows filled the room and he slipped inside. The curtains were still pulled on the balcony doors. He went through the room fast, seeing only Kergan's body on the floor. He flicked on the light switch.

He was about to check Christie's room, but something odd about Kergan caught his eye. The body lay closer to the wall than when they had left. He walked over to look more carefully.

Kergan's hands were wrapped around the umbrella's handle, the tip of it under his chin. The small extension cord from the umbrella's handle was plugged into the wall and Kergan's stiff, frozen finger still depressed the umbrella's trigger.

Steel unplugged the umbrella.

He bolted to Christie's room. Her purse was on the bed. His pulse took a small skip and he wondered where she could be.

Looking at all that was there, he searched for a clue to tell him the story, but came up empty.

He dumped the contents of her purse onto the sheets. The Glock fell out. He picked it up, turned off the light, and sat in the shadows with a dead man to wait.

The call came in an hour. He picked up the phone with a sweaty palm.

The voice was muffled.

"Waianapanapa Cave, Steel. One hour, alone, or she dies."

The phone went dead.

He was already out of his chair.

# CHAPTER 89

TRIGGERS WERE GOING OFF in Steel's head over the call and the destination. Waianapanapa Cave was on the far eastern end of the island. A small cave, it lay near another one of similar size and shape, the pair the result of a lava tube cave-in long ago. He had visited it several years ago with Rachel.

Someone knew about his past, knew he used to be a caver, and planned on using that in a deliberate way to unsettle him. He had banned himself from all caves except one since Rachel's death, but it wasn't that fact that sparked his eyes and hunched his shoulders. It was Christie.

By giving up on Carol, he had freed another part of himself that had been chained for the last year to a dead marriage. And maybe his attempt to hang on to Carol was also his fear that he couldn't love again or be loved. If he couldn't succeed in ten years with Carol, how could he succeed with anyone?

Thoughts about Christie flashed through his mind. Their conversations, the moments shared at his house, her betrayal. And that she had risked her life twice to save his.

She had often been playing a game with him. Still on an intuitive level he also knew there was more. Her deception had triggered a reaction in him that was in part due to the pain he held from Carol's betrayal. If he had been in Christie's position, with his superior officer and the CIA director telling him someone was guilty, he wondered what he would have done.

And just as she had kept secrets from him, he had withheld information from her, putting her in danger. She was at risk now in part because of him.

The more telling thing for him was his feelings for her at a gut level. Something was there, some affinity they shared. It came down to his ability to trust again, his ability to love again.

He tried to focus on the caller. The position in which he had found Kergan indicated someone who enjoyed brutality. He remembered finding Rusack in his sensory deprivation tank, the way he was killed, slowly and with lots of pain. He was sure it was the same man who now ordered him to go to a cave.

This man knew how to hurt people, psychologically and physically. And enjoyed it. He was also good at it.

He tried not to imagine Christie in this man's hands and wondered if she was alive. Wondered if the man had already tortured her. Wondered too many things to feel stable or prepared.

He accelerated the Jeep.

It was near dark when he pulled into Waianapanapa State Park. He drove past cabins near the seashore, which were located in a thick stand of bushy hala trees—their exposed roots sticking vertically into the ground like exposed six-foot bones.

The turn he was looking for suddenly loomed in his headlights. A bumpy dirt road that wound toward his destination. The cave was located far enough away from the ocean so that the black sand beach and waves were out of sight.

He turned off the lights on his car and stopped. With the Glock tucked in at his back, he limped the rest of the way through ferns, brush, and trees.

Memories of Rachel returned. Memories of her laughing and grabbing his hand to pull him faster.

*Come on, Dad.*

He swallowed.

# CHAPTER 90

A SMALL FRESHWATER POOL BLOCKED the entrance to the cave. Without hesitation he waded into the cold water and swam.

At the rock wall entrance he treaded water, took a deep breath, and dove. He swam down eight feet and then level a dozen yards beneath rock to get to the inner cave.

He surfaced quietly in darkness. A small light blinked on farther back. Keeping his breath silent, he pulled his Glock and swam a quiet sidestroke toward the faint glow, holding the gun out of the water. His arm and leg ached with the exertion.

He hoped he held the element of surprise.

Abruptly a bright light shone in his eyes. It was pulled back out of his gaze just as fast. His pupils adjusted again. A lantern was turned up until the cave was brightly lit. The ceiling was a dozen feet above the oblong pool, which was thirty feet wide and not much longer. The lantern hung from a climbing piton driven into the wall one foot above Major Flaut's head.

Flaut was sitting on a short but wide ledge on the left side of the cave, barely visible. Christie sat in front of him, her feet dangling off the ledge, her back against Flaut's drawn-up legs, her head in front of Flaut's, blocking any possibility of a shot. It looked like her hands were tied behind her back. Flaut held one of his arms tightly around her neck with his gun barrel pressed against the side of her head. That she was still alive gave Steel hope.

"The gun, Steel. Toss it."

He threw it across the pool and it plopped and sank into the water.

"The knife too," Flaut said curtly.

Steel repeated his action with the OTF blade.

"Now swim to the other side, directly across from me."

He swam forward to the other side of the pool, directly across from Flaut, and found a handhold in the rock wall to grip.

In the few seconds it had taken him to do that, Flaut had shoved Christie off the ledge into the water, his bare feet on her shoulders.

Gasping, Christie struggled to keep her head above the water, her eyes wide, her wet hair trailing around her neck. Her soft gasps and splashing sounds broke the silence, tensing Steel's shoulders.

In one hand Flaut held a rope tied around her neck, while in his other he held a Walther PPK/S.

Steel remembered a Walther had been used to kill Tom and Janet Bellue. His jaw clenched.

Flaut smiled at him and pushed Christie's head under the water. After several moments he allowed her to surface and she gasped for air. "The great Steel. I have some questions for you."

Steel remembered the interrogation after the Komodo Op, the obsession Flaut had shown over the details of violent acts. And he remembered Flaut's interest during the Serpent debriefing regarding the torture Alvarez had used on the captured DEA agent.

Flaut lifted the rope. "But first I should tell you the penalties for wrong answers. Christie has her hands tied behind her back, and she's worked very hard for some time before you arrived to keep her head above water." He smiled. "If you don't answer a question truthfully, I'll have to punish her."

Steel saw the desperation in Christie's eyes. "Who do you work for?" he asked.

Flaut pushed Christie under water. "Only talk if spoken to. Understand?"

Steel remained silent, focused on the water above Christie's submerged head.

Flaut repeated, "Understand?"

"Yes." His hand tightened on the rock as he waited for Christie's face to reappear.

Flaut allowed her back up. Her gasp for air sounded painful.

Steel saw fear in her eyes.

Flaut shrugged. "Actually I've worked for Torr and Danker, but most recently I've been working for myself to tie up some loose ends. I think I'm as tired as you are of following orders." He paused. "This is pleasure."

Steel stared at Flaut. For the first time in many years fear bubbled to the surface, through his guard, spreading out into his stiffening limbs. Not fear for himself, but for Christie. She didn't deserve to die like this, to have her life wasted for Flaut's amusement.

Flaut continued. "Here's what I want to know first. How does it feel to be in this cave, when you haven't been in it since you lost your daughter?"

He swallowed. "Empty."

"Does it bring back good memories of you and your daughter?"

"Go to hell," gasped Christie, fighting to stay above the water.

Flaut pushed her down, looking at Steel. "Beg me to let her back up."

"Please." There was a dark swirl of eddies. Steel's grip on the rock tightened. "Please," he said louder.

Flaut eased his feet off her shoulders, and Christie's head exploded out of the water. She coughed harder this time, struggling to regain her breath.

"She's a tough one, Steel, isn't she? Anyway, I hope you appreciate the setting for our rendezvous. I've admired you for some time. You probably didn't know Danker had me on every Blackhood Op you participated in, except Hellfire and Serpent. I was the one who questioned you after Hellfire."

Steel remembered the cold manner of the man who had interrogated him after the Hellfire Op.

Flaut flashed another smile, toying with Christie's cheeks with his toes. "Actually, Steel, I'm just following Danker's orders. You, Christie, Torr, and Sotelo were the targets of the last Blackhood Op Danker ran. Torr paid for it and offered me more money to kill Sorenson and Danker."

He set the Walther down and held the line around Christie's neck with both hands. "Do you want to know what the Op was called?"

Steel concentrated on Christie, meeting her gaze. He almost didn't realize Flaut was waiting for a reply until the man's eyes narrowed. "Yes."

"Dragon. I seriously doubt there will be Blackhood Ops for some time to come, so this one is special in a way, isn't it?"

"Yes, it is." His chest heaved, his eyes still on Christie. There was something forlorn in her expression and he wanted to sweep it away. But he couldn't see a way out of this. He felt helpless before Flaut, like Tom and Janet Bellue, Rusack, Danker, Sorenson, and he guessed a long line of others. Flaut always had the upper hand going in. It was how he operated. The man didn't make mistakes or make himself vulnerable.

Rage erupted deep inside him for the swath of destruction Flaut had cut through so many lives. And he hadn't forgotten the promise he had made to Janet Bellue. There had to be a way.

He estimated the distance to Flaut. Ten yards. Ten strokes. Flaut would shoot him and Christie before he was halfway across.

"You're an expert at torture," he said.

Flaut sat back, his feet stiff on Christie's shoulders. Then he nodded and relaxed his legs. "I'll take that as a compliment, Steel, so I'll let it pass." He paused. "I killed the man who shot your dog—I was coming to check out your virtual reality system and found him instead. I have a dog myself so I know how it must have felt. Does that make you feel better?"

"No."

"It wouldn't help me either."

Steel flicked his gaze from Christie to Flaut, desperately running through strategies.

"Now we come to the central issue." Flaut's hands tightened on the rope around Christie's neck. He gave a little jerk and she coughed, barely able to keep her mouth above water. "What exactly happened on the Serpent Op? I listened to you in the debriefing. Your story was believable, but I have experience with these sorts of things. I know you lied. I knew you lied to me after the Hellfire Op too, but we'll let that go."

Steel's arm grew rigid.

Flaut's face sharpened with eagerness as he leaned forward. "What happened to Alvarez and his woman, Marita?" He gave another jerk on Christie's noose, which tightened further, making her cough and choke for air. "The truth, Steel. Did Alvarez try to kill you?"

He held Christie's eyes. "No."

Flaut looked at him carefully. "What was it? You untied Alvarez, told him to run for it?"

He couldn't answer. The image of Marita floated in front of his eyes again.

Flaut straightened his legs.

Steel said softly, "I cut him loose and injured him."

Flaut relaxed his legs. "Then you killed him?"

"Yes."

"Why?"

Steel glared at Flaut. "I was hurt. He posed a risk."

Flaut smiled. "How did you kill him?"

"A knife."

"In the back?" asked Flaut.

"Yes." Steel saw that Flaut reveled in the details.

"Up close?"

"Yes."

Flaut paused. "What's the real reason you killed him?"

"Security." Steel could hear Christie's fatigue in her gasping breaths, but he knew Flaut wouldn't be rushed.

"You didn't trust his thirst for revenge?" Flaut said it more as a statement than a question.

"Yes."

Flaut looked at him hard. "You killed him because you had to."

"Yes."

Flaut nodded slowly. "And Marita told you she was the DEA informant."

"Yes."

"Did you believe her?"

Steel swallowed. "Not at first."

Flaut leaned forward. "Why didn't you bring her back?"

"I couldn't find her."

Flaut considered his answer. "She ran while you hunted Alvarez."

"Yes." Steel's words were mechanical.

Christie jerked her chin slightly to the left.

"She was scared you were going to kill her too," said Flaut.

"Yes." His voice was a whisper.

Christie jerked her chin left again, her eyes rolling to the left too.

"Why?" asked Flaut.

Steel spoke softly, sorrow filling his words. "Before I injured Alvarez, I was delirious. Alvarez believed I was going to kill both of them. Marita didn't trust me."

"But you went after her?" Flaut sounded eager.

"Yes."

Flaut's eyes shone. "Called for her in the jungle while she hid from you?"

"Yes."

"What did you say?"

Steel hesitated. "You're safe."

"Over and over again?"

The memory made Steel feel empty. "Yes."

"And she didn't believe you."

"No."

"Beautiful." Flaut smiled, his eyes bright with satisfaction.

Steel felt naked, stripped in front of this man. Intuitively he also knew Flaut had extracted what he wanted from him. Their time was up. Beneath the water he braced the soles of his feet against the wall. Ready.

Christie jerked her left shoulder back. Flaut's foot slipped forward, and she twisted her head and sank her teeth into his toes, and then allowed herself to sink below the water.

Steel pushed off.

Flaut screamed as Christie's weight pulled him off the ledge. He kicked at Christie with his free foot, while he reached for the Walther.

Steel estimated the distance that separated himself from Flaut. Too far.

Flaut grabbed the Walther.

Steel dove. The lantern's light reflected on the water above him. He didn't see Christie. But as he neared the ledge he saw a pale foot slide up out of the water, another leg drawing up after it.

Grabbing Flaut's ankle, Steel braced his feet against the ledge, still under the water, and pushed against the rock. His head and shoulders splashed free of the surface.

Flaut tried to swing the Walther, firing before he could aim it. The explosion echoed in the cave. Steel shoved them both off and Flaut crashed into his arms.

Wrapping himself around Flaut, Steel sucked in air and pulled him down. Flaut struck his head with the Walther and tried to turn the barrel in against him. Frantic, Steel used one of his arms to block the gun.

Flaut banged his forehead into Steel's sternum, driving air from his lungs.

They thrashed with each other just below the surface. Steel's lungs ached, while Flaut writhed with wild, jerking movements to get free.

Flaut's face appeared in front of him. Steel jammed his forehead into it. He couldn't hang on any longer and let go. Kicking his feet, he drove his head out of the water where he gasped for air, cold liquid splashing around his shoulders.

Flaut came up in front of him, the Walther first—already aimed. Steel weakly grabbed Flaut's gun wrist with both hands and twisted his body.

Another deafening shot rang out, echoing off the ceiling and walls.

Steel kicked at Flaut's midsection with his injured leg. Pain shot up to his hip. Water poured into his mouth, but he still clung to Flaut's gun arm.

Flaut kicked out, using his free arm to strike Steel's face. The blow glanced off Steel's cheek, but one of Flaut's feet caught his ribs.

Gasping, Steel released Flaut's arm and kicked himself forward, driving a forearm into Flaut's face.

Flaut coughed for air, laid back, and brought his own legs up to kick at Steel, swinging the Walther toward him again.

Steel kicked forward again and drove rigid fingertips into Flaut's eyes.

Flaut cried out and dropped the Walther, his hands jerking to his face. Steel struck him again, twice in succession in the front of the neck with a rigid hand, crushing his larynx.

Limp, arms outstretched, Flaut sank.

Steel treaded water, his lungs desperate for air, his legs and arms aching. But something even more crucial than his survival prompted him to swallow what air he could and dive.

His hands groped in the cold darkness while his aching lungs screamed for oxygen. He found her crumpled like a fetus on the bottom. It took all his strength to drag her up to the surface.

Gasping, he hung onto the ledge. Everything hurt as he pulled himself up onto it, still holding the rope tied to her neck.

His chest heaved as he lifted her out of the water by her shoulders. She was lifeless as he undid the rope around her neck and rolled her onto her side. Lifeless as he tried to empty water from her lungs. Lifeless as he began CPR.

Her skin was cold and clammy, her eyes closed. He wasn't sure if Flaut had broken her neck with his kicks, and he had the desperate feeling that he was too late again. Too late for Janet Bellue and John Grove. Too late for Rachel. The wrong decisions at the wrong time. Carol. Marita. Christie.

His lungs heaved. Again he rolled her onto her side to see if more water would come out, and then continued. *Please. Not too late.*

The time for possible revival seemed too long. Brain damage. A flood of grief made him shudder. The thought of losing her crystallized all of his uncertainties, doubts, and concerns about her, stripping them away. He was surprised by what was left.

He wasn't conscious of the cold water that dripped down his body or the pain in his arm, leg, and lungs. He was only aware of the silence, broken by his hurried gasps, and his thoughts that he was too late.

And then she breathed.

# CHAPTER 91

THE PRESIDENT AND HULM smiled at each other, though Hulm knew it wouldn't last. Still he hoisted his glass of champagne in the cabin of Air Force One and clinked it with the president's.

"We got the bastard." The president's gaze rested on Hulm. "You're sure we got all the recordings? Really sure?"

Hulm smiled. The president had asked the same question fifty times already. "If Torr had another hidey-hole, it would have to be on a different planet. Our mole got us access to everything. Bank accounts—secret and otherwise—dummy corporations, everything the man has ever touched in fifteen years. Like I said, we found the recordings in one safe deposit box, in one bank, which Torr had under an assumed name in New York. It's over, we're free."

The president beamed. "I've been liberated from jail and the warden is dead. You've done well, Hulm."

Hulm didn't trust the president's smile. The man would get rid of him if he could in the near future. Hulm had no leverage on him.

There was a knock on the cabin door.

The president ignored it so Hulm asked, "What is it?"

"The vice president sent an urgent message for the president."

"Bring it in." The president rolled his eyes. "It's about a bill in Congress we're backing."

The aide walked in, looking bright and efficient in his blue suit. He handed an envelope to the president and left quietly, closing the door behind him.

The president opened the envelope and read the printed message with silent, moving lips. His face paled.

Hulm's stomach took a dive. "What is it?" He tried to keep his voice even.

"Oh, nothing," the president said quietly. "The vice president says he got a call from our press secretary, who got a call from a man by the name of Rich Plugh, a lawyer for some environmental groups, who says he recently received an email from the mother of one Colonel Danker. The email had an attachment, a report that Danker's mother has on a flash drive which her son sent to her.

"Apparently the email attachment is an audit report from some due diligence work performed on the Paragon missile project, and it has some interesting names in it. Plugh says he wants to know if we have any comments, since the report is going to be discussed in the next New York Times' issue, which," the president checked his watch, "will be on the sidewalks and online in a few minutes." He lifted his head. "Do we have any comments?"

Hulm had to duck the president's champagne glass.

# CHAPTER 92

STEEL WORE A GREENSAVE green baseball cap, jeans, and a green flannel shirt. Sitting atop the cliff seventy-five feet above the beach, he lifted the binoculars and scanned the crowd below. He estimated a hundred thousand, with another one billion television viewers.

The bright sun shone down on San Diego's North Pacific Beach. The sky was clear, the air pleasantly warm, the sand white, and the blue waves nicely sedated.

He traded the binoculars for the G28 sniper rifle lying in the grass beside him, resting the camouflage green and brown rifle across his bent knees.

The speaker system on the beach carried up the last of Francis Sotelo's words to him.

"We must treat each other and all of God's creatures as our brothers, sisters, and children, and take care of them with equal love by our actions. Otherwise what we are doing is choosing who to love and who not to love. And that isn't love at all. Love all creation as you love yourself. Love everyone as your family. Then we can save it all."

The friar stood behind a thick, plexiglass bullet-proof shield that protected him on three sides. He waved to everyone, turned one-hundred-eighty degrees, and walked away from the cameras and down the beach to the water's edge. There he was assisted into the black and white thirty-five-foot Chaparral Signature cruiser, which took him and his protection contingent a short distance offshore.

Francis moved to the bow of the boat, which gently bobbed up and down, his arms raised. The sun shone on him like a bright spotlight as scores of seagulls descended around him in a blanket of white. Dolphins leapt out of the water near the bow of the boat.

Voices and movement faded from the crowd on shore until only silence remained.

It was a surreal sight that held the promise of something beautiful and new, full of peace. Steel felt its effects deep within his spirit even as he sighted on the friar.

He shifted the rifle slightly to check on the four alert bodyguards in the boat, their weapons ready. Next he swung the rifle ninety degrees to the left, and one-eighty right, sighting on the other two men with rifles to make sure all were alert. Then he began to scan the crowd.

His phone rang and he answered, speaking into his Bluetooth.

"All clear, boss," came the voice.

"The name's Jack, Harry."

"Sorry, boss."

Steel smiled. "Very funny. You have your sister's sense of humor, Harry."

"Nah, she stole it from me. And for the record, I'm happy for both of you."

"Thanks, Harry. All right, make sure we have Francis' exit locked down. I'm leaving now."

"Okay, Jack."

A sigh of relief escaped his lips. Every event posed different risks and unknowns, but Christie again had planned things perfectly. Helicopter Francis in, boat ride out, meet him in the Jeep away from the crowd. The San Diego police had cleared the cliffs above the beach for the event, and the beach was cleared of all activity today except for Francis' visit.

Steel had obtained permission to provide additional security for Francis—it was a condition of the friar's visit. They had screened people coming in from the south and north—everyone had to have bags searched and pass through a metal detector set up in a break in the fencing that ran from the water up to the cliffs.

Their protection agency, Greensave, was starting out with just a few assignments. He could be choosy and focus primarily on Francis until things settled down. Francis had support from every social and environmental group on the planet, and some heavy hitters were paying for his protection.

The president and CIA Director Hulm were in jail. That threat was over. But Francis would probably always need protection now. Even though the friar had put politics aside, he was being proclaimed the next St. Francis of Assisi, and killing a supposed saint was too tempting a target for all kinds of reasons for all kinds of wackos.

Still it was a good beginning, to protect the man who was trying to protect all people and life on the planet. He also saw it as a way to honor the deaths of Grove, Tom and Janet Bellue, Marita, and those killed on the Komodo and Serpent Ops. Something to give those deaths meaning.

He sent a monthly check to Grove's wife, anonymously through his lawyer. It was probably of small comfort to her. But he needed to do it for himself—though Grove's death was a debt that could never be repaid. He still thought of Grove, Janet Bellue, and Marita often, but the nightmares had mostly ended and he often slept in peace.

He carried the rifle and binoculars to the black Jeep parked behind him. He would drive south to meet the boat, get Francis, and take him out the preplanned secure exit route.

Francis sometimes complained, but the friar knew his safety was important. Francis had learned his lesson a year ago when he had been shot. He wasn't invincible. Since then he always wore a Kevlar vest at events.

Steel started the Jeep, put on his sunglasses, and drove down the road. He was already looking forward to getting home. To Christie.

# CHAPTER 93

OW DID IT GO? Tell me."

Steel smiled. Barely out of his Jeep and Christie was already coming out of the house, asking him about San Diego. "Perfect, as usual. You did a great job setting it up."

"What did you expect?" She smiled. Wearing shorts and a Greensave baseball cap, she looked ready for a run. Her tanned face shone in the sunlight. She hugged him and met his lips with hers for several seconds. "Welcome home, babe."

He pulled back. "I'll always want to come home now."

"I'll always be here." She smiled at him.

"They think Florida will be the biggest live crowd yet. Maybe a half-million." His arms tightened around her. "It'll take some time to set that one up."

"Don't worry about it. That's my job."

"Harry says hello."

"Hello to brother Harry." She paused. "I'm happy for Francis. For us." She smiled again, light shining in her green eyes as she playfully patted his shoulder. "We're going for a run. Want to come?"

"Sure." He looked at her, all bright and alive. The warm sun danced on her brown and blond-streaked hair. Sliding his arm around her shoulders, he kissed her cheek. He had let her deeper into his life in one year than he had Carol in ten. She knew about the tunnels, safes, and secret hideaways. No more secrets. Refreshing.

"Where's our girls?" he asked.

Christie gave a whistle. From around the corner of the house and under the sycamore tree, Spinner and a golden retriever streaked across the grass.

Steel stroked both dogs while they danced around their legs. Flaut's statement about having a dog had made him look into it. He was glad he could give Lacy a home.

"Where have you been, Lacy and Spinner?" Christie playfully patted the dogs. She looked up. "Think you'll have trouble keeping up with us?"

"Maybe. I've got a bum leg." He laughed.

She chuckled. "Right." She stroked his arm. "It's good to hear you laugh, Jack."

"It's good to be able to laugh." Warmth filled him. Despite all of his mistakes and the losses he had suffered, he could offer love freely to those around him again. And with Christie he had a chance at lasting happiness and peace in a relationship they both cherished.

He scanned the trees along the driveway. The leaves had turned again, already reds, yellows, and oranges splashing some of the branches. A gray fox sat fifty yards away and stared at him. A woodpecker hammered in the distance. And ruby-throated hummingbirds took nectar from feeders hanging from the sycamore.

All that remained for him was Rachel's memory, which no longer brought him pain. All the suffering had been worth it. The other side was worth seeing. That thought made him smile.

A mole kingsnake wound its way across the driveway.

His phone rang.

"Jack? Jack?" It was Carol and she sounded hysterical.

She had been doing better in the last months, returning to her legal practice and slowly recovering from Kergan's deceit.

They had gone through a quick, amicable divorce. Yet his chest tightened reflexively, protectively, when he heard her concern.

"What's wrong, Carol?"

Silence, maybe a sob.

He pressed his ear hard against the phone. "Talk to me. I'll come over right now if you need me. I'll..."

"Jack!" Carol was shouting.

Uncontrollable sobs filled his ears.

His fingers tightened on the phone. He couldn't tell if it was fear or something else that motivated her words. "Where are you, Carol? I'm coming right now."

He walked toward his Jeep, swinging around to look at Christie.

She hurried after him, her brow wrinkled.

"They found her, Jack. They found her. Oh, Jack." Carol's voice was out of control.

A deep welling of sorrow and fear and desire all mixed together swept through his torso, constricting his throat. His eyes blurred. His feet locked to the ground. For a wild moment his gaze caught and held the swing under the sycamore tree.

"Where are you, Carol?!" he yelled, just noticing the police car coming down the drive.

"You were right, Jack! You never let her go. Oh, Jack. Our beloved Rachel's alive, Jack." Carol was whispering now. "She's coming home. Rachel's alive."

The squad car stopped and Carol tumbled out with a smaller figure with auburn hair and wearing sweats.

Steel ran, at the side of the car in seconds as Rachel rushed into his arms. Numb, he gripped her, his throat tight with happiness and disbelief. All the searching. All the money spent. All the time. He couldn't believe she was in his arms. Christie was beside him, her eyes filled with tears. Spinner was barking and jumping up and down near Rachel.

Carol wiped tears from her face. "A delusional, grieving woman kidnapped Rachel to replace the loss of her own daughter. The woman had been watching Rach for months before she took her. She pulled up in a RV and asked Rachel for help. Rachel felt sorry for her. For two years she was just a three-hour drive away." She let go a half-sob, half-chuckle. "But she escaped and the woman's in a psych ward. She's the one that made the call telling us Rachel was okay."

Rachel looked up at him, her eyes brimming with tears. "I did what you told me, Dad."

"What was that, honey?" He nearly choked on the words, still not believing he was holding his daughter.

"Stay calm, assess options, look for a solution." She made a fist and thumped his arm gently. "What you always told me to do in an emergency when we were caving. Don't you remember?"

"I remember." He had to wipe his eyes. "I do remember."

"You saved me, Dad."

The thousands of self-recriminations he had hurled at himself over the last two years washed away. Tears streamed down his face. He had saved her after all. She had survived because of him. "Oh, Rachel."

"Rachel." Carol sobbed softly, kneeling and holding her daughter.

"I'm okay, Mom."

"I'm so proud of you, honey." He held onto her, never wanting to let her go again.

"I missed both of you so much." Rachel gripped him tighter, her cheeks wet, her hair shining in the sunlight.

"I missed you so much it hurt every day, Rach."

He saw Carol smiling up at him. For one moment he worried about Rachel returning to a broken home, with two years of her life wasted. But he shoved it aside. They were still a family. Rachel would be okay, he would make sure of it, and Carol would be okay too. She had her daughter back. It would help her with other pain.

Christie smiled at him. She understood.

He couldn't think of anything better than what he had.

Dear Reader, I have a favor to ask.

If you enjoyed this book, please leave a review
on Amazon—even 1 sentence!
Every review helps! Thank you!

See how the Jack Steel series began!
For email updates on new books, deals, and free review
copies of new releases from Geoffrey Saign and for your
FREE copy of *Steel Trust* go to
www.geoffreysaign.net

Turn the page to read an excerpt from Book Two
in the Jack Steel series

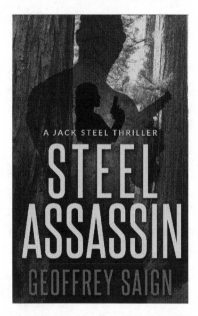

A JACK STEEL THRILLER

STEEL
ASSASSIN

GEOFFREY SAIGN

**Jack Steel's life is turned upside down when he's
blackmailed by a past enemy to murder cartel leadership in
order to save his family.**

*Excerpt from STEEL ASSASSIN*

# CHAPTER 1

JACK STEEL STOOD AT the back of the stage, watching for any movement in the crowd. The lighting over the audience was subdued. However his view was unobstructed.

He wore black jeans and a black collared shirt, invisible to anyone in the auditorium because the floor lights in front of him were aimed forward at the speaker—Afia Ameen.

A petite woman with black hair and delicate features, Afia was dressed in western clothing; a long colorful dress and long-sleeved blouse.

Steel admired her. She was courageous to give public talks. A cleric of the Muslim Brotherhood had issued a fatwa calling for her execution after she had begun talking about how Islamic extremists use Sharia law to brutalize Muslim women and limit their rights.

Afia's own story was one of rape and torture—she had survived acid thrown in her face—and she eventually fled a forced marriage in Iraq. She was a symbol for women oppressed everywhere and had gained a large following.

Since she started speaking publicly there had been several attempts on her life. Tonight her usual security agency had a commitment elsewhere. They had asked Steel months ago to cover today's event with his own protection agency, Greensave.

Afia had been in hiding for a year but decided to risk coming out for this interview. It had been well-publicized. The Muslim cleric that had issued the fatwa said Afia was going to die tonight if she spoke publicly again.

Steel took the threat seriously. He felt proud that his agency was protecting someone like Afia from violent men. Protecting the innocent had always been a cornerstone of his previous military career.

The interviewer was a local female news anchor. She was asking Afia about her views on Islam, and if she believed Sharia law ever honored women as equals.

Steel half-listened as he scanned the crowd.

They had searched the auditorium earlier. And attendees had been forced to pass through metal detectors as they entered. Yet someone could have hidden a weapon inside beforehand with a plan to charge the stage.

The Macky Auditorium at the University of Colorado in Boulder seated two thousand and every seat was filled. Several hundred people were standing. The Thursday night interview was also being broadcast live to millions.

In the middle of Afia's response, a young man in the audience stood up and began shouting, "You are a disgrace to Muslim women and a traitor to Islam! You deserve the fatwa made against you!"

The man kept shouting, amid boos from the crowd.

Steel ignored the gangly-looking student. He worried the young man was a decoy to occupy his security people, while the real attack would come from elsewhere.

Two of his security detail rose from their seats in front of the stage and hurried to the man. They dragged him into the aisle and forced him toward the doors. The man kept shouting. More people in the crowd booed the student on his way out.

Steel whispered into his throat mike, "Stay alert, everyone. A few angry people in here. Harry, check the immediate area."

"Roger that," said Harry.

"On it," said Christie.

Christie and her brother, Harry, were outside with the exit vehicle. It was Christie's first field assignment with Greensave, but Steel was confident of her skill set. And Harry was an ex-Marine and thus capable of handling tough situations.

Steel had personally trained them both to ensure their expertise, using his state-of-the-art military virtual reality program to refine their techniques to the nth degree.

"That was horrible," said the news anchor. "No one deserves such threats for speaking out. Are you alright, Afia?"

Afia spoke calmly. "I have heard this many times before. It is an example of how radical Islam is converting people to their cause. They wish to spread their version of Sharia law everywhere, as they have done in the UK, Germany, France, Sweden, and Austria. The men threaten violence if anyone criticizes them.

"And their women are not free as they are in U.S. Not free to get jobs on their own. And not free to divorce men as easily as men can divorce them. Women face the ongoing threat of violence for disobedience. Beatings, forced marital sex, and child abuse is common."

Stepping to his right, Steel thought he saw movement in the far aisle. He moved closer to the lights for a better vantage point.

Just someone leaving.

As the interview continued Steel looked at his watch. And smiled. He did that often. Random smiling. Christie said it was because he loved her and had everything anyone could want. She was right. He loved his life, loved her, and loved his daughter, Rachel.

When Carol had asked him for a divorce, he didn't think he would ever find someone to love again. But he and Christie had been together for over a year now. She gave his life more meaning, depth, and beauty. They were a better fit than he and Carol had ever been and he couldn't imagine his life without her.

The last year had erased a year of hell before it, as if it had never existed. Sometimes a few faces from the past still haunted his dreams, but he could live with them for now.

He was also hungry. Christie's other two brothers, Dale and Clay, had flown in from Montana to eat dinner with them tonight. Friday and Saturday they all planned to do some hiking together.

As small as Boulder was, Steel couldn't wait to get out of the city and into the mountains. It made him realize how lucky he and Christie were to have a home surrounded by forest. Though Virginia was his home, his heritage was from Louisiana and Cajun creole—Spanish, French, Native American, and Caribbean—which gave him a light olive color skin.

On Sunday Christie's three brothers were leaving. Then he and Christie were taking their first road trip together. Hikes, lounging, sightseeing. He smiled again.

The interview ended and the audience stood, cheering and applauding.

He talked quietly. "Interview is over."

"Exit area secure," said Harry.

"The car's running," said Christie.

Steel scanned the crowd again. "Be ready. Here she comes."

Afia crossed the stage toward the side door to the left.

Walking behind the lights, Steel quickly crossed the back of the stage. Afia didn't want to give anyone the image of her being guarded or scared, and thus didn't want Steel or his crew visible. He understood.

Afia exited the door ahead of him.

Seeing movement, he paused, remaining at the rear of the stage.

A bearded man in his mid-twenties was climbing onto the stage to the right. The man was swift and solid looking, matching Steel's six-two height and one-ninety weight. Security tried to grab his leg and he lashed out. The security man went down.

Steel stiffened when he saw something black in the man's hand. A knife. Maybe a graphite utility knife or hard plastic.

Running across the stage, the man slashed at the news anchor. Crying out, the woman stepped back, her forearm bleeding.

The attacker continued toward the door Afia had exited. The crowd erupted with shouts and yells.

Steel strode past the lights, his Glock 19 up and aimed.

The man didn't notice Steel until he was reaching for the door knob, and then whirled with his knife up.

Steel shot him in the head and the man collapsed.

Swinging open the door, Steel glimpsed another man climbing the stage closer to him. He couldn't take a shot with the crowd as a backdrop. "Two attackers in here, one down," he said.

"Ready here," said Harry.

Intuiting that the main attack would be outside, Steel ran down the hallway. In seconds he burst through the exit door. The warm mid-September air hit his face as he scanned the immediate area.

Their exit SUV was parked twenty feet to his right, parallel to the sidewalk in the curved lot reserved for performers and speakers. Afia was hurrying down the wheelchair ramp alongside the building. The sun was going down. Shadows filled the area past the SUV.

Harry stood beside the open SUV rear door, Glock in hand. Wearing jeans, boots, and a western shirt, he was built like a thirty-year-old linebacker. Six-three, broad-shouldered, and lean.

Steel stopped on the stoop. Footsteps. He whirled.

The second man. Running down the hallway toward him. Black knife again. No gun. Steel raised the Glock but glanced once more at Afia and Harry.

Beyond Harry, a man slipped from the cover of one of the large pine trees on a small section of ground five feet higher than the sidewalk that bordered the lot. Steel tensed as the man ran toward Afia, arm extended, a gun visible in his hand. Harry and a few trees blocked Steel's shot.

"Harry!" yelled Steel. "Get down, Afia!"

Afia gasped and crouched on the ramp. Bullets bit the wall above her head.

Whirling, Harry shot the shooter in the chest and head.

The attacker stumbled forward and fell off the raised ground, landing hard on the pavement bordering the lot. He didn't move.

"Afia!" Harry waved her to the SUV.

Running bent over, Afia ducked into the back seat of the SUV.

Steel slammed the door into the attacker who was almost upon him. Half-dazed, the man still managed to push open the door and step out, swinging his knife backward at Steel.

Sliding behind the door, Steel shot the man in the side of the head, sending him to the pavement.

Three muted rifle shots hit the back window of the SUV, putting divots into the bulletproof glass. That sent chills down Steel's back. Silenced guns. Pros. They had to get out.

"Go, Christie!" he yelled into his mike. "Meet at rendezvous A."

The SUV roared toward the exit.

Turning, Steel aimed his Glock across the street. Fifty feet away a man holding a rifle stood in the middle of a dozen trees. He was already disappearing into the shadows as Steel fired two shots. What puzzled Steel was that the man could have shot Afia earlier if he wanted to. But maybe the ramp door had blocked his line of sight.

He turned and watched the SUV rocket toward the lot exit. No shooter visible in the street. He glanced back across the street. The man with the rifle was gone.

A jarring crash of metal and glass filled his ears. The SUV had been broadsided in the middle of the road by a small, white pickup truck with a cargo bed cover.

Steel jumped off the stoop and ran across the lot.

Tinted windows hid the pickup driver. The truck had a metal pole on its roof, bent lower by a tie-down attached to the front bumper. The pole had shattered the SUV's rear passenger window.

Steel swore. "Harry?"

"We're okay." Harry's voice sounded stressed.

More rifle shots came from the shadows across the street, hitting the front driver's side window of the SUV. Steel's chest tightened over the possibility of Christie dying here.

"Christie!" Stopping, he aimed his Glock at the trees across the street, not seeing a target. The man with the rifle had to be hiding in the shadows. He hesitated to fire blindly in case there were pedestrians beyond the trees. "Christie!"

"I'm good." She sounded calm.

"Stay in the vehicle! Get out of here!" Keeping his gun up and watching the trees, Steel stepped sideways toward the SUV, and froze.

The white pickup had backed up five feet. But a short man wearing a black hood was standing next to Harry's smashed-in window, holding something inside the SUV.

Steel swung around to fire but checked his trigger finger upon hearing the man's voice on their coms; "I have a bomb. If my finger comes off the trigger, we all die. Coms, phones, and guns on the back seat."

Harry's voice burst through Steel's earpiece. "Don't shoot, Jack! Don't come any closer!"

Steel gripped the Glock, glancing back across the street. No shooter. He heard the man with the bomb say, "Get into the back of the pickup, Harry. Now!"

The rear passenger door opened and Harry got out. He walked past the hooded man to the rear of the pickup, where he climbed into the truck's cargo bed. Someone shut the tailgate. In moments the truck took off down the street.

The man at Harry's door had already entered the back seat of the SUV and shut the door.

"Harry!" Panicked that he had been too passive, Steel expected the SUV to take off. He sprinted for the vehicle, while the pickup sped away with Harry.

The white pickup took a right at the far corner, heading north. Expecting the SUV to take off too, Steel was surprised when it didn't move.

Reaching the rear door, he shoved his Glock inside the corner of the broken window, relieved to see Christie and Afia alive. Christie's face was pale as she stared at the back seat. Afia sat rigidly. They both eyed the same thing.

On the seat next to Afia sat the short man, wearing jeans, a black hoodie, and a black face mask. The front of the man's hoodie was unzipped, revealing a vest with two C-4 blocks fitted with detonators. Wires led from the detonators to a hand switch.

The man's thumb kept the switch depressed.

If the man's thumb released the switch, the bomb would go off.

# CHAPTER 2

A PHONE RANG.

Beside the man a burner phone lay among Harry's and Christie's guns, smartphones, earpieces, and throat mikes.

"It's for you." The man with the bomb had a Latino accent and sounded young. The mask hid everything except his eyes and mouth.

Steel reached in and picked it up, answering it. "What do you want?"

"Put the phone on speaker and keep it on speaker."

Steel complied. The caller had a Colombian accent, but he didn't recognize the voice.

"Drop your gun, personal phone, and coms in the back seat, and get in the front. Tell Christie to drive away. If the police stop you before you leave Boulder, my friend detonates the explosives and we kill Harry. Take highway ninety-three south to six west, into the mountains. We're all ready to die if you don't obey."

The caller hung up. The man's accent seemed at odds with Muslim radicals trying to kill Afia. Steel guessed the caller was in his fifties. Possibly the man with the rifle he had spotted across the street.

Wary, Steel set his gun, earpiece, throat mike, and phone on the back seat, and got into the front.

Christie quickly drove away. She glanced at Steel, her hair in disarray like her black pant suit and white blouse. Her green eyes were steady though.

Steel saw the bullet divots in her window. A powerful rifle would have punched through. The shooter had just wanted to scare Christie, keep her attention focused on the window. He wiped sweat from his brow.

Christie brushed back strands of her brown-and-blond streaked hair and lifted her chin to him. He gave her a slight nod.

Sirens could be heard in the distance. Christie stepped on the gas.

Steel twisted to study Afia.

"I'm all right," said Afia. She appeared calm.

"No talking!" said the man in the back seat.

Steel searched for answers but couldn't find any. Too many things didn't fit. The man Harry had shot tried to kill Afia. If these men wanted to kill her, why go to all this bother? Were they handing Afia off to someone for torture or to videotape her beheading? Maybe Harry was collateral to force their cooperation.

Their kidnappers wanted something, otherwise they would have blown up the SUV already. Maybe they wanted to torture him, Christie, and Harry too—to make an example of anyone protecting someone with a fatwa on their head.

Or maybe they just wanted Harry out of the way. The more he thought about it, he began to suspect that these men might not be connected to Afia and the fatwa.

He twisted to face the man in the back seat. "What do you want?"

"Shut up. Speak one more time and I release it!" The man held the switch in his hand a few inches higher.

Few people had the ability to become suicide bombers, but the young man fit the profile. Steel guessed he was in his twenties. Easy to brainwash. And the man's tone held an edge of vehemence

Steel had heard before in people willing to die for causes. He turned around and kept his mouth shut.

He glanced at Christie, regretting bringing her—he had to shove that aside and focus. He was missing something, but when he ran through possible enemies he couldn't find a fit. Trying to think of a way to deal with the man in the backseat proved fruitless too. He had to wait for an opportunity.

Christie dropped her right hand onto the divider between the bucket seats. Steel grasped and squeezed it. She squeezed back several times before releasing him.

While she drove, he ran through every possible scenario he could think of to get free of their situation. There was always a way out of seemingly impossible situations—Kobayashi Maru didn't exist for him. All of his virtual reality training centered on placing himself in impossible situations until he found a solution.

His own personal motto, *Stay calm, assess options, wait for a solution,* guided him when things got ugly.

In a half hour they were on highway six, headed west into the mountains. It was dark and the traffic was light. Christie flicked her gaze to the rearview mirror several times. Steel understood. They were being followed.

The phone rang and he answered.

"Phone on speaker." The Colombian.

Steel complied.

"Park at the next scenic overlook and turn off your headlights. Stay on the phone and roll down all your windows."

Christie powered down all the windows, letting in the cooler air. In a few minutes she rounded a curve and pulled off the road into a scenic overlook.

The small parking area was empty except for two sedans parked at the far end. When Christie cut the headlights, darkness surrounded them. The full moon gave them some light.

A small pickup pulled off behind them.

Steel readied himself. Slowly he worked his right hand to the horizontal belt-sheath built into the back of his belt. It held a Benchmade 3300BK Infidel auto OTF blade. He pulled it out. Transferring it to his left hand, he placed his right hand close to the door handle to be able to open it fast.

He still had to account for the man with the bomb. He didn't have a solution to him. But if the kidnappers planned to kill them here, he resolved to do something.

A man appeared in his side-view mirror, wearing a black hood and holding a sawed-off shotgun aimed at his head. Through the driver's side passenger window he glimpsed another man on Christie's side. Identically dressed and also holding a sawed-off aimed at her.

Both men stood five feet back from the front doors to minimize any chance of attack. Professionals.

"Jack Steel."

Steel glanced over his shoulder at the speaker, whose voice fit the man on the phone. The man's height and general build also fit the rifle shooter in the trees.

"Face forward," the man said roughly.

He did—and considered opening the door and ducking low.

"If the door so much as cracks open, I step back and shoot you."

Steel swallowed. He believed the man.

"Here's the good news, Steel. You're all going to live. All three of you are going to get into the closest sedan parked at the far end. When you reach Idaho Springs, pull off the highway at the first gas station you see. Then open the trunk. There's a phone inside. Have someone pick up Miss Afia. She isn't part of this. I admire her courage. I'll call with instructions. Do as you're told or your brother dies. You do want to see Harry again, don't you, Christie?"

Christie glanced over her shoulder at him, biting her lip as she faced forward. "Yes."

"Call in the police or any law enforcement, and Harry's dead. We're monitoring everything. We so much as see a police car or roadblock on the road and Harry's finished."

Both men backed up from the doors. The man on Steel's side said, "Get out. Leave the burner phone on the car seat. Go to the sedan. Hurry or I won't be so nice."

Steel exited the SUV along with Christie and Afia, keeping his knife hidden behind his leg as he faced the man with the shotgun.

The shotgun had a pistol grip, and the Latino held it stiffly to absorb recoil, sighting on him, both arms up, left leg and arm forward. He knew what he was doing. Maybe ex-military.

Afia and Christie hurried around the rear of the SUV and joined him. Christie carried her small purse.

The younger man with the bomb got out on the other side of the SUV, still holding the switch. He didn't look experienced like the other two men—who were also huskier and taller.

Steel turned to go, but the older man's voice made him pause.

"Steel, one last reminder. You and Christie are on your own. Call in anyone else to help—outside of picking up Miss Afia—and you can say goodbye to Harry and everyone you both love. When we talk, I'll explain that last point in detail. And if you and Christie split up, same result. You'll be watched."

Steel tensed over the threats but said nothing. Wanting to get Afia and Christie away from the men as fast as possible, he strode across the dirt to the sedan. He glanced at the second car parked a little farther away. Empty.

Christie took the driver's seat, he the front passenger seat, while Afia ducked into the back. The keys were in the ignition. In seconds Christie pulled the car onto the highway. They rapidly pulled away from the SUV and armed men.

Steel put his knife away. After a few miles he concluded the sedan didn't have a bomb hidden in it.

"That was strange." Afia sat up and fanned her face with her hand. "But I give thanks that we're all still alive!"

Steel agreed on both counts. "I'm sorry you had to go through that, Afia."

She sat back. "Thank you for protecting me at the auditorium, Jack and Christy. I hope Harry will be all right."

"Glad we were there to help," said Steel.

"Why Harry?" Christie sounded shaken. "Do you know any of those men, Jack?"

"I didn't recognize their voices." Once more he ran through all the contacts and people he knew. The Colombian's accent reminded him of the Serpent Op in Colombia last year.

A Colombian cartel leader had threatened him with retribution. But these men and their orders didn't strike him as originating from a cartel. Other connections to the Serpent Op didn't fit either.

He checked his sideview mirror, but in the dark it would be hard to see if any of the three men were following them. He assumed at least one was.

They drove to I-70 and arrived at Idaho Springs in twenty minutes. Christie pulled into the first gas station. Steel asked her to back the car into the shadowed rear corner of the large lot.

They exited the car, and he told the two women to move away before he checked the undercarriage and engine compartment for any sign of a bomb. Nothing.

After pulling the trunk release, he crouched and carefully opened the trunk. No explosion.

There was a large zippered duffel bag inside, which he opened. He gaped. It was full of weapons. Two Glock 19s, two Sig Sauer P320s, and three SIG MCX Rattlers—rifle-caliber machine guns with optical sights and carry straps. Along with silencers, ammo clips, knives, zip ties, duct tape, two night-vision goggles, binoculars, gloves, and two black face masks.

Ten thousand dollars in weapons and accessories. The Rattlers had folding stocks and were easy to conceal. The guns also told him the Latino had experience with weapons, supporting his earlier guess of ex-military. It made his mouth dry. His first thought was that he had to get Christie out of here.

A phone lay next to the bag. He grabbed it, zipped up the duffel bag, and shut the trunk. Apprehensive, he rejoined Christie and Afia.

"What's in the trunk?" asked Christie.

He gave a slight shake of his head. "The phone and a few other things. I'll show you later."

Christie nodded. "I'll call Clay and Dale. They'll take care of Afia."

He handed the phone to her. "Alright. And maybe your brothers can search for Harry."

"Agreed." She hesitated, staring at the phone.

He understood and took it back. Taking off the back, he examined the interior, then put it back together. "I don't think it's bugged."

"Thanks." She walked away to make the call.

He didn't want to call the police or FBI. Not with Harry in play. And not until he understood the kidnapper's threat to his family. At least Afia would be safe. All of Christie's brothers had military backgrounds.

He turned to Afia. "Can I ask a favor?"

"Anything." She looked up at him, her brown eyes serious.

"I would appreciate it if you just told the police that your head was down the whole time so you don't know where we are. Tell them we're worried and still checking on other concerns so we dropped you off with Christie's brothers. I don't want them chasing us, since that man threatened to kill Harry if the police are brought in."

He shrugged. "It's a lot to ask."

"Hah. You just saved my life! I am happy to do that." She stepped closer. "I worry for you, Jack. Take care."

"Thank you, Afia. I admire your strength."

Her voice lowered. "Violence never solves anything, and revenge only makes things worse. I hope these men can see that soon."

"So do I." He doubted that would happen.

"The mountains are so beautiful, Jack, but this is ugly."

He grimaced. The weapons in the trunk promised things were going to get a lot uglier.

# CHAPTER 3

C HRISTIE RETURNED. "THEY'LL BE here in twenty minutes. I told Clay that Harry was kidnapped and we needed their help to get Afia out of here. I left out the rest of the details. Otherwise Clay would have questioned me for a half hour."

"Good." Steel remembered the first conversation he had with Clay, her oldest brother, nearly a year ago. A week after he and Christie had survived a harrowing Op in Hawaii, Clay had asked him if he could keep his sister safe.

At that time Christie wasn't going with him on Greensave field assignments. She was just doing the planning. He had answered Clay by saying whatever Christie did, it was her choice. But Clay's words had always nagged at him.

It was a half hour before a blue rental car pulled up alongside their car.

Dale and Clay appeared as solidly built as Harry. Dale was in his late twenties and shorter, Clay in his late forties with a moustache. Both had short hair and wore jeans, denim jackets, and boots. Clay wore a cowboy hat.

Steel liked both of them. Ex-Army. Dependable. Solid. He had visited their homes in Montana and watched some of the winter Korean Olympics with them. They had been welcoming to him, but now they looked serious as they gave Christie a big hug and shook his hand firmly.

"Let's go, Afia." Clay motioned to their car.

Afia hugged Christie, whispering, "I hope you get your brother back."

"Thank you, Afia." Christie held her tightly.

Afia grabbed Steel next. "Thank you for protecting me."

He pulled back. "Anytime."

Once Afia was in the car, Clay shut the door and stepped up to them. His voice was terse, his face drawn. "Who has Harry?"

"Yeah, what gives?" asked Dale.

"We don't know," said Christie. "Harry is in the back bed of a small white pickup truck with a cargo bed cover. Most likely Latinos are driving it."

"Hell, who would do something like that?" Dale frowned.

Clay was silent, staring at Steel.

Steel looked each of them in the eye. "The man in charge is Colombian. I recognized his accent, but I don't know who he is. We're being watched. If we call in the police or any law enforcement they said they'll kill Harry."

Clay stuck his hands in his pockets. "Do you believe them?"

"One of their men held a bomb in our SUV and was ready to die if we didn't do what we were told." Steel waited, concerned Clay wouldn't go along with it.

"I disagree." Clay grimaced. "We need to call in the FBI. They're trained to handle this kind of stuff."

Steel nodded. "The Colombian has something else over me, because he said all our loved ones will die if we don't do as he says. He's going to call me and explain that to me so I think we have to wait to hear what it is before we call anyone in."

He paused. "The way they took us was very carefully planned. They knew where we would be, how to make it succeed, and pulled it off without a mistake. The Colombian is a pro and we have to take him seriously."

"Hell." Clay bit off his words. "I always felt something like this would happen with your background, Jack."

"That doesn't help us, Clay," snapped Christie.

Clay stared at them. "All right. We see what the Colombian has to say and then we revisit this decision, agreed?"

"Agreed." Steel nodded.

"How can we help our brother?" Dale frowned. "We gotta do something."

Steel said, "After you drop off Afia, get a different color rental car and head north on highway six, past Boulder. I think that's a decent bet for where they took Harry, but it's still a long shot." His voice hardened. "I won't let anything happen to your brother."

"Why the different color car?" asked Dale.

"I think they're watching us so they'll pass along the color of the car you have now to whoever is driving the white pickup." Steel assumed Clay and Dale wouldn't be followed. "We have to be cautious."

Clay motioned to their car. "We'll drop Afia off at the Boulder police station. Then we'll swap cars and drive north. We'll wait for your update."

Steel gestured to him. "Thanks. I'm sorry about all this."

"We'll sort it out," said Dale.

"Can I talk to you alone for a moment, Jack?" Clay stared at him steadily.

"Whatever you have to say, say it in front of both of us, Clay." Christie's voice was firm.

Clay frowned. "All right. I might lose a brother over something I don't understand. I don't want to lose a sister too." He looked at her. "I think you should come with us."

Christie stared at him. "If we split up, the Colombian said he'll kill Harry and our families."

Clay's forehead wrinkled. "Why is he making you stay with Jack?"

Christie shrugged. "We don't know."

Clay shook his head, looking frustrated. "Damn."

"Let's see what develops," said Dale. "If we get moving, maybe we can find Harry quick and end all this."

Clay regarded Christie and Steel for a few moments. "Okay. We'll do it your way for now."

"Be careful." Christie hugged her brothers once more.

Clay returned to the passenger seat of the rental car. Dale climbed in behind the wheel.

Steel tapped on Clay's window. When he powered it down, Steel said, "Hang on." He motioned to Christie. "Come on."

He opened the trunk of their car, unzipped the duffel bag, and looked at Christie. "I want to give two guns to your brothers. Do you want a SIG or Glock? There's two of each." She preferred the SIG's steady trigger pull and ergonomics, but she practiced with both.

She gaped at the weapons. "SIG."

"Alright." He preferred the grip of a Glock anyway. He took out one SIG and one Glock, and an extra mag for both. Hesitating, he said, "Let's check them quick."

He handed her the SIG, he took the Glock. They ejected the full magazines, checked the chambers, took off the slides, recoil springs, and barrels.

"Clean." Christie reassembled it.

"Mine too." He put the Glock back together, took the SIG from her, and said, "Walk in front of me to Clay's window so no one can see the guns."

She did. Remaining close behind her, he unobtrusively handed the guns to Clay. "You might need these. We just checked them. Clean and ready."

Clay raised his eyebrows, but he took the guns. "I expect you to take care of my sister, Jack."

"Nothing will happen to her, Clay. You have my word."

Clay and Dale drove away.

Steel stared after them, vowing silently to live up to his promise.

# CHAPTER 4

CHRISTIE NUDGED STEEL'S ARM. "Ignore Clay. Big brother crap. He's always been protective of me."

Steel kept silent, knowing his own concerns for her wouldn't allow him to dismiss Clay's comments so easily.

She walked back to view the weapons in the trunk. "They're arming us. For what?"

"We're going to find out. Let's check the other guns quick."

They both examined a pistol and Rattler, field-stripping them and examining magazines again. Everything was functional. They were finished in minutes and he shut the trunk.

Christie walked into his arms, whispering, "I'll die if anything happens to Harry."

He held her close, his stomach wound tight. "We'll make sure nothing does."

The phone rang and he answered, putting it on speaker.

The Colombian's voice was matter-of-fact. "Here it is, Steel. Op Retribution. Remember Marita? You abandoned our compatriot, refusing to give her asylum, and thus allowed her to be raped, tortured, and killed by Gustavo Alvarez's men in the Choco jungle on your last Op."

He remembered. The DEA informant, Marita, had died on the Serpent Op. He had considered the possibility that the Colombian kidnapper was somehow connected to Marita but had rejected it as too unlikely. A sinking feeling hit him. He had caused all of this. The past wouldn't let go.

Christie's brow furrowed and he saw worry in her eyes. He felt it too but controlled his features.

The man kept talking. "We're holding you responsible for what happened to Marita. You're going to kill the men who participated in her death. We know everything about you, gringo, and if you do anything we don't like, Harry dies. Your first target is in Vail. Garcia Rincón. He's vacationing with his wife and two children, using the alias of Rodrigo Garcia."

A photo of Garcia arrived on Steel's phone. Moustache, dark hair, mid-forties. He showed it to Christie.

The Colombian continued. "He's a cousin of Gustavo Alvarez, the drug lord you killed. He's also one of the men who ruined and killed our beloved Marita. He has four guards. Three are men living in the U.S. but connected to the cartel. The fourth is his most trusted guard, Hernando. Hernando also participated in Marita's death.

"Kill Garcia and Hernando tonight or Harry dies. If you let the other guards live, the cartel will have an easier time finding you. It's up to you. Garcia has rented a house. I'll text you the address. We'll know if you succeed."

Anger and panic rose in Steel's throat. "I won't do anything until I talk to Harry to make sure he's alive."

"Take the phone off speaker and walk away from Christie."

Christie's eyebrows raised, but he did as requested, holding the phone up to his ear.

"I'm texting you a photo of our compatriot."

The photo arrived. It was a shot of Marita's face and shoulders post-mortem. The torture wounds were obvious and horrible. It made him sick to his stomach, and remorseful again that he had allowed it to happen. Hers was one of the faces that still sometimes haunted his dreams at night.

"Now ask yourself if you want this to happen to Christie. To your daughter, Rachel. To your ex-wife, Carol. To Harry. I'll release Christie's photo and photos of everyone in both of your families to the cartel if you fail or if you call in the police or law enforcement."

He felt his world caving in, and he wanted this man dead. "I tried to save Marita."

"Go to hell, gringo."

"This is between me and you. Let's meet."

"I could have put a bullet in you or Christie long ago, but then your deaths would be too easy. I want you to suffer like Marita did."

"Why now?" He glanced around the station, knowing the Columbian wasn't far away.

"Opportunity. I had to act when Marita's killers came north."

"How do you know me?" Steel searched for a way out.

"Information is always available for a price."

He had been sold out on the Serpent Op, his name given to the target—the drug lord Gustavo Alvarez. It wasn't a surprise that the Colombian had traced his name. Gustavo Alvarez had also threatened revenge from the cartel. It hadn't happened, but it had kept Steel on edge over the last year.

He casually strolled farther away from Christie. "Christie had nothing to do with Marita's death. Leave her out of this."

"I want you to worry about losing someone you love dearly, all the while knowing that it's your fault if she dies."

Steel's free hand bunched into a fist, but he kept his voice calm. "If you want revenge, I'll be more effective if I operate alone. Christie will just get in the way."

"That's part of the fun, amigo."


AVAILABLE ON AMAZON NOW

For email updates on new releases, deals, and free review copies from Geoffrey Saign and for your FREE copy of **Steel Trust** go to www.geoffreysaign.net


Get updates on Jack Steel and Alex Sight thrillers at www.geoffreysaign.net

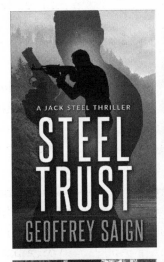
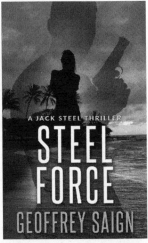
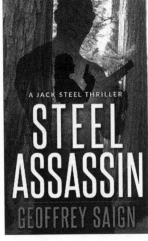
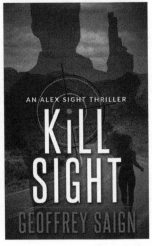

# ACKNOWLEDGMENTS

I WANT TO THANK MY friend Stanley Blanchard who used his extensive military background to strengthen the military scenes and give Jack Steel the nuances he needed to play the part. Any mistakes or omissions in anything military is my fault alone. Thanks to Steve McEllistrem, cousin and fellow writer who gave the book a read for grammar. I also wish to thank my parents for their critiques—they have always had a sharp sense of what makes a great action thriller.

Jack Steel is a character whose discipline gives him advantages over his enemies. As someone who did four-hour workouts nearly daily for five years in kung fu, I thought it would be interesting to create a character who used virtual reality to hone his skills to the nth degree, and then throw him into trouble.

The crimes in *Steel Force* stem from greed and a corporation. Corporations are the new feudal lords of today's world, often pulling the strings of politicians and world leaders to gain influence and get what they want. The ability to organize via the Internet is the single biggest weapon citizens have today to keep corporations honest. What used to take months to learn about via mainstream news, now takes minutes. Secrets are shared with the public before they can become secrets.

The character Jack Steel follows his values above all else. Doing the right thing is something you learn from the adults around you. My parents did a great job of teaching that to me.

Lastly, I wish to thank all the men and women who act heroically every day to ensure our safety. We owe you our thanks, gratitude, and support.

Award-winning author GEOFFREY SAIGN has spent many years studying kung fu and sailed all over the South Pacific and Caribbean. He uses that experience and sense of adventure to write the Jack Steel and Alex Sight thriller action series. Geoff loves to sail big boats, hike, and cook—and he infuses all of his writing with his passion for nature. As a swimmer, he considers himself fortunate to live in the Land of 10,000 Lakes, Minnesota.

For email updates from Geoffrey Saign and
your FREE copy of *Steel Trust* go to
www.geoffreysaign.net

Made in the USA
San Bernardino, CA
11 December 2019

61271104R00236